MW01141277

MURDER ON THE
ROPES

Also available in this series from New Millenium Press

Murderers' Row, Original Baseball Mysteries

MURDER ON THE ROPES

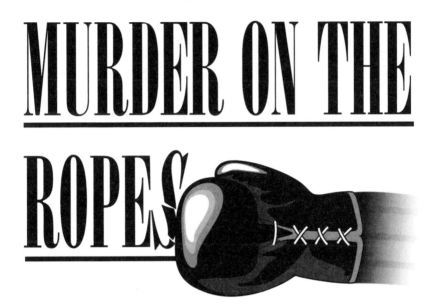

ORIGINAL BOXING MYSTERIES

EDITED BY OTTO PENZLER

NEW MILLENNIUM PRESS
Beverly Hills

Text Design by KL Design
Printed in the United States of America

Library of Congress Cataloging-in-Publication Data

Murder on the Ropes: original boxing mysteries / edited by Otto Penzler.—1st ed.
    p. cm.
Includes bibliographical references (p.).
ISBN 1-893224-33-3
    1. Boxing stories. 2. Boxers (Sports)—Fiction. 3. Detective and mystery stories, American. I. Penzler, Otto.

PS648.B67 M87. 2001
813'.087208355—dc21

        2001055866

New Millennium Press
A Division of NM WorldMedia, Inc.
301 North Canon Drive
Suite 214
Beverly Hills, CA 90210

10 9 8 7 6 5 4 3 2 1

For Larry Kirshbaum
With deep respect and
heartfelt affection

CONTENTS

INTRODUCTION

Boxing, known also as pugilism, prizefighting and the manly art, is among the oldest of all sports, with evidence of its existence in ancient Crete in 1500 B.C, Even the epics of Homer describe in breathless prose the heroic adventures of fighters:

"So, when their fists were bound with thongs of force-giving ox-skin/Coiling the long bands round their arms, they met in the mid-ring/Breathing slaughter against each other...."

Although the rules of boxing have changed dramatically over its long history (indeed, in its earliest years, it would be hard indeed to find *any* rules), some of the practices have changed less than purists might wish.

There was no footwork in the beginning age of boxing (though fans of George Foreman, Jimmie Thunder and Michael Grant might wonder how much that has changed), it being regarded as cowardice to avoid a punch (by which standard Arturo Gatti must be regarded as the most courageous fighter of his time, since he has yet to avoid his first one). Wrestling was allowed (a sadly uninformed "Bonecrusher" Smith evidently was kept in the dark about this rule change) until the marquess of Queensberry rules were adopted in 1867 and initiated the modern era of boxing.

In much of the long history of prizefighting it was permissible to gouge, kick, head-butt, punch below the belt and bite (as boxing historians will recall, the notion that these offenses against good sportsmanship were outlawed in 1839 must have failed to reach the ears of such gentlemen of the ring as Mike Tyson and Andrew Golota, who clearly retain a great affection for the early traditions of the sport). Those only occasionally followed proscriptions were known as the London Prize Ring rules, which brought some semblance of organization to boxing.

In an attempt to make the sport more palatable to a higher class of people, John Sholto Douglas, the eighth marquess of Queensberry, lent his name to the new rules, which were regarded by the toughs of the ring as effete. These included the now fundamental tenets of boxing: three-minute rounds with a one-minute rest period between rounds; a ten-second count if a fighter was knocked down, and the fight ended if he could not get up unaided; and padded gloves. When John L. Sullivan, king of the bare-knuckle fighters, finally agreed to fight under those rules (not to help the sport, but to get a bigger payday), they became part of the boxing scene forever.

While there are plenty of exceptions, boxing has traditionally appealed to tough, uneducated young men, often the victims of prejudice and bigotry, who have seen the sport as a means of literally fighting their way out of squalor and deprivation to fame and fortune.

Not surprisingly, perhaps, for a sport in which few make it to the top and many attempt it, and which features one man against another, not an entire team against another, boxing has been a rich breeding ground for corruption and related crimes.

In no other contemporary sport does an athlete put so much at stake (often his very life) for such small rewards ($50 for a preliminary club fight is not unusual). Can anyone be surprised that a better payday for taking an early dive is appealing to some fighters, whose managers, trainers, and others connected with them stand to make a little killing (so to speak) by placing the right bet?

Everyone wants to watch a championship fight these days. Promoters are eager to give fans what they want, so there are more sanctioning bodies with more initials than a truckload of Campbell's alphabet soup. And there are so many weight divisions ranked by these organizations (junior middleweight, middleweight, super middleweight, etc.) that there are guys carrying spit buckets who get ranked, especially if the promoters are paid off. No, don't be too shocked. It has actually happened. And some judges, bought and paid for by the likes of Don King, the colorful impresario who makes fight fans long for the relatively clean days of Blinky Palermo and Frankie Carbo, make Ray Charles seem eagle-eyed.

So why does boxing appeal so deeply and relentlessly to so many of us? Perhaps because, in the midst of all the muck, there is something inherently pure about two men, physical equals, matched in a visceral *mano a mano* contest, with no one to turn to during the three minutes that can seem like three hours when someone is hitting you very hard.

The violence that is so inherent in the very definition of boxing has resulted in serious injuries in the ring over the years, and occasionally even some deaths. There are also crimes, including murder, associated with boxing that have occurred outside the ring. (Let's have a moment of silence for such upstanding citizens as Charles "Sonny" Liston and Oscar Bonavena.) There are more than a few episodes (mainly fictional) that fill the following pages, and these stories are narrated by some of the finest crime writers in the United States.

Doug Allyn majored in criminal psychology at the University of Michigan, served in military intelligence during the Vietnam War and followed those career paths with twenty-five years as a rock guitarist. He began his mystery writing career fifteen years ago and has published five novels and nearly sixty short stories, winning or being nominated for every major literary award in his field, including the Edgar Allan Poe Award for 1995.

Andrew Bergman, in addition to being the author of three novels featuring Jack LeVine, has for more than a quarter-century been one of America's most successful screenwriters, especially of such comic masterpieces as *Blazing Saddles, Fletch, The Freshman, Honeymoon in Vegas, Soapdish,* and *The In-Laws.* "In the Tank" is his first short story.

Lawrence Block enjoys both critical and popular success as one of the most prolific and versatile writers in the mystery world, with works ranging from the brooding darkness of the Matt Scudder series to the light comedy of his novels about the burglar and bookseller Bernie Rhodenbarr to the perfectly crafted stories about his amoral hit man, Keller. He is a multiple Edgar winner and Grand Master of the Mystery Writers of America.

Brendan DuBois is the author of four novels, one of which, *Resurrection Day*, will soon be made into a major motion picture. He has received even more acclaim for his short stories, which appear regularly in *Playboy* and *Ellery Queen's Mystery Magazine.* Two have been selected for *Best American Mystery Stories of the Year* and one, "The Dark Snow," was named to *Best American Mystery Stories of the Century.*

Thomas H. Cook has written more than a dozen books, three of which have been nominated for Edgars in three different categories, with *The Chatham School Affair* winning for Best Novel of the Year in 1997. His only previous mystery short story, "Fatherhood," won the Herodotus Award as Best Historical Short Story of the Year.

Loren D. Estleman has written many novels of crime, mystery and suspense, as well as several highly regarded westerns. His hard-boiled novels about Amos Walker, set in Detroit, are among the genre's favorites. Estleman, once a boxer himself, says, "There isn't a day goes by, particularly when I'm shaving in the morning and listening to the rush-hour traffic reports, that I don't thank God I wasn't a better fighter."

James Grady, a former Senate aide and investigative reporter for columnist Jack Anderson, is the author of numerous detective stories and thrillers, the best known of which is *Six Days of the Condor,* filmed as *Three Days of the Condor* with Robert Redford and Faye Dunaway.

Edward D. Hoch is one of the most creative and prolific short story writers ever to have produced mystery fiction. His stories have appeared in every issue of *Ellery Queen's Mystery Magazine* for more than twenty years, during which time they have been frequent nominees for most major mystery awards. He won the Edgar Allan Poe Award for Best Short Story of the Year in 1968 for "The Oblong Room." He is a former president of the Mystery Writers of America.

Clark Howard, a former boxer, has had three short stories nominated for Edgars and a fourth, "Horn Man," won the award from the Mystery Writers of America in 1981. He has also had Edgar nominations for two true crime books, *Six Against the Rock* (1977) and *Zebra* (1979), his account of the notorious "Zodiac" murders in San Francisco.

Stuart M. Kaminsky's enormously successful series about 1940s Hollywood detective Toby Peters has featured his involvement with Charlie Chaplin, Humphrey Bogart, Mae West and Joe Louis, among others. He also writes books about Abe Lieberman, a Chicago detective, and Porfiry Rostnikov, a Russian policeman who starred in 13 books, including the Edgar-winning *A Cold Red Sunrise*.

Mike Lupica is an award-winning sportswriter and columnist for the *New York Daily News*. He is also one of the stars of the popular weekly television program *The Sports Reporters*. His mystery writing career includes the Peter Finley series, the first of which, *Dead Air*, was nominated for an Edgar and then was filmed for CBS as *Money, Power and Murder.*

Joyce Carol Oates is perhaps the most critically acclaimed writer of her generation. Nominated for six National Book Awards and winner of that prestigious honor, as well as of the PEN/ Malamud Award for Achievement in the Short Story, her short fiction has been published in *Best American Short Stories of the Century, Best American Mystery Stories of the Century, The O. Henry Awards, The Pushcart Prize,* and every other collection of importance. Her essay "On Boxing" is one of the most perceptive pieces ever written about the sport.

John Shannon is the author of four novels about Jack Liffey, who has a talent for finding lost children: *The Concrete River, The Cracked Earth, The Poison Sky* and *The Orange Curtain.* The character, the novels and the author have been praised by Michael Connelly, George Pelecanos, James Crumley, Robert B. Parker, Thomas Perry, James Sallis, Kent Anderson and *The New York Times,* the *Chicago Tribune,* the *Los Angeles Times* and countless other publications.

F.X. Toole is the pseudonym of Jerry Boyd, a longtime boxing trainer and cutman who has previously been an actor, Teamster, salesman, bartender and bullfighter. His first book, *Rope Burns: Stories from the Corner,* was selected by *The New York Times* as one of its Notable Books of the Year 2000.

Now that you have been introduced to the principals...let's get it on!

—Otto Penzler

SUNLIGHT SHINING ON WATER

by Doug Allyn

Mick never saw the punch. Caught him by surprise in the third round of a two-bit preliminary bout.

Shouldn't have signed for the fight at all. Took it on short notice for short money. But it had been a thin year and there was an outside chance the bout might be televised.

His opponent was Kid Ibo, a Nigerian fighting out of Chicago. Middleweight. Black and hard as an ebony club. Tribal scars gouged in his cheeks. Ibo looked like he ate lions for lunch. Fought like it too.

First round, Mick and the Nigerian both came on strong, trading inside, testing each other, throwing a lot of leather but blocking most of it. The crowd cheered the action but it was all sizzle, no meat to it.

Kid Ibo had power, though. Mick felt it when he slipped a right cross Ibo aimed at his throat. The punch grazed his shoulder. And widened his eyes. The Nigerian was for real. Dangerous.

Fully focused now, Mick picked up the pace and took Ibo to school. Boxing 101. Hammering the Kid's body with sharp combinations, following immediately with a cross to the head.

The Nigerian went for it. Started raising his guard a tad after the last body shot, anticipating a head shot. Big mistake.

As the round wound down, Mick suddenly reversed his pattern, started low, then went lower, digging a hook under the

Nigerian's elbow as he raised his hands, drove it halfway to his liver, saw him wince.

Ibo backed away, grinning, shaking his head like the punch was nothing.

Yeah, right. Mick quickly worked the same combination again before the Nigerian could figure it out, jammed another hook into the same spot, flat-footed, with serious steam on it.

No clowning this time. Eyes narrowing in pain, Ibo backpedaled, dancing away from Mick, dancing the last fifteen seconds of the round. Danced all the way back to his freakin' corner at the bell.

Hurting. Definitely.

"You got him goin', Irish," Nate Cohen grinned as Mick dropped onto his stool, breathing deep, nostrils flared, sucking in all the air he could hold, smelling the crowd, the smoke, the whiskey rolling off Nate like aftershave. Ignoring it, Mick focused on the Nigerian across the ring.

Tall for a middleweight, Ibo was rangy, long arms like Tommy Hearns. The tribal scars gleamed beneath the Vaseline on his cheeks, giving him a fierce, predatory look.

But beneath it, Mick sensed Ibo's pain. Brow furrowed, teeth bared, the Nigerian couldn't straighten up on his stool, even when his cornerman tugged on his waistband, trying to relax his abdominals.

Mick knew that pain. Knew Ibo felt broken. Mick had taken a shot like it in his only championship bout. Hadn't finished him at the time, but it set him up for the knockout in the seventh.

Now it was Ibo's turn. Only Mick couldn't wait for the seventh. This was a lousy four-round preliminary. Only two to go. He had to take him out quick.

Deacon Washburn was yelling instructions in his ear, had been since Mick sat down. Tuning him out, Mick checked the crowd. Fight night at a Detroit Ojibwa casino. Mom-and-pop weekend gamblers who wouldn't know a right hook from bad nookie. They knew the fight was strictly from hunger, though. A warmup, two nobodies killing each other, killing time before the main event, an IABF cruiser-weight title bout.

Mick glanced up. The club's TV cameras were running, red eyes glowing in the smoky haze over the ring. If he could put Ibo down hard, maybe he'd make ESPN's highlight film. Have to do it with style, though. And fast.

"Seconds out," the timekeeper called, banging on the ring for emphasis.

"Have you heard a fuckin' word I said?" Washburn demanded.

"Sure," Mick said. "Work the body, stay on him." It was what Wash always said. "How about I finish him instead?"

"Then do it, Irish," Wash growled, rinsing Mick's mouthpiece, sliding it in. "We need this win bad. Don't let him get away." Grabbing the stool, he hoisted himself through the ropes.

Mick frowned. Wash sounded worried, which was odd. Wash never worried. Through bad times and good, his faith in Mick never wavered. What was up with him?

Didn't matter. Mick was on his own once the bell rang. Always had been. That was the beauty of the game. In the end, it came down to the two guys inside the ropes. Nobody else.

At the bell, Ibo came out in high gear, flailing like a windmill. Wired up on adrenaline and pain. And fear. Mick knew the feeling. Been there.

He let Ibo swing away, catching everything on his arms and elbows, waiting for his opening. Headhunting. Looking for a one-punch knockout.

And there it was! Ibo threw a left hook so hard it carried him around when it missed, leaving his jaw wide open for a counter.

Perfect! Mick brought the right full force, swiveling his hips into the punch—and walked into Ibo's desperation roundhouse right, catching it flush on the temple.

Totally focused, Mick barely felt Ibo's punch. Until he was stumbling off balance into the ropes. And going down. What the hell? And the ref was counting.

Mick jumped up immediately, more embarrassed than hurt. Ibo was dancing in his corner, arms raised in victory, showboating for the crowd. And they were eating it up. Even morons could understand a knockdown. Damn it!

"You okay?" The ref was peering into his eyes intently.

"Hell yes!" Mick roared around his mouthpiece.

"What?"

Mick nodded vigorously, desperate to get the ref out of the way and get back into the fight. Grabbing his gloves, the ref wiped them off on his white shirt, then stepped back and waved them on.

Mick charged into Ibo's corner, but the Nigerian danced away, grinning, hot-dogging around the ring for the last half minute of the round.

"You're blowin' it," Wash barked as Mick sagged on his stool. "Dammit, I told you—"

Mick leaned back, closed his eyes, tuning Wash out. Shit! Decked by a dumb-ass lucky punch. Ibo hadn't laid a hand on him all night. Wouldn't have to, now. The knockdown would decide the bout. Wash was ranting, wired up, worried. So was Mick.

"Last round," the ref said, leaning in over Wash's shoulder. "Touch 'em up when you come out. You okay, Shannon?"

"Terrific," Mick snapped.

"Glad to hear it," the ref said mildly, trotting over to remind the Nigerian's corner it was the last round. Mick noticed he didn't bother asking Ibo if he was okay. The fight was already over unless he could catch Ibo in the last round and put him down...

He couldn't. They did the traditional glove touch before starting the last round. It was the closest Mick came to landing a punch.

Ibo danced the round away, running for his freakin' life but looking good doing it, getting on his bicycle every time Mick tried to close with him, confident he had the fight in the bag. Which he damn sure did.

The ref warned him once, but it didn't mean dick at that

4

point. Ibo was still dancing at the final bell. Five seconds to confer with the judges and the ref was raising Ibo's hand in victory while the ring announcer bellowed the unanimous decision as the crowd ordered drinks or hit the johns before the next not-shit warmup bout.

"Lucky punch," Deacon Washburn said glumly, easing his bulk down at Mick's table in the casino lounge. Wash's black shark-skin suit and old-timey Afro attracted a few stares, tourists wondering if he was Fats Domino. "You rocked him in the second. What the fuck happened? I told you to work Ibo's body—"

"Screw that, Wash. I blew it, okay? Dropped a fight I should've won. That's on me and I know it. I also know it was a crummy match. Why'd you stick me in a four-round prelim with a no-namer like Ibo?"

"He was the best we could do. And Ibo ain't a no-name, he's a new name, which is more than I can say for Irish Mick Shannon. Ibo was eight wins, no losses coming into this, now he's nine-zip, Mick. What's your record?"

"Sixteen and five—no, sixteen and six after tonight. Sweet Jesus, Wash, I'm only a couple of losses away from Palookaville."

"C'mon, Mick, it ain't as bad as all that," Nate Cohen said, joining them, carefully placing two drinks on the table before sitting down. Both drinks were his. "You got time to turn things around. You're still a young man."

"I'm twenty-eight, Nate."

"Like I said." Nate licked his lips before knocking back the first scotch. "A young man."

"Compared to you, George Foreman's a punk kid, Nate."

"Don't be raggin' on Nate," Wash said. "He didn't deck you."

"I know, dammit. Look, Wash, just give me my money and let me get out of here. I'm not in a party mood, okay?"

"I can't," Wash said slowly. "I, um, I bet our front money on you, Mick. Nate's kicked in his share too. We knew you could take

Ibo and…" He swallowed. "Anyway. It's gone."

"What the hell, Wash, you had no right to do that! How much did we lose?"

"All of it. And a lot more. I gave him odds."

Mick froze, staring at him. "What odds? Who'd you bet with?"

"You know Tom Ducatti? Owns a couple bars, a car dealership in Royal Oak?"

"Tommy Duke? I've seen him around the game. Enough to know he's mobbed up. How much are we out? Exactly?"

"Three grand at three to one. We're down nine."

"Nine! Jesus! Have you got nine, Wash? I sure as hell haven't."

"You know I ain't got spit either, Mick. I figured it was our chance to get ahead, but…anyway, maybe it'll work out. Tommy's backin' a new fighter, a guy from L.A., Calvin Kroffut. I seen film on him. Looks bad to the bone, gang-banger tattoos, dreadlocks. Learned to box in prison and he's already eighteen and one. Killed a Messican kid in a bout down in Tijuana. Killer Kroffut, they're callin' him now, Big K. Sells a lot of tickets."

"So? What's that got to do with us?"

"K's eighteen wins were nobodies, mostly Latins or convicts. Hell, south of the border everybody's forty and two and Kid Gavilan was they daddy, you know? Tommy's lookin' for local bouts. He, um, he wants to talk to you, Mick."

Wash looked away, unable to meet Mick's stare. "My god," Mick groaned. "What you really mean is, Tommy's lining up tomato cans his boy can knock down to pump up his record, right?"

"Maybe," Wash admitted. "But it don't matter. You've gotta talk to him, Mick. We're in a lot of trouble here."

Mick found Tommy Duke holding court at a table on the dais overlooking the casino's main floor. A dozen people around him, two chicks, half in the bag, Tommy's bodyguard, a hawk-faced Mex in a gray silk suit, narrow tie. Ramos? Something like that.

Tommy's new fighter was at the end of the table. Wash was

right. Even in a suit and tie Kroffut looked super bad.

So did Tommy Ducatti, but in the original sense of the word. Big, fleshy, with thinning black hair, Tommy looked like a jock going to seed. Fast. His ruddy face was seamed with smile lines from his salesman's pasted-on grin. Carousing himself into an early coronary, laughing all the way.

"Mr. Ducatti? My manager said you wanted to see me?"

"Irish Mickey Shannon," Tommy said, not bothering to offer his hand. "Hey everybody, say hello to Irish Mick." No one looked up but Ramos, who nodded. Mick didn't return it. Guys like Ramos were all over the fight game like lice. "Siddown, have a drink," Tommy slurred. "Can probably use one, right?"

"One," Mick sighed, taking a chair opposite Ducatti. "A beer would do fine."

"Beer here," Tommy bellowed at a passing waitress, who bustled off. "Have you met Killer K yet?"

Kroffut eyed Mick, nodded, then shook his hand. Gently, Spanish style. "Saw you fight, Shannon. Bad luck."

"I make my own luck, good or bad," Mick shrugged. "Haven't seen you yet. People say you're good."

"People are right," Tommy interrupted. "I know you must be tired, Shannon, so let's get to it. I got a problem I figure you can help me with."

"A fight?"

"Somethin' like that. It's my sister. Some asshole is hittin' on her, givin' her a bad time, you know? I need somebody to straighten him out. Seriously. Know what I'm sayin'?"

"You want me to...work somebody over?" Mick couldn't freakin' believe it.

"That's what you do, isn't it?" Duke said, leaning forward, booze sour on his breath. "I don't care how you handle it, but I want the guy out of the picture, you know? Guy's name is Tony Brooks, runs some kinda half-ass karate school on Dequinder. That's where Maria—"

7

"Whoa, we've got a mix-up here." Mick rose, trying to hide his rage. "I'm a boxer, Mr. Ducatti. A pro, not some nickel-dime hood—"

"Siddown," Ramos snapped. "Man's not finished talkin'."

"I'm finished," Mick countered. "If you got a problem with that, pal, take your best shot."

"Whoa, whoa, everybody chill," Tommy said, waving Ramos off. "Look, Shannon, your manager's into me for nine large, which he lost bettin' on you. I figure that makes you and your cornerman responsible, you know? All in it together. You got my money?"

Mick shook his head.

"Didn't think so. Okay, you owe me big and I need a favor. Seems fair enough to me."

"Why me? Isn't your rat-faced buddy up to it?"

"People know Ramos works for me. If he handles it, cops might trace it back to me. You and me got no connection, Shannon. Until now. So. You gonna do this? Or do I send Ramos around to collect from your friends?"

"They haven't got the money either."

"That's not my problem." Tommy leaned back, confident now. "Lemme put it to you straight, Irish. Your career's in the toilet, going round and round. I can help you out. Or flush you down. What's it gonna be?"

Mick didn't answer. Couldn't. He wanted to puke. Or punch Tommy's lights out. He glanced out over the casino floor instead.

Acres of slots, blackjack and craps tables. Monte Carlo, Motown style. Cash and major credit cards accepted. No personal checks, no dress code. No class. An hour ago he'd fought a warrior from Africa to entertain these stiffs. For what?

He turned back to Tommy Duke. "What did you say the guy's name was?"

Mick's car had been repo'd months before. Had to catch an early crosstown bus to the address Ducatti gave him. Found

Brooks' studio with no trouble, a storefront dojo a few blocks off the Cass Corridor. Martial Arts, Self-Defense, Fitness. Shotokan Karate, Tai Chi Chuan. Personal Training by Master Tony Brooks. By appointment only. Right.

Mick bought coffee at a corner deli, took up position across from the dojo in an alley. Lurking. Feeling like a goddamn mugger. Brooks didn't show till noon, a tall, light-skinned black, shaved head, goatee, wearing a maroon Nike running suit. Sore and surly, Mick trotted across the street, braced Brooks just as he put his key in the door.

"Mr. Brooks? Can we talk a minute?"

Brooks looked him over. Liquid brown eyes. Intelligent. No fear. Only curiosity. "Sure, come on in."

Mick followed Brooks inside. Big room, gleaming hardwood floor, Asian flags on the walls, racks of Oriental weapons: swords, staffs, daggers, some wooden, some chrome steel. Smelled clean, not like a real gym. "What can I do for you, Mister...?"

"My name doesn't matter. We've got trouble, you and me."

"Trouble?" Brooks seemed more puzzled than worried. Up close he looked big, light on his feet. "Don't I know you?"

"Nope, but you know Maria Ducatti, don't you?"

"Maria? Shit, is that what this is about?"

"You're gonna stay away from her, sport. Out of her life. You don't see her, don't call her anymore. Understand?"

"I understand that psycho bitch went cryin' to her big brother, laid a load of crap on him and he sent you, right?"

"It doesn't matter who sent me."

"Irish Mickey Shannon." Brooks snapped his fingers. "Knew I knew you. Saw you fight a couple years ago at the Palace. Title fight. You looked awful that night."

"Had the flu. And this isn't a social call."

"Right," Brooks said, unzipping his jacket, tossing it aside. Well built, golden skin. Long ropy muscles, like a swimmer. Like a young Ali. "You here to work me over, Mick? Defend the lady's honor?" He was edging toward a rack of swords as he spoke.

"I just want to talk," Mick said, stepping between Brooks and the weapons—and then he was flying. Dropping to a crouch, Brooks kicked his legs out from under him. Mick landed hard, flat on his ass. Swiveling like a ballerina, Brooks plucked a wooden sword from the rack. Swished it through the air, testing its heft, eyeing Mick.

"Stay down," Brooks said mildly. "No need for anybody to bleed here. Not over Maria Ducatti."

Mick shrugged, opening his hands. "Whatever you say, sport. You're the guy with the sword."

"Want me to loan you one?"

"I'd rather have a thirty-eight so I could shoot myself in the head, save you the trouble of whackin' me to death. Jesus, I'm havin' a crummy week, you know?"

"Things must be pretty thin for you if you're into this kind of work, Irish."

"I'm not. I mean, it's the first time I ever mugged anybody. Guess it shows. Maybe I'm not cut out for a life of crime."

"The whole fight game's one big crime, you ask me." Brooks lowered the sword point to the floor. But kept it. "So what happened after you lost to the champ?"

"Fought too soon, tryin' to salvage my career. Screwed it up instead. And here I am."

"Well, for what it's worth, you came for nothing. I'm not bugging Maria Ducatti, she's after me. Ever seen her?"

Mick shook his head.

"Butt-ugly as her brother and twice as dumb. Hired me as her personal trainer, figured it included stud service. Shows how dim she is. She's not my type. You might be if you weren't straight. Follow?"

"Yeah. Sooo...I guess I can tell Tommy Duke his sister's safe from your unwanted attentions?"

"Oh, definitely. Tell him you kicked my ass if it'll get her out of my life. Unless you still figure on trying it?"

"No," Mick said positively. "We're done, Mr. Brooks. In fact, I'm done with the goon business. It's not me."

"Wise choice."

"Can I get up now?"

Brooks eyed him a moment, still hefting the sword. "Sure," he said, offering him a hand up. "You okay?"

"People keep asking me that," Mick sighed, brushing off his pants. "Makes a guy wonder."

"You still fighting?"

"Fought four rounds last night. Lost. That's why I'm here."

"Then I wish you'd won."

"So do I, believe me. Thanks for not taking my head off with that thing."

"No charge. If you run into Maria, just tell her you scared me so bad I never want to see her again. Fair enough?"

"Yeah, only...how did you do that?"

"Do what?"

"Put me down like that."

"I swept your legs. A basic karate move. It mostly worked because you weren't expecting it. Why?"

"Like you said, things are thin for me. Maybe you can show me something that can help."

"They don't allow leg sweeps in boxing. Or spinning back-fists or wheel kicks or most of the other stuff I teach."

"So what are you saying? All this Oriental shit is just window dressing?"

"No, it's real," Brooks said, unoffended. "But...look, here's the thing about karate. You learn moves, kicks, punches, blocks. Practice them over and over, same way every time, until they become reflexes. You with me?"

"Reflexes, right."

"If you have to think about it, any physical action takes three-fifths of a second, minimum. A reflex only takes two. That's why someone who knows karate can usually beat anyone who doesn't. Their reflexes are quicker. There's no magic to it. How long have you been boxing?"

"Since I was fourteen. Why?"

"A long time. Let me show you something. I'll try to slap your face. You just defend yourself. And please don't hit me, okay?"

Mick crouched. Brooks had quick hands, brought them from all directions. Mick had no trouble blocking them.

"See," Brooks said, grinning, straightening up. "You've got reflexes up the wazoo already, Irish. Umpty years worth. I can't unteach them, wouldn't if I could. Sorry."

"But there must be something. You weren't even looking at me when you swept my feet. That's why it worked so well. How did you do that?"

"Oh, that," Brooks nodded. "A Zen technique. There's a lot of Zen in the martial arts. That one's called Sunlight Shining on Water."

"Sunlight...what?"

"Shining on Water. It sounds hokey, but it's a simple technique. Remember what I said about reflex time versus thought-driven actions?"

"Yeah, reflexes are quicker."

"Right. The Sunlight technique gives your brain something to think about, takes it out of the circuit, frees up your reflexes. Instead of looking at your opponent, you picture sunlight shining on calm water. Pure golden light."

"You mean...you do this while you're fighting?"

"Exactly. You don't close your eyes or lower your guard. Everything's still working. But if your opponent makes a move, your reactions will be pure reflex. It sounds a little nuts but it really works. Try it. Put your hands up. Now, picture a lake, sunlight shining on it. No waves, no breeze, just golden light shining on the water..."

The punch came out of nowhere. Mick blocked it on reflex,

barely kept himself from drilling Brooks with a counterpunch.

"Whoa, whoa," Brooks said, stepping back. "Peace, bro. So? Did it work?"

"Yeah, I think it did a little," Mick nodded, still pumped.

"Your reaction seemed a tad quicker to me," Brooks said. "Damned near fatal, in fact. But that's you and me in an empty room. Do you figure on trying it in the ring?"

"Maybe."

"Then I'll try to make your next fight, see how it works. Thing is, I'm not sure I did you a favor, Shannon. From sixteen to twenty-four, reflex speed stays roughly constant. After twenty-five it slows. A little more each year. No technique can change that, not Sunlight Shining on Water or anything else. It's simple mathematics."

"Simple to you, maybe," Mick smiled. "Me? I was always lousy at math."

Brooks was right. The Sunlight thing was a gimmick, nothing more. But sometimes sugar pills cure cancer. Mick practiced the technique as he jogged the five miles back to the Alamo Apartments. Most days, not having a car was major-league inconvenient. Not today. It made his timing perfect.

He'd been trying to meet the woman from the fourth floor for weeks. She was just starting up the outside stairs carrying an armload of books. Small and slender with cinnamon skin, she was classier than most Alamo transients. Short, shaggy dark hair, probably styled it with her fingertips. Dressed well, though, dark suits, heels. A teacher, somebody said.

Mick couldn't guess her age. Twenty-five? Thirty-five? Didn't matter. She had the most penetrating brown eyes he'd ever seen.

"Hi," Mick said, overtaking her at the first landing. "Can I help you with those?"

"No thanks, I can manage."

"You'd be doing me a favor. I need the exercise. I'm Mick

Shannon. I live upstairs on seven." He held out his hands.

She eyed him warily, then shrugged and gave him the books. "Theresa Garcia. You're the boxer, right?"

"Guilty. Irish Mickey Shannon. You a fight fan?"

"No. Someone mentioned your name and I...wondered about it."

"Wondered what?"

"No offense, but it's kind of redundant, isn't it? Isn't a person named Mickey Shannon automatically Irish?"

Mick almost gave her a song and dance about Great Irish Fighters. John L. to Sean O'Grady. Didn't though. He was having a strange day. A day for truth.

"In Ireland, any Mick Shannon would probably be Irish," he conceded. "In Detroit, Irish Mick on a fight card means I'm white. Saves promoters the trouble of printing my picture."

"I don't understand. What difference does your color make?"

"Inside the ropes, none. But the fight game's a business. Most Motown fighters are black. A white guy helps sell tickets."

"So you're...what? A token white guy?"

"Not a token. More like a condiment. To spice up the mix, you know? And not just me. There are Korean fighters, Russian fighters. Couple years ago there was even a guy from New Zealand made some noise. Had the tribal tattoos and all. What do they call those guys?"

"Maoris?"

"Yeah, that's it. Name was Thunder. Heavyweight. Real strong, real slow."

"And did you ever fight this...Mr. Thunder?"

"Me? No, I'm a middleweight. Fought a Nigerian, though. Last night, in fact."

"Last night? Really? Aren't you exhausted?"

"Nah, it was only a four-rounder. I can go ten rounds easy, went twelve once a few years ago. Not so much lately, though. Mostly shorter stuff."

"Why is that?"

Mick swallowed, choking back his bitterness. Luckily, she was looking down, didn't notice.

"Prelims are all I can get," he said carefully. "My career's in kind of a slow phase now. But it's looking up."

"I'm sorry to hear it," she said wryly, her smile taking any sting out of her words. A good smile. He wanted to see it again.

"Why should you be sorry?"

"Because if things get better, you'll be fighting more, won't you? You might get hurt. Are you married, Mr. Shannon?"

"Nope. But this is so sudden, Miss Garcia. We only just met."

"It's Mrs. Garcia and I'm semiserious. I can't imagine a man like you having a wife. My ex-husband was a cop. I had trouble with his job being so dangerous. What do you do? I really don't understand it at all."

"And I had such high hopes for us. Some fighters are married, though. Heck, some fighters are women."

"I know. I'm sure you think I'm a hopeless square, but you seem reasonably bright—"

"Thank you."

"—and you even have a certain charm," she continued, smiling again, white teeth flashing against caramel lips. No lipstick, no need. "I guess I'm asking why you do it. Surely you must be able to do something else?"

"I plan to someday," he shrugged. "Nobody boxes forever. But...the truth is, Shannon's not even my real name. I got dumped at an orphanage, one of the sisters was from Shannon, Ireland, and she named me. Lucky thing too. Baby Doe's a terrible name for a fighter."

Another quick smile. Good.

"Anyway, I grew up going in and out of foster care. Learned to box in Boys' Club. It was the first thing I was ever good at, I mean really good, you know? People noticed me. Made nice. Went in the Marines after high school to earn money for college, wound up

15

boxing in the Corps too. I even went to the Olympics. In Barcelona."

"Really?" Impressed at last.

"Wasn't that big a deal. I was only an alternate. De la Hoya won everything that year. But I got to march into Olympic Stadium wearing American colors, eighty thousand people on their feet... I'm babbling, aren't I?"

"No. I had no idea. So, all this time, you've been trying to...what? Recapture that feeling again?"

"Not that so much. I didn't win anything at the Olympics. Didn't prove anything. I want to make a mark, you know? Win a belt. Be somebody."

"I don't have a championship belt," she noted quietly. "Does that mean I'm nobody?"

"Of course not, but...I guess I didn't explain it very well."

"You did fine. It doesn't make sense to me, but I can see why it matters to you. A little anyway."

"And that's good?"

"I don't know. You're not at all what I expected..." She reached up, her fingertips hovering near the scar tissue around his eyes. "It must be very hard," she murmured, as much to herself as to him, "to love something that can't love you back."

"Or someone."

"Or someone," she agreed, smiling, meeting his eyes. He almost kissed her. Sensed a gap in her guard, could have moved through it. But she sensed it too and stepped back, startled by the intensity in the air. "Thanks for carrying my books, Mr. Shannon," she stammered. "This is my floor."

"I'll walk you to your door."

"No need. Good luck with your career." And she was gone.

"Thanks," he muttered to himself. "Same to ya."

Kayoed. Another loss. So what? She wasn't so special. Except she was. Not like the bimbos and star-fuckers around the arenas. Theresa was bright and pretty and...she said he wasn't

16

what she expected. So maybe she'd noticed him too. And wondered.

Or maybe not. One thing for sure. She might think a belt didn't matter. Mick knew better. Everybody loves a winner. Nobody knows you when you lose. Ten years of hard training, hitting, getting hit. He didn't have a belt, didn't have a goddamn car and was halfway to getting his legs broken by Ducatti's goons. He needed to win something. Fast. But first he had to get out from under.

Tracked down Tommy Duke at his New Millennium Motors operation. Premium Pre-owned Vehicles, Fleet Leases and Repossessions. A used-car lot, but a posh one.

Tommy's office was just as posh. Thick green carpet, a carved desk, a brag wall displaying dozens of awards and color photographs. Tommy with Ali, with Evander. At Kronk's gym with Emmanuel Lewis, at a banquet with Mayor Archer and Coleman Young.

The man himself looked like a before-and-after commercial. Tommy at the casino was before, today was after.

Eyes red-rimmed, hands trembling, skin patchy, he was morphing into Mick's cornerman, Nate Cohen. Hag-ridden by permanent thirst.

His bodyguard, Ramos, was leaning against one of the narrow windows, looking out over the lot. Could have been wearing the same gray silk suit from the casino.

"It's about time, Irish," Tommy said absently, scanning some paperwork. "I was beginning to wonder. Thought we might have to go lookin' for you."

"No need. I talked to Brooks. He won't hassle your sister anymore. Ever."

"Roughed him up pretty good, did you?"

"No place that shows," Mick said evenly. "But if he sees her coming he'll run the other way. I guarantee it. And we're even now, right?"

"Even? You've gotta be kidding. Nine large to straighten

somebody out? That's a five-cee job, Shannon. You and your pals are still down eight and a half large."

"Dammit, you said if I handled Brooks—"

"I said I'd take care of you. And I will. You met my boy Kroffut last night. He scare you?"

"Hell no. I'll fight him in your garage if you want. Even money."

"Jesus H. Christ, Shannon. Have you got a death wish? You couldn't handle K on the best day of your life."

"Couldn't even handle Kid Ibo," Ramos sneered.

"You want your money and I need the work," Mick said stubbornly. "Besides, we both know his wins were nobodies. I'm not a big name, but I was a contender a few years back and K needs legit fights to get anyplace."

"Not just fights, Irish. Wins."

"You just said you think he can take me. So what are you afraid of?"

"Afraid?" Tommy rolled his eyes. "Afraid's got nothin' to do with it, you stupid bastard. It's business. You been around long enough to know the game. I paid seventy grand for K. If we pad a half dozen wins onto his eighteen I can get him a title bout. Win or lose, my end of that fight will be half a mil, easy. I'm not riskin' that kind of money against the chump change you owe, punchy. You want to fight K, Irish? I can arrange that. But only if we can work a deal."

"What kind of a deal?"

"I'll write off your debt and pay you...six grand on top to fight K, a four-round warmup bout in say, three weeks? Six thousand. Two grand a round. For three rounds. You followin' me? You're gone in the third."

"No fuckin' way. I'm not taking a dive, not for six grand or sixty."

"You don't get it, do you? You can't beat K in a straight fight anyway, Irish. He'd kill you. This way you get a payday, K gets a workout and pads his pedigree. Everybody wins."

"I don't."

"Sure you do, only you're too dumb to see it."

"But if I beat him—"

"—it would only prove K's as big a nothin' as you are. Nobody'd care and I'd be out seventy grand. So that ain't gonna happen, understand? K may lose to the champ, but not before. That's the deal, Irish. Three rounds, six grand. Do you want the gig or not?"

"Stick it up your ass."

"How about I stick my nine-millimeter up yours?" Ramos said, coming around the desk, reaching under his coat.

"Whoa, not here," Tommy said, waving him off, his eyes still locked on Mick's. "Irish Mick's a real tough guy. Stupid, but tough. So we'll save him for last. You'd better talk to your management about this. Because your dumb ass isn't the only one on the line here. Now get the hell out. While you still can."

Papa Doc's Soul Barbecue, best babyback ribs in Eastpointe. Papa Doc, a squat ex-welterweight, parked a tall diet Coke on the counter as Mick walked in. Mick carried it to the back corner booth where Deacon Washburn did breakfast, lunch and business every day from ten till two. Nate Cohen was with him, sipping Irish coffee, wispy hair awry. His face was bruised, his left eye swollen nearly shut. Mick stared down at him a moment, then slid into the booth across from Wash.

"Ramos?" he asked grimly.

Wash nodded. "He was waitin' outside Nate's place this morning. To send us a message."

"I'm going to find that skinny sonofabitch and—"

"Hold on," Wash said, grabbing his arm, pulling him back. "You find him, so what? Tommy'll just send somebody else."

"It's okay," Nate slurred. "I took plenty worse back when I was fightin'. Back in '78 I went six rounds with—"

"Cork it, Nate," Wash snapped, cutting him off, "we got troubles of our own. I take it negotiations with Tommy didn't go real well?"

"He wants me to fight Kroffut. For three rounds of a four rounder. I told him to stick it."

"Pretty bold, Mick. Only Nate paid the tab for it."

"I'm sorry, I never—" Mick shook his head. "I'm sorry."

"It's not your fault," Wash said. "Nate put his money down same as I did and he was old enough to vote last time I checked. The question is, what do we do now?"

"I'm not going in the tank, Wash."

"Nobody said you should. Only..."

"Only what?"

Wash sipped his coffee, considering. "We've been friends a long time, Irish. Too long, maybe. Makes it hard to see what's right in front of you sometimes. Hard to say what needs to be said."

"Like what? Like you said, Wash, we're friends. Say your piece."

"Okay, then, here it is. You can still fight, Mick. You train hard, you're smart..." He looked away, avoiding Mick's eyes. "Smart enough to know there's no belt waitin' with your name on it. Ibo got lucky with you the other night. Couple years ago, he couldn't have. You've paid your dues to the game, Mick. Maybe it's time the game paid us back."

"By losing, you mean?"

"Losing to Kroffut will get us out from under. If I put the word around we're dealin', we could line up half a dozen bouts in a hurry. You could bank maybe sixty, seventy grand by Christmas, then get the fuck out. Maybe make some kinda life with that little honey you been moonin' over. What's her name?"

"Theresa. Look, I know it doesn't make sense, Wash, but I just can't do it."

"Why the hell not? You think you owe the fight game somethin'? Like what? Your brains? Your life? You want to end up like Ali or Jerry Quarry or ol' Nate here?"

20

"There must be some other way. Can't you get me another fight?"

The fat man's shrug said it all. "Sure, Mick, you can fight a few more kids like Ibo. I can even get you a rematch with him if he's stuck in your craw. But you already know what it pays. And how it's gonna turn out."

"That's not much of a choice, Wash."

"Listen to me, Irish. You've been living in the same dump ten years waiting to move up. You got no car, no prospects. It's time to pack it in. Don't do it for me or Nate. Do it for yourself. Let me make the calls."

Mick glanced away, idly touching the bruises on Nate's cheekbone. "Okay," he said, taking a deep breath. "Do it."

"You sure?"

"I said so, didn't I? What's the matter? I turn crooked and suddenly my word's no good?"

"Nope. Man, I didn't think you'd ever wise up."

"Thanks, Wash, I appreciate that."

Wash eyed him oddly. "All the years I been with you, Irish, and I still can't tell when you're kiddin'. I ain't jokin' now. We talkin' serious shit here, with serious people. You even think about welshin' or backin' out, they'll come after us. All of us."

"I know. Go ahead, make your calls."

"Not from here," Wash said, easing his bulk out of the booth, brushing off his vest. "Some deals you don't do over a phone. But don't be piggin' out on me now. You still gotta make weight and look good on fight night, same as always."

"Not quite the same," Mick said.

Nate toyed with his coffee after Washburn left, a faint smile crinkling his swollen mouth.

"What?" Mick demanded. "Spit it out."

"I'm glad," the old man said simply. "Wash is right. Best to step away, before you get hurt."

"And the right and wrong of it?"

"The game belongs to the promoters, Mick, not the fighters. Always has. In the old days, gamblers ran it. Now it's all TV. A guy like K with a dead man in his record draws big ratings. Kinda like that *Survivor* show in reverse. People tune in hopin' he'll kill somebody up close and personal. He might, too. I've seen film on him. He's for real. A serious slugger."

"He's got no reason to come after me. Hell, I'm bought and paid for."

"Wouldn't count on that. Deal or no deal, he likes to hurt people. Why do you think Tommy Duke gave you the gig? Because you're such big pals? When are you supposed to fall?"

"In the third," Mick said slowly.

"Right. Assuming you make it that far."

Staring at Nate's battered face, Mick began to understand what he'd bought into. All of it.

"Did you say you had film on this guy?"

They watched it on the old Motorola TV in Wash's dingy office at the back of the gym, footage from a club fight in Tijuana. Jerky images, filmed in black and white with a hand-held camera. K and a Mexican. No sound.

At the casino in a suit, K looked somnolent, like a sleepy crocodile. In the ring, he was transformed. Bowlegged, barrel-chested, with jailhouse chains tattooed around his biceps and waist, K fought like a pit bull on amphetamines. Marched out of his corner at the bell, hands down, daring his opponent to hit him. When he tried, K slipped his punches and countered with brutal body shots, low and hard. Mick winced in sympathy.

"Carries his guard low," was all he said.

"Muhammad Ali started that shit," Nate grunted. "Young fighters oughta ask him what he thinks of it now. Only they wouldn't understand his answer. Ali don't talk so good anymore. What do you think of Killer K?"

"I can take him," Mick said automatically, then caught himself. Nate was grinning, shaking his head, then they both burst out laughing, roaring, a manic mix of despair and absurdity, laughing at themselves, their lives, the universe. Laughing until the tears came, laughing until...

K put his man down on the small screen. Hooked him to the liver, dropped him like a rock. The Mexican tried to rise, fell back. Then went utterly still.

The ref waved in the ring doctor, a pudgy chump in a rumpled suit who knelt over K's opponent. The screen went to static.

His smile fading, Mick glanced the question at Nate.

"They said it was an aneurysm," Nate shrugged. "Cranial blood vessel burst. Died in the ambulance."

"But K didn't hit him in the head. It was a body shot."

"It's always an aneurysm down south. No liability for the promoters that way. A guy takes a thousand punches that'd kill a gorilla, but when he croaks it's always from a vessel he coulda popped while he's bangin' his wife. Funny. You ever hear of a fighter screwin' himself to death?"

Mick shook his head.

"Me neither. Want me to run it again?"

"No. I've seen enough."

But he hadn't apparently. The video's grainy images kept popping onto the viewscreen of Mick's mind at odd moments. K's opponent hitting the canvas like a sack of cement, the ref counting, then waving for the ring doctor...

He knew better than to dwell on it. He'd handled fear before, knew how to squeeze it down, lock it away in a small corner of his gut. But in the past, he'd had his hunger to counter it. His hopes. His will to win.

Not anymore. He'd crossed the line now, sliding into the gutter with Tommy Duke and the rest. All he had left were his waning skills. And his guts.

And Sunlight Shining on Water.

At first he practiced the technique haphazardly, when he

was jogging or out walking in a crowd. Eyes wide open, he'd try to visualize a lake with sunlight glittering on its surface. Couldn't manage it. Decided the vision was too big. Tried a pond instead, on a farm he'd visited as a kid...

That worked. After a few days, he could dissolve reality at will, filling his mind with liquid golden light. But still reacting to the world around him. Roadwork became less of a grind, more relaxing. Instead of pushing himself, he seemed to settle into a natural lope that felt like it could go on forever.

In the gym, working the heavy bag or the speed bag, he found himself extending his drills, enjoying the workout instead of slave-driving himself through it. Going for the burn. Getting back into top shape.

Was the Sunlight actually helping? Hard to tell. After the first week, his punches seemed a bit more fluid, perhaps more accurate. But the improvement was slight, marginal at best. Maybe even imaginary. Seen because he needed to see it.

The change in his attitude was real, though. Working with the Sunlight technique made old skills seem fresh again. Brand new. Reminded him of the way he felt in the beginning. When his life was unrolling in front of him like a red carpet.

Perhaps it was because he could see the end of the Game now, a last round looming in the hazy distance ahead. At first he could hardly imagine it. But as the weeks passed, a new future began to take shape.

College. He still had tuition grants he'd earned in the Marines. With the money he'd get for his final half dozen losses and a part-time job, he could get by. Maybe get serious about Theresa Garcia...

Assuming he lived that long.

He started seeing Ramos around at odd times. Cruising past while Mick was running. Parked in front of the Alamo late at night. They never spoke. No need to. Mick got the message. Ramos could find him. Anytime.

Big K was haunting him as well. Or rather his video image was. Something about the snuff film kept chewing on him. K, rude and tattooed. Standing over the dead man in the ring.

Eventually, Mick figured out what bothered him about it.

Not the stiff. He'd seen men knocked cold before. Put a few in that condition himself.

It was K's reaction to it. None. No excitement, no dismay. Shuffling his feet in his corner, coolly scanning the corpse for movement. A tic, a twitch, anything. Waiting to finish him.

When the ref waved in the ring doctor and K realized the fight was over, he simply raised his hands in victory, marched around the ring, then waited with his handlers for the final announcement.

Never looked at the dead man again. Not once. Putting people down was his trade. If they didn't get up afterward, that was their problem.

How would he react to a fixed fight? Treat it as a workout? Dancing for dollars? Or would he try for kill number two? Either way, Mick figured tangling with Big K might be the longest three rounds of his life.

Naturally, the three weeks between were the shortest.

Two days before the fight, out for a run, he met Theresa Garcia in the park. Dressed in faded jeans and a Pistons sweatshirt, she looked like her own younger sister.

Her daughter was with her, a six-year-old stunner with chestnut hair and her mother's dark, intelligent eyes.

And Mick was lost.

Either girl could have melted the heart of a stone statue. Together, they were overwhelming. He wanted them. Both of them. A family. More than he'd ever wanted a championship belt. More than...anything.

Theresa seemed pleased to see him, even introduced him to her daughter as a friend. Then sent the girl off to play on the swings.

"I got your present," Theresa said. "Thanks."

"Present?"

"Tickets to the fight on Friday. To be honest, I wasn't sure whether to go or not. You know how I feel about violence, but...I think I'll be there. If you care so much about boxing, it can't be so terrible. Maybe we can have coffee or something afterward. If you'd like."

"Coffee or...something would be good," Mick said, trying not to grin like an idiot. And failing.

"Fine. See you then," she said. "And good luck." Kissing him lightly on the cheek, she trotted off to collect her daughter.

Mick trotted off also, collecting his thoughts. Tickets? Wash must have sent them. A three-hundred-pound Cupid in a silk suit. The question was, did Mick really want her there?

He'd always been a fighter, always defined himself as one.

And now? He'd be fighting, but he wasn't sure what it meant anymore.

He turned to tell her not to come. And found her watching him from across the park. He recognized that look. She was measuring him. Sizing him up. He didn't know why. But she was. And when she waved goodbye he simply waved back.

He saw an alternate version of that measured stare the next morning during the barely controlled chaos of the weigh-in. Stripping in a roomful of people, answering loaded questions from the press, and doing it all with K checking him out with his reptilian eyes, sizing him up for a body bag. His variation of The Look.

Sonny Liston, Roberto Duran, even Mike Tyson in his prime could psych out opponents with The Look, a dead-eyed, savage stare. When it worked, their fights were half over before the opening bell.

Mick didn't avoid K's glare. Didn't have to. He was seeing Sunlight instead. Sunlight Shining on Water. Kept the image bright in his mind during the tedious process of stepping on scales, having a ring doctor check his eyes and heartbeat.

Afterward, Wash took him aside to ask if he was stoned.

He'd been smiling the whole time.

Wasn't smiling that night, though. Hurriedly arranged, the bout was part of a low-budget card at the Motown Athletic Arena, a remodeled movie theater that hadn't shown a first-run film since *Night of the Living Dead*. Place smelled like some of the flick's zombies were rotting in the basement.

Lying on the training table, Mick listened to boos and catcalls raining on the poor slobs shambling through the first bout. He knew how they felt, laying your soul and body on the line to entertain people you'd cross the street to avoid.

Maybe the crowd wasn't seeing Leonard/Hagler II, but the punches still hurt, the blood was real. Rendered hopelessly hyper by TV remotes and hip-hop videos, fight fans figure anything slower than Mortal Kombat III is snail-speed.

As the bell sounded the end of each round, Mick got up and shadowboxed for sixty seconds, staying warm, staying loose. Then relaxing again. Or trying to.

Ordinarily, arenas had separate dressing rooms for the fighters. Here only a blanket divided the combatants and their handlers. Mick could see K every time he got up. Not that there was much to see.

Wearing a black silk hooded warm-up suit, K was sitting in a metal chair against the wall. Silent. Still as death. Not asleep, his eyes were half-open. But Mick got the sense the Killer was far away, cruising some primordial sea like a shark. Waiting for the taste of blood.

Just before the final round, the promoter stuck his head in the door. "Shannon, Kroffut, you're up. Show 'em somethin', okay? The natives are gettin' restless."

Mick was already up, shadowboxing, breaking a serious sweat. If K heard the promoter, he gave no sign. Nor did his handlers say anything to him. He never moved.

Good. Mick had always been a quick starter, liked jumping on guys too lazy to warm up—he shook off the thought. He wouldn't be jumping his man tonight. Tonight he'd be fighting to win a new future. No point in planning ahead. Follow K's lead, make him look good. Earn the damned money.

K didn't glance up as Mick followed Wash and Nate out of the dressing room to wait in the shadows at the rear of the arena. In the ring, the two tired fighters touched gloves, then plodded through the last round. After a brief delay for commercials, the announcer bellowed the decision to the muttering crowd. No one even bothered to boo.

And then it was Mick's turn, trotting down the aisle with Nate massaging his shoulders, the old excitement galvanizing his guts.

Crudely assembled in the center of the huge room, the ring was circled by roughly two hundred metal chairs. Fewer than half were occupied, street toughs and gang-bangers mingling with Ecorse rednecks and yuppie execs from the Renaissance district. Typical Motown fight crowd.

With one exception. Theresa Garcia was seated fifth row back, near the center. Wearing a fashionably battered leather jacket, with her hair tied back, she looked like a college freshman on a first date. But, she seemed to be alone. The seat beside her was empty. Good.

Scanning the crowd as he neared the ring, Mick spotted Tony Brooks, impeccably turned out in a fawn Armani jacket. Brooks rose, applauding as Mick passed, nodding a hello.

The only other suits in the arena were the ring judges and Tommy Ducatti's crowd. Tommy Duke had taken an entire row at ringside, close enough that his cigar smoke was wafting into the video lights overhead, close enough that his three-thousand-dollar blue pinstripe was already spattered with bloodstains.

Mick drew a smattering of applause as he stepped through the ropes. Not much. Once, he'd been a white hope. Now...?

In his corner, dancing in place while Nate massaged his shoulders, Mick realized he couldn't remember the last time a crowd had cheered him, even when he won. Should have listened to that silence. They'd seen this night coming a long time ago.

He did a perfunctory circuit of the ring as his name was called, then waited for K, who was taking his sweet time. Playing the big star already.

K was only halfway down the arena aisle as the announcer roared his name, hands on his trainer's shoulders, face hidden by his black cowl. As he stepped through the ropes, the crowd fell strangely still. It was Kroffut's first Detroit appearance but every fan in the joint knew his story. Boxing is a blood sport, unarmed combat with serious injury or death always a possibility.

K gave that possibility a shape and the crowd recognized it. In his hooded suit, K couldn't have symbolized Death any better if he'd carried a scythe.

The silence turned to a buzz as he shed his suit. Black trunks, black shoes. The Tyson Ensemble, no frills, all attitude. Mick's emerald green trunks seemed boyish as the two stood in ring center, ignoring the ref's mumbled balderdash about protecting themselves at all times. Eyeing each other.

K was giving him The Look again, and this time Mick felt its impact. The ferocity. Any doubts about Kroffut's mind-set vanished in that instant.

K didn't give a damn about any fix. He meant to make himself a reputation. That's why Tommy changed his mind, gave Mick the fight. And offered him money by the round. This was a payback for mouthing off.

Trotting back to his corner, Mick felt his belly clench into an icy knot. Worse than fear. Despair. The price for selling out was going to be a lot steeper than he'd thought. And it kept going up.

As he scanned the crowd, Mick realized the seat beside Theresa wasn't empty anymore. Ramos was there. Theresa was waving at Mick, cheering him, unaware of who Ramos was. But he was definitely aware of her. As his eyes met Mick's over the crowd he raised his hand in the shape of a gun. And smiled.

Instant chill. Turning back to face K, Mick felt like he'd been kicked in the belly. Sweet Jesus, they weren't taking any chances. A setup. All the way.

Okay. He was a pro. All he had to do was get through this. Stay with the guy, throw enough leather to make it look legit. Take a few lumps if he had to. How tough could it be?

He found out at the bell. K came charging out of his corner like a freight train, straight up, fists at his waist, head and upper body unguarded. No feints, no bobbing, he came in firing body shots with both hands, belt level.

Mick caught the first few on his elbows, felt the full power of them. On film they hadn't looked like much. Easily blocked. Which is exactly what K wanted.

Forget the corpse and the string of knockouts. K was a pure body puncher. Using the leverage of his squat frame, he'd hammer an opponent's arms until his defenses slowed, then dismantle him. *Knock down the body, the head falls with it.* The crude strategy made Joe Louis a legend. Now it was K's turn.

Sidestepping left, Mick fired a right cross, snapping Kroffut's head back, trying to slow the onslaught. It didn't.

Swiveling like a tank turret, K followed him, still punching. Backpedaling now, Mick blocked a half dozen powerful shots with his forearms and biceps. Felt like he was being beaten with a baseball bat. Then K was on him again, and all he could do was trade inside, trying to drive him off.

And even as he was fighting for his life, Mick couldn't shake the picture of Ramos beside Theresa. His fault. He'd bought into this. But what it meant was even worse...

He'd lost focus. Big mistake. Three punches into a combination, K slipped a hook under Mick's guard. Mick deflected part of the blow with his elbow, but it still bit into his rib cage like a meat axe.

Mick felt himself hunching over, knew it would be fatal, and fired off two quick jabs as he backed out. He had nothing on them, but the second jab derailed K's timing a tad and his next punch missed.

A good thing. The right cross blazed past his chin like a lightning strike, so close Mick felt the breeze. Missing the punch threw K off balance, spinning him halfway around...

And there it was. For a split second, Mick saw the opening. A clean shot past K's shoulder to his jaw. Almost took it. Almost blew his payday. And perhaps Theresa's life. And then the gap slammed shut as K pivoted, coming on again, hammering Mick's midsection like a wrecking ball.

Mick survived the round, barely. K caught him in the corner at the ten-second warning, might have driven him through the ring post if the bell hadn't sounded.

The ref, a retired light-heavy named Grissom, had to pull K off. Nearly caught one himself as K whirled on him in a killing fury. Mick could almost hear the clank as K's brain registered the difference between the tall black man in the white shirt and the Irish pug in green trunks crouching against the ropes.

Shaking off Grissom, K stalked angrily to his corner while Mick shambled to his, collapsing on the stool. Nate pulled out his mouthpiece, Mick rinsed his mouth and spat into the bucket, then leaned back, breathing deeply.

Crowd sounded unhappy. Mick wondered if they were bitching about his lousy showing or because K hadn't killed him. Yet.

As Nate sponged him down, Wash knelt beside Mick. But for the first time in four years and a dozen fights, the fat man was silent. No chatter, no coaching. No need.

Leaning forward, Mick whispered to Nate, gesturing into the crowd.

"What the hell you doin'?" Wash asked.

"Showing him my girl," Mick groaned, slumping back on the stool.

"Screw that. Get your head back in the ring, Irish. K's tryin' to make his name on you."

"Think what his gate'll be if he kills two guys. Any advice,

Wash?"

"You doin' all right. You still here."

"Glad to hear it. I was wondering."

"Seconds out!" the timekeeper called.

Nate slid in Mick's mouthpiece, then ducked through the ropes and hurried off. Mick stayed on the stool, resting until the last possible second, rising at the bell.

K came storming out like The Terminator, irresistible, bent on destruction. This time Mick tried circling right, jabbing, staying on the outside, away from K's crushing body blows.

And it worked. For nearly half the round, he kept K at arm's length, trading long-range leather. Boxing, not slugging. Crowd didn't like it much. K didn't either. Mick didn't care. Fighting outside was his best chance to reach his third-round payday alive. The extra few inches K's punches had to travel gave him the split second he needed to block them with his gloves rather than his arms.

Visibly frustrated, K's swings were getting wilder, showing Mick some openings. The guy was ferocious but not invincible. Mick even risked a quick glance into the crowd at Theresa—

But K spotted the lapse. And lunged! Enraged by the booing, he slammed into Mick like a linebacker, knocking him off balance. As Mick stumbled into the ropes, K hammered two vicious shots to his midsection, following with a murderous right cross.

This time it didn't miss. Mick saw it coming, turned his head away but couldn't avoid it. Took it flush on the jaw.

Felt his legs dissolving, turning to water. Mick tried to clinch but K shoved him off, hitting him twice as Mick stumbled to his knees, fouling him so clearly that the ref grabbed K's arms, wrestling him away.

Furious at being manhandled, K wasted precious seconds struggling with Grissom, delaying the count. Not that it mattered much.

Still on his knees, swaying like a willow in a hurricane, Mick was two thousand miles and ten years away. Walking into Olympic

Stadium with hundreds of athletes, hearing the crowd roar like great waves breaking. Yet somehow he didn't fall. He looked up instead, into the glare of the television lighting, into the golden sunlight above the stadium, feeling its warmth on his face.

Wanting to feel more of that sun, he tried to stand. Heard a voice in the distance...

"Stay down! Forgodsake, Mick!" Nate was yelling at him. Couldn't make sense of it. Realized he was on one knee. Unless he got up, the parade would pass him by...and suddenly he was back.

The ref had parked K in a neutral corner. And he was counting Mick out.

Damn! He'd been knocked down. Okay. Been here before. Mick waited till the ref said seven, then staggered to his feet, wobbled, almost fell again.

"You okay?" Grissom yelled in his ear. Crowd was roaring, drowning him out. "Take a minute if you want! You got fouled! Want to walk it off?"

"I'm okay."

"Kroffut! Get back in your corner!" The ref roared as K came charging across the ring. Seeing K jolted Mick a notch closer to reality. But when Grissom asked again if he was all right, Mick said yes because he was still in Barcelona's Olympic Stadium on the sunniest September morn of his life.

Mick's serene glow continued even as Grissom was cleaning his gloves, signaling for the bout to continue. And perhaps the Olympic sun saved him. Dazed, rubber-kneed, Mick instinctively danced away from K. After weeks of practicing Sunlight Shining on Water, the sunglow in his mind freed a lifetime of trained reflexes to trigger automatically.

Staying outside, only vaguely aware of his surroundings, Mick managed to deflect most of K's punches. The pain of those that struck home gradually dragged him back from Barcelona, to Detroit, to the arena. Into the ring. And the lights, and the roaring crowd.

Felt his legs coming back, firming up. Realized he was in a

Sunlight on Water mode. And that it was working. Sort of. K was helping. Enraged at seeing his easy knockout slip away, he'd reverted to the street fighter he was, windmilling wild haymakers at Mick's head. Deadly punches, but easy to slip.

The timekeeper's ten-second warning sent K's fury over the edge. Desperate to finish Mick before the bell, K lunged again. But this time Mick sidestepped the rush, firing off a machine-gun combination that caught K full in the face, snapping his head back, bloodying his nose.

K was so surprised he stood like a stone after the bell rang, the two of them glaring at each other until Grissom stepped between, waving them to their corners.

Slumping on the stool, Mick sagged against the turnbuckle pads, sucking air, grateful for the support of the ropes. Grateful to be breathing.

Half his consciousness was still dreaming in the golden Barcelona sun. Seeing faces reflected in the light. A high school teacher. Math? Couldn't think of her name. Dead now.

Theresa and her beautiful daughter. "It must be hard to love something that doesn't love you back..." Theresa. Swiveling slowly, he searched the faces in the crowd. And found her. She was on her feet, moving toward the aisle with Tony Brooks. Ramos was slumped in his seat, out cold. Brooks caught Mick's eye, grinned and gave him a thumbs-up. Okay.

"Mick?" Wash's voice seemed to come from far away. "We're almost there. Third round's coming up. Just walk out, mix it up a little and go down. You hear me?"

Mick didn't answer. Closed his eyes instead, shutting out everything, then took a deep, ragged breath and let it out slowly.

"No," he said.

"No? No what?"

"No to all of it," Mick swallowed. It was hard to concentrate. Part of him wanted to return to Olympic Stadium, hearing the crowd, feeling the sun on his face. "No dive. No deal. I can take this guy."

"What! Are you nuts? He's killin' you! You've earned your money! Go down!"

"No. The fix is off, Wash. Theresa's safe and Ramos is out of the picture. K's on his own now. So am I."

"But you made a deal! I made one!"

"I know you did. You were in it with Tommy from the first, weren't you? Had to be. You were the only one who could tell him who Theresa was. A little insurance to make sure I stayed fixed, right? You sold us out, Wash. Me and Nate both."

"Dammit, Mick, you're past it and you wouldn't listen. You gotta listen now. Tommy Duke—"

"Fuck Tommy Duke! You think after fightin' this guy I'm worried about Tommy fuckin' Duke? But you better worry about him, pal. Because he paid you to fix me and I'm done playin' along. Hope you and Tommy both bet real heavy on this fight, Wash, because I'm about to put his boy down."

"Seconds out!" the timekeeper called.

"Mick, don't be stupid! You'll walk away with nothin' if you walk away at all. It's crazy!"

Mick didn't answer. Couldn't. Wash was right. He probably was past it. Time to get out. But not Tommy Duke's way. Or Wash's.

Maybe he was crazy to care about this game. But you can't choose what you love. It chooses you. You can only honor it. Or not. And that choice is what you are.

Biting down on his mouthpiece, Mick stared up into the TV lights. Almost went into Sunlight Shining on Water. But didn't.

Instead, he breathed deeply, smelling the crowd, hearing their rumble like distant thunder. Then he stood up, steadying himself, staring across the ring at K.

He wanted to remember this. The noise. The pain. All of it. Clear and clean. Maybe he was getting punchy. Because he felt eighteen again. Olympian. Eager for the bell to sound.

When it rang, K came charging out of his corner, teeth bared, furious. Mick marched calmly out to meet him. And lightly tapped his gloves.

Startled, K glanced at the ref. Both of them looked so surprised Mick couldn't help grinning around his mouthpiece.

"Last round," he said.

IN THE TANK

by Andrew Bergman

Jerry Merman was a pudgy and freckled guy of about thirty-five who proudly introduced himself as a second cousin of the comedian Morey Amsterdam and then waited for a boffo reaction. He didn't get one. I asked him to sit down and he did, but the Negro kid who had come in with him remained standing. When I suggested that he sit down also, the kid didn't budge, and when I asked him his name, he looked questioningly over at Jerry Merman.

"His name is Typhoon Walker," Merman answered, taking a white handkerchief from the pocket of his blue suit jacket and patting down his brow. It was a gray but humid Wednesday afternoon in the spring of 1952, and my fan wasn't working much better than usual.

"Interesting name," I said. "He a weatherman or a fighter?"

"Correct on the second guess," Merman said pleasantly. "He's a pugilist, a light-heavy." He dabbed at his neck. "You know they sell air conditioners these days, Mr. LeVine."

"I think I read about that in *Popular Science*." I looked over at the young fighter. "Take a load off your feet, Mr. Walker."

Walker didn't make eye contact; he stood staring at the floor, his large fists knotted together in front of him. It was obvious that sitting down in a white man's office didn't come any easier to Typhoon Walker than asking for a job running the Bank of New York.

"You from the South, Mr. Walker?" I asked.

The light-heavy nodded in the affirmative, moving his lips as if in silent prayer.

"Bull's-eye, Mr. LeVine." Merman dove right in again. "Guess you're a private dick for a reason. Typhoon's from Mississippi, doesn't get any more South than that. You could tell because he's so shy, is that it?"

"Something like that," I told him. Walker had a long, sorrowful face, and his biceps rolled like dark music from beneath his short-sleeved white shirt. His hair was cut close to his well-shaped skull and his ears weren't much bigger than a child's. Despite the impressive musculature, he looked less than intimidating. In point of fact, he looked frightened.

"Go ahead and sit, kid," Merman told him. "Do what the man asks." Typhoon Walker finally sat himself down in a most gingerly fashion, as if my oak chair held an electric charge.

I leaned back behind my desk and started unwrapping a stick of Wrigley's Spearmint. I had quit smoking precisely sixteen and a half days before. "So what can I do for you gentlemen?"

Merman cleared his throat noisily. "I have a problem," he began. "Typhoon is on the undercard of the Billy Graham–Rocky Castellani fight on Friday. You follow boxing, Mr. LeVine?"

"I do. Not avidly, but I know who's who. Graham–Castellani could be a decent fight."

"Could be, unless Graham plays it cute, which he has a tendency to do." Merman took a small cigar from his pocket and stuck it in his mouth. "Won't smoke it," he said, too eager to please by half. "Just like to chew it."

"You can smoke it or stick it in your ear. All the same to me." I smiled at Merman affably, and for the first time I saw a flicker of a smile twitch at the corner of Typhoon Walker's mouth. "Are you Typhoon's manager, Mr. Merman?"

"Call me Jerry." A drop of sweat hung from the tip of his substantial nose and then dropped onto his shirtfront. It was warm, but not that warm, and I wondered if Merman wasn't a doper of some kind. "Yes, I have a half-interest in Typhoon with a few other sportsmen. I'm an investor by trade, but I enjoy the sporting life."

This guy seemed as much like an investor as I do a ballroom dancer. "What do you invest in?"

"Talent," he said with some pride. "Talent of all kinds. Some singers, a couple comedians, and a few fighters."

"So you're an agent then?"

He shook his head. "I don't like that word, right, Typhoon?" He looked at the kid from Mississippi, and for the first time Typhoon spoke a complete and comprehensible sentence.

"That's right, Mr. Merman, you sure don't," is what he said, and then he resumed examining his hands.

"And who are your partners?" I asked Merman.

"Different people for different ventures. Obviously, handling a young fighter like Typhoon is a different enterprise than handling a chanteuse like the inimitable Lily Francoise, who's opening a limited engagement this Friday in the Champagne Lounge at the Drake."

"And you have a problem concerning your fighter, which is why you came here with him?"

"We have a big problem." Now it was "we."

He dug into his jacket pocket and handed me an envelope. I leaned across the desk and took it. Across the front of the envelope was written in perfect calligraphy:

Mr. Jerry Merman
Personal & Confidential

"Nice handwriting," I said.

"I'd call it exquisite, actually," Merman said.

I opened the envelope, which had not been glued shut, but sealed with a gold adhesive circle on the back. Typhoon Walker leaned forward in his chair as I lifted the gold seal, as if to get a better look.

The letter was brief and to the point, and rendered in the

same silken hand as the envelope.

Merman—
Your light-heavyweight, Walker, will
be shot to death if he does not go down
and stay down in the third round on
Friday night. This is not an idle threat and
do not take it as such.

Friends of White Athletes

I placed the letter and the envelope on my desk.

"Not a pleasant thing to receive," I said.

"I'm terrified," Merman said, but he didn't sound terrified, not even close. His fighter licked his lips and stared at the floor.

"How about you, kid?" I said to the light-heavyweight.

"I don't know," he said softly, examining the parquet floor. "Seem pretty crazy."

"How do you mean crazy?"

Merman piped up again. "He means someone has to be crazy..."

"Mr. Merman," I told him with some force, "if I ask your fighter a question, it means I want him to answer it. If you keep up this ventriloquist act, I'll give you the names of a half dozen perfectly competent shamuses who'll be more than happy to humor you as long as you pay them in U.S. currency."

Merman spread his hands in a gesture of good fellowship.

"I was just trying to speed things along."

I turned back to the fighter. "Tell me what you think, kid."

Walker wet his lips once more. "This a four-round fight, mister. Why should anybody care what happen? Bet big money on a four-round fight? Don't make no sense."

The kid sat back in his chair, as exhausted as if he had just completed a filibuster on the floor of the United States Senate.

"'Friends of White Athletes.'" I said to no one in particular. "Sounds like a race thing, not a gambling thing, unless that's just a red herring. Or a white herring."

"Plenty of colored fighters," Merman said. "Why my kid? To make him an example? Makes no sense, just like he said."

I held the letter up to the light, as if looking for a secret message. All I saw was a watermark.

"Let me see what I can do," I told the two men. "And I need to hang on to this letter. My fee is fifty dollars a day, plus expenses."

Merman rubbed his nose. "That means you work exclusive for us?"

"That means I charge fifty dollars a day plus expenses. You don't like my work, you're free to dump me at any instant. And I want a hundred in advance."

Merman smiled, but only with his mouth; his brown eyes didn't join in the fun. "You're a tough son of a bitch. That's just what Typhoon and I need." He took a billfold from his inside jacket pocket, removed five twenties sharp enough to slice cheese with, and laid them flat on my desk, along with his business card. Then he and his fighter arose and headed for the door.

"Time to train."

"Where do you train, kid?" I asked Typhoon Walker.

The fighter stared at his sneakers. "They got me over at Hochstein's."

"Where else," Merman said brightly. Then he opened the door for his fighter, winked at me for no reason I could fathom, and left the office.

Over a solitary lunch at the Stage Delicatessen, I ate a whitefish platter and studied the letter. The handwriting was truly exquisite, which was not only incongruous but confounding. It was the type of calligraphy that nuns had taught childhood friends of mine who suffered through their Catholic educations with reddened knuckles and sore behinds. The beauty of the script only made the note more sinister. Beyond that, I was clueless, which was perfectly appropriate for this stage of the investigation, to wit,

41

the stage where I have lunch and wonder why the hell I wasn't born rich. I polished off my last pickle and decided to go downtown and see what was happening over at the legendary Hochstein's Gymnasium.

Hochstein's gym was an ancient establishment on West Twenty-ninth Street that was unprepossessing on the outside and got a lot worse once you stepped through the door. It was badly lit and echoed with the sounds of leather being struck and young men grunting and not infrequently farting as they aimed their fists at objects both animate and inanimate. Hochstein's existed on two floors, with boxing rings on each and a full array of light and heavy bags, plus rooms for showering and changing. Men of varying ages and shapes stood almost motionless and watched the boxers train, commenting to each other from the sides of their mouths or not saying anything at all. Some of these men were professionals, some were bookmakers, some were undoubtedly criminals, and others were like me, curious and oddly startled, like visitors to a city zoo.

At the time of my entrance, a couple of lightweights were enthusiastically banging each other around the front ring. They wore protective headgear and oversized gloves. A diminutive trainer wearing a porkpie hat stood beside the ring holding a stopwatch; he directed a steady stream of advice toward the taller of the two skinny kids.

"Downstairs, Chico! Downstairs!" the trainer hollered.

The taller kid responded by firing a couple of left hooks deep into his sparring partner's ribs. The sparring partner's face reddened behind his headgear and he countered with a right uppercut that the tall kid blocked with his forearms. The tall kid missed a wild left to the head, but came right back with a right to the shorter man's stomach, then danced away before the little trainer said "time." The two fighters turned and leaned over the ropes; they were both breathing hard.

"Better, Chico," the trainer said in a hoarse croak. "Not so much head-hunting." He waved at the sparring partner. "Okay, Vinnie, that's it." Vinnie nodded like a vaudeville horse, then climbed out of the ring with surprising grace. Chico stood and awaited further instructions.

The trainer threw him a towel. "Go take your shower, kid. Then we'll talk."

Chico hopped childlike over the ropes and jogged toward the shower room. I smiled amiably at the little man in the porkpie hat.

"Quick hands," I said.

The trainer took a Tiparillo from his shirt pocket and stuck it in his mouth. "If his brains were that quick, we'd be in business. Only had ten fights. We'll see." He squinted at me and lit his cheap cigar, which ignited like yesterday's funnies. "You got a fighter here?"

"Nope. I'm just a tourist." I handed him my card, which he took and studied for so long I began to wonder if he was literate.

Finally he looked up. "You know an Abe LeVine?"

"No."

"He was in the dress business, had a stroke, then retired. Had a piece of a middleweight I trained, Johnny Nitro." The trainer slid my card into his shirt pocket, then extended his small work-ingman's hand. "Barney Adelman. What can I do for a private dick?"

I asked him if he knew anything about Typhoon Walker or Jerry Merman and he nodded.

"I seen Walker train around here and he definitely has pos-sibilities—very quick, long reach, tremendous jab and straight right. Quiet kid, almost retard-quiet, but he ain't a retard 'cause I heard him talk a couple times." Adelman looked over my shoulder and waved at a heavy-set man who had just entered the gym. The man was wearing a fur coat and a fedora. "Hiya, Nick," the trainer said.

The heavy-set man grunted in reply and when he passed us by, the trainer said, "Nick Thomopolous. Has a piece of about thir-ty fighters. Gotta be nice to him."

"What's with the coat."

"Wears it winter, fall, and spring. Summertime he gives it a rest. He's a little nuts, is what he is. Maybe a lot nuts. Hard to tell."

I watched as Thomopolous strolled over to the far ring, where a baby-faced light-heavy in gold trunks was dancing circles around a sparring partner who looked old enough to have gone ten rounds with Teddy Roosevelt. People immediately clustered around the man in the fur coat and you knew he was two hundred and fifty pounds of dread and money.

I turned back to the trainer.

"What about Merman."

Adelman's face remained blank. "What do you want to know?"

"What kind of guy is he?"

"He hire you, Merman?"

"Maybe."

The trainer flashed a sour smile. "Watch your back. On his good days, he's a two-bit cocksucker."

"What about his bad days?"

"I heard he killed a guy. Maybe two."

"Really."

"Yeah." Adelman waved a copious cloud of smoke away from his kisser. "That's what I hear."

"Who?"

"Who what?"

"Who'd he kill?"

"Somebody who owed him. That was years ago. He doesn't do his own work anymore."

"He's a shylock?"

Adelman shrugged. "He always made a living, that's what I know. How come he hires you?"

"The kid was threatened. Walker."

"Threatened?"

"Got a note, fancy handwriting, says if he doesn't take a flop in his prelim on Friday he gets drilled."

Adelman took the Tiparillo from his mouth and scratched the back of his head.

"That makes no fucking sense."

"I agree."

"If there was big money moving on a prelim it'd stick out like a boner in a steam room. Can't hide that."

"The note was signed 'Friends of White Athletes.'"

Adelman remained mystified, then turned and whistled at a swarthy, heavy-set trainer across the room.

"Eddie, who's Typhoon Walker fighting on Friday?"

The heavy-set trainer didn't hesitate. "Sweet Eddie O'Brien."

Adelman turned back to me. "Sweet Eddie O'Brien."

"I heard."

"Knocky O'Brien's kid."

"Who?"

"Knocky O'Brien." Adelman stared at me as if I had just drawn a blank on my own name. "The Nazi guy."

An hour later I was sitting in the Old Seidelburg saloon with my pal Toots Fellman, a reporter for the *Daily News* and former house dick at the late and unlamented Hotel Lava, a fleabag on West Forty-fourth where Toots had received his bachelor's and master's degrees in human depravity.

"American Patriots Party," Toots said with a mouth full of bratwurst. I nursed a cup of coffee. "He's an ex-cop from Staten Island. His wife was killed, stabbed maybe forty times, they made a colored guy for the murder and Knocky went batshit. I mean seriously batshit."

"How batshit is seriously batshit?"

"Started dressing up in brown outfits, hung a swastika from his roof, began having meetings in his basement. It's legal."

"He have any kind of following?"

"Marginal, but its growing faster than you might imagine. A lot of extreme anti-Commies running around, and it attracts the more dim-witted of them."

"I thought the Bund had been outlawed."

"This isn't the Bund and they don't strictly call themselves Nazis. 'Patriots' is the dodge, but they're getting money from various Jew-haters and all these anti-Soviet groups."

"You ever meet him?"

"Knocky?"

"Yeah."

"Heard him speak once. Couldn't tell if he was really nuts or it was just an act." Toots finished his brat and wiped his hands. "Let me see that note."

I handed the letter across the table.

"I'm thinking that a New York guy named O'Brien, odds are he went to Catholic school," I said.

"You talking about the handwriting?"

"Correct."

"'Friends of White Athletes.'" Toots stared at the letter, then handed it back to me. "Almost too neat somehow."

"I thought the same thing. And his kid is Typhoon's opponent? It's so..."

"Obvious," Toots finished my sentence. "Obvious out of stupidity or obvious in a perverse sort of way."

"A blind alley."

"Exactly." Toots looked around. "I need some more coffee." He waved in the direction of our waiter.

"What are you doing this afternoon," I asked him.

"Getting laid or taking a nap, depending on my luck."

"I have a better idea. When's the last time you visited Staten Island?"

"Oh, go screw yourself, Jack," said Toots. "Do your own goddamn sleuthing."

That was just his way of saying yes.

An hour or so later, I drove my Buick Roadmaster off the Staten Island ferry and into the hills of New York's smallest and most verdant borough. Toots consulted a road map and aimed me in the direction of 28 Mohawk Lane, which is where Knocky O'Brien maintained his residence and the world headquarters of the American Patriots Party. As we turned on Choctaw Avenue, a Dodge station wagon came racing straight toward us, then swerved, went up on the road shoulder and roared past.

"Jesus!" Toots shouted and whirled around to look at the speeding car.

"What the hell was his problem," I asked. "Could you see who was driving?"

"Not really. A guy, his head was turned," Toots said, then pointed out the window. "This is it."

"This is what."

"We're at Knocky's."

Knocky O'Brien lived in a white two-story frame house that needed a paint job and significant roof work. The lawn and back-yard appeared well maintained but lacked any sign of human habitation. There were no bicycles or lawn chairs, no clotheslines or bird feeders. The place was quiet and altogether unremarkable, except for the large red-and-white swastika that hung from the roof. That was an eye-catcher.

"Am I the only one who feels nauseous here?" asked Toots.

"Goes right through you, doesn't it?" I said through clenched teeth. "If I had any hair, it'd be standing on end."

We each took a long breath, then started up the walkway. Toots and I were going to play it as straight as possible—he the earnest and inquiring reporter with an interest in Knocky's hard-luck story, me the warm-hearted private dick.

Toots rang the front doorbell. I expected it to play "Deutschland über Alles," but it just rang sharply. We waited, looked at each other, then looked at our shoes. After a minute of utter silence, Toots rang again.

Nothing.

I tried the door and it swung open easily. Toots stared at me.

"What the hell," I said, and we walked inside.

We entered and walked into a vestibule that contained a worn throw rug and an umbrella stand. The umbrella stand had been knocked on its side. Toots raised an inquiring eyebrow. There was a second door. I turned the knob; the door opened to a small living room. A portrait of Adolf Hitler in all his brown-shirted glory hung over the sofa and dominated the room. Dominated it until your eyes traveled from the picture down to the sofa itself where Knocky O'Brien lay sprawled out, but not comfortably. His arms were flung wide and his mouth was wide open, as was the rest of his head.

"Holy fuck," said Toots.

The room had the acrid reek of gunpowder and looked to have been thoroughly tossed. Chairs and a breakfront were over-turned; a coffee table was upside down. Books and pamphlets were scattered across Knocky's fraying carpet.

"Guess he put up a fight," I told Toots.

"Holy fuck," he repeated.

"That, too."

I walked over and took a closer look at Knocky, not that I was eager to. From casual observation, it looked to me that he had been shot at close range at least three times.

"Guess you have an exclusive," I told Toots.

"I guess I do. We gotta call the law, Jack."

"Give me a second." I wandered around the living room, opening drawers and sticking my fingers into cubbyholes. I came up with a couple of thumbtacks and fourteen cents in loose change.

"Jack, come on," Toots repeated. "We gotta make the call."

"Hang on," I told him. I walked over to a rickety bookcase that had been pushed over on its side. It contained some recent fiction, some racy paperbacks of the suburban housewives variety, a few volumes of American history and a copy of *Mein Kampf*. I pulled Hitler's treatise up out of the fallen bookshelf and it immediately felt strange in my hands, and not for reasons of ideology.

It was hollow.

I opened the cover and found myself staring at a rectangular compartment that held a taped-in plastic bag containing about a pound of white powder. I turned to Toots and showed him my discovery. He whistled.

"This gets more warm and fuzzy by the minute, doesn't it," he said.

Eventually we called the cops, of course, and in a matter of minutes two homicide bulls named Murphy and Clark arrived and came charging into the house like they had trapped Dillinger in the bathroom. We told the bulls what we knew, carelessly omitting the part where I found the pound of heroin. Toots said he was a *News* reporter doing a feature on the Patriots party, and I said I had just come along for the ride. The bulls didn't quite buy it, but Toots' press credentials were unmistakably legit. After they had asked us the same questions a couple of hundred different ways, they let us go, but not before Murphy told us, "He was good folks, Knocky."

I went into neutral. "Really."

Murphy's eyes were blue and very hard.

"Yeah, really. And he was my brother-in-law. My wife was sisters with his ex."

"I'm very sorry," I said.

"You're very sorry," said Murphy. "Glad to hear that. I'm going to take this matter very personal. Like I say, he was good folks..."

His partner, Clark, tried to hush him up. "Joe..."

"Shut the fuck up," he told him. "Good folks he was. All he wanted was to get these fuckin' Commies out of this good country."

I checked out the shine on my shoes. No way I was going to start jousting with this maniac.

"So I'm going to break some balls before this is over," Murphy declared, as if reading from the Declaration of Independence. "That understood?"

Toots and I nodded, then we shuffled out of the house and out to the street and into my faithful Roadmaster. I started the engine.

"A dead Nazi who dealt heroin," said Toots. "You found yourself a swell case, Jackson."

An hour and a half later, after dropping Toots off at the *News,* I pulled up to my apartment house in Sunnyside and found Jerry Merman pacing in front of the building. When I got out of my car, he practically jumped into my arms.

"Did you hear?" he asked.

"Hear what?" I said, "and how the hell did you get my home address?"

"Typhoon is missing."

"Excuse me?"

"I was supposed to meet him at Hochstein's at three o'clock. I get there, no Typhoon, and this kid is never late. I wait a half hour, he don't show. I call this fleabag in Harlem where he's parked, they tell me they haven't seen him all afternoon. I tell them to check his room; they go up there, and everything's in order."

"Maybe he found a girl for the afternoon."

"That ain't Typhoon, believe me. I know him over a year, you can set your watch by him."

"That's beside the point. He's walking around knowing maybe somebody's going to ice him. Thing like that's going to make anybody skittish."

Merman put his hand to his chin, as if in deep thought. "That's a valid point. He's frightened."

"It's not a particularly esoteric concept, Jerry. And how, I repeat, did you get my address?"

"I asked around. How about I come up for a couple minutes?"

"You want to talk to me, come to my office. This is my home."

"Fair enough," Merman said. "But I'm worried. Maybe you're right, maybe he just panicked. I just wanted to come up and try calling his hotel again, but I can do that from a pay phone, right? No need to invade your privacy. Can I call you later?"

"You have my number?"

"I'll get it if I need it," he said with a smile, walking in the direction of a dazzling salmon-and-white Kaiser parked in front of Al Deutsch's candy store.

"Jerry?" I called out.

"What?" He kept walking.

"What do you know about Knocky O'Brien?"

He stopped in his tracks. "You know about Knocky? That's fast work, Jack."

"What do you mean, 'know about him'? Know what about him?"

"He's a Nazi, hates Jews and colored." Merman nodded with some agitation. "You think he's behind this? Interesting theory."

"He was murdered this afternoon. That's even more interesting."

Merman didn't move a single facial muscle. "Who was murdered?" he finally said.

"Knocky." I liked saying his name. "Three shots to the head at close range."

"Holy shit." He paused with his hand on the fabulously beautiful Kaiser. "You sure I can't come up and talk to you about this?"

"I'm sure."

"Makes me extremely nervous, hearing that about Knocky," Merman said, "and knowing my kid is unaccounted for all afternoon. Not that I think he would do such a thing in a million years."

"Did Typhoon even know about him?"

"About Knocky?" He liked saying it, too. "I doubt it, but you never know. Maybe somebody at the gym told him."

"Didn't it figure that the note might have come from Knocky? He's a white supremacist, his kid is fighting Typhoon?"

Merman shook his head. "Too obvious, don't you think?

Plus, Knocky's kid fought colored before and nobody ever got threatened."

"You're right," I told him, and he was. This didn't add up at all. "So why start with Typhoon?"

"Hey, Jack," Merman said, "who's the detective, me or you?" He opened the car door. "I gotta go find my kid. This ain't good...he might have panicked, who knows? You can get a gun up in Harlem as easy as you can get a platter of chicken."

Merman got in his car and drove away. I turned and walked into my building with a sinking sensation in my guts. This case had started out sour; now it was getting positively rancid.

I sank further when I got out of the elevator at the third floor and found Typhoon Walker seated on the windowsill directly across the hall from my apartment. The sill was wide and faced the windows that looked out over the front courtyard of my building,

"Evening, mister," he said. "Sorry to bother you, but I have to talk." He watched me take out my keys. "Can I come in?"

"Sure." The door to the neighboring apartment opened and Mrs. Campanella stuck her large head out. She was wearing a house dress and an apron, and the aroma of veal parmigiana coming from her apartment was overpowering.

"Everything okay, Mr. LeVine?" she asked with some trepidation. Well-muscled Negroes in their early twenties were not a common or comforting sight in the building.

"Everything's great," I told her, and gestured to Typhoon. "Come on in, kid." Typhoon entered my apartment. Mrs. Campanella crossed herself and went back into hers.

I locked the door behind me and when I turned around Typhoon was staring out my living room window at the street below.

"You're in training so I won't offer you a beer, but how about a soda, kid?" I said to him.

"Just water, mister, if that's okay," he said.

I walked into the kitchen, took a Blatz out of the refrigerator for myself and poured some water into a glass I had bought at the Futurama exhibit of the '39 World's Fair. When I came back into the living room, Typhoon was still on his feet, staring out over the streets of Sunnyside like he was getting his first look at Paris.

"What's on your mind, kid?" I asked him, handing him the glass of water.

"He come out here?"

"Your manager?"

"Yes, sir."

"Yeah," I told him, and took a long cool swallow of my Blatz. "He just left in that Kaiser."

"Some car that is, mister."

"Sure is." I sat down on my couch. "I'd ask you to sit down, but my guess is you're gonna keep standing."

"I ain't much good at sitting down, mister," the kid said.

"You're scared."

"Yes, sir." He was figuring how much to tell me, but coming to my apartment obviously meant that he trusted me already. "Yes, sir," he repeated, taking a delicate sip of his water. "I think Mr. Merman's the one wants me to sit down on Friday night."

This was getting to be really fun.

"Why do you think that, kid?"

"He got money problems, I think. He got a lot of problems."

"He a dope addict by any chance?"

Typhoon rubbed his nose like it was a magic lamp, then he nodded. "Yes, sir. I believe he is."

"Heroin?"

Typhoon nodded again. "I don't want to take no dive, mister. I'm a good fighter and I could make money someday. Got a big family down in Hattiesburg. Five brothers and four sisters."

"I understand." I drank a little more Blatz and tried to sort this all out. "You think Merman is supporting a habit. That gets very expensive."

"Yes, sir."

"But how much could he or anybody make betting a four-rounder? You can't stake a bundle on a prelim; the commission would know about it in a heartbeat. Suspend the purses, nobody would collect anything."

"Maybe it ain't just about the fight, mister."

"You mean, maybe it's like a gesture of good faith."

Typhoon finally sat down in an easy chair across from me. He crossed his long legs.

"Yes, sir. Maybe."

"A small favor that would prove he could do big ones."

Typhoon rubbed his hand across his face. "Thing is, once a man doing heroin, he ain't thinking straight anymore." This was a very bright kid. Not book-smart, I'd bet he had never made it out of the eighth grade, but he obviously had a growing sense of how things worked in the low lives of the city.

"So you think he came to my office just to throw you off the scent, to look like he was legitimately concerned."

"Maybe. I don't know." Typhoon looked around the room. "Think he got your name out of the phone book."

"Really."

"Yes, sir." He bounced up again. "I better go."

"Want to stay here tonight?"

He turned his steady gaze back at me.

"In your house?"

"Yeah. This couch folds out. If you're that concerned about Merman."

"Couldn't do that, mister; hotel I'm staying in up in Harlem plenty good enough. Nobody gonna hurt me there."

"Fair enough. I'll see you at the gym tomorrow. We gotta play this straight, like Jerry's telling the truth and nothing but."

"Okay." He handed me his empty glass. "Thanks for the water, mister."

"Anytime," I told him.

Typhoon wiped his hands on his slacks and headed for the door.

"Kid, you ever hear Jerry say anything about a fella named Knocky O'Brien?" I said as he prepared to exit.

The young fighter shook his head. "No. Guy I'm fighting, his name O'Brien."

"Knocky's his father." I didn't want to say "was." Typhoon had enough on his mind already. "How about Nick Thomopolous? Ever hear that name?"

Typhoon bit his lip and nodded. "Yes, sir. Own a lot of fighters. I ain't sure, but I think Mr. Merman buying his drugs from him."

"That's where he gets his heroin?"

"I seen them talking quiet in the corner at the gym and sometimes Mr. Merman get real nervous until he see him."

"Strung out."

"Yes, sir. Don't relax till he see him."

"That figures."

"Yes, sir. Thanks again for the water."

Typhoon was about to leave when the doorbell rang. His eyes got very wide.

"Go in my bedroom and stay there," I told him.

He turned without a word and sped into the back. When I heard the bedroom door close, I opened the front door.

Standing in the hallway were Staten Island's elite homicide bulls, Murphy and Clark. Murphy looked happy, Clark appeared uncomfortable and gassy.

"We know he's here," Murphy said, just like he'd learned it at the movies.

I didn't say a word. Murphy reached into his pocket and extracted a sheet of paper. "This is a warrant for the arrest of Charles Walker, also known as Typhoon Walker."

"You're kidding," I said.

Murphy's eyes froze over. Clark rubbed his stomach. I figured him for a guy still getting over a late lunch.

"Not kidding, asshole," Clark said, stifling a belch.

"Kidding?" Murphy said softly, but with great force. "This dinge is going to fry for killing my brother-in-law."

With that the two cops entered the apartment and jogged toward my bedroom.

"Kid," yelled Murphy, "do yourself a favor and get the fuck out of that bedroom right now."

When nothing happened, Clark kicked the door open and I could see Typhoon Walker standing on the fire escape outside my bedroom.

"Kid, come back in," I yelled, but it was like trying to shout instructions to a deer standing in a meadow during hunting season. Typhoon just stared at me and the next thing I knew Murphy had shot him twice in the chest. The kid gripped onto the edge of the fire escape for a couple of seconds and then just slumped down, bleeding right through the rusting metal slats onto the African violets that Mrs. Leitner kept on the floor below. Then Murphy aimed one more time and basically blew Typhoon Walker's head off.

I sat down on my bed, sick to my stomach.

Clark looked at me. "Don't look so blue, Jack. We just saved the state of New York a bunch of dough. Keep this bum in the Death House through all the fuckin' appeals? Come on, we put him out of his misery."

I turned to Murphy.

"Hope this makes your wife happy."

He put his gun away and wiped his mouth, as if he had just ingested the juiciest of steaks. "You don't know how she suffered, you fuckin' Jew bastard, when that nigger offed her sister. This is just a little gift for her, like a pin or something."

"Joe, relax," said Clark.

"This kid didn't do it," I told him.

Murphy smiled, if you want to call it that.

"The fuck he didn't. He just tried to shoot me, didn't he?"

An hour later, after Typhoon Walker had been wrapped up like a Persian carpet and carried out of my apartment, I picked up my phone with still-shaking fingers and dialed Jerry Merman's number. I wasn't at all surprised to see that it had been disconnected. He had fingered his own kid, undoubtedly followed him out to Queens, and then dropped a dime on him. I wanted to kill him with my bare hands.

But I didn't have to.

At ten o'clock my phone rang, and it was Toots Fellman, calling me from his desk at the *News*.

"Thought you'd be interested to know that we just got a report that Jerry Merman was found in his apartment. Heroin overdose."

I just stared at the phone for a minute.

"That's three dead people today," I told Toots when I had regained my powers of speech.

"Well, that's heroin," Toots said simply.

"Bet you anything they had Merman bump off Knocky, because he owed them, and then they nailed him just to shut him up."

"Because you can't ever trust a junkie."

"Particularly this junkie. Jesus, did I screw this up."

"You're a detective, Jack. Not a fucking psychic. Have a drink and go to sleep."

I hung up and went to take a shower. A long hot one. When I got out, I toweled myself off and turned on my television. The Graham–Castellani fight was starting, and seated at ringside were Nick Thomopolous and beside him, smiling ever so happily, was Lieutenant Murphy.

I got up and shut off the set, then poured myself a bourbon and said kaddish for Typhoon Walker, whose ghostly presence filled the apartment.

YOU DON'T EVEN FEEL IT

by Lawrence Block

She found them at the gym, Darnell in sweatpants and sneakers, his chest bare, Marty in khakis and a shirt and tie, the shirt a blue button-down, the tie loose at the throat. Marty was holding a watch and Darnell was working the speed bag, his hands fast and certain.

She'd been ready to burst in, ready to interrupt whatever they were doing, but she'd seen them like this so many times over so many years, Darnell working the bag and Marty minding the time, that the sight of them stopped her in her tracks. It was familiar, and thus reassuring, although it should not have been reassuring.

She found a spot against the wall, out of his line of sight, and watched him train. He finished with the speed bag and moved on to the double end bag, a less predictable device than the speed bag, its balance such that it came back at you differently each time, and you had to react to its responses. Like a live opponent, she thought, adjusting to you as you adjusted to it, bobbing and weaving, trying not to get hit.

But not hitting back. . .

From the double end bag they moved to the heavy bag, and by then she was fairly certain they had sensed her presence. But they gave no sign, and she stayed where she was. She watched Darnell practice combinations, following a double jab with a left hook. That's how he'd won the title the first time, hooking the left to Roland Weymouth's rib cage, punishing the champion's body until his hands came down and a string of head shots sent the man to the canvas. He was up at eight, but he had nothing left in his tank, and Darnell would have decked him again if the ref hadn't stopped it.

"The winner, and...new junior middleweight champion of the world...Darnell Roberts!"

He'd moved up two weight classes since then. Junior middleweight was what, 154? And middleweight was 160, and he'd held the IBF title for two years, winning it when the previous titleholder had been forced to give it up for reasons she hadn't understood then and couldn't remember now. The sport was such a mess, it was all politics and backroom deals, but all of that went away when you got down to business. You sweated it out in the gym, and then you stepped into the ring, you and the other man, and you stood and hit each other, and all the conniving and manipulation disappeared. It was just two men in a pure sport, bringing nothing with them but their bodies and whatever they had on the inside.

He was a super middleweight these days. That meant he'd have to be under 168 when he weighed in the day before the fight, and seven to ten pounds more when he actually stepped into the ring. You wanted those extra pounds, she knew, because the more you weighed the harder you punched.

Of course your opponent had those extra pounds, too, and punched harder for them.

Darnell had run through his combinations, and now he was standing in and slugging, hitting the bag full force with measured blows that had all his weight behind them. And Marty was standing behind the bag, holding on to it, steadying it, while Darnell meted out punishment.

Marty saw her then. Their eyes met, and she didn't see surprise in his, which meant she'd been right in sensing he knew she was there.

Other hand, Marty hardly ever looked surprised.

She drew her eyes away from Marty's and watched Darnell

as he hit the bag with measured lefts and rights. He weighed what, 185? 190? But he wouldn't have trouble making the weight. He had two months, and he was just starting to train. All he had to do was work off twelve or fifteen pounds. Rest was water, and you sweated it out before you stepped on the scales, then drank yourself back to your fighting weight.

She always used to love to see him hit the heavy bag. It was fun to watch him train, watch that fine body show what it could do, but this part was the best because you saw the muscles work beneath the skin, saw the blows land, heard the impact, felt the power.

Early days, watching this, she'd get wet. Young as she was back then, it didn't take much. And, young as she was, it embarrassed her, even if nobody knew.

Fifteen years. They'd been married for twelve years, together for three before that. Three daughters, the oldest eleven. So she didn't get wet pants every time she watched him work up a sweat. Still, she always liked the sight of him, digging in, setting himself, throwing those measured punches.

She wasn't liking it much today.

"Time," Marty said, but he went on holding the bag, knowing Darnell would throw another punch or two. Then, when his fighter's hands dropped, he let go of the bag and stepped out from behind it, smiling. "Look who's here," he said, and Darnell turned to face her, and he didn't look surprised either.

"Baby," he said. "How I look just now? Not too rusty, was I?"

"I heard it on the news," she said.

"I was gonna tell you," he said, "but you was sleepin' when I left this morning, and I didn't have the heart to wake you."

"And I guess it was news to you this morning," she said, "even if you signed the papers yesterday afternoon."

"Well," he said.

"Last I heard," she said, "we were thinking about quitting."

"I been thinkin' on it," he said. "I not ready yet."

"Darnell…"

"This gone be an easy fight for me," he said. He had the training gloves off now, and he was holding out his hands for Marty to unwind the cotton wraps. The fingers that emerged showed the effects of all the punches he'd landed, on the heavy bag and on the heads and bodies of other fighters, even as his face showed the effects of all the punches he'd taken.

Well, some of the effects. The visible effects.

"This guy," he said. "Rubén Molina? Man is made for me, baby. Man never been in against a body puncher like me. Style he got, I can find him all day with the left hook. Man has this pawing jab, I can fit a right to the ribs in under it, take his legs out from under him."

"Maybe you can beat him, but——"

"Ain't no maybe. And I won't just beat him, I'll knock him out. All I need, what you call a decisive win, an' then I get a title shot."

"And then?"

"Then I fight, probably for the WBO belt, or maybe the WBC. And I win, and that makes three belts in three different weight classes, and ain't too many can claim that." He beamed at her, and she saw the face she'd seen when they first met, saw the face of the boy he'd been before she ever met him. Under all the scar tissue, all the years of punishment.

"And then I hang 'em up," he said. "That what you want to hear?"

"I don't want to wait two more fights to hear it," she said. "I worry about you, Darnell."

"No call for you to worry."

"They had this show on television. Muhammad Ali? They showed him talking before the Liston fight, and then they showed him like he is now."

"Man has got a condition. Like that actor used to be on

Spin City."

"That's Parkinson's disease," Marty said. "That Michael J. Fox has. What Ali has is Parkinson's syndrome."

"Whatever it is," she said, "he got it because he didn't know when to quit. Darnell, you want to wind up shuffling and mumbling?"

He grinned, did a little shuffle.

"That's not funny."

"Just jivin' you some," he said. "Keisha, I gonna be fine. All I's gonna do is win one fight and get a title shot, then win one more and get my third belt."

"And take how many punches in the process?"

"Molina can't punch worth a damn," he said. "Walk through his punches, all's I gotta do."

"You think Ali didn't say the same thing?"

"It may not have been the punches he took," Marty put in. "They can't prove that's what did it."

"And can you prove it isn't?" She turned to her husband. "And Floyd Patterson," she said. "You don't think he got the way he is from taking too many punches? And that Puerto Rican boy, collapsed in his third professional bout and never regained consciousness."

"That there was a freak thing," Darnell said. "Ring ropes was too loose, and he got knocked through 'em and hit his head when he fell. Like gettin' struck by lightnin', you know what I'm sayin'? For all it had to do with bein' in a boxin' ring."

If the boy hadn't been in the ring, she thought, then he couldn't have got knocked out of it.

"You worry too much," Darnell said, and gathered her in his arms. "Part of bein' a woman, I guess. Part of bein' a man's gettin' the job done."

"I just don't want you hurt, Darnell."

"You just don't want to miss the lovin'," he said, "the whole last month of training. That's what it is, girl, innit?"

"Darnell——"

"All that doin' without," he said, "just make it sweeter afterward. You think about that, help you get through the waitin' time."

"Tell her," Darnell said. "Tell Keisha how it went."

"He had a brain scan and an MRI," Marty told her. "This was to make you happy, because he had a scan after his last fight and there was no medical reason for another one."

"He's been slurring his words," she said. "Don't you call that a reason?"

"He sounds the same as ever to me," Marty said.

"Maybe you don't listen."

"And maybe you listen too hard."

"Hey," Darnell said. "Maybe I gets a little mushmouth some of the time. Sometimes my lips be a little puffy." He tapped his head. "Don't mean nothin's messed up inside."

"All the punches you've taken—"

"Let me tell you something about the punches," he said. "Gettin' hit upside the head? Nine times, you don't even feel it. It don't hurt. Body shots, a man keeps beating on your ribs, man, that's a different story. Hurts when he does it and hurts the next day and the day after. Head shots? Don't mean nothin' at all. Why you lookin' at me like that?"

"Nine times."

"Huh?"

"'Nine times, you don't even feel it.' That's what you just said."

"So?"

"Nine times out of ten, you meant."

"What I said."

"No, you just said nine times."

"Well, shit," he said. "You tellin' me you didn't know what I meant?"

"I'm telling you what you said. You left out some words there."

"Man, there's a sign," he said heavily. "I must have brain

damage, leavin' out 'out of ten' like that."

"It's cumulative, Darnell."

"What you talkin' now?"

"Punches to the head, the effect is cumulative. Even if you barely feel them—"

"Which I just said I don't."

"—they add up, and you reach a point where every punch you take does real damage. It's irreversible, you can't turn it back, and once you see signs—"

"Which there ain't yet."

"If you're slurring words," she said, "then we're seeing signs."

"What happens," he said, grinning, "my tongue gets in the way of my teeth an' I can't see what I'm sayin'. Why you lookin' at me like that?"

"Your tongue gets in the way of your eye teeth," she said, "and you can't see what you're saying."

"What I just said."

"Except you left out 'eye'," she said. "You said your tongue got in the way of your teeth, and that doesn't mean anything."

"But you know what I meant."

"And I also know what you said."

"Damn," he said. "We just had the tests. Didn't have to, had 'em to just keep you happy, and look at you. You ain't happy!"

Marty said, "What's that, a Coke? You want something stronger?"

"This is fine."

"Because you're not in training. You can have a real drink if you want."

"No, I'm fine."

"Well, I want a drink," he said, and ordered vodka on the rocks. "I'll tell you," he went on, "I won't pretend I wanted to be having this conversation, but we ought to have it. Because you really got to cut the guy some slack, Keisha."

"I've got to cut him some slack?"

"Molina's style is tailor-made for Darnell," Marty said, "just like he says it is. You look at tapes of his fights, that jumps right out at you. But that doesn't mean this is gonna be a walk in the park. Molina's ten years younger."

"Eleven. He's twenty-six and Darnell turned thirty-seven last month."

"Can we compromise? Call it ten and a half?" His smile was disarming. "Keisha, what I'm getting at, he should have training on his mind and nothing else, and what he's got is you hammering away at him, telling him he's slurring his words. He's training hard, he's tired by the end of the day, and is it any wonder his speech might be the least bit blurry? Time the day's done, I'm slurring my own words, come to that."

"Just let him see a doctor," she said.

"Keisha, he saw one. He had a scan and an MRI, remember?"

"A doctor to test his speech," she said. "There's a specialist, I wrote the name down. All Darnell has to do is sit down and talk with him, and he can tell whether there's been any damage."

Marty was shaking his head. "We looked at the brain waves," he said, "and he got a clean bill of health. No evidence of damage."

"Or proof there hasn't been any."

"You can't prove a negative. There's no evidence of any organic brain damage, Keisha, and he's been pronounced okay to fight by experts. You sit him down, have some quack listen to his speech and measure how his tongue moves, and it's a judgment call on his part, got nothing to do with anything you can put your finger on. And if he gets it into his head that there's something wrong, the fight's off. Doesn't matter that your expert turns out to be full of crap. The fight's off and Darnell's chance at a third belt's down the toilet."

"He doesn't need a third belt."

"He wants it, Keisha."

"And you? What do you want, Marty?"

"I want him to have a shot."

She looked at him. "The money doesn't mean a thing to you," she said.

"Not as much as it means to Darnell," he said. "His fight with Molina's on the pay-per-view undercard. He's getting eighty thousand dollars for it, Keisha. He's had title bouts where he didn't get that."

"We don't need the money."

"That's not how he sees it. What he sees is he can stand in there for ten rounds and put eighty grand in his pocket."

"Minus your cut, and training camp expenses, and everything else that takes a bite out of his check."

"Including taxes, which gets a lot more of his money than I do, and a lot more of mine, too. But ten rounds is what, thirty-nine minutes, start to finish? You do the numbers, Keisha, you're the one's good at numbers, but it's better than anybody ever made bagging groceries at the Safeway."

She looked at him. He met her gaze, then picked up his drink and drained it.

"And if he gets past Molina," he said, "which he will, and it won't take all ten rounds either. I can get him a title shot, prolly WBO but it could be WBC, and for that he'll make close to a million. And if he wins it, which there's no reason why he can't, then he's a man won three different belts in three different weight categories, and he's that much more desirable when it comes to endorsements and public appearances, because that's the only way you can make any money after you hang the gloves up. You show up at a dinner, you make a little speech—"

"How's he going to make a speech," she demanded, "if he can't talk straight?"

"He sounds fine to me," Marty said. "Maybe you got ears like a dog, hear things I don't, but he sounds fine to me. And nobody is gonna expect him to perform Shakespeare. All they want is for him to show up, three-time champion of the world, sign some autographs and pose for some snapshots. Keisha, all this is beside the point. It's what he wants, this fight and the fight after. Then he'll quit winners and hang 'em up."

"Will he?"

"He'll have no choice," he said. "I'll insist on it. I'll tell him I'm quitting him, and he'll have to quit."

"You could do that now."

"There's no reason."

"I already told you the reason, Marty. His head's the reason. All those punches he's taken, aren't they enough of a reason?"

"The man's never been knocked down."

"That Cuban fighter, had all those tattoos—"

"You didn't let me finish. The man's never been down from a blow to the head. The Cuban kid, what the hell was his name, they coulda called him the Human Sketchpad—"

"Was it Vargas?"

"Vargas, yes, and he had a funny first name. Filomeno, something like that. That was a shot to the liver put Darnell down, and that's a punch'll floor anybody, it lands right, and what did he do, Darnell? Got up, took an eight count, and hit Vargas hard enough to erase half his tattoos. Knocked him out, remember?"

"I remember."

"He's lost four fights, Darnell, his entire career. One early decision, it was the other kid's hometown, no way you were gonna get a decision there. You didn't see that fight, Keisha, it was before you were in the picture, but believe me, we got robbed." He shrugged. "It happens. It still pisses me off, but that's the kind of shit that happens. He lost that fight, and he lost a decision to Armando Chaco that could have gone either way, and he was stopped twice. One was a head-butt, the other fighter couldn't continue, and they went to the scorecards and two judges had the other kid ahead." He closed his eyes, shook his head. "The other was when he lost the 160-pound title, and you couldn't argue with it. Darnell was taking way too much punishment, and the ref was right to stop it."

"That's not how you felt at the time."

"Darnell wanted to go on, and he's my fighter. I got to want what he wants. But we looked at the films afterward, and we both agreed it was the right thing, stopping it. Look, Keisha, can't you stop making it harder for him? He's gonna have this fight, and one more for the title. He's got his hands full training for it. Why give him a hard time?"

"Gee, I don't know, Marty. Maybe because I love him."

"You think I don't? Keisha, don't be like that. Sit down, have another Coke, a real drink, whatever. Listen, Darnell's gonna be fine."

She started to say something, but what was there to say?

She was seated at ringside when he fought Rubén Molina.

At first she hadn't intended to be there. "I can't watch," she told him. "I can't."

"But you always there," he said. "You my good luck, don't you know that? How'm I gonna get in the ring, my good luck charm ain't there?"

She didn't believe she brought him luck, wasn't sure she believed in luck at all. But if he believed it...

She kept opening and closing her eyes. She couldn't watch, couldn't not watch. Every time Molina landed to Darnell's head, she felt the impact in the pit of her stomach. Molina didn't have much of a jab, he just stuck it out and groped with it, but he had an overhand right that he sometimes led with, and he was able to land it effectively.

In the third round, one of those right-hand leads snapped Darnell's head back, and he grinned to show it hadn't hurt. Fighters did that all the time, she knew, and it always indicated the opposite of what they intended.

Darnell stayed with his fight plan, working the body, punishing Molina relentlessly with hooks to the rib cage. In time, she knew, the body blows would slow Molina, taking the spring out of his legs and the power out of his punches, but meanwhile he kept landing that right, and Keisha winced every time he threw it, whether it landed or not.

Couldn't watch, couldn't not watch...

Midway through the sixth round, Darnell double-jabbed, then missed with a big left hook. Molina hit him with a right hand and put him on the canvas. She gasped—the whole crowd gasped, it seemed like—and he was up almost before the referee started counting, insisting it was a slip. He was off balance, that much was true, but it was a punch that put him down, and he had to take a count of eight, had to meet the ref's eyes, had to assure the man that yes, he was fine, yes, he wanted to keep fighting. Hell, yes.

He kept his jab in Molina's face for the rest of the round, and hurt him with body shots, but Molina landed an uppercut during a rare clinch and it snapped Darnell's head back. And there was another right hand at the bell, caught Darnell flush, and she saw his eyes right before the ref sprang between the two fighters.

The doctor came over to the corner between rounds, said something to Darnell and to Marty, shined a flashlight in Darnell's eyes. The ref came over to listen in. Oh, stop it, she wanted to shout, but she knew they weren't going to stop it, and the doctor returned to his seat and the bell rang for the seventh round.

And the seventh round was all Darnell's. He was determined to make up for the knockdown, and he pressed his attack, throwing three- and four- and five-punch combinations. The bodywork brought Molina's hands down, and a right cross with thirty seconds left in the round sent Molina to the canvas.

Stay down, she prayed. But no, he was up at eight, and the bell ended the round before Darnell could get to him.

The round took a lot out of both fighters, and they both coasted through the eighth. Molina kept his jab in Darnell's face through most of the round and landed the right once or twice, with no apparent effect.

At the bell, Darnell stood still for a moment, and she caught a look at his eyes. Then he recovered and loped over to his corner, and she got to her feet and pushed her way through, reaching a hand through the ropes and tugging at the cuff of Marty's pants. He was busy, talking to Darnell, using the Endswell to bring down a mouse under his right eye, holding the water bottle for him, holding the spit bucket for him. If he was aware of Keisha he gave no sign, but when the warning buzzer sounded and he came down out of the ring he didn't look surprised to see her there.

"You got to stop it," she told him. "He didn't know where he was, he couldn't find his corner."

"You don't know what you're talking about," he told her.

"Marty, his eyes aren't right."

"They looked fine to the doc. Keisha, he's winning the fucking fight. The other guy's got nothing left and Darnell's prolly gonna take him out this round, and if he doesn't that's fine because we're way ahead on points."

"He was knocked down."

"He swung and missed, and it was his momentum knocked him down more than anything else. Next round he came back and knocked the other guy down, and came this close to knocking him out. Another thirty seconds in the round and the fight'd be over and we could go home."

"Marty, he's hurt."

"I don't agree with you," he said. "And if I did, which I don't, and I tried to stop it? He'd kill me. He's winning the fight, he's winning impressively enough to get a title shot, and—Keisha, sit down, will you? I got work to do here, I got to concentrate."

Toward the end of the ninth round, Darnell caught Molina with a big left hook and dropped him. Molina got through the round, but in the tenth Darnell got to him early, putting him down with a body shot, then flooring him a second time with a hard right to the temple. The referee didn't even count but stopped it right there, and the place went wild.

On his way out of the ring, Darnell told the TV guy Molina was a tough kid, and no, he himself was never hurt, the knockdown was more of a slip than anything else. "He hit me a few shots," he allowed, "but he never hurt me. Man punches like that, hit me in the head all day long. You don't even feel it, you know what I'm sayin'?"

Later, when they replayed the interview, they pointed out that Darnell had slurred his words, that his speech was hard to make out.

In his dressing room, Darnell was grinning and laughing and hollering along with everybody else. Until his eyes went glassy and he mumbled that he didn't feel so good. He collapsed and was rushed to the hospital, where he died three hours later without having regained consciousness.

He was wearing khakis, she noted, and a shirt and tie, but he'd added a navy blazer with brass buttons, and brown loafers instead of his usual sneakers. He said, "Keisha, I don't know what to say. I tried to see you, I don't know how many times, but I was told you weren't seeing anybody."

"I had to be by myself."

"Believe me," he said, "I can understand that. I didn't know whether it was everybody you weren't seeing or if it was just me, and either way I could understand it. I left messages, I don't even know if you got them, but I don't blame you for not calling back." He looked away. "I was going to write a letter, but what can you say in a letter? Far as that goes, what can you say in person? I'm here now and I don't know what to say."

"Come in, Marty."

"Thank you. Keisha, I just feel so awful about the whole thing. I loved Darnell. It's no exaggeration to say he was like a son to me."

"Let me fix you a drink," she said. "What can I get you?"

"Anything, it doesn't matter. Whatever you've got."

"Vodka?"

"Sure, if you've got it."

She put him in the overstuffed chair in the living room, came back with his vodka and a Coke for herself. And sat down across from him and listened to him talk, or tried to look as though she was listening.

"Another drink, Marty?"

"I better not," he said. "That one hit me kinda hard." He yawned, covered his mouth with his hand. "Excuse me," he said. "I feel a little sleepy all of a sudden."

"Go ahead and close your eyes."

"No, I'll be fine. 'Sfunny, vodka never hit me so sudden."

He said something else, but she couldn't make out the words. Then his eyes closed and he sagged in his chair.

She was sitting across from him when his eyes opened. He blinked a few times, then frowned at her. "Keisha," he said. "What the hell happened?"

"You got sleepy."

"I had a drink. That's the last thing I remember."

He shifted position, or tried to, and it was only then that he realized he was immobilized, his hands cuffed behind him, his ankles cuffed to the front legs of the chair. She'd wound clothesline around his upper body and the back of the chair, with a last loop around his throat, so that he couldn't move his head more than an inch or two.

"Jesus," he said. "What's going on?"

She looked at him and let him work it out.

"Something in the vodka," he said. "Tasted all right, but there was something in it, wasn't there?"

She nodded.

"Why, Keisha?"

"I didn't figure you'd let me tie you up if you were wide awake."

"But why tie me up? What's this all about?"

That was a hard question, and she had to think about it.

"Payback," she said. "I guess."

"Payback?"

"For Darnell."

"Keisha," he said, "you want to blame me, go ahead. Or blame boxing, or blame Darnell, or blame the Molina kid, who feels pretty terrible, believe me. Son of a bitch killed a man in the ring and didn't even win the fight. Keisha, it's a tragedy, but it's not anybody's fault."

"You could have stopped it."

"And if I had? You think it would have made a difference if I threw in the towel when you told me to? He didn't get hit more than a couple shots after that, and Molina didn't have anything left by then. The damage was already done. You know what would have happened if I tried to stop it then? Darnell would have had a fit, and he probably would have dropped dead right then and there instead of waiting until he was back in his dressing room."

"You could have stopped it after the knockdown."

"Was that my job? The ref looked at him and let him go on. The ringside physician looked at him, shined a light in his eyes, didn't see any reason to call a halt."

He went on, reasoning with her, talking very sensibly, very calmly. She stopped listening to what he was saying, and when she realized that he was waiting for a response, an answer to some question she hadn't heard, she got up and crossed the room.

She picked up the newspaper and stood in front of his chair.

He said, "What's that? Something in the paper?"

She rolled up the newspaper. He frowned at her, puzzled, and she drew back her arm and struck him almost gently on the top of the head with the rolled newspaper.

"Hey," he said.

She looked at him, looked at the newspaper, then hit him again.

"What are you doing, trying to housebreak me?"

The newspaper was starting to unroll. She left him there, ignoring what he was saying, and went into the other room. When she returned the newspaper was secured with tape so that she wouldn't have to worry about it unrolling. She approached him again, raised the newspaper, and he tried to dodge the blow but couldn't.

He said, "Is this symbolic? Because I'm not sure I should say this, Keisha, but it doesn't hurt."

"In the ring," she said, "when a fighter tries to indicate that a punch didn't hurt him, what it means is it did."

"Yeah, of course, because otherwise he wouldn't bother. And they know that because they notice it in other fighters, but it's automatic. A guy hurts you, you want to make him think he didn't."

She raised the newspaper, struck him with it.

"Ouch!" he said. "That really hurt!"

"No, it didn't."

"No, it didn't," he agreed. "Why are we doing this? What's the point?"

"You don't even feel it," she said. "That's what Darnell always said about blows to the head. Body shots hurt you, when they land and again after the fight's over, but not head shots. They may knock you out, but they don't really hurt."

She punctuated the speech with taps on the head, hitting him with the rolled newspaper, a little harder than before but not very hard, certainly not hard enough to cause pain.

"Okay," he said. "Cut it out, will you?"

She hit him again.

"Keisha, what the hell's the point? What are you trying to prove, anyway?"

"It's cumulative," she said.

"What are you talking about?"

"The same as it is in the ring," she said. "Rubén Molina didn't kill Darnell. It was all those punches over all those years, punches he didn't even feel, punches that added up and added up and added up."

"Could you quit hitting me while we're talking? I can't concentrate on what you're saying."

"Punch after punch after punch," she said, continuing to hit him as she talked. "Down all the years, from playground fights to amateur bouts and pro fights. And then there's training, all those rounds sparring, and yes, you wear headgear, but there's still impact. The brain gets knocked around, same as your brain's getting knocked around right now, even if you don't feel it. Over a period of years, well, you got time to recover, and for a while that's just what you do, you recover each time, and then there's a point where you start to show the damage, and from that point on every punch you take leaves its mark on you."

"Keisha, will you for Chrissake stop it?"

She hit him, harder, on the top of the head. She hit him, not quite so hard, on the side of the head. She hit him, hard, right on the top of the head.

"Keisha!"

She set down the rolled-up newspaper, fetched the roll of duct tape, taped his mouth shut. "Don't want to listen to you," she said. "Not right now." And, with Marty silent, she was silent herself, and the only sound in the room was the impact of the length of newspaper on his head. She fell into an easy rhythm, matching the blows with her own breathing, raising the newspaper as she inhaled, bringing it down as she breathed out.

She beat him until her arm ached.

When she took the tape from his mouth he winced but didn't cry out. He looked at her and she looked at him and neither of them said anything.

Then he said, "How long are you going to do this?"

"Long as it takes."

"Long as it takes to do what? To kill me?"

She shook her head.

"Then what?"

She didn't answer.

"Keisha, I didn't hit him. And I didn't try to make him do anything he didn't want to do. Keisha, there was no damage showed up in the MRI, nothing in the brain scan."

"I said for you to let an expert examine him. Study his speech and all. But you wouldn't do it."

"And I told you why. You want me to tell you again?"

"No."

"Keisha, he had an aneurysm. A blood vessel in the brain, it just blew out. Maybe it was from the punches he took, but maybe it wasn't. He could have been a hundred miles away from Rubén Molina, lying in a Jacuzzi and eating a ham sandwich, and the blood vessel coulda popped anyway, right on schedule."

"You don't know that."

"And you don't know any different. Keisha, you want to let me up? I gotta go to the bathroom."

She shook her head.

"It's your chair. You want me to make a mess on it?"

"If you want."

"Keisha—"

"Some of them," she said, "the ones who took too many punches, they get so they can't control their bladders. But that's a long ways down the line. Slurred speech comes first, and you aren't even slurring your words yet."

He started to say something, but she was pressing the tape in place. He didn't resist, and this time when she picked up the rolled newspaper he didn't even attempt to dodge the blows.

A WINNING COMBINATION

by Brendan DuBois

It was dusk when Jerry Hughes stepped out of his car, slipping his reporter's notebook into his inside coat pocket. He shivered, and hoped he had shivered just because of the October air, and not because of the surroundings. He was in part of the city he had never been before, not once, and he made sure all of the doors to his six-month-old car were locked. His own newspaper had run glowing stories these past months about how the city of Cooper, Maine, was recovering nicely, with federal building funds and grants, but he felt like he had been transported into some industrial stretch of New Jersey or New York.

The streets were cracked and potholed, and most of the buildings had blank storefront windows, with cardboard signs wilting against the dirty glass, offering the spaces for lease or rent. Besides his own Toyota, not a single vehicle parked in view had an undented surface or uncracked windshield. Paper and other trash filled the gutters, and the few men strolling by—no women in sight—gave him a quick and blank gaze of hostility he had never seen before, up in Federal Hill, the arts district, Harbor Point, or even City Hall.

He shivered again and started walking. Before him, on a street corner, was a dirty brick building that extended out, with a cracked cement stoop. The sign above the double-glass doors said ROLAND'S GYM, and as he got closer, Jerry heard some laughter. He stopped, looked across the street. Three or four guys were hanging around a variety store that had bars over its doors and windows— the first time he had ever seen such a thing in Maine—and they seemed to be pointing and laughing at him. His hands felt tingly and he looked to the dirty glass of the doors to the gym. Just a minute ago the place seemed frightening, depressing, a place he would never look at twice for anything.

But now, with those guys across the street looking at him, the place looked as inviting as DisneyWorld. He opened the glass doors and walked in.

Earlier in the day, Jerry was at his desk at the Cooper *Sentinel*, trying to decide which upcoming event he should highlight for his weekend column, "Port of Call." The newsroom was fairly quiet, nothing like the old days, some of the old-timers complained, but Jerry rather liked the stillness that came over the place during the afternoon. The old-timers would talk about the times when the floor was tiled and typewriters were still used, along with the old teletype machines, and when it came close to deadline, there would be a low roar that would get louder and louder, from phones ringing and editors yelling and reporters typing.

Now there was the occasional *blew-bleep* of a phone ringing, and the constant, almost monkish *clack-clack* of computer keys, and except for the vibration that one could feel every afternoon at 1 P.M. when the presses started up in the basement, a visitor could be in an insurance or bank office.

Jerry looked through the offerings yet again. A press release from a woman sculptor who was opening her own one-woman show at the Cate Gallery in the Port District, and the gallery owner had called yesterday, saying the woman had a great story to tell, that she had left an abusive relationship and was now on her own, creating dark pieces of wood sculpted to reflect her inner turmoil. The other possibility was about a poet who was slowly going blind and was writing furiously, as fast as he could, because he could only create his best works by taking an old-fashioned fountain pen to white paper and—

"Jerry? My office, okay?"

He looked up, saw the receding form of his new editor, scratching at his butt and heading into his office. He sighed, picked up a notepad, followed the man in. Rick Burrows, one of the old-timers and one who hated anything soft about the newspaper. Soft news, soft features and especially, soft columns. Rick had been an assistant city editor until the features editor had left, and he was warming that seat until a new editor could be hired. A month ago Jerry didn't know how good he had it with Rhonda Owens. The two of them worked well together, explored the art and history of the old port city, and while she could be a tough editor, she had loved his copy and loved his stories even more. But now she and her partner had gone out west to Santa Fe, leaving him behind. He still couldn't shake off the feelings of abandonment, as silly as it sounded.

Rick sat down at his desk, breathing hard, his thin black hair not even coming close to hiding a large bald spot. He was close to three hundred pounds in weight and sucked a lot of hard candies, since the office was a no smoking area and it seemed his editor didn't like making the fifty-yard walk to smoke outside. The office was a mess: old coffee cups, file folders, filing cabinets so full that the drawers couldn't shut. Rhonda's office, at the other side of the newsroom, was still dark and closed, almost like a shrine. Days like this one, Jerry thought, he considered lighting a candle outside of Rhonda's office, still mourning for her passing.

Rick coughed. "I'll get right to it, Jerry. There's gonna be some changes in your column."

Jerry said, "Well, I could try writing them in French, but it's been a while. Those damn verbs keep tripping me up."

Rick's eyes narrowed. "What you call your sense of humor won't go far with me, or anybody else in this paper."

"Thanks for the heads up."

"You didn't mean that, so I won't say you're welcome," Rick said. He opened the top drawer of his desk, pulled out five or six lottery scratch tickets. In his large hands the quarter he used to rub off each ticket looked as small as a nickel. "Let's see. Last column you wrote about a high school dance club that needs to raise money for a trip to Augusta. Week before that, you wrote about a songwriter whose favorite guitar got stolen. And the week before that, a story about a glassblower who burned his right hand and can't work as well anymore. You see a pattern here, Jerry?"

He was going to say something wise about a collection of prize-winning pieces for next year's New England Press Association Awards, but he didn't like the way Rick wasn't even looking at him, how he was concentrating on carefully scratching off each lottery ticket. Little bits of gray fluff started piling up around his hands. "No, I don't see a pattern," Jerry said.

"Well, I'm glad to clue you in, me being your editor and all. Those stories are heart-tugging pieces about the artists in our fair city and the troubles they face. In other words, about losers that nobody cares about."

His hands tightened about his notebook. "I care about them. And so do our readers."

"Wrong," Rick said. "You care about them and hardly anybody else does. Which means your columns are going to take another tack, Jerry. You're going to start doing stories about real people in the city. And you're gonna start with this one."

Rick wrote something down on the back of an empty envelope, passed it over. "Here you go. Sonny Gaston. At Roland's Gym. Get there this afternoon."

Jerry didn't pick up the scrap of paper. "Who's Sonny Gaston?"

"Kid about twenty, twenty-one. Has had some rough times growing up. Nice feature piece."

He picked up the envelope. "All right, who is he? A gymnast?"

Rick laughed. "Yeah, in a manner of speaking. He's a boxer."

"A fighter?" Jerry asked, looking up in surprise.

"Yeah, a boxer."

"You want me to do a story about a guy who fights somebody else? On purpose?"

"Sure seems that way."

Jerry pushed the paper back. "No. I won't. I've got a reputation with my readers and the paper. Look, Rick. I'm a features column. I do pieces about the art life in Cooper, culture and—"

"Wrong," Rick said, returning to his lottery tickets. "You're a columnist in the features section of the *Sentinel*. You do columns about feature stories that take place in Cooper. You're going to do a column about this kid boxer. And it's going to be a good column. And if you start whining and thinking of excuses for not doing it, here's a news flash. Your old editor's out west with her girlfriend. Her old job may not be filled. There may be cutbacks coming down the pike for the *Sentinel*, which means I'm doing everything to keep my job 'cause I got tuition to pay for two daughters. And the first ones out the door will be writers who don't listen to the editors. There. Clear enough?"

Jerry just nodded. Picked up the old envelope and left without a word.

Inside the gym the air seemed like it came from another planet, perhaps Venus of the old science fiction pulp magazines. It was thick and hot and muggy, and filled with powerful scents that almost made him gag. There was a reception desk of sorts that was empty and some old easy chairs kept together by duct tape and stitching. The tile floor looked like it had been white once, and was now a dull yellow. He followed the noise down a small corridor, and then paused as he entered the gym, now breathing through his mouth because the smell was so thick. The first thing he noticed was the crowded condition of the gym, followed instantly by the noise, the loud sounds coming from every part of the room. There was a series of rapid *slap-slap-slap* sounds, coming from boxers doing jump-rope exercises, their black-booted feet pounding the floor, and another, harsher, *slap-slap-slap* sound came from other boxers in the corner, striking at hanging punching bags with such speed that their gloved hands were a blur. There were deeper, thumping noises as other boxers struck heavier punching bags, the chains holding them up jangling with each blow. Dominating the room were two raised platforms, bounded on all four sides by ropes. Rings, Jerry thought, though why in hell would they be called rings if they were square?

In each ring were two fighters, seemingly egged on by coaches from the sidelines. The fighters wore shorts and tank-top T-shirts, and each wore a padded helmet. In addition to the noises of the jump roping, the bag punching, and the feet slapping the ground, there were sounds from the boxers and coaches themselves. Grunts, snorts, puffing sounds like locomotives from the breathing of the boxers, and the shouts from the coaches: "Jab! Jab! Duck now! Keep your elbows in!"

Jerry felt like he had been upended from a safe and secure platform and dumped into a swamp of scents and sounds he had never experienced before. The young men in here were hitting each other, were actually striking blows against one another, and he felt nauseous at hearing the sounds of the gloves striking flesh. He remembered reading somewhere that boxing was called "the sweet science," but he didn't see anything sweet here, not at all. One young boxer sat down on a stool, breathing hard, sweat making his dark skin glisten, as an older man leaned over and yelled in his ear. The boxer nodded blankly, took a swig of water and leaned over and spat it onto the dirty floor.

Sweet science indeed.

He looked around, trying to spot somebody in charge, but everybody seemed locked in their own little world. The fighters at the different punching bags were eyeing what they were doing, and the boxers in the rings were either fighting their opponent or listening to their coaches. No one paid him any mind at all, and he looked at the large clocks on the stained walls, at the signs that said THINK LIKE A CHAMP, HIT LIKE A CHAMP and peeling posters from boxing matches from years gone by. Finally, a slim man in trunks and T-shirt came by, wiping at his face with a towel, and Jerry said, "Excuse me?"

"Yeah?" came the voice, partially muffled from the towel.

"I'm looking for the owner," he said. "Or the manager. Or somebody in charge."

The towel came down, exposing a puffy lip and swollen cheek, but the guy didn't seem upset by his injury. "That'd be Tom. Tom Hart. The guy over there in the corner."

"Thanks," Jerry said, but the young man had already left. Jerry walked over to the corner, where a man in his early forties was examining a clipboard. He was about Jerry's size but his shoulders were wider. He had a thick black moustache and prominent ears. He looked up as Jerry approached and said, "You're the guy from the *Sentinel*."

"Yes, I am," he said. "Jerry Hughes. I'm sorry, have we met before?"

Tom laughed. "No, I was expecting a guy from the paper to stop by, and don't be offended, pal, but you sort of don't fit in. You know?"

Jerry knew it well, felt that flush of shame that came from being a good student in grammar school and high school, good enough with books and assignments, never quite good enough for sports or girls. "Yeah, I know. I'm not quite meeting the dress code around here."

Tom smiled. "Good call on your part. I know your editor, Rick. Looking for Sonny, right?"

"That's right."

Tom pointed over to the far corner, where a young boxer was punching a suspended bag, his moving hands a blur. "That's him. Go on and talk to him, but good luck."

Jerry didn't like being told good luck in a place where men were pounding on each other. "What do you mean, good luck?"

Tom smiled again, showing surprisingly good teeth, or the results of a good dentist. "I mean I talked to him about an article, and he's not too crazy about it. See, he's a good kid, big heart and fast hands. He just hasn't had many breaks. He's got a big fight coming up in a couple of days that he's gonna lose, and well...I thought something like this might make it better. Give him something positive before he gets whaled on."

Sure, Jerry thought, that's what his column was designed for. To make slow-thinking punchers feel better. "All right, I'll see what I can do. Thanks."

"Sure."

Jerry walked over to the corner, feeling exposed again. At least Tom seemed friendly and cheerful enough. He almost wished Tom had escorted him over to the fighter, and then pushed that thought aside. Sure, he wasn't a fighter, but he was an up-and-coming columnist. He had nothing to apologize for.

He stood near Sonny, watching him work the bag. The sound of the gloves striking the leather was a constant noise that sounded like a fast engine, whirring along. He tried to catch the boxer's eye but the young man stared straight ahead. He had on black shorts with red stripes, a tank-top T-shirt in the same color scheme, and the gloves were a dull red. His black hair was cut short. Sweat was rolling down the side of his face and along his thick neck. He was breathing hard, the noise almost as loud as the punches, and then he said "Hah!" and gave the bag one more punch and stepped back. He looked over and wiped his face clumsily with the back of one glove.

"Didn't mean to ignore you," he said. "Thing is, I'm working, and I don't like being disturbed. Gotta finish this part of the workout. What's up?"

"Jerry Hughes from the—"

Sonny nodded, wiped his sweating face again. Each glove

had EVERLAST on the cuff. "Yeah, I know, the *Sentinel*. Tom told me all about it. You wanna do a story on me, right?"

"That's right," Jerry said, thinking maybe a half hour or an hour with this guy, and he'd be back home in his apartment in the harbor district. With a nice glass of wine. "A profile for my column."

Sonny shook his head. "Nope."

Jerry said, "It'll be a nice feature, with a photo and everything."

Sonny started tugging the gloves off and walked out of the corner. Jerry stuck close as he said, "What do you think I am, stupid? Talk to you and get my pic in the paper? Think I'm that hard up for attention?"

Jerry said, "Look, I thought this was all cleared with your, um..."

Sonny got one glove off, revealing a hand wrapped in some sort of cloth strip. "Manager? Owner? Tom's a nice guy and he does manage a bunch of us, but trust me, I'm just one guy. And mister, this wasn't cleared with me. He thought a story about me would be interesting. Bah. I know the friggin' drill. Poor kid trying to claw his way out of the projects by boxing, keeps on going though he's never won a real bout. Sorry, don't need the grief. Tom thought it might change people's minds about his gym and such, and I don't care. I told him that and I'll tell you. I don't need the grief."

By now Sonny's voice was raised such that a few other fighters in training noticed it, and they looked over at them. Jerry suddenly felt outnumbered. Still, he reached into his coat pocket, pulled out his business card. "I sure wish you'd change your mind. It would be a nice story. I can guarantee you that. I'm not an investigative reporter, trying to sniff something out. Just a human interest story, that's all."

Sonny took the card, tucked it into the front of his shorts. "My mind might get stirred up now and then, but I don't think I'm gonna change it. Look, it's time for me to shower up and get out of here. See ya."

Jerry saw him walk down another corridor, thought about chasing him into the locker room and decided arguing with a naked man who settled questions with his fists wasn't a good idea. He looked around for Tom, the gym owner and manager, and spotted him in one of the rings, working with a fighter who didn't look more than fourteen or fifteen. Jerry waited, thinking maybe he could talk again with Tom and figure something out, but after a while, the noise and the smells and the humidity just got to be too much. It was time to leave.

Outside it was dark and the cold air seemed as sharp as razors. Jerry coughed and zipped up his coat. A bust, but it wasn't his fault. He'd talk to Rick tomorrow, see if he could work something out. Maybe Rick could get a hold of the gym owner—Rick was an old-timer, and no wonder he knew the guy—or maybe Rick would assign him something else. And nothing against the gym or the boxers, but he felt like his clothes would need to be dumped in the laundry hamper when he got home.

Home. There was a thought. Ahead was his car, still looking lonely in the cluttered street, and he wondered how he would approach Rick tomorrow when he told him what had happened.

He was still thinking about his options when they jumped him.

The noise of their feet came first, as they raced out of an alleyway, and he turned just as a fist struck him in the chest. He coughed and tried to shout out as more fists pummeled him, as he hit the ground, dimly recalling the group of toughs who had been eyeing him earlier from across the street.

"Move, move," one said harshly. "Grab the loser's wallet!"

He rolled, tried covering his head with his hands, tried to say something but he couldn't catch his breath, couldn't do a damn thing, as the kicks and punches continued, and then—

A yelp. Another yelp. "Damn it, who the—"

Another shout.

He rolled on his back, tried to sit up. His hands were shaking. Two of his attackers were on their hands and knees, trying to crawl away. A third seemed to be helping yet another as they went back into the alley.

Then a shape came toward him, knelt down. It was Sonny, breathing hard, dressed in jeans and a gray sweatshirt.

"You okay?" he asked.

"No," he said. "I'm not."

Sonny laughed. "It's okay. You'll feel worse tomorrow. Here, let me help you up."

A half hour later they were in an all-night diner, sitting in a booth in the far corner. Sonny ordered a cup of coffee and a slice of apple pie, while Jerry made do with a tall glass of ice water. He took some of the ice cubes out and wrapped them in his handkerchief, which he pressed against his left cheek. Sonny nodded and said, "You've also got some scrapes on your hands, but you're okay. I've seen worse."

Jerry felt the shakes continuing in his legs as he kept the ice and handkerchief against his face. "I don't see why you thought calling the cops would be a waste of time."

Sonny shrugged, poured some sugar into his coffee. "Where do you live?"

"Harbor Point."

"Nice place. You call there about being roughed up, you'd get a couple of squad cars, maybe even a detective assigned to look into the case. Down here, same call would have a cruiser come by when they had a chance. Maybe a ten, twenty-minute wait for someone to show up. You want to keep on hanging out there, waiting for a cop to show up? Maybe those guys would come back later, with their friends. Doesn't sound like much of a choice. I thought we made the right call."

Jerry moved his tongue slowly about his mouth. All his teeth seemed okay, but there was a wound inside his cheek where he had bitten himself. "Thanks," he said. "I should have said thanks."

Another shrug. "No big deal. Four on one isn't real fair. I decided to even things up."

"By going against four? Really?"

He sawed into the piece of pie with his fork. "Sure. Those clowns didn't know how to fight."

Jerry shifted the ice pack against his face, winced at the sharpness of the pain. "Really? Seems like they did all right to me."

Sonny smiled. "No offense, but it wasn't a fight until I got there. Those four guys were whacking you, but there wasn't anything pro about it. Just fists and kicks. I got there and scattered them out with a couple of good jabs. That's all. They had no punches, no brains, no strategy."

Jerry watched Sonny as he picked up the piece of pie, chewed and swallowed. "Strategy?"

"Sure. Strategy. Oh, I get it. You think I'm a dumb guy, a guy who can only think with his fists, right?"

"Ah, no, not really..."

"Don't worry, I won't get pissed. I know what you're thinking, and that's fine. I get that all the time. Look, tell me, when's the last time you've been in a fight. Not counting tonight."

"Tonight?" Jerry thought back, went through, thinking and examining, going back and back and... "Grammar school. I think. Fourth or fifth grade, in a schoolyard. Nuns came and broke it up. That was that."

"Uh huh," Sonny said, working on another piece of pie. "Since you're so quick to judge who I am and what I do, here's a taste of it for you. Nuns, huh? Private school, nice little neighborhood, high school and college. Safe career, working with your mind. Nothing physically demanding. Nothing like shingling a roof in a rainstorm, or framing a house in a cold breeze. Both parents alive and loving and all that good stuff. A good guess?"

Ice water was starting to dribble down his wrist, and he wondered for a moment why he was here, listening to this nonsense. Another tremble from his legs. And that's why. He owed this guy. Owed him a lot.

"Not complete but yeah, pretty close."

"And never a physical confrontation, never a fight, never a punch in your nose, all those years. Right?"

"Correct."

Sonny grinned, speared the piece of pie. "Nice story. Here's mine. Grew up a few blocks from here in the projects. Single mom who worked a lot. Got knocked flat on my ass when I was ten. Then a couple more times. Then I got tired of being knocked around. Came down to the gym, started learning how to fight. And when I knocked a few other guys down, they left me alone. Simple survival. Muddled through high school. Did okay but not great. College not even a possibility. Now I do construction days, boxing nights and weekends. And there you go."

"How far can you take boxing?"

"As far as I can."

Jerry got a few more ice cubes out of his glass, his fingers numb. "Tom said you had a big fight coming up. Said...well, he didn't seem too confident about your chances."

"'Confident about your chances,'" Sonny repeated. "That's a fancy way of saying he expects me to get my clock cleaned. Yeah, he's probably right."

"So why do it?"

"What makes you think I have a choice?" Sonny said.

"Don't you?"

Sonny finished his pie. "Tell you what. Let me show you. Okay?"

Jerry said, "Okay. Only if I can bring this ice pack."

"Deal."

They were now back inside the gym by themselves—Sonny said he had a key because he sometimes swept up on weekends for a few bucks—and were standing by one of the large hanging punching bags. Sonny had taken off his sweatshirt and was in jeans and a white T-shirt. "First thing first," he said, wrapping a long strip of cloth around his wrist, hand and fingers. "Get your hand nice and wrapped tight, give you support. You want to know a secret?"

"Sure."

"You know when you're wrapped too tight?"

"Nope."

Sonny smiled, starting work on the other hand. "When your fingers turn red and start to tingle, cutting off the circulation. Real fights, you use gauze and tape, but practicing like this, a cloth wrap is just fine. Okay, here we go, put on a pair of ten-ounce gloves, help me with this, will you?"

Jerry held the glove open and against his chest, as Sonny pushed in his hand. He felt himself move back as Sonny increased the pressure, and then they did the other glove. Sonny reached down to a folding chair, where he picked up a mouthpiece. "Not only protects your teeth, but it keeps your jaw firm. Good punch comes in, prevents your jaw from swinging around and getting fractured."

The mouthpiece slipped in, and then Sonny's voice changed. "That's why you hear that puffing noise when we're in the ring. Hard to breathe good with the mouthpiece in. So we breathe, hard through the nose. Okay, watch."

Sonny went after the bag, snapping into action from one heartbeat to the next. The heavy bag was hanging by a chain from a metal frame, and Jerry saw four 50-pound weights holding down the frame, but the punches from Sonny came so fast and hard that the frame and punching bag started dancing into a corner. Sonny came back, breathing hard. "See? Did you see that?"

Jerry reluctantly shook his head. "Well, I'm not sure what I saw. I saw a number of punches."

"Right, right, but they're different. All of 'em. Here, watch."

And Jerry watched over the next half hour as the young

boxer demonstrated his jab, his uppercuts and overhand punches, the way the hips rolled with each punch, adding that much energy, the way the left shoulder was hunched up, protecting one's face, how the elbows and wrists were held in close, to protect the ribs. The punches went out, dancing the bag yet again, and he remembered once, a year ago, touring a utility power plant and walking past the electrical generator. From this young boxer he felt the same humming power, coming at you almost in a subconscious way. He also recalled the first time he had come into the gym, how out of place he had felt, and how superior he was, in working with his mind and not his fists. Now he was embarrassingly aware that he had broken the first rule of journalism: assuming you knew a damn thing about something you had never encountered before.

Sonny paused, breathing harder, his T-shirt now sweated through. "All right, those are the basic punches. Takes you a while to learn them. But fighting somebody else is a hell of a lot different from punching a bag. Here, punch me in the face."

Jerry said, "Excuse me?"

A confident nod. "C'mon, hit me in the face. And don't worry. You won't hurt me. Put up your hands, just like a boxer."

He felt ridiculous doing as he was asked, posing as a boxer, but he did just that. He put up his hands, held in his arms tight—just like Sonny had done—and the boxer nodded and said, "Go on."

Jerry swung out with his right hand, which was swatted away in a matter of seconds, and then there was a blur, as Sonny's right hand flew up and stopped, seemingly millimeters away from his ribs. Jerry flinched and stepped back.

"See?" Sonny asked. "Quick. You gotta be quick. You come at me to my face, and I work quick enough, I can batter away your punch. I do that, it opens you up for a good undercut. See?"

Jerry wasn't too sure but he went along with a few more exercises, feeling like a six-year-old being invited to pitch against a major-league baseball player. The young man was so confident, so strong, and so able to block away the feeble punches that Jerry was throwing, it was almost humiliating. And it would have been humiliating, except for the serious way Sonny was going at it.

Then the young boxer stopped, spat out his mouthpiece into his hand. "There. That's some of the moves. But I left out one thing. The strategy."

"What do you mean, strategy?"

Sonny started tugging off his gloves. "I know what you're thinking. The whole object is to beat the crap out of your opponent, right? So where's the strategy in that? Let me clue you in, Jerry. You've got four rounds, of three minutes apiece, to fight your opponent. Twelve minutes total. So you gotta use your mind, too. You find out who your opponent is, you watch some videotapes, you figure out the kind of moves he likes to use. Does he like to work from the ropes? Does he push you in with his feet? Does he have a particular combination he uses? If he's hit in one spot, how does he respond? Let me tell you, a good strategy and good jabs can mean a winning combination, every time."

Jerry watched as Sonny started undoing the wraps from his hands. "Suppose the moves and strategy don't count. Maybe your opponent's been told to...well, you know..."

"Oh. Throw the fight, huh? Maybe in some places, but not here. Look. I'm a boxing amateur. No money, just trophies or certificates if I win something. Maybe there's betting on the side, but I don't see none of it. Nope, I keep my nose clean, do the best I can, work my way up through the Golden Gloves tournaments. Keep on doing that and you get noticed by the guys working for the Olympic team. That's what I want to do, Jerry. Fight my way up there and be somebody. Then maybe turn pro. We'll see. If not, well...back to construction and nothing else. But at least I gave it a shot."

"But what about this fight coming up in a couple of days?" Jerry asked. "You said you expect to get beat. Even Tom Hart, the gym owner, he thinks you'll be beat. Doesn't that bother you?"

Sonny didn't seem enthused anymore, and he sat down, still

unwrapping the long pieces of cloth from his wrists and hands, carefully rolling them up. "Yeah, it bothers me. What do you think? You go in a ring, you're standing there, exposed. It's you against the other guy. Everything's on the line. You're either coming out of that ring a winner or a loser. There's no middle ground. There's a finality to it, you know? And sure, it stinks that the odds are against me, that everybody thinks I'm gonna lose this Saturday. But that's part of the deal. To get noticed."

"Who are you fighting?"

"Some kid from Portland. Luis Romero. Has hands like concrete, they say." Sonny finished with the wraps, stuck them inside the gloves, looked up. "But I'm gonna fight. It's my first real bout, and I can't back away. I just can't. Not after all the years of running, weight lifting, training. I can't back off."

Jerry looked at that determined face, the sweated-out T-shirt. He said quietly, "My column."

"Yeah?"

"I'd still like to do it."

Sonny placed the gloves in his lap, like they were tiny objects of affection. "You would, huh?"

"Yes."

Sonny shrugged. "Oh, what the hell, I guess so."

Three days later, Jerry was in his apartment, all the windows and doors locked, sipping a glass of Bordeaux, listening to a jazz station from Portland, looking out at the harbor. This was his quiet time, his special time after work, to be here alone with his books and slowly building antique collection. It was a time to relax and forget the outside world, to enjoy the simple pleasures of life. He sighed, sipping the wine.

It wasn't working.

It hadn't worked for days, and it scared him so.

The column had gone well, the morning after his visit with Sonny. He had written so fast and furious that for the first time in a long time, he spell-checked his column twice before submitting it. He wrote about Sonny, about the man in the ring, about how he was scheduled for a fight he knew he was going to lose. He quoted Theodore Roosevelt's saying about the man in the arena being the only one that counted. He noted that boxing had an ancient lineage, dating back five thousand years to the Sumerians and then up to the Greeks and Romans. He touched briefly on the marquess of Queensberry rules, the legacy of John L. Sullivan, all the way through the boxing greats of the 1920s and 1930s, up to Muhammad Ali and beyond. When the column was finished and he sent it over to Rick for review, he was actually physically tired. Nothing like that had ever happened to him before, writing about musicians or poets.

And then, a few minutes later, Rick had shambled by, grinning. "Great column," he had said. "Really well done."

He took another sip from his glass. That bout of praise had felt good. So why hadn't it lasted?

Jerry looked around the apartment, at the locked doors and windows. That's why. Having written the column and gotten the praise from the editor should have set everything right, but no, things had gotten worse. And he knew exactly why. Every time he closed his eyes, every time he walked out on the streets, every time he looked in a damn mirror, he remembered the helplessness of being on the ground, of being punched and kicked and slapped. He had thought that after a few days, he would have gotten over it, but it hadn't happened. If anything, it had gotten worse. Seeing a beat-up car drive by the office or his apartment building made him stop with fear, wondering who was in there. Loud voices, small groups of men, a ringing phone would start him shaking. He would wake up at 2 A.M., staring at the ceiling, wondering if perhaps those guys who had beaten him up, maybe they had noted his license plate. Maybe they knew his name. Maybe they knew where he lived.

So he would lie there, waiting for the door to be broken in. Or to hear the phone ring.

And the cops? Please. It had been days. He didn't know their names, wasn't even too sure what they looked like.

All he knew is that they had pummeled him like they owned him, that in addition to hurting his jaw and scraping his hands, they had also shattered his little cocoon, his safe haven. He no longer felt safe either here or at work or even in his car.

And all the good words from his editor weren't going to change that.

He finished off the wine, felt an urge to get another glass. Jesus, that wasn't good, not at all, and to keep his mind off having another drink, he picked up a copy of that day's *Sentinel*—a free copy, one of the few perks in the job—and idly leafed through the pages, even going into the sports section, where a little headline caught his eye.

LOCAL BOXER IN SURPRISE WIN

He sat up, scattering the other pages of the newspaper in the process.

LOCAL BOXER IN SURPRISE WIN

Jerry got up and grabbed his coat, and left the place that was still his home, but no longer a safe place.

Back into the gym, back to the noise and the smells and the shouts, but this time he recognized what was going on, how the punches were being thrown, the way the boxers were circling around, trying to gain an advantage. Tom Hart gave him a crisp nod as he walked by, and there was Sonny, working out by himself, striking a hanging bag by himself. Jerry walked right up to him and grabbed a shoulder, and Sonny spun back, holding up his gloves in a fighting stance, until he grinned and spat out his mouthpiece into a glove.

"Hey, how's it going," he said. "Sorry I didn't get a chance to call and thank you for that column. I guess I've been busy."

"Yeah," Jerry said, "I guess you have." He held the sports page under Sonny's nose. "Care to explain this?"

A shrug. "I won. There you go."

"Right, there you go. A fight you were supposed to lose. A fight you weren't suppose to win. Hell, even you said that guy had fists of concrete."

"He surely did," Sonny said, smiling, and Jerry noticed a swollen bruise above the boxer's right eye. "But I also found out he had a glass jaw."

"And when did you find that out? Before you went into the ring, or before you scammed me?"

Sonny's face darkened and he said, "Watch your mouth."

"Those guys who beat me up. That part of the deal or just a coincidence?"

Sonny said, "I don't know those guys, not at all. I...I was coming out of the gym, to grab you before you left. To tell you that I changed my mind. That's when I saw them beating you up."

"Maybe so," Jerry said. "But everything else was a scam. Right?"

Sonny was silent.

Jerry went on. "What do you think I am, an idiot? I know what you did. I know what happened. This was your real strategy, your real winning combination. You and the gym guy and whatever, you got together to pump up this little bout. You needed some publicity, about the up-and-coming kid who couldn't make it happen but still had a heart. Get interest in the fight, get a lot of betting action going on. Everybody wanting to get in on the action, thinking they had a sure thing. But you went in and spoiled the story, right? Turns out you did the whacking around, not the other guy. So. How much did you get?"

Sonny spoke slowly. "Like I said. I got a small trophy. Nothin' else."

"You're saying a lot of money didn't pass hands last night?"

Sonny leaned in, gently pushed at Jerry's chest with his gloved hand. Jerry moved back. "I'm sure some money passed around. That's what happens. But I didn't see any of it. And if you're so smart, tell me who sent you here? Okay? I sure as hell didn't call you, did I?"

Then it all made sense. His old-timer editor, Rick, who knew this gym and the manager. In his office, complaining about paying tuition for his daughters. Worried about cutbacks. Scratching out lottery tickets in his office, looking for that winning ticket...

Jerry tried not to let it show on his face, what he had just figured out, but he also felt a little flush of victory. When he got back to the newspaper office and had a chat with Rick, it was back to the old ways, writing the columns he wanted to do. But here, right now, he pressed on. "No, you didn't call me. But you know what? I just had an idea for another column. An investigative piece. About scamming in boxing, and what you told me and what really happened. All those years of work and training, what's that going to matter if I put a story out, tainting your first real victory? How does that sound?"

Sonny started breathing hard, stepped in even closer. "You wouldn't dare."

"Or what? Are you going to punch me out, right here? Go right ahead. I'll call the cops and that will make it real special, add to the column about you. Hot-blooded boxer beats up defenseless newspaper writer. Sonny, that's what I'm planning, and that's my strategy. What do you think about that?"

The young boxer remained silent, staring at him, gloved fists at his side, sweat trickling down the side of his face. Jerry added, "Unless..."

Sonny said, "Unless what?"

"Unless we can work out a deal."

Sonny rubbed a glove against his face. "What kind of deal?"

Jerry took a breath, remembering that burning humiliation, of being on his hands and knees and having his safe world taken away. "Here's the deal. I don't do the column. Not a word. In exchange for something from you."

"And what's that?" he asked suspiciously.

"That you teach me."

Sonny shook his head. "Teach you what?"

"Teach me how to fight," Jerry said, not really believing what he was saying, but knew it made sense, made the only sense, if he ever wanted to sleep and rest and work in peace.

"You're kidding," Sonny said.

"Not for a moment," he said.

"It's going to take a lot of work, a lot of practice, a lot of exercise," Sonny said cautiously. "Your legs and arms will burn, you'll feel like puking up half the time, and you'll get battered around in these rings like a Ping-Pong ball. That's what it's gonna take. You think it's worth it?"

He looked at the confidence in the man's eyes, and looked around at the other boxers, the ones he had dismissed a few days ago as being ill-bred hulks who could only punch. Maybe so, but look at them, look at all of them. Not a single one of them was afraid.

"Yes," Jerry said. "I think it will be worth every second."

THE FIX

by Thomas H. Cook

It could have happened anytime, on any of my daily commutes on the Crosstown 42. Every day I took it at eight in the morning, rode it over to my office on Forty-second and Lex, then back again in the evening, when I'd get off at Port Authority and walk one block uptown to my place on Forty-third.

It could have happened anytime, but it was a cold January evening, a deep winter darkness already shrouding the city at six P.M. Worse still, a heavy snow was coming down, blanketing the streets and snarling crosstown traffic, particularly on Forty-second Street, where the Jersey commuters raced for a spot in the Lincoln Tunnel, clotting the grid's blue veins as they rushed for the river like rabbits from burning woods.

I should tell you my name, because when I finish with the story, you'll want to know it, want to check it out, see if I'm really who I say I am, really heard what I did that night on the Crosstown 42.

Well, it's Jack. Jack Burke. I work as a photographer for Cosmic Advertising, my camera usually focused on a bottle of perfume or a plate of spaghetti. But in the old days, I was a street photographer for the *News*, mostly shooting fires and water main breaks, the sort of picture that ends up on page 8. I had a front page in '74, though, a woman clinging with one hand to a fire escape in Harlem, her baby dangling from the other hand like a sack of potatoes. I snapped the button just as she let go, caught them both in the first instant of their fall. That picture had had a heart, and sometimes, as I sat at my desk trying to decide which picture would best tempt a kid to buy a soda, I yearned to feel that heart again, to do or hear or see something that would work like electric paddles to shock me back to my old life.

Back in those days, working the streets, I'd known the Apple down to the core, the juke joints and after-hours dives. I was the guy you'd see at the end of the bar, the one in a rumpled suit, with a gray hat on the stool beside him. It was my seed time, and I'd loved every minute of it. For almost five years not a night had gone by when I hadn't fallen in love with it all over again, the night and the city, the Bleeker Street jazz clubs at three A.M. when the smoke is thick and the riffs look easy, and the tab grows like a rose beside your glass.

Then Jack Burke married an NYU coed named Rikki whose thick lips and perfect ass had worked like a Mickey Finn on his brain. There were lots of flowers and a twelve-piece band. After that the blushing bride seemed to have another kid about every four days. Jack took an agency job to pay for private schools, and that was the end of rosy tabs. Then Jack's wife hitched a ride on some other guy's star and left him with a bill that gave Bloomingdale's a boner. The place on Eighty-fifth went back to the helpful folks at Emigrant Savings, and Jack found a crib on West Forty-third. Thus the short version of how I ended up riding the Crosstown 42 on that snowy January night in the Year of Our Lord, 2000.

The deepest blues, they say, are the ones you don't feel, the ones that numb you, so that your old best self simply fades away, and you are left staring out the window, trying to remember the last time you leaped with joy, laughed until you cried, stood in the rain and just let it pour down. Maybe I'd reached that point when I got on the Crosstown 42 that night. And yet, I wasn't so dead that the sight of him didn't spark something, didn't remind me of the old days, and of how much I missed them.

And the part I missed the most was the fights.

I'll tell you why. Because all the old saws about boxing are true. There's no room for ambiguity in the ring. You know who the winners and the losers are. There, in that little square, under the big light, two guys put it all on the line, face each other without lawyers or tax attorneys. They stare at each other without speaking. They are stripped even of words. Boxers don't call each other names. They don't wave their arms and posture. They don't yell, Hey, fuck you, you fucking bastard, you want a piece of me, huh, well, come and get it, you fucking douche bag....while they're walking backward, glancing around, praying for a cop. Boxers don't file suit or turn you in to the IRS. They don't subscribe to dirty magazines in your name and have them mailed to your house. They don't plant rumors about drugs or how maybe you're a queer. Boxers don't come at you from behind some piece of paper a guy you never saw before hands you as you step out your front door. Boxers don't drop letters in the suggestion box or complain to your boss that you don't have what it takes anymore. Boxers don't approach at a slant. Boxers stride to the center of the ring, raise their hands and fight. That was what I'd always loved about them, that they were nothing like the rest of us.

Even so, I hadn't seen a match in the Garden or anywhere else for more than twenty years when I got on the Crosstown 42 that night, and the whole feel of the ring, the noise and the smoke, had by then drifted into a place within me I didn't visit anymore. I couldn't remember the last time I'd read a boxing story in the paper, or so much as glanced at *Ring* magazine. As a matter of fact, that very night I'd plucked a *Newsweek* from the rack instead, then tramped onto the bus, planning to pick up a little moo shoo pork when I got off, then trudge home to read about this East Hampton obstetrician who'd given some Jamaican bed-pan jockey five large to shoot his wife.

Then, out of the blue, I saw him.

He was crouched in the back corner of the bus, his face turned toward the glass, peering out at the street, though he didn't seem to be watching anything in particular. His eyes had that look you've all seen. Nothing going in, precious little coming out. A dead, dull stare.

His clothes were so shabby that if I hadn't noticed the profile, the gnarled ear and flattened nose, I might have mistaken him for a pile of dirty laundry. Everything was torn, ragged, the scarf around his neck riddled with holes, bare fingers nosing through dark blue gloves. It was the kind of shabbiness that carries its own odor, and which urban pioneers inevitably associate with madness and loose bowels. Which, on this bus packed to the gills, explained the empty seat beside him.

I might have kept my distance, might have stared at him a while, remembering my old days by remembering his, then discreetly stepped off the bus at my appointed stop, put the whole business out of my mind until I returned to work the next morning, met Max Groom in the men's room and said, Hey, Max, guess who was on the Crosstown 42 last night? Who? Vinnie Teague, that's who, Irish Vinnie Teague, the Shameful Shamrock. Mother of God, he's still alive? Well, in a manner of speaking.

And that might have been the end of it.

But it wasn't.

You know why? Because, in a manner of speaking, I was also still alive. And what do the living owe each other, tell me this, if not to hear each other's stories?

So I muscled through the crowd, elbowing my way toward the rear of the bus while Irish Vinnie continued to stare out into the fruitless night, his face even more motionless when looked upon close up, his eyes still as billiard balls in an empty parlor.

The good news? No smell. Which left the question. Is he nuts?

Language is a sure test for sanity, and so I said, "Hey there." Nothing.

"Hey." This time with a small tap of my finger on his ragged shoulder.

Still nothing, and so I upped the ante. "Vinnie?"

A small light came on in the dull, dead eyes.

"Vinnie Teague?"

Something flickered, but distantly, cheerlessly, like a candle in an orphanage window.

"It's you, right? Vinnie Teague?"

The pile of laundry rustled, and the dull, dead eyes drifted over to me.

Silence, but a faint nod.

"I'm Jack Burke. You wouldn't know me, but years ago, I saw you at the Garden."

The truth was I'd seen Irish Vinnie Teague, the Shameful Shamrock, quite a few times at the Garden. I'd seen him first as a light heavyweight, then later, after he'd bulked up just enough to tip the scales as a heavyweight contender.

He'd had the pug face common to boxers who'd come up through the old neighborhood, first learned that they could fight not in gyms or after-school programs, but in barrooms and on factory floors, the blood of their first opponents soaked up by sawdust or metal shavings in places where no one got saved by the bell.

It was Spiro Melinas who'd first spotted Vinnie. Spiro had been an old man even then, bent in frame and squirrelly upstairs, a guy who dipped the tip of his cigar in tomato juice, which, he said, made smoking more healthy. Spiro had been a low-watt fight manager who booked tumbledown arenas along the Jersey Shore, or among the rusting industrial towns of Connecticut and Massachusetts. He'd lurked among the fishing boats that rocked in the oily marinas of Fall River and New Bedford, and had even been spotted as far north as coastal Maine checking out the fish gutters who manned the canneries there, looking for speed and muscle among the flashing knives.

But Spiro hadn't found Vinnie Teague in any of the places that he'd looked for potential boxers during the preceding five years. Not in Maine or Connecticut or New Jersey. Not in a barroom or a shoe factory or a freezing cold New England fishery. No, Vinnie had been right under Spiro's nose the whole time, a shadowy denizen of darkest Brooklyn who, at the moment of discovery, had just tossed a guy out the swinging doors of a women's shelter on Flatbush. The guy had gotten up, rushed Vinnie, then found himself staggering backward under a blinding hail of lefts and rights, his head popping back with each one, face turning to pulp one light-ning fast blow at a time, though it had been clear to Spiro that dur-ing all that terrible rain of blows, Vinnie Teague had been holding back. "Jesus Christ, if Vinnie hadn't been pulling his punches," he later told Salmon Weiss, "he'd have killed the poor bastard with two rights and a left." A shake of the head, Spiro's eyes fixed in dark wonderment. "I'm telling you, Salmon, just slapping him around, you might say Vinnie was, and the other guy looked like he'd done twelve rounds with a metal fan."

Needless to say, it was love at first sight.

And so for the next two years Spiro mothered Vinnie like a baby chick. He paid the rent and bought the groceries so Vinnie could quit his prestigious job as a bouncer at the women's shelter. He paid for Vinnie's training, Vinnie's clothes, Vinnie's birthday cake from Carvel, an occasion at which I was present, my first view of Irish Vinnie Teague. He was chewing a slab of ice-cream cake while Spiro looked on, beaming. Snap. Flash. Page 8 over the lead-line, UP AND COMER BREAKS TRAINING ON HIS 24TH.

He'd continued upward for the next four years, muscling his way higher and higher in the rankings until, at just the moment when he came in striking distance of the title, Irish Vinnie had thrown a fight.

There are fixes and there are fixes, but Irish Vinnie's fix was the most famous of them all.

Why?

Because it was the most transparent. Jake La Motta was Laurence Olivier compared to Vinnie. Jake was at the top of the

Actors Studio, a recruiting poster for the Strasburg Method, the most brilliant student Stella Adler ever had...compared to Vinnie. Jake LaMotta took a dive, but Irish Vinnie took a swan dive, a dive so obvious, so awkward and beyond credulity, that for the first and only time in the history of the dive, the fans themselves started swinging, not just booing and waving their fists in the air, not just throwing chairs into the ring, but actually surging forward like a mob to get Vinnie Teague and tear his lying heart out.

Thirty-seven people went to Saint Vincent's that night, six of them cops who, against all odds, managed to hustle Vinnie out of the ring (from which he'd leaped up with surprising agility) and down into the concrete bowels of the Garden where he sat, secreted in a broom closet, for over an hour while all hell broke loose upstairs. Final tab, as reported by the *Daily News*, eighty-six thousand dollars in repairs. And, of course, there were lawsuits for everything under the sun so that by the end of the affair, Vinnie's dive, regardless of what he'd been paid for it, had turned out to be the most costly in boxing history.

It was the end of Vinnie's career, of course, the last time he would ever fight anywhere for a purse. Nothing needed to be proven. The *Daily News* dubbed him "The Shameful Shamrock" and there were no more offers from promoters. Spiro cut him loose and without further ado Vinnie sank into the dark waters, falling as hard and as low as he had on that fateful night when Douggie Burns, by then little more than a bleeding slab of beef, managed to lift his paw and tap Vinnie on the cheek, in response to which "The Edwin Booth of Boxers," another *Daily News* sobriquet, hit the mat like a safe dropped from the Garden ceiling. After that, no more crowds ever cheered for Vinnie Teague, nor so much as wondered where he might have gone

But now, suddenly, he was before me once again, Irish Vinnie, the Shameful Shamrock, huddled at the back of the Crosstown 42, a breathing pile of rags.

"Vinnie Teague. Am I right? You're Vinnie Teague?"

Nothing from his mouth, but recognition in his eyes, a sense, nothing more, that he was not denying it.

"I was at your twenty-fourth birthday party," I told him, as if that was the moment in his life I most remembered, rather than his infamous collapse. "There was a picture in the *News*. You with a piece of Carvel. I took that picture."

A nod.

"Whatever happened to Spiro Melinas?"

He kept his eyes on the street beyond the window, the traffic still impossibly stalled, angry motorists leaning on their horns. For a time he remained silent, then a small, whispery voice emerged from the ancient, battered face. "Dead."

"Oh yeah? Sorry to hear it."

A blast of wind hit the side of the bus, slamming a wave of snow against the window, and at the sound of it Irish Vinnie hunched a bit, drawing his shoulders in like a fighter...still like a fighter.

"And you, Vinnie. How you been?"

Vinnie shrugged as if to say that he was doing as well as could be expected of a ragged, washed-up fighter who'd taken the world's most famous dive.

The bus inched forward, but only enough to set the straphangers weaving slightly, then stopped dead again.

"You were good, you know," I said quietly. "You were really good, Vinnie. That time with Chico Perez. What was that? Three rounds? Hell, there was nothing left of him."

Vinnie nodded. "Nothing left," he repeated.

"And Harry Sermak. Two rounds, right?"

A nod.

The fact is, Irish Vinnie had never lost a single fight before Douggie Burns stroked his chin in the final round on that historic night at the Garden. But more than that, he had won decisively, almost always in a knockout, almost always before the tenth round, and usually with a single, devastating blow that reminded people of Marciano except that Vinnie's had seemed to deliver an even more deadly killer punch. Like Brando, the better actor, once said, he "coulda been a contendah."

In fact he had been a contender, a very serious contender, which had always made his downfall even more mysterious to me. What could it have been worth? How much must Vinnie have been offered to take such a devastating dive? It was a riddle that only deepened the longer I pondered his current destitution. Whatever deal Spiro Melinas had made for Vinnie, whatever cash may have ended up in some obscure bank account, it hadn't lasted very long. Which brought me finally to the issue at hand.

"Too bad about..." I hesitated just long enough to wonder about my safety, then stepped into the ring and touched my gloves to Vinnie's. "About...that last fight."

"Yeah," Vinnie said, then turned back toward the window as if it were the safe corner now, his head lolling back slightly as the bus staggered forward, wheezed, then ground to a halt again.

"The thing is, I never could figure it out," I added.

Which was a damn lie since you don't have to be a rocket scientist to come up with the elements that make up a fix. It's money or fear on the fighter's side, just money on the fixer's.

So it was a feint, my remark about not being able to figure out what happened when Douggie Burns' glove kissed Vinnie's cheek, and the Shameful Shamrock dropped to the mat like a dead horse, just a tactic I'd learned in business, that if you want to win the confidence of the incompetent, pretend to admire their competence. In Vinnie's case, it was a doubt I offered him, the idea that alone in the universe I was the one poor sap who wasn't quite sure why he'd taken the world's most famous dive.

But in this case it didn't work. Vinnie remained motionless, his eyes still trained on the window, following nothing of what went on beyond the glass, but clearly disinclined to have me take up any more of his precious time.

Which only revved the engine in me. "So, anybody else ever told you that?" I asked. "Having a doubt, I mean."

109

Vinnie's right shoulder lifted slightly, then fell again. Beyond that, nothing.

"The thing I could never figure is, what would have been worth it, you know? To you, I mean. Even, say, a hundred grand. Even that would have been chump change compared to where you were headed."

Vinnie shifted slightly, and the fingers of his right hand curled into a fist, a movement I registered with appropriate trepidation.

"And to lose that fight," I said. "Against Douggie Burns. He was over the hill already. Beaten to a pulp in that battle with Chester Link. To lose a fight with a real contender, that's one thing. But losing one to a beat-up old palooka like—"

Vinnie suddenly whirled around, his eyes flaring. "He was a stand-up guy, Douggie Burns."

"A stand-up guy?" I asked. "You knew Douggie?"

"I knew he was a stand-up guy."

"Oh yeah?" I said. "Meaning what?"

"That he was an honest guy," Vinnie said. "A stand-up guy, like I said."

"Sure, okay," I said. "But, excuse me, so what? He was a ghost. What, thirty-three, four? A dinosaur." I released a short laugh. "That last fight of his, for example. With Chester Link. Jesus, the whipping he took."

Something in Irish Vinnie's face drew taut. "Bad thing," he muttered.

"Slaughter of the Innocents, that's what it was," I said. "After the first round, I figured Burns would be on the mat within a minute of the second. You see it?"

Vinnie nodded.

"Then Douggie comes back and takes a trimming just as bad in the second," I went on, still working to engage Irish Vinnie, or maybe just relive the sweetness of my own vanished youth, the days when I'd huddled at the ringside press table, chain-smoking

Camels, with the bill of my hat turned up and a press card winking out of the band, a guy right out of *Front Page*, though even now it seemed amazingly real to me, my newspaperman act far closer to my true self than any role I'd played since then.

"Then the bell rings on Round Three and Chester windmills Douggie all over again. Jesus, he was punch-drunk by the time the bell rang at the end of it." I grinned. "Headed for the wrong corner, remember? Ref had to grab him by the shoulders and turn the poor bleary bastard around."

"A stand-up guy," Vinnie repeated determinedly, though now only to himself.

"I was amazed the ref didn't stop it," I added. "People lost a bundle that night. Everybody was betting Douggie Burns wouldn't finish the fight. I had a sawbuck said he wouldn't see five."

Vinnie's eyes cut over to me. "Lotsa people lost money," he muttered. "Big people."

Big people, I thought, remembering that the biggest of them had been standing ringside that night. None other than Salmon Weiss, the guy who managed Chester Link. Weiss was the sort of fight promoter who wore a cashmere overcoat and a white silk scarf, always had a black Caddie idling outside the arena with a leggy blonde in the backseat. He had a nose that had been more dream than reality before an East Side surgeon took up the knife, and when he spoke, it was always at you.

Get the picture? Anyway, that was Salmon Weiss, and everybody in or around the fight game knew exactly who he was. His private betting habits were another story, however, and I was surprised that a guy like Irish Vinnie, a pug in no way connected to Weiss, had a clue as to where the aforementioned Salmon put his money.

"You weren't one of Weiss's boys, were you?" I asked, though I knew full well that Vinnie had always been managed by Old Man Melinas.

Vinnie shook his head.

"Spiro Melinas was your manager."

Vinnie nodded.

So what gives, I wondered, but figured it was none of my business, and so went on to other matters.

"Anyway," I said. "Chester tried his best to clean Douggie's clock, but the bastard went all the way through the tenth." I laughed again.

The bus groaned, shuddered in a blast of wind, then dragged forward again.

"Well, all I remember is what a shellacking Douggie took."

Vinnie chewed his lower lip. "'Cause he wouldn't go down."

"True enough. He did the count. All the way to the last bell."

Vinnie seemed almost to be ringside again at that long-ago match, watching as Douggie Burns, whipped and bloody, barely able to raise his head, took punch after punch, staggering backward, fully exposed, barely conscious, so that it seemed to be a statue Chester Link was battering with all his power, his gloves thudding against stomach, shoulder, face, all of it Douggie Burns, but Douggie Burns insensate, perceiving nothing, feeling nothing, Douggie Burns in stone.

"Stayed on his feet," Vinnie said now. "All the way."

"Yes, he did," I said, noting the strange admiration Vinnie still had for Douggie, though it seemed little more than one fighter's regard for another's capacity to take inhuman punishment. "But you have to say there wasn't much left of him after that fight," I added.

"No, not much."

"Which makes me wonder why you fought him at all," I said, returning to my real interest in the matter of Irish Vinnie Teague. "I mean, that was no real match. You and Douggie. After that beating he took from Chester Link, Douggie couldn't have whipped a Girl Scout."

"Nothing left of Douggie," Vinnie agreed.

"But you were in your prime," I told him. "No real match,

like I said. And that...you know...to lose to him...that was nuts, whoever set that up."

Vinnie said nothing, but I could see his mind working.

"Spiro. What was his idea in that? Setting up a bout between you and Douggie Burns? It never made any sense to me. Nothing to be gained from it on either side. You had nothing to gain from beating Douggie...and what did Douggie have to gain from beating you if he couldn't do it without it being a....I mean, if it wasn't...real."

Vinnie shook his head. "Weiss set it up," he said. "Not Mr. Melinas."

"Oh, Salmon Weiss," I said. "So it was Weiss that put together the fight you had with Douggie?"

Vinnie nodded.

I pretended that the infamous stage play that had resulted from Weiss's deal had been little more than a tactical error on Vinnie's part and not the, shall we say, flawed thespian performance that had ended his career.

"Well, I sure hope Weiss made you a good offer for that fight, because no way could it have helped you in the rankings." I laughed. "Jesus, you could have duked it out with Sister Evangeline from Our Lady of the Lepers and come up more."

No smile broke the melancholy mask of Irish Vinnie Teague.

I shook my head at the mystery of things. "And a fix to boot," I added softly.

Vinnie's gaze cut over to me. "It wasn't no fix," he said. His eyes narrowed menacingly. "I didn't take no dive for Douggie Burns."

I saw it all again in a sudden flash of light, Douggie's glove float through the air, lightly graze the side of Vinnie's face, then glide away as the Shameful Shamrock crumpled to the mat. If that had not been a dive, then there'd never been one in the history of the ring.

But what can you say to a man who lies to your face, claims he lost the money or that it wasn't really sex?

I shrugged. "Hey, look, it was a long time ago, right?"

Vinnie's red-rimmed eyes peered at me intently. "I was never supposed to take a dive," he said.

"You weren't supposed to take a dive?" I asked, playing along now, hoping that the bus would get moving, ready to get off, be done with Vinnie Teague. "You weren't supposed to drop for Douggie Burns?"

Vinnie shook his head. "No. I was supposed to win that fight. It wasn't no fix."

"Not a fix," I asked. "What was it then?"

He looked at me knowingly. "Weiss said I had to make Douggie Burns go down."

"You had to make Douggie go down?"

"Teach him a lesson. Him and the others."

"Others?"

"The ones Weiss managed," Vinnie said. "His other fighters. He wanted to teach them a lesson so they'd..."

"What?"

"Stay in line. Do what he told them."

"And you were supposed to administer that lesson by way of Douggie Burns?"

"That's right."

"What'd Weiss have against Douggie?"

"He had plenty," Vinnie said. "'Cause Douggie wouldn't do it. He was a stand-up guy, and he wouldn't do it."

"Wouldn't do what?"

"Drop for Chester Link," Vinnie answered. "Douggie was supposed to go down in five. But he wouldn't do it. So Weiss came up with this match. Between me and Douggie. Said I had to teach Douggie a lesson. Said if I didn't..." He glanced down at his hands. "...I wouldn't never fight no more." He shrugged. "Anyway, I wasn't supposed to lose that fight with Douggie. I was supposed to win it. Win it good. Make Douggie go down hard." He hesitated a moment, every dark thing in him darkening a shade. "Permanent."

I felt a chill. "Permanent," I repeated.

"So Weiss's fighters could see what would happen to them if he told them to take a dive and they didn't."

"So it wasn't a fix," I said, getting it now. "That fight between you and Douggie. It was never a fix."

Vinnie shook his head.

The last words dropped from my mouth like a bloody mouthpiece. "It was a hit."

Vinnie nodded softly. "I couldn't do it, though," he said. "You don't kill a guy for doing the right thing."

I saw Douggie Burns' glove lift slowly, hang in the air, soft and easy, drift forward, barely a punch at all, then Irish Vinnie Teague, the Shameful Shamrock, hit the mat like a sack of sand.

The hydraulic doors opened before I could get out another word.

"I get off here," Vinnie said as he labored to his feet.

I touched his arm, thinking of all the times I'd done less nobly, avoided the punishment, known the right thing, but lacked whatever Irish Vinnie had that made him do it, too.

"You're a stand-up guy, Vinnie," I said.

He smiled softly, then turned and scissored his way through the herd of strap-hangers until he reached the door. He never glanced back at me, but only continued down the short flight of stairs and out into the night, where he stood for a moment, upright in the elements. The bus slogged forward again, and I craned my neck for a final glimpse of Irish Vinnie Teague as it pulled away. He stood on the corner, drawing the tattered scarf more tightly around his throat. Then he turned and lumbered up the avenue toward the pink neon of Smith's Bar, a throng of snowflakes rushing toward him suddenly, bright and sparkling, fluttering all around, like a crowd of cheering angels in the dark, corrupted air.

FLASH

by Loren D. Estleman

Midge was glad he'd put on the electric-blue suit that day. He could use the luck.

Mr. Wassermann didn't approve of the suit. At the beginning of their professional relationship, he'd introduced Midge to his tailor, a small man in gold-rimmed glasses who looked and dressed like Mr. Wassermann, and who gently steered the big man away from the bolts of shimmering sharkskin, the concern kept in stock for its gambler clients, and taught him to appreciate the subtleties of gray worsted and fawn-colored flannel. He cut Midge's jackets to allow for the underarm Glock rather than obliging him to buy them a size too large, and made his face blush when he explained the difference between "dressing left" and "dressing right."

The tailoring bills came out of Midge's salary, a fact for which he was more grateful than if the suits had been a gift. He was no one's charity case. The distinction was important, because he knew former fighters who stood in welfare lines and on street corners, holding signs saying they would work for food. Back when they were at the top of the bill, they had made the rounds of all the clubs with yards of gold chain around their necks, girls on both arms, and now here they were, saying they would clean out your gutters for a tuna sandwich, expecting pedestrians to feel guilty enough to buy them the sandwich and skip the gutters. Mr. Wassermann never gave anyone anything for nothing—it was a saying on the street, and Midge had heard him confirm it in person—and the big ex-fighter was proud to be able to say in return that he never took anything from anyone for nothing.

He liked the way he looked in the suits. They complemented his height without calling attention to his bulk, did not make him look poured into his clothes the way so many of his overdeveloped colleagues appeared when they dressed for the street, and if it weren't for his jagged nose and the balloons of scar tissue around his eyes, he thought he might have passed for a retired NFL running back with plenty in Wall Street. Of course, that's when he wasn't walking with Mr. Wassermann, when no one would mistake him for anything but personal security.

Today, however, without giving the thing much thought, he'd decided to wear the electric-blue double-breasted he'd worn to Mr. Wassermann's office the day they'd met. He'd had on the same shade of trunks when he KO'd Lincoln Flagg at Temple Gate Arena and again when he took the decision from Sailor Burelli at Waterworks Park. He'd liked plenty of flash in those days, in and out of the ring: gold crowns, red velvet robes with Italian silk linings, crocodile luggage, yellow convertibles. Make 'em notice you, he'd thought, and you just naturally have to do your best.

But then his run had finished. He lost two key fights, his business manager decamped to Ecuador with his portfolio, the IRS attached his beach house. The last of the convertibles went back to the finance company. In a final burst of humiliation, an Internet millionaire with dimples on his forehead bought Midge's robes at auction for his weekend guests to wear around the swimming pool. When Midge had asked Mr. Wassermann for the bodyguard job, he'd been living for some time in a furnished room on Magellan Street and the electric-blue was the only suit he owned.

It had brought him luck, just as the trunks had. He'd gotten the job, and right away his fortunes turned around. Because Mr. Wassermann preferred to keep his protection close, even when it was off duty, he had moved Midge into a comfortable three-room suite in the East Wing, paid for his security training and opened an expense account for him at Rinehart's, where well-dressed salesmen advised him on which accessories to wear with his new suits and supplied him with turtle-backed hairbrushes and aftershave. On the rare occasions when his reclusive employer visited a restaurant (too many of his colleagues had been photographed in such places with their faces in their plates and bullet holes in their heads), he always asked the chef to prepare a takeout meal for Midge to eat when they returned home. These little courtesies were offered as if they were part of the terms of employment.

Because there were other bodyguards, Midge had Saturdays off, and with money in the pocket of a finely tailored suit, he rarely spent them alone. The women who were drawn to the aura of sinister power that surrounded Mr. Wassermann belonged to a class Midge could not have approached when he was a mere pug. While waiting for his employer, he would see a picture of a stunning model in *Celebrity* and remember how she looked naked in his bed at the Embassy.

There had been a long dry spell in that department after his last fight. True, his face had been stitched and swollen and hard to look at, but that wasn't an impediment after the Burelli decision, when eighteen inches of four-oh thread and a patch of gauze were the only things holding his right ear to his head; he'd made the cover of *Turnbuckle* that week and signed a contract to endorse a national brand of athlete's-foot powder. He'd considered hiring his own bodyguard to fight off the bottle-blond waitresses. But that was when he was winning. The two big losses and particularly the stench that had clung to the twelve rounds he'd dropped to Sonny Rodriguez at the Palace Garden might as well have been a well-advertised case of the clap.

The fans had catcalled and crumpled their programs and beer cups and hurled them at the contestants. The Palace management had been forced to call the police to escort them to their dressing rooms. Three weeks later, the state boxing commission had reviewed the videotape and yanked Midge's license.

The irony was, he hadn't gone into the tank. He'd taken the money when it was offered, and since he considered himself an ethical person he'd fully intended to fake a couple of falls and force a decision against him, but he hadn't gone three rounds before he realized he was no match for the untried youngster from Nicaragua. He was out of shape and slow, and Rodriguez was graceless for all the fact that any one of his blows would have knocked down a young tree. Even the fellow who had approached Midge and ought to have known a fix from a legitimate loss called him afterward to tell him he was a rotten actor; he feared a congressional investigation.

Midge had considered returning the money, but integrity had proven to be a more complicated thing altogether than he'd suspected. He was both a fighter who had sold out and a fighter who had never thrown a fight. Just trying to think where that placed him in the scheme of things gave him a headache. It hurt worse than the one he'd suffered for two weeks after he went down to Ricky Shapiro.

On this particular Saturday off, he'd broken a date with a soap opera vixen to meet a man with whom Mr. Wassermann sometimes did business. Angelo DeRiga—"Little Angie," Midge had heard him called, although he was not especially small, and was in fact an inch or two taller than Mr. Wassermann—dyed his hair black, even his eyebrows, and wore suits that were as well made as Midge's new ones, from material of the same good quality, but were cut too young for him. The flaring labels and cinched waists only called attention to the fact that he was nearing sixty, just as the black hair brought out the deep lines in the artificial tan of his face. The effect was pinched and painful and increased the bodyguard's appreciation for his employer's dignified herringbones and barbered white fringe.

Little Angie shook Midge's hand at the door to his suite at the King William, complimented him upon his suit—"Flash, the genuine article," he said—and invited him to sample the gourmet spread the hotel's waiters were busy transferring from a wheeled cart to the glass-topped mahogany table in the sitting room.

Midge, who knew as well as Little Angie that the electric-blue sack was inappropriate, did not thank him, and politely refused the offer of food. He wasn't hungry, and anyway, chewing interfered with his concentration. Too many blows to the head had damaged his hearing. High- and low-pitched voices were the worst, and certain labials missed him entirely. By focusing his attention on the speaker, and with the help of some amateur lip reading, he'd managed to disguise this rather serious disability for a watchdog to have from even so observant a man as Mr. Wassermann; but then Mr. Wassermann spoke slowly, and always around the middle range. Little Angie was shrill and carried on every conversation as if he were on a fast elevator and had to finish before the car reached his floor.

When the waiters left, the two were alone with Francis, Little Angie's bodyguard. He was a former professional wrestler who shaved his head and had rehearsed his glower before a mirror until it was as nearly permanent as a tattoo. As a rule, Midge got on with other people's security, but he and Francis had disliked each other from the start. He suspected that on Francis' part this was jealousy; Mr. Wassermann's generosity to employees was well known, while Little Angie was a pinchpenny who abused his subordinates, sometimes in public. On Midge's side, he had a career prejudice against wrestlers, whom he dismissed as trained apes, and thought Francis disagreeably ugly into the bargain. When they were in the same room they spent most of the time scowling at each other. They had never exchanged so much as a word.

"I know Jake the Junkman's been white to you," Little Angie seemed to be saying. "Too good, maybe. Some types need to be put on an allowance. A lot of smart guys can't handle dough."

Midge didn't like what he'd heard. Everyone knew Mr. Wassermann had made his first fortune from scrap metal, but most respected him too much to allude to his past in this offensive way. He wondered if it was his place to report the conversation to his employer. So far he didn't know why he'd been invited here.

Little Angie reached into a pocket and took out a handful of notepaper on which Midge recognized his own scrawl. "You ain't hard to track. Everywhere you go, you leave markers: Benny Royal's floating crap game on the South Side, the roulette wheel at the Kit-Kat, Jack Handy's book up in Arbordale. There's others here. You owe twelve thousand, and you can't go to Jake for a loan. He's got a blind spot where gambling's concerned. He don't forbid his people from making a bet now and then, but he don't bail them out either. Tell me I'm wrong."

Midge shook his head. Mr. Wassermann had explained all this his first day. Midge hadn't known then that the new class of woman he'd be dating liked pretty much the same entertainments as the old.

"See, that's a problem. I spent more'n face value buying these up. I'm a reasonable man, though. I'll eat the difference. You got twelve grand, Midge?"

"You know I don't."

Little Angie smacked his face with the markers. Midge took a step forward; so did Francis. Little Angie held up a finger, stopping them both. "Let's not be uncivil. There's a way you can work it off. You won't even have to pop a sweat."

Midge heard enough of the rest to understand. Mr. Wassermann, who had the ear of a number of important people, had promised to spoil an investment Little Angie wanted to make. The important people, he hinted, would be in a position to listen to reason if Mr. Wassermann were not available to counsel them otherwise. All Midge had to do to settle his debts was stand at his usual station outside the door to Mr. Wassermann's office the following morning and not leave it, no matter what he heard going on inside.

"What if I just owe you like I did the others?" Midge asked.

"They was getting impatient. If I didn't step in, you'd be wearing plaster instead of that flashy suit, peeing through a tube. And I got to tell you, patience ain't my what-you-call forte. Francis?"

The ugly bald wrestler produced a loop of stiff nylon fishline from a pocket. Midge knew he could prevent Francis from making use of it, but there were others in Little Angie's employ who knew what a garrote was for. He couldn't fight them all. Sooner or later he'd run into a Sonny Rodriguez.

"I know what you're thinking," Little Angie said. There's always a place in my organization for a fellow knows the score. You won't be out of a job."

Midge hadn't been thinking about that at all. "Can I have time to think it over?

"If I had time I'd wait for Jake to die of old age."

Midge agreed to the terms. Little Angie leered and tore up the markers. Francis looked disappointed as well as ugly.

.

The next morning outside Mr. Wassermann's office was as long a time as Midge had ever spent anywhere, including seven and a half rounds with Lincoln Flagg. Mr. Wassermann had some telephone calls to make and told him he'd be working through lunch, but that he'd make it up to him that night with the full twelve courses from Bon Maison, Midge's favorite restaurant back when he was contending. He had an armchair for his personal use in the hallway, but today he couldn't stay seated in it more than three minutes at a stretch. He stood with his hands folded in front of him, then behind him, picked lint off the sleeve of his new gray gabardine, found imaginary lint on the crease of the trousers and picked that off too. He was perspiring heavily under his sixty-dollar shirt, despite what Little Angie had said; he, Midge, who used to work out with the heavy bag for an hour without breaking a sweat. This selling out was hard work.

Too hard, he decided, after twenty minutes. He would take

his chances with Little Angie's threats. He rapped on the door, waited the customary length of time while he assumed Mr. Wassermann was calling for him to come in, then opened the door. The garrote didn't frighten him half as much as the anticipation of the look of sadness on Mr. Wassermann's face when he told him about his part in Little Angie's plan.

Mr. Wassermann was not behind his desk. But he was.

When Midge leaned his big broken-knuckled hands on it and peered over the far edge, the first thing he saw was the tan soles of his employer's hand-lasted wingtips. Mr. Wassermann was still seated in his padded leather swivel, but the chair lay on its back. Mr. Wassermann's face was the same oxblood tint as his shoes and his tongue stuck out. Midge couldn't see the wire, but he'd heard it sank itself so deep in a man's neck it couldn't be removed without getting blood on yourself, so most killers didn't bother to try.

A torch lamp behind the desk had toppled over in the struggle and lay on the carpet, its bulb shattered. Both it and Mr. Wassermann must have made more than a little noise. The door that was usually concealed in the paneling to the left stood open. It was used by Mr. Wassermann's congressmen and the occasional other business associate who preferred not to be seen going in or coming out. It was one of the worst-kept secrets around town.

Midge felt sad. He walked around the desk, stepping carefully to avoid grinding bits of glass into the Brussels carpet, and looked down into his employer's bloodshot eyes.

"The thing is, Mr. Wassermann, I didn't really go into the tank."

Mr. Wassermann didn't say anything. But then Midge probably wouldn't have heard him if he had.

THE CHAMPIONSHIP OF NOWHERE

by James Grady

Gene Mallette and the kid named Sandy were wildcatting a double shift on an oil derrick fifty-five afternoons before Independence Day. Drill and generator motors pounded May's prairie air. Sandy laughed about something and smiled. Then a drill chain broke, whipped like a silver tie around his neck and rocketed him to the top of the fifty-foot rig. His body swung there while pipes clattered and a driller screamed and all Gene could think about was Sandy's teenage face smeared oil black except for his happy eyes and the glint of white teeth.

The chain unraveled with a spin and Sandy crashed to the derrick floor.

Gene and another guy rode to town in back of the flatbed truck with Sandy's body laid at their boots. There'd been a spring snow two weeks before, so the truck didn't kick up much dust from the dirt road. The earth smelled damp and good. He heard the foreman in the truck cab say maybe the drought was over. They saw a skinny deer grazing by the walls of a deserted sod house. They saw the blue misted Sweet Grass Hills rising from the yellow prairie between them and Canada. Those three volcanic crags would have been mountains anyplace else but here in Montana. The foreman drove to the Shelby undertaker parlor. As they lifted Sandy off the truck, Gene heard the mortician's hand jingling silver dollars for those happy eyes.

"I'm done," said Gene, and walked to the boardinghouse.

He put a shower and a tub soak on his tab. Sat at the dinner table with other boarders and ate stew he didn't taste. Walked out to the sidewalk to sit on a bench, watch the people and cars around the Front Street speakeasies and make himself think about nothing, nothing at all.

Least I got that, he thought.

Just before sunset a rancher named Jensen staggered out of a speakeasy called the Bucket of Blood, walked to a roan horse cinched to one of the new electric light poles, pulled out a silver pistol and shot the horse smack between the eyes. The roan plopped to the ground so hard it snapped the cinch. Jensen pumped slugs into the beast, filling the town with the roar of the gun. He had gone through a full reload of the revolver and had its cylinder swung open for more bullets when the black Ford with a big white star painted on each of its front doors pulled up behind the dead horse. Texas John Otis unfolded his grizzly bear body to climb out of the car, sheriff's badge on the left lapel of his black suit, a dead German sniper's ten-inch broomstick handle Mauser in his right hand. Sheriff Otis ripped the shiny revolver away from Jensen and slammed the Mauser against the rancher's skull.

"You dumb son of a bitch!" roared the Sheriff. "You shot your own damn horse!"

But by then Jensen lay draped unconscious across that bloody roan.

Gene turned away and saw her walking toward him.

He'd seen her before, back in '06 when she was nine and he was fourteen. Her white father moved her and her kid brother off the Blackfeet Rez to educate in Shelby instead of being sentenced to an Indian boarding school. Gene'd seen her every day when he was a high school senior. She'd skipped a grade so she was a shy freshman who wore her black hair like a veil. Gene just knew she wouldn't talk to him. Then he couldn't talk to her while she was still in high school and he was a graduated adult doing a man's job as a gandy dancer building railroads to bring homesteaders out West and ship the loot of the land back East. He'd seen her almost every week, often trying to corral her wild brother. Gene had seen her at the train depot the day he shipped out to the Marines for the Great War against the Kaiser. That day, damned if he wouldn't before he died doing what had to be done, he'd gone up to her, said: "Good-bye." She'd flinched—then lanced the gloom with her smile. When he came home from Europe with no visible scars, he'd seen her in the Shelby cemetery putting flowers on the influenza graves of the homesteader she'd married who'd been old enough to be her dad and the baby girl she'd let that dreamer father. After bloody California, as Gene's parents and their ranch died, he had seen her move to town when the great winds of 1920 ate the homestead she'd tried to keep going while working the schoolmarm job her husband had been white enough to let her get and the town had been Christian enough to let her keep for the full year of widow's black. Gene had watched as she waitressed at the Palace Hotel where she lived in the back room, sometimes with her brother when he was in town trying to find dollars for ivory powder he pumped into his arm. And Gene'd seen her sad smile two months earlier when he'd asked her out. She'd whispered: "I got nothing that's worth it for you." He'd seen her not believe him when he swore she was wrong, seen her walk away so she wouldn't see tears fall she couldn't catch.

But that night, he saw her and knew she was walking toward him.

She blocked the red ball of the setting sun as she drew near. They were together inside a crimson lake. He could barely breathe and the water of this moment turned her walk into a slow swim toward him, her hair undulating out from her shoulders, her dress floating around her calves. He remembered forever that dress was the blue of morning sky. She wore no makeup on her skin, the color of milked coffee. The scent of purple lilacs came with her. Gene felt like Sandy spinning free of the chain that hung him high above the

127

earth as he fell into her midnight eyes.

He knew he said "Hello Billie" and she said "Hello Gene."

Maybe they tried to say more but they couldn't, not until she said: "I need your help. I need you to meet with some men. They sent me to get you. They want you to do something. It might save me, but it won't be anything but trouble for you, no matter what they promise. But I had to come. I had to ask. I had to do that much. I'm sorry."

All of a sudden it was night. Lights came on throughout the town. The glow from the street lamp on the corner yellowed her skin.

"Is it a long walk?" said Gene.

"I've got their car."

The license plate on the Ford bore the county ID numbers from Butte, 200 miles to the south, the only place rougher than Shelby in the whole state. Butte was a smokestack city of 60,000 people, tough Bohunk miners digging up the richest hill on earth for Irish robber barons who ran the place with Pinkertons, dynamite and satchels of cash they spent to fight off Wobbly labor organizers and Ku Klux Klan Catholic haters and reform meddlers from back East. On a good day, Shelby only had 1,200 people crowded into its prairie valley, busted-out honyockers who'd believed the Iowa newspapers' lies about homesteading, ranchers like Jensen and cowboys who cut barbed wire fences whenever they rode up to one, Basque sheepherders who couldn't converse with two-legged creatures, Blackfeet and Gros Ventre and even Cheyenne stepped off their scrub reservations hunting for hope or honor or a last resort hell of a good time, railroad men, shopkeepers and saloon tenders and border runners and streetwalkers and roughnecks like Gene had become who were trying to cash in on the Great North Country Oil Strike of 1921 that had filled every hotel hallway with dime-a-night cots.

Gene liked the no-nonsense way Billie drove, shifting when she had to, not afraid to let the engine whine and work it up a steep grade rather than panic-shift to high, stall and maybe die. She drove them east, out of town past the railroad roundhouse and the mooing slaughterhouse pens, up and over the rim of the valley. Lamps of the town winked away in the Ford's mirror. Somebody'd shotgunned a million white stars in the night overhead. The sky shimmered with green and pink sheets of northern lights, and the yellow cones of the car headlights showed only a narrow ribbon of oiled highway.

"This road goes all the way to Chicago," said Gene.

"We can't," said Billie. "I can't."

She drove into the night.

"Why me?" he asked.

"Because of who you are. What you can do. California."

"Because I'd come if you asked."

"I don't know what to say about that."

"We never did."

"No." She steered the car toward a farmhouse. "We didn't. Neither of us."

She stopped the car in the dark yard beside a Cadillac Gene thought he recognized.

"I'll take you back right now, if you want," she said.

"Will you stay with me?"

He saw her head shake.

"Then let's go," said Gene as he got out of the car. "They're waiting."

Her brother opened the farmhouse door. He wore a frayed white shirt unbuttoned at the collar, loose pants and a pencil pusher's black shoes that were as dull as his droopy eyes. His right hand that pumped Gene's was strong enough to deal cards at the Palace Hotel but not much more, a weak grasp that whispered he was a man who couldn't cover his bets.

"Zhene Mallette!" he slurred. "What d'you say, what d'you know, good ta see you!"

"How you doing, Harry?" said Gene, though he knew enough

to know that answer and sent all the question's sincerity to the man's sister. Gene's fingers brushed Harry back into the living room where the two men who mattered waited, and though he silently prayed otherwise, he sensed Billie step into the farmhouse behind him and shut the door.

The Cadillac in the yard belonged to the pudgy Shelby banker standing by the table supporting a bottle of pre-Prohibition whiskey and glasses. The brass nameplate on his desk in the bank read PETER TAYLOR—VICE PRESIDENT. He had a knotty head of not much hair and reminded Gene of a grinning toad who never said no to another fly.

"Good evening, Mr. Mallette," said Taylor. "Thank you for coming."

"Wasn't for you," said Gene.

"We know," said the other man, the one Gene had never seen. Least, he'd never seen that particular black-haired city-suited man who hadn't bothered to get up off the couch—or to either fill his hand with the .45 on his lap or hide the gun. Gene'd seen those eyes and that set of face once in the trenches, another time in a Tijuana cantina, a third time ringside at a smoker in Fresno, and the last and worst time in a set of chains headed through the work camp to the scaffold at San Quentin. Wasn't that the man was tough, though Gene knew he could take a beating and then some, it was that he'd crawl up off any floor you knocked him down on to tear your heart in two and suck in the sound of ripping flesh.

"Please," said the banker, "have a chair. Call me Peter."

"Never figured on calling you at all."

"Life adds up like we don't expect. Please, sit down. There, beside the woman."

"Where should I sit?" said her brother, but his words went into the night as *didn't matter*.

Gene eased himself into the folding chair closest to the couch and acted like his legs weren't coiled springs. Banker Taylor settled into an easy chair and filled glasses with whiskey. Harry

Larson strutted to the folding chair close to Gene, grandly lowered himself but misjudged his balance and almost crashed to the floor. By the time he got himself stable, his sister stood behind him, a hand on his shoulder. The man on the couch didn't move.

"Nice night for a drive." Gene sent his words to the banker, kept the man on the couch in his gaze. "But that whiskey is illegal. Seems like a man in your position would be more careful."

"Laws like Prohibition are for people who fear man's nature." Taylor held a whiskey toward Gene. When Gene didn't take it, Taylor sat the glass on a milk crate near Gene's legs. "Wise of you not to drink, given the opportunity in front of you. As for what's legal, a man like you who's served time in a prison work camp can't be sanctimonious."

"Your friend on the couch there would know more about prison than me."

"Never been," said the man on the couch. "Witnesses never make it to the trials."

Banker Taylor extended a glass of whiskey to the black-haired man. "Gene, you'll find that Norman here—pardon my manners, this is Norman Doyle—Mr. Doyle is a lucky man."

Doyle took the whiskey glass with his left hand; the butt of the .45 faced his right.

"You don't need a glass, do you, Harry? You took care of yourself as soon as your sis left for town. Your vice is still legal, though the politicians are going to fix that, too. And you, Wilemena —or should I call you Widow Harris? You know, Gene, she's been without a man for a long time. A broke-in mare without a saddle for the itch. I don't think we'll give her a glass. She's a woman, plus whiskey and Injuns don't mix, even if they are breeds."

"Get to it," snapped Gene.

"How you doing in the market?"

"What?"

"The stock market," said the banker. "Everybody plays the market these days. Going up, up, up. Going to make everybody a millionaire. How you doing in the stock market?"

"You know I'm not that kind of guy."

"You mean you can't be. 'Cause you don't have the money. So how you going to get rich? This is America. Everybody wants to get rich. Can't get a good car or the woman you want if you don't have silver dollars to jingle. Are you going to get what you want, what you need, by roughnecking other people's oil out of this God-forsaken ground?"

"I get by."

"And that's all you're getting. By. Passed by. Till one day the wind just up and blows you away like you were never here. Forgotten. But tonight, you're a lucky man. If you got the guts to be who you are and do what you can do better than any man in this state."

"Tell me."

The banker said: "You're a boxer."

Harry Larson blurted out: "Everybody knows, Gene! We all heard. You're the best!"

Billie squeezed her brother's shoulder and he shut up.

"I gave that up," said Gene. "I'm not ever going back in the ring."

Doyle said: "Yet."

"California rules don't matter up here," said the banker. "What that judge said—"

"It isn't about that."

"Maybe you don't have the guts for it anymore," said Doyle.

"It's not guts," said Gene. "It's the stomach."

"Killing a man should be no big deal for a war boy like you," said the man with the gun.

"I didn't kill him. We fought. I hit him. He went down. He didn't get up. He died."

"Oh." Doyle smiled. "So *you* didn't do it. What happened? Did some angel come down to the canvas and snatch his soul?"

"I don't know. Angels don't tell me their secrets. The only

reason the night court judge called it reckless misadventure was to keep the locals from lynching me. Banning me from boxing in the state and sticking me in the work camp for ninety days got me out of town. When I got out, nobody cared anymore. Except me. I went home. So what's my boxing to you?"

"It's what it is to our whole damn town," said the banker. "We got us a heavyweight championship of the world going to be fought here. Jack Dempsey against Tommy Gibbons."

"That's just a joke going around," said Gene.

"Yes, it started that way. A joke. A telegram from a civic leader that was a publicity stunt to get Shelby a little free fame. As if anything is free."

"Who cares about fame."

"Be a modern man, Gene. Modesty is over. Useless. So is reality. Image is everything. What's true for a man is true for a town. This is a dirt road nowhere, but so what? If it can become famous, a celebrity, then riches and the happy-ever-after good life will surely follow."

"That's a load of crap."

"Maybe, but it's the way things work nowadays. The joke telegram was going to get us a few newspaper stories back East, a publicity stunt. But Dempsey's manager Jack Kearns called the bluff, agreed to his boy fighting for the championship in Shelby. Nobody out here wants to be a back-down kind of guy. So now this 'joke' thing has grown a life of its own, a bigger one every day. Dempsey's been guaranteed a hundred thousand dollars. Now accountants are estimating a total cash gate of a million to a million point four."

"What does that have to do with me?" Gene nodded his head to take in Billie. "With us?"

"We're going to heist the fight."

"What?"

"I don't believe the million-dollar-gate hype," said the banker. "But figure it's half that, and figure our plan will get us half of that half. A quarter of a million dollars split up among we five won't make us famous, but these days, that much cash will still buy us some sweet years."

"You're nuts!"

"No, I'm the inside man. If these locals knew the strings I've been pulling the last few years, they'd lynch me. I've been a public naysayer on this fight, but a whisper here, a question phrased just so, and suddenly people get an idea they think is their own. That's how I put this in place, that's how we'll take it.

"To make it work," said the toad, "we all need to be insiders. I inspired the idea that to perfect our glorious Dempsey–Gibbons fight, we need a preliminary bout: the heavyweight championship of Shelby. That'll put us all on the inside. That's how we'll rip it off."

"You want me to be your man in that prelim fight. Your boxer."

"Don't care if you win," said the pudgy banker in the lantern-lit farmhouse. "Don't care if you lose. All we care about is that you fight, that you make it go the distance, and that you climb out of the ring alive with enough left in you to do the job."

"Getting out of the ring alive seems like a good idea," said Gene.

"We're good idea men," said the banker. "The question is whether you got the guts and the smarts to be one, too. You can say no, walk out of here right now. If you're dumb enough to tell anybody what's what, we'll call you crazy and a liar. They'll believe us, not you."

"This hard world is Hell on liars." The black-haired man reclined on the couch, made a show of keeping his eyes on Gene and the .45 automatic on his lap.

"How is it on crazies?" said Gene.

"Depends." Norman Doyle didn't smile.

"What if they have to carry me out of the ring?"

Doyle said: "Don't bother to wake up."

The hophead beside Gene looked at nobody.

134

"So what's it going to be?" said the banker. "Yes or no?"

"Never happen." Gene shook his head: "Forget about whether the heist would work, the crime thing isn't what I do."

"Then you can say goodnight and leave," said the toad. "Your Billie girl will drive you back to that charming boarding-house. Say goodbye to her, then, too. She'll be leaving town.

"You see," continued the toad, "there've been expenses. Bringing Doyle up from Butte. Guaranteeing debts Harry incurred 'round the state. He was the one who knew of your fondness for his sister. She's a hell of a woman. A fine worker. But schoolmarming and waitressing won't settle Harry's debts. Bankruptcy foreclosure from the people Harry owes is permanent. So if our scheme 'never happens,' then Doyle will drive her to Butte so she can work buying her brother's lifeblood a few dollars at a time in an establishment whose proprietor I happen to—"

Gene was on his feet, the folding chair spinning behind him before he knew it, but not before Doyle'd filled his hand with the .45.

"You did this whole thing!" he told the banker.

"Let's say I brought elements together for a successful business venture," said Taylor. "Now you choose. What do you want that business to be?"

The black hole of the .45 watched Gene's heart. The banker watched his eyes. Harry Larson slumped with his face in his hands.

His sister stood behind him. Gene saw her soft cheek he'd never touched now scarred by a wet line.

Must have been deep into the twenty-first century before he said: "Who do I have to fight?"

"Doesn't matter," said Doyle.

"No," said Gene, "I guess it doesn't. How long do I have to get ready?"

"Seven weeks and change. You fight on the Fourth of July."

"That's not enough time."

"Make it be," said Taylor. "Inspired local sponsors 'found' Doyle to manage you. The mayor's sending an offer. Accept it. Also, cultivate your mustache: in your pictures, that's what we want people to see and remember, for your sake. Tomorrow, Billie will fetch you out to the old Woon ranch. The four of you will live there while you train."

"One of you might be able to run away for a while," said Doyle. "I'd catch you, but you'd have a while. But the three of you...easy pickings."

"I have enough running to do for the fight," said Gene.

"Good," said Taylor. He raised his whiskey glass: "And good luck...champ."

She drove him back to town. They didn't talk. The envelope with the offer from the mayor was in his mailbox. Gene scrawled *OK*, signed his name and gave the club-footed desk clerk two bits to deliver it. Gene settled his tab through the morning and stretched out on his last honest bed. Trains clattered through town on the tracks fifty yards from where he lay, but he let them go without him to clean forests and seaside towns.

Billie picked him up after breakfast. The highway snaked through erosion-farmed prairie spreading sixty miles west to the jagged blue sawtooth range of the Rocky Mountains. That highway beneath heaven's blue bowl sky led to Mexico. She turned left off that oiled route, put the Rockies at their backs as they followed a graveled snake trail. The farmland became hilly with the breaks for the river named Marias after some woman in Meriwether Lewis' life. Gene thought Lewis was damn lucky to be able to do that for her.

The peeling Woon house and barn stood against the horizon at the end of the road.

"There's two bedrooms upstairs, one down, and a room in the barn," said Doyle as he came off the front porch to where Gene and Billie parked. "I got the downstairs where I can hear the screen doors creak. You're upstairs, palooka, the woman, too. Hophead is in the barn."

Doyle led them into the barn where the oven air was thick with the scent of hay and manure. Flies buzzed. A black horse whinnied from a stall. A heavy punching bag hung down into the open other end from one beam, while another dangled a speed bag. Dumbbells waited on a table next to boxing gloves, rolls of tape, and five pairs of canvas shoes.

"Taylor guessed about your size," said Doyle. "We'll get other stuff if you need it."

"I've got my own shoes and gloves for the fight." Gene picked up a pair of sneakers. "These'll work in the meantime."

From ten feet away, Doyle said: "So what now?"

"You got a knife?"

Doyle's right hand snapped like a whip to drop a switch-blade out of his sleeve. Light flashed between him and Gene and with a *thunk* the knife stuck into a stall wall. "Help yourself."

So I gotta watch out for that, too. Gene pulled the knife from the barn wood and cut his pants into shorts. Tossed the knife to the dirt in front of Doyle's shined shoes. Gene took off his shirts, changed his work boots for the new sneakers, said: "Time to train."

Working the oil rigs had kept him strong with endurance. That was crucial, but he'd need explosive power, too. He spent an hour working with dumbbells while telling Harry how to construct a flat bench for chest presses. He put a ten-pound weight in each hand to shadowbox. When his arms were on fire, he put on train-ing gloves and moved first to the heavy bag, then to the speed bag. Gene's arms were so heavy that even if he'd had his old timing, the twenty-minute display of *tap tap miss* he gave the watching Doyle, Billie and Harry would still have been pitiful.

"Seems you're working it backward," said Doyle. "Skill stuff should come first."

"Find out what skill you got when you're at your worst." Sweat covered Gene's bare chest. "Then you know how much fur-ther you've got to make yourself go."

"'Pears to me you'll be lucky to make it out of this barn."

"I might not be the only one."

"'Least you talk like a fighter." Doyle spit. "Woman: I'm hungry. Go make lunch."

"Make your own lunch," said Gene. "I need a spotter for road work and I don't fancy your company or figure Harry can handle the heat."

"Your job ain't to figure, palooka."

"Fine. You explain to Taylor how you chose to screw up me getting ready."

"I explain nothing to nobody." Doyle'd taken off his suit jacket so his white shirt showed dampness around the leather straps of the .45's shoulder holster.

But you won't push things too far, thought Gene. Not yet.

Doyle said: "I'm going to the house."

As he walked away, Gene told Billie what he needed.

She bridled the black horse. Didn't even look for a saddle. Swung herself up on its back, her dress swirling, hiking up past her knees. Her feet were bare, as were her legs that gripped the naked flanks of the black horse. Harry draped glass jars of water on each side of the quivering animal's neck. Billie tapped her heels against the animal, and he carried her out of the barn, her round hips split evenly along the beast's spine and rocking with the rhythm of each step. When she got into the sunlight, she turned back, gave Gene a nod.

Gene ran.

Out of the barn, through the yard, along the gravel road. Dust filled his panting mouth. Rocks stabbed the soles of his feet. He followed a wagon trail along the crests of the river breaks. A quarter mile and the house vanished behind rises and dips in the land. He dropped the strong set of his shoulders. Heard the *clump clump* of the horse behind him, the rattle of the glass water jars. A half mile and he vomited, staggered and would have fallen but somehow she was down on the ground beside him, holding him up as he wheezed and gasped and the world spun in bright explosions of light.

She poured water over him, made him wash his mouth and

drink. "Can you do it?"

"Have to, don't we?"

Billie touched his sweaty chest. His slamming heart made her hand twitch. "Thank you."

"Have to run ten miles a day by end of next week."

She got back on the horse. He stumbled along for another three minutes before he turned around and made his mind see him running back to the house. He wouldn't let Doyle see him have to be carried back. Billie made Gene eat four scrambled eggs for lunch. Hosed him off behind the house. Laid him down on the bed upstairs while she unpacked his suitcase with his clothes, the canvas bag with his still supple ring shoes, blue satin trunks and those blood-smeared black gloves. Before dinner she held his ankles while he did sit-ups until his mid-drift cramped at ninety-seven and he thrashed out of her control on the barn's dirt floor. He sparred with the heavy bag and the speed bag and lost both times. She watched for the five minutes he hung swaying from a pipe by both arms to stretch out and give himself a whisker longer reach. She couldn't tell that he'd tried to finish with a set of pull-ups and failed. Hosed him down again. Dinner was whatever and he ate it all, including the nighttime-only bone-building milk that could cut his wind. Upstairs, in only his underpants, he lay helpless while she sponged his face in the pickle brine he'd made Doyle get from town. Some trickled in his eye, but she was fast and put her hand over his mouth so his scream stayed muffled in the bedroom walls. She eased both of his hands into other bowls of brine: working the rigs had toughened their flesh, but every trick mattered. The brine stung in the dozens of cuts on his hands. He was too tired for pain.

"Would he do it?" said Gene. "Your brother. Make you...let them force you into..."

"Harry would hate that but he already hates himself. He'd shoot up and believe it was a trick of fate he couldn't help and can't help, something that'll go away if we just get through it."

"What about you?"

She turned away. "My mom died. My baby died. My brother's all I've got left to lose."

"There's you."

"You're the only one who cares about that." She shook her head. "Besides, they wouldn't just kill Harry, they know he wouldn't care. So they'd kill me, too, to prove the point to the world. At least if the two of us are still alive...we've got that."

She turned back to him. "You know that...whatever you want from me, you can have."

"I don't want anybody to hurt you. I don't want you to ever have to cry."

Billie left the bedroom. He lay there with his hands in the bowls of brine. *If the house catches fire, here's where I'll die.* The bedroom door opened and she came in carrying a roll of blankets and a pillow. She made a bed for herself on the floor, took his hands out of the bowls, pulled a blanket over him, but then he was gone into a sleep beyond rest.

The next day was worse. And the day after that. Bone-thumping soreness. Muscles of rubber, lungs of fire. Half the time he couldn't think straight as he lifted weights, tried not to trip and kept failing as he jumped rope. He'd hang from the pipe first thing every morning, drop down to bend and twist every way he could before Billie bridled the horse, filled the water bottles and followed his stumbling run across the prairie. Heavy bag, speed bag, more rope, shadowboxing, then another run before dinner. Brine sponges and soaking. And always Doyle watching, hanging around, eating across from him and Billie, and when he wasn't on the needle, brother Harry, who kept trying to joke, who talked of what a fight it would be, of how all Gene's road work was building them streets of gold, a highway to heaven.

On the fifth night at the farm, Taylor snuck out to see them.

"They found your opponent," said the pudgy banker. "Eric Harmon. He's got twenty pounds of muscle and two inches on you, and he's only two years out of high school. Won the Golden Gloves down in Great Falls, and he's got glory in his eyes."

"He can have it," said Gene.

"That's right. As long as you don't let him finish you off getting it."

Taylor left them a radio and left them alone.

Training the next day was Hell. And the next. Nights while he soaked his hands, Billie read Sinclair Lewis to him as music played on the radio downstairs where Doyle smoked and watched the door. Gene could read just fine, but her voice was magic. He'd ask her questions. Knew she answered him with the truth, perhaps saying it for the first time in her life without qualification. About how her father bought her mother. About how Billie always knew she never belonged, not white, not Indian, not a man with power, not a woman with respect. How freedom only came when she lost herself in a book or at a movie or in a song on the radio. Or sometimes on a horse, galloping over empty prairie. How the only time she ever felt real was when she was teaching and some kid's face lit up as he got it, whether "it" was the Pythagorean theorem or the glories of Rome. How she took pity on the fatherly man who begged to marry her, gambled that he'd at least keep her safe. How he gave her baby Laura, who fiercely stirred her soul. How daughter and husband died coughing while Billie watched.

Gene answered her questions, too. About how after the blood of Belleau Wood he'd rotated to England where a sergeant gave him a choice of boxing or the Front. The ring seemed saner. Learning to slip and bob and weave, combinations and counters and timing.

"And I found out that while I could do a lot, I was only truly good, really good, born in the blood special good for one thing: boxing."

"Then knowing and having that makes you lucky."

"You'd think so, wouldn't you," he said.

She said nothing. Blew out the bed lantern and lay down on her floor.

The next morning he ran clear and cool in his head, heard the horse trot to keep up behind him. He went three hills farther than he'd ever gone before and ran back without stopping. Took only one jar of water from Billie. He used heavier weights, did more sit-ups, made the jump rope sing and swirl. Slipped on training gloves. The heavy bag hung in the sunlit barn. Gene glided to it on feet that didn't stick to the earth. He felt the rhythm of a breeze. Feinted once, twice—

Hit the heavy bag with a right jab that shook dust off the barn beam, a great slamming *thwack* that made the horse jump in his stall.

Gene turned and grinned at Billie. Saw her want to smile back, and that was something, almost enough. The heavy bag cried in pain for half an hour of his punches. He worked the speed bag like a machine gun. Doyle came out of the house, the leer gone from his face. Harry pranced around the barnyard like a chicken chirping: *What'd I tell you! What'd I tell you!*

And Gene breathed as a boxer.

That night Billie blew out the lantern on the bedside table, but instead of lying down on her floor, she stood there looking at him on the bed as moonlight streamed through the open window. The breeze stirred her hair and her long white nightshirt.

"You lied to me," she said.

"That's one thing I'd never do."

"You said you were only truly good at one thing, at boxing. But you're the best in the world there ever could be at this. At risking everything to save me. No one could do that better and there's sure no one who would ever want to."

The bed floated in front of the light of her eyes in that shadowed room.

"Do you think we're going to get out of this alive?" she whispered.

"Or die trying."

But she didn't laugh. Said: "Either way, just once, for one

thing, I want to choose."

"That's what I want for you, too."

She lifted the nightshirt off over her head like a white cloud floating away to let her bare skin glisten with the lunar silver glow. The bed squeaked as she knelt on it, as she lay beside him. He'd never been so afraid of doing the wrong thing. She took his right hand and pressed it on her breast, filled it with her round warm stiffening flesh, and he felt her heart slamming as hard as his as she said: "Everything I can, I give to you."

"But do you want to?" he whispered.

Her breath came quicker, shallower, like she was running. Her long legs stirred against his. He pulled back, her face held away from his, her lips parted but unable to reach him and he held her away until he heard her whisper *Yes!* she whispered *Yes!* she told him *Yes!* and as her bare leg slid up his thighs he moved into their kiss.

In the morning Gene found the edge. That knife line border where strength and hunger meet. That fury place when you sink into your eyes and your spine steels. You no longer walk, no longer run: you are a tight wind with legs like thunderclouds and lightning bolt arms. The smile on your skull is death and your mouth's coffee-metal-salty taste for blood doesn't care whose. He devoured ten miles of road with the scent of her on him, her hips bouncing up and down on the black horse. He shadowboxed in the barn with her watching everywhere and not there at all. Bare-fisted, slew the heavy bag with his favorite three-punch staccato rhythm and whirled without losing cadence to make the speed bag sing, then spun to snatch a horsefly out of the air with his right jab. He was totally in the moment of that hay-stinking, dusty, oven horse barn even as he was absolutely in eternity's every four-cornered canvas ring. Pain simply didn't matter. He was a boxer.

"Clean up," said Doyle. "We're all going to town, show the yokels we're for real."

Doyle drove and made Gene sit up front with him. Harry was a wire in the backseat beside Billie. She wore that blue dress.

143

Shelby'd been full before the fight announcement. Now Gene felt like he was in a beehive swelling with hot air from the beating of a million wings. The town had six dance halls for workers who'd flooded in to hammer up the eight-sided, 40,000-seat wooden arena rising like a toothpick skeleton on the edge of town. On the prairie across the tracks from the fight site stood an encampment of Indian tepees. Cars jammed Main Street. People stared and pointed. Men took it upon themselves to clear a slot for them in front of the movie house, holding up traffic, beckoning Doyle into the parking spot. When they got out of the car, hands appeared from everywhere to shake Gene's, to touch him on the back, the shoulders. The crowd stared at the Larsons, who followed in the wake of the fighter and his trainer, knew these merely local half breeds were now somehow sacred, too. Fans smiled a dark hunger. An oilman's blond daughter whose eyes Gene had never marked now pulled at the gladiator with her sapphire gaze.

Harry jumped out front: "Let us through! Let Gene through!" They entered a barbershop. A white-shrouded half-clipped customer leapt out of his chair and Doyle nudged Gene to obey the barber's plea to take that throne.

"On the house for you two boys," said the barber. "On the house."

"What two boys?" said Gene.

The back room curtain opened and out came a husky giant whose muscles bulged his shirt sleeves. Eric Harmon said: "Me and you."

The good part of Gene, the old part, the real part wanted to say: *You were here first, Eric. Take the chair.* But the boxer he was now smiled and leaned back for the barber's clip.

"I won't be long," said Gene. "Then you can have your turn."

"Don't I know it," said Eric.

Only the *snip snip* of scissors sounded in the barbershop as Eric leaned against the wall. Doyle sat, nodded for Billie and Harry to sit, too. Two other customers pretended to read magazines. On the street outside the window, none of the shoulder-to-shoulder crowd moved, all of them faced every which way they could to keep that glass in the corner of their eyes.

"Is that okay?" whispered the barber after he spun Gene around to look in the mirror.

"Looks damn fine," said Gene. "I look damn good, don't I?"

Thought: *Please Billie, know I don't mean it!*

"Never thought of you as a pretty boy," said Eric.

"I never thought of you at all." Gene got out of the chair, tossed the barber a quarter. Told the scissors man: "You do such fine work, think I'll hang around and watch."

Eric shook his head and took the chair. The white sheet whipped around him. Gene noticed the barber's shaking hands.

"Careful there, Pete. Don't nick our boy and make him red out too soon."

"Doesn't matter if he uses the razor," said Eric. "I don't bleed easy."

"We'll see." Gene looked across the room. "Mind if I put on your radio?"

The barber didn't break his concentration as he cut the younger man's hair and Gene walked over, tuned the radio to some hot New York jazz. Gene turned the volume up.

Gene said: "I got to wash up. But not as much as some."

Then he walked through the curtain to the sink and the bathroom. The sound of radio jazz blanketed the room outside the curtain. Nobody could hear anything from the washroom. Gene turned on the water and didn't look around as he heard the curtain swing open, get pulled shut.

"Think we gave them enough show, Eric?" Gene took a towel off the rack, turned around, drying his hands. The younger fighter stood watching him. At least two inches. At least twenty pounds.

"This isn't a show for me," said Eric. "We never met, not really, but I know who you are, seen you around. Always kind of admired you. So you should know this isn't personal."

"At least you're that smart."

"This is about winning. About who's a champion. And that'll be me. I'll fight you fair, but I'll beat you."

"Eric, don't kill yourself over—"

"California was a long time ago. Not long for people out there in the street, but for guys like us who have to climb into the ring, damn near the weight of forever ago. I got no feelings for what you did, except sorry for you and the guy who fell."

"I knocked him down."

"You'll have to do more than that to me. This is my only chance to prove I'm somebody."

"No it's not."

"Sure it is. Just look at you."

Then the younger man stuck out his hand. When they shook, he didn't try to crush Gene's fingers and Gene suddenly loved him for that.

"Give me a good fight," said Eric. "I want to know I won something hard."

Gene didn't know what to say. Let him leave with silence. Gene gave him time to get clear of the barbershop, swept open the curtain, and there stood Sheriff John Otis.

"'Pears I didn't have to hustle down here after all," Texas John's eyes pulled back from Gene to take in Billie, trembling Harry. Doyle. "Don't see no trouble to put down."

"Could have been," said the barber. "Why—"

"My law ain't about 'could be.' 'S about what I see with these two good eyes." Those two good eyes rode Doyle. "Though just 'cause I size up a son of a bitch doesn't mean I'll give him what he deserves. But when he makes his wrong play, I drop the curtain."

"Just like you were in a movie, huh?" said Doyle. "Not out here in the real world."

The sheriff laughed and his suit coat *coincidentally* opened with his swinging arms. Gene saw the Colt Peacemaker holstered on Texas John's hip like it had been in his Ranger days. Saw the wooden stock for the Mauser slung under Otis' right arm, knew that thousand-yard sniper automatic hung near the sheriff's heart.

"This ain't the real world, this is Shelby."

"Imagine that," said Doyle.

"Don't have to," answered Texas John. "I'm here. And we got phones and everything. And when I called around about a curly-haired fancy-dancy with a Butte license plate who claims to be a boxing manager, the boys down there wondered how you ended up in an honest game."

"Just lucky, I guess."

"Luck is a fragile thing," said Doyle. "Be sure to watch it close. You can bet I will."

The sheriff told Gene: "You in with some fine people, Hometown."

His black cowboy boots shook the barbershop as he tromped out to Main Street.

"We're back to the ranch," said Doyle.

Great by me, thought Gene. Every day his training ran him like a growing steel tiger. Every night he lay beside Billie. He needed less sleep and more of her. She gave him all she could reach. She'd ask questions, care about his answers.

"What was the hardest thing to learn about boxing?" asked Billie.

"Making yourself pull down into the fighter's crouch where you could hit and where you could get hurt. Getting past the terror. Your mouth all dry, your stomach heaving in and out, and you look across the ring and see that steely stare coming back at you and you hope he doesn't see your stomach fluttering and then you see his and it's jumping like mad, too, and oh Christ, any second they'll ring that bell."

He told her how easy it was to forget to keep your guard up. How his favorite combination was a lightning left-left-right, and when you throw the left jab, how you had to remember to bring it back at eye level, quick and straight. How after the second left, your dance had to move your left foot four inches to the left so your shoulders squared up and gave your right jab the snap that created power. How the uppercut was easy, go pigeon-toed and corkscrew your punch. How the hook took him months to learn, how he practiced a million times with each fist until he could keep his elbow up and whip it out tight and close, just eighteen inches of loop—two feet and it's an arm punch, a pillow, a joke, a nothing and left you only with how lucky you were in dodging the other guy's coming-in cannonball.

"But besides being good at it, what do you like about boxing?"

Took him all the next day to find the answer. That night they lay like spoons in the darkness, his face brushed by the perfume of her hair, her bare spine pressed against the mass of his chest, the two of them alone on the white sheet of their starlit bed.

"In the ring," he whispered, "what's happening is real. True. Even the feints, the fakes and the cheats. You use every single bit of yourself and find more you didn't know was there. No chain is gonna whip out of the sky and hang you dead and dropped before you know it. You're not gonna need to shoot your own damn horse. You know exactly who you are. Where you are. It's a fight. You're a boxer."

She said nothing.

Then told him: "This here with you is the closest I've got to that."

Told him: "You say the one special thing you can do is boxing. The one special thing I can do is make you love me."

Billie curled into a ball, away from him and into him at the same time, her head pulling away on the sheet from his kisses even as her round hips pushed back against his loins, pressed against him, rubbing, and Gene gave himself to her.

Nine nights before the fight Doyle threw open their door, stood backlit in the entrance as Billie jerked the sheet over her nakedness and Gene snuck one bare foot down to the floor.

"Wake up and dress, palooka. I need a driver."

"That's not my job."

"The hophead's too shaky, so it's either you or the woman. If it's her, the coming back to you will take a good while longer. That's okay with me."

Gene made the time as midnight when he drove Doyle away from the farmhouse.

"They say a woman weakens a boxer," said Doyle. "Steals his legs. His wind."

"Only way to find out is to get me a sparring partner. Why don't you volunteer?"

"You'd like that, wouldn't you, punchy?"

"I'm just doing the job I said I'd do."

"No. Tonight you're driving. Like I say you'll do."

Doyle made him take a back road into Shelby. Music came from the joints on Front Street. Doyle had him park on an alley slope up from the drop-lit rear door of Taylor's bank.

"Shut off the lights and engine, but keep your hand on the starter."

"We meeting the man?"

"Might say that if you weren't supposed to keep shut up."

Doyle bent over to hide the strike of a kitchen match that let him check his watch: ten minutes to one. Doyle puffed out the blue flame. Sulphur smoke soured the darkness. He eased out the passenger door, flapped his suit coat so it was loose.

"When I come running, you start the engine. Keep the lights out." Doyle crept to a shed where the shadows hid him from the alley below, stood there like a rock.

Gene knew time in three-minute increments. In the middle of the sixth round, way down the slope, between two Main Street buildings, Gene spotted the hulking figure of a man walking toward the alley. The man stepped out of the passageway: Sheriff Otis.

From that distance, the car with Gene was an innocent shape, one of the new vehicles crowding into town for the oil rigs or the railroad spur they were building for the chartered trains from back East. Even if the ex–Texas Ranger spotted the car, its engine was off, its doors were closed. Shadows cloaked Doyle. Sheriff Otis walked along the flat stone wall of a building and into the cone of light dropping down over the bank's rear door. Otis wrapped his gun hand around the bank's doorknob to be sure it was locked tight.

Gene barely heard Doyle's whisper: "Draw!"

Saw the shadowed man's solo hand clear his suit coat and snap straight out toward Otis.

Saw the flash of the pistol and heard its roar as a blast of crimson graffitied the bank's cement wall below the doorknob and Otis flipped into the air and crashed to the alley.

Doyle leapt into the car and they sped to the back road south.

"Got the son of a bitch just like I wanted!" yelled Doyle.

"Sucker shot!"

"Depends on which side of the trigger you're on. Besides, I could have put the pill through his black heart, but instead he'll get to gimp around and play the local hero."

"What makes you so kind?"

"A dead lawman brings heat from everywhere. A cripple is a joke."

"Hope he doesn't bleed out."

They hit a bump.

Doyle said: "Those are the risks you take."

Three nights later, six days to the fight, Taylor drove out, told Doyle: "Perfect job. The town fathers gave a local guy the badge. Otis is parked in his house on the east end, sitting on the porch with his gun on his lap, his leg cemented up, watching the trains go by and cursing like a son of a bitch. Somehow everybody's talking about two guys with Texas accents who blew into town and now can't be found anywhere. Almost like they never existed, but they must have been the ones. A man's past come back to haunt him. Happens all the time."

"Will he walk again?" asked Gene.

"Who cares?" said Doyle. "The law dog's not gonna be there to figure what he can't see, he's not gonna be able to run after no robbers."

"You will have to run," said the toad to Gene. "In all the confusion, our locals won't piece it together but, quick enough, they'll take it to the real lawman. He'll figure your part, especially since he already's got a bead on Doyle. But Doyle's good shot bought you half a day at least.

"After the heist, this is the first place they'll look. Doyle'll plant a burned map of Mexico in the trash ashes. But you go east to that farm where we met. Cut up the cash. Hide my share in the lockbox under the living room floor. Harry, leave the money you owe. Doyle will peel off extra bills for expenses. There'll be scissors, hair dye. A razor for your mustache, Gene. If you're banged up from the fight, there'll be a sling for your arm and doctor's papers about a farm accident. Only lie when you have to. A close trim, a henna and Billie'll look respectable. The shed has a change-up car. Alberta plates. Harry knows the bootlegger trail into Canada. The four of you'll hit that whistle-stop depot at Aden before the evening papers. Doyle'll have train tickets to Vancouver for Mr. and Mrs. Louis Dumas. Doyle figures he'll like New York: Anybody can be anybody there. Harry, you can help Doyle drive to the big time or he'll let you out on the way, your choice."

"What about you?" said Gene.

"I stay here to keep messing with the minds of our friends and neighbors. A year from now, I regretfully leave this paradise for a better job. Six months later, I vanish a free man."

"What's to stop us from keeping all the money?" said Gene. "You won't go to the cops."

"You're too smart to risk running from my insurance men plus hiding from the law." Taylor smiled. "Besides, you and the Larsons are fundamentally honest people. A banker learns how to judge that real quick."

That moonlit night as she floated on his chest, Billie whispered: "Would Doyle double-cross our banker?"

"No. Not as long as it's all working. They're both too clever for that."

"What about us?" whispered Billie.

"Yeah." A breath made his chest rise and fall. "Anyway you look at it, what about us."

On the first day of July the thermometer said it was 92 degrees in the shade. Doyle was gone, Harry was stoned. After his morning run and workout, Billie stretched Gene out on their bed, rubbed him down, lay beside him like every morning. They napped. Something woke Gene before the ticking alarm clock. The window glowed like molten white gold. He shielded his eyes and shuffled to the edge of the fluttering curtains.

Out there. By the barn. Doyle closing the trunk of his Ford and carrying a shovel back into the barn where maybe it hadn't been hanging that morning.

That night, Gene told Billie: "Tomorrow I need you to go to town. With Doyle. If Harry comes, even better, but you've got to get Doyle away from here and keep him away for at least half a day. Say it's for supplies or whatever, but you've got to get me free of him." She nodded in the darkness and he hated them both for the creeping fear.

The next day, the second day of July, two days before the fight, he watched as Billie drove away from the farm toward Shelby. With Doyle. Doyle alone.

Gene ran to the barn, found Harry slumped on a stool. Harry sat in that manure oven, his shirt sleeves buttoned tight on his wrists, flies crawling untroubled on that face where the eyes clung to open above a slack-jawed smile. Gene said: "What kind of man are you?"

"Wasted," answered Harry.

"Can you still lie and do it good enough to save your sister?"

Harry stared at ghosts standing witness. Licked his lips,

told Gene: "I'm the kind of guy who says *whatever* and then believes it's true. Believing a lie helps sell it. So you're telling me that for once in my stupid life, what I gotta do is just be myself? Even I can't screw that up."

Can't do it like Billie, thought Gene as he saddled the black horse while lecturing her brother: "If Doyle beats me back, tell him I took the horse to ride out my crazies. Sell him that. If I get back first, we got to get this horse in his stall like he never left it."

As he galloped away, Gene didn't look back at the man slumped in the barn door.

Way he figured it with Billie's talk about the Pythagorean theorem, from the barn on the ranch south of Shelby to the farmhouse east of that town was just under 14 miles. But that was one way, and across fenced rolling prairie and farmland where somebody might see him.

Somebody, but not Doyle. He'd be busy. In town. With Billie.

Gene boot-heeled the horse's flanks. *Not for nothing. Not all this for nothing.*

Misted indigo humps of the three Sweet Grass Hills rode a horizon of blue sky. Fields of wheat Gene and the horse charged through were losing green to gold, baking to an early harvest in the 95-degree heat. The horse reeked of wet sweat. *Would Doyle's nose pick up that scent rubbed on a man? When he got back. With Billie.* A circling hawk watched Gene cut the first of many barbed wire fences. *I'm just like an old-timer now, he thought as he rode through the savaged fence. What was it like for them? Fields of horse belly-high buffalo grass instead of sodbuster ruined scrub and wheat planted for starving Boston urchins. What was it like for Billie's people who rode this endless open with a hundred million buffalo?* Gene heeled his horse.

He spotted the farmhouse. Nobody else had seen him, though he'd seen a wagon ferrying a Hutterite family in their religion's strange black pants, homemade checkered shirts and plain faces. They'd ignored a frantic horseman who galloped past them, cutting fences before they were even out of sight. They'd tell no one outside their colony what they'd seen: nothing outside their community of God mattered.

Gene sat in the saddle on the heaving horse. Watched the farmhouse for ten minutes. Saw nothing move. He made the horse trot forward.

"Hello?" he called. No answer. He reined in the horse by a garage window. Gene peered inside: dusty sunlight showed him a coupe with Alberta license plates. And only two seats.

Took him one loop around the farmhouse to spot what he hadn't found at Woon's ranch. Behind a shed was a freshly shoveled solo hole in the earth, six feet long and four feet deep, its dirt pile waiting beside that gaping maw.

Call me a lucky man, thought Gene. Not many people get to see this.

Doyle, you lazy bastard. Four feet isn't deep enough for even one in this coyote country.

From the saddle, he nudged open the shed door and saw three sacks of quicklime.

Gene pulled the door shut, then jerked the reins and kicked the frothing horse home.

In a gully a mile from the Woon barn, the horse staggering beneath him, Gene glanced over the ridge toward the highway: two cars turned off that main road toward the ranch.

"Go!" he kicked his boot heels. The exhausted black beast stumbled through the rocky gully circling Woon's ranch. If Gene rode low and kept the horse's head down, maybe no one driving up in a car would spot him. He risked a scouting peek over the sagebrushed ridge.

Saw Doyle's Ford and toad Taylor's Cadillac closing in on the ranch.

From the barn ran Harry, stumbling into the path of the cars so they had to stop, had to not get to the ranch as he waved his arms and ranted like a man poisoned with monsters.

"*Hya!*" Gene charged the horse through the gully, around the back of the ranch, up out of its shelter and into the barn as car engines whined closer. Gene rode the white-foamed black horse into the open stall, flipped off the saddle and almost ripped the teeth out of the wheezing horse's mouth as he stripped off the bridle, let it fall to the stall floor as car engines stopped. Gene raced toward the mass of sunlight filling the barn door—

Out, charging toward the two cars emptying of Doyle and Taylor and caught-a-ride Harry. And Billie. Gene yelled: "Where the hell have you been!"

"In town!" called Billie. Her face told him the truth: "Just in town."

Gene whirled to Taylor: "Why the hell are you here?"

"The town dispatched me to brief you on their plans." The toad smiled. "And I'll tell you ours. All that sweat: you've been working out. Good. But rest now. Hot out here, let's go inside."

Gene snapped: "The barn?"

"I'm no animal," said Taylor, and led everyone into the house.

Sitting in the Woon living room, Gene told Taylor: "Sounds like we ain't going to have a fight. The radio says the chartered trains from back East have all canceled. No money, no fight, nothing for us to steal. Dempsey's boss Jack Kearns says—"

The toad lunged across the room to scream at the sitting boxer: "The fight is happening! Don't you say that! The fight is happening and we're...we're..."

"You're wound tight," said Gene. "Just as tight as one of the real boosters."

"Worry about you!" Taylor's hands shook. "You got to fight fifteen rounds and still be workable! Don't worry about Kearns! The fight's going to happen! They're meeting in a bank right now getting seed money! People will show up with cash they owe for tickets! And the chartered trains! They're going to run full speed from St. Paul and Chicago and fifty dollars ringside! They're bringing all that money so we can take it! Nobody's going to keep it from us!"

Gene shrugged. "You're the boss."

Saw Doyle staring at the trembling toad.

"Yes," said Taylor. "Yes I am. And this is how it works.

"Under that wooden arena are four rough dressing rooms, one for each fighter. And a collection room for all money coming through the gate. By the sixth round of the Main Event, accountants figure ninety percent of the gate cash will be in. To get it to the bank, they'll send a posse in the seventh round. Kearns will make Dempsey take it that long so people get their money's worth. Everybody knows Dempsey can put Gibbons away, so they all be glued to the ring for the first rounds, for the quick knockout. Guards will be on the gates leading down into the dressing rooms and collection area. But inside there'll only be fighters, their trainers, a couple counting room clerks—and all that cash.

"You've got to take Eric the full fifteen rounds so you'll have an excuse to still be inside when the Dempsey fight starts. Change fast. Pillow case masks and gloves go inside with you. Soon as the crowd roars with the bell starting Round One, you three run to the counting room, muscle inside, tie up the clerks, grab the cash, walk out with everything stuffed in your gear bags. Billie picks you up out front during the fifth round while the posse is still at the bank. You're gone before anybody knows anything is wrong."

"No killing," said Gene.

"I'm not a necktie fool," said Doyle. "We got handcuffs and tape strips for the clerks. Shouldn't be more than two of them. I'll be gun man, you truss them up, Harry scoops up cash."

"You know the rest of the plan," said Taylor.

"Yes," said Gene, "I do."

"So," said the banker to Gene as he stood to leave: "How you gonna do in the fight?"

"Swell."

"Glory," said Doyle. "Ain't it great."

That night Gene and Billie made love for the last time before the fight.

"We have to beat everybody," Gene whispered to her. "Even Harry, and we have to clue him in as much as we dare. We have to do the holdup. Not let anybody die. Get to the car. Then take over Doyle, wrap him up. Drive out east to Texas John's, dump the whole true thing on him and convince him ours was the only way. If we turn in the cash plus the guy who shot him and stole it, we got a chance. Maybe Doyle will rat on Taylor, too, buy himself a deal. The men Harry owes won't go after you two: you're not worth it to be roped in as accessories. I'll do time if I have to. No matter what, you'll be free."

"You mean from all this."

"From all that you want free of."

"It's a terrible plan."

"Yes," he said. "I know."

Heaven moved aside and let the noon sun boil down on a bull's-eye boxing ring that Fourth of July, 1923, a black-roped canvas square centered in the heart of an octagonal sloping wooden arena on a sallow dust prairie. Gene wore those bloodied black gloves, blue satin shorts and his second skin shoes. For a long count he existed alone in the hollow, dry breeze, floating in slow motion, bouncing on the balls of his feet, jabbing air that was as thick as invisible molasses. He lived in the belly of a blazing whiteness. He heard his rasping breaths, his cannon heartbeat. Then gravity's roar rocketed him back to a box of glory in Shelby, Montana, to Doyle and Harry wearing cornermen's white shirts and bow ties and sweating at their post, and Gene knew everything had gone terribly wrong.

"Nobody's here!" he yelled to Doyle. "Look out at the stands! Like three rows of people! Maybe three hundred at most! Empty bleacher seats stretching all the way up to the sky!"

Toad Taylor bobbed outside the ring beneath their corner, a ridiculous straw skimmer knocked off-center above his crimson face as he shook both hands in the air and hissed at them: "They're coming! The charter trains! Don't believe them when they say they didn't go! We stopped the rumors about no fight! We did! So they have to go! They have to be here! Plus the crowds outside! Thousands of them! You're just the throwaway! The time filler! The real people will be here! They'll bring the big money! They have to! They must! This is the heavyweight championship of the world!"

But not for Gene.

Or for Eric Harmon, younger, taller, heavier muscled and abruptly materialized in the opposite corner. The sheen on Eric looked like the boy had oiled himself, but Gene knew it was sweat: Eric would not cheat. Eric's eyes were bullets. As their gloves fell away from the referee's handshake, Gene felt Eric drop benevolence he'd cradled for a lifetime.

Then rang that bell.

A whirling fury charged across the ring to Gene, gloves hooking and jabbing and feinting fast, so fast, trees falling on his raised arms as Gene backpedaled, saw flashes of sky and flesh flung his way. Eric connected with a right hook Gene blocked with his shoulder. Gene spun—

Hit the canvas and bounded up before the referee could count two. The bell rang.

"He's killing you out there!" screamed Doyle in the corner as he sponged Gene's face.

"He's trying."

"The fight's gotta last!" Doyle glared into Gene's face. "Decide how you want to die."

Ding!

Gene took the ring and meant it. Eric rained blows at him. Gene slipped a punch and fired his jab back along the younger man's arm in a blow that shook Eric's face. But Gene pulled the last two punches of his combination. Eric didn't care. Round Two, Three, Four, Five. Eric matched each ticking second of the clock with a punch, a move, a charge.

Round Six Eric bloodied Gene's mouth. Not much. A trickle

of salty wet inside his cheek. The bell rang. Gene went to his corner. If Doyle or Harry said anything, he heard them not. He swallowed. When the bell rang, a new beast pranced out to meet Eric.

All fights have a rhythm, a jazz that is the two combatants and the fight itself, a music that shimmers beyond the sum of its parts into a set with its own time and place and fury. Often individual elements of a fight so dominate that the jazz is muted or lost to naked eyes and souls. But even then, the jazz is there. The true boxer senses that jazz in his bones, a feeling he can't create alone but one which he can slip into, and through it, become it. And command.

Round Seven came the jazz, and the jazz was Gene. Eric's punches hit him and hurt, damaged and didn't matter. Gene's jabs slammed into the bigger man on time, in rhythm. Gene's mind cut a deal with the jazz to play long enough to keep the set alive as Gene's gloves smacked the meat of a young man. Here the ribs. There a hook to the face. Left-left-square up right *bam!* Over and over again. Round Seven. Eight. Nine. Ten. Eric fought with everything he had and more, but in this music *that* was his sound, his damning sound: Eric was a fighter fighting. Gene was a boxer. Force against finesse. Strength against science. Work against art. Eric had a heart full of prayers but the angels' chorus was jazz.

Round Eleven. Blood ran from Eric's ears and nose. He threw off the referee. *Come on!* his gloves beckoned Gene. *Come on!* Round Twelve. Thirteen. Gene danced him into a clinch.

"You can have it!" whispered Gene. "I'll take a dive in the fifteenth! Don't make me do this!"

Eric pushed off him and wildly swung-missed. Spit out his mouthpiece. Through broken teeth yelled: "Hell wi' you! I'm real!"

The low punch Eric threw might have hit home in Round One, but now Gene slid back and let it fan. Without thought, Gene's right counter slammed his opponent's jaw. Eric hit the canvas so hard Gene bounced. *Stay down!* Gene willed. Eric staggered up on the seven count.

Round Fourteen. Eric stood in the center of the ring like a heavy bag absorbing punch after punch from Gene, who for a fury-blind minute couldn't stop. Then he backed away, only bobbed back in close when it looked like the referee would call it.

Fifteen. Final round. Strings down from the sky plucked Eric off his corner stool and puppeted him toward Gene. Blood and sweat trickled down both of Eric's arms to drip on the canvas. His guard didn't rise above his belt. Gene tapped his face twice. Eric staggered back—

A roar from the soles of his shoes tore through the state. Eric charged, his arms swinging slow wild haymakers like a baby, his eyes drowned by gore streaming from his splattered forehead as he yelled: "W're are 'ou? 'Hre 'ou? Fight me! Fight me!"

No one should lose like that. Gene snapped up a perfect guard, danced in. As softly as he dared, Gene hooked a right into the staggering man's cheek and felled him to the canvas.

The referee stood there, not bothering to count ten. The last bell rang.

Gene knew the referee raised his hand. Knew Harry gave him water, wiped him down. Knew the mayor bounded into the ring and hung a gold-painted brass medal around his neck. Men carried Eric out of the ring. Gene saw his chest move and knew that boy's hands still clung to life inside bloodied boxing gloves. And as Gene staggered between the ropes Doyle held and saw an arena over-flowing with empty seats, he knew that now began his real fight.

Momentum pulled him to the arena corridor. As they walked past the stands, Gene saw a man pass a mason jar to the only other two people sitting in the row. Gene knew the mason jar didn't hold the concession stand's lemonade. Going down the corridor's ramp, Gene and his crew met a squad of trainers and corner-men coming up with night-haired Jack Dempsey.

Dempsey hit Gene with eyes that were black ice and saw everything about him, the sheen of sweat, the glint of brass around his neck, the blood splattered on Gene's chest. I'm taller than him, thought Gene as they drew close. That flicker of arrogance whispered to Dempsey. His gaze jabbed Gene's soul and Gene knew: never had a day that good, never will.

The paltry paid crowd roared when they saw the true champion emerge into the sunlight.

The lone guard on the door to the walled-in area for the dressing and other rooms told Gene's crew: "Not a single chartered train came! And everybody else is still hanging outside!"

"Nothing changes!" hissed Doyle as they hurried to the pine-planked sweat chamber the promoters grandly called a dressing room.

Inside, door closed. Harry threw a bucket of water over Gene, wiped him with a towel. Kept muttering: "Great fighter, you're a great fighter, great fight. Not me, you. 'S' thing to be". From a duffel bag, Doyle pulled pillow cases cut for masks and money hauling, his .45 shoulder rig, a suit jacket. He tossed revolvers to Harry and Gene.

"Don't worry, Champ. They ain't loaded."

Gene said: "If the trains didn't come—"

"We take what's there!" said Doyle. "You better pray there's enough!"

Gene had only his shirt left to button when a thunderous *creak!* rolled through the wooden arena. The room around them bent and screamed. From outside came a great roar. Three would-be holdup men ran into the dungeon of rooms built under the area. The dim hall was empty. They ran to the corridor door. No guard. They hurried up the ramp into a blast of sunlight. Dempsey and Gibbons danced in the ring for Round One, but the great rolling-herd roar of a thousand voices caught even their attention.

In they came from every entryway. Men in suits and straw hats, work boots and denim. Women in long skirts and yellow scarves. Umbrellas and pocket flasks. Clothes ripped by the barbed wire and turnstiles they'd torn down to storm inside for free. Damn the big money they'd never have: no one would keep them from their championship.

"Look!" Harry pointed to a corridor a hundred feet away.

A toad of a man, his straw hat askew, hopped back and forth in front of a stampeding phalanx, his hands outstretched to hold them back, screaming so loud that even Gene and his crew heard him: "Go back! You didn't pay! You've got to pay! Everybody's got to pay!"

Laughter drowned him out as he spun into the ranks of wild-faced men and cackling women. Gene lost sight of Taylor as the crowd swirled. The banker popped out, pressed against a railing as elbows and shoulders slammed his back. The toad's face was a purple moon with craters for eyes and the scream of his mouth. Taylor's hands clutched his chest like he'd been punched, clawed at his throat fighting a strangler. A well-wisher poured amber liquid from a pocket flask into the uptight banker's maw. Taylor choked, gurgled. He flopped over the rail as the crowd surged into the arena. Revelers plucked the banker from the rail and dragged him along until he sprawled into a hatless toad heap on a bench, reeking of bootleg whiskey like he was dead drunk, but Gene knew the toad was just dead, that he'd bake in the sun until the cleaning crew and newspaper eulogies told about an innocent casualty of championship fever.

"Gone." Harry trembled as he stared at the chaos. "'Sall gone to crazy!"

"Come on!" yelled Doyle as the crowd of twelve thousand gate crashers scrambled in and the bell rang the end of Dempsey–Gibbons Round One. "We've got a job to do!"

"No good," muttered Harry as Doyle marched them back down inside the bowels of the arena, past the unguarded corridor door. "Nothing's no good 'less you're a fighter."

"Shut up!" snapped Doyle as they hurried back to Gene's dressing room.

Harry plucked at Doyle with a trembling hand: "No good, you're no good, this is all gone no good and we know what you're going to do!"

Shut up, Harry! willed Gene.

Harry chose to fight for the first time in his life. He jumped on Doyle: "Get him now, Gene! Don't wait!"

Doyle threw Harry into Gene. Gene shoved Harry back toward Doyle as that man's right hand whirled. A heartbeat before the crowd outside roared the start of Round Two, Gene heard *snick* and saw *light flash* in the dim wooden cavern. Crimson misted the air between Harry and Doyle. Harry spun to show Gene his new wet red collar. The inertia of the switchblade slash turned Harry all the way around to face Doyle again. Doyle pushed the dying man aside. Harry fell between wooden beams to lay underneath the arena until the demolition crew found him two weeks later, long after insects and animals finished with his flesh. The law chalked up his bones to a worker who'd gone missing after cops ran two Wobbly labor organizers off the construction site, one of those tragic industrial accidents that happens all the time.

Doyle stabbed at the boxer but Gene still had the jazz. He batted the knife out of Doyle's hand with a left slap and slammed his right fist straight into the killer's jaw. Fifteen rounds earlier, that punch might have put Doyle out for good; now it dropped him out but breathing.

Finish him—No! Gene dragged the moaning man to his dressing room, threw him inside and slammed the door: no lock. He wedged the knife in the doorjamb and snapped off the blade.

Doyle won't be out for long. The wedged door won't hold him long. *Think!* Won't let us get away, we're witnesses, 'n' he doesn't need no other reason than rage.

But first he'll go to the money. Try to feed his money hunger first, then revenge.

Gene ran to the counting room. Get there first! Tell them Doyle'd gone crazy! Killed Harry! Was going to hold them up. With a clerk, maybe two, maybe guns with bullets, they could ambush Doyle and the clerks would be witnesses to Gene's story, to him being a hero, to him and Billie being innocent, safe, fr—

The counting room door stood ajar.

The crowd roared as Gibbons split open an old cut over Dempsey's eye in Round Four.

A short guy in a good suit stood in the counting room. Four chairs behind the long table were empty. Notebooks and tills were strewn everywhere. But no silver dollars. No stacks of greenbacks. The short guy stared at the big man in the doorway whose hand dangled a revolver.

"If you've come for money, you're too late," said the short guy. "Someone beat you to what little of it they had. Got them to give it up to him. Then once the bust-in riot started, the clerks knew it was over and they all left to see the big fight."

"You're Dempsey's manager. Jack Kearns."

"Guilty. And with that gun in your hand, you're a man looking for trouble."

"Doesn't have any bullets."

"A man with a gun and no bullets is a man who's *in* trouble." Kearns squinted. "I saw you fight, Mallette. You held back. Got size, speed, strength, technique. But give it up. You got no future as a real champ. Inside you there's no killer."

"You'd be surprised."

"Not likely. What did they promise you for winning?"

"Wasn't about the money."

"For you, probably not. But how much to be the champ of this town?"

"A thousand."

"They cheaped you. You'll never get it anyway. This crazy day cheated them, too. They'll all go bust." Kearns held a fold of bills toward Gene. "Every winner deserves a purse. Five hundred, and keep this between you and me. Call yourself lucky to get it and get gone before your half-assed manager comes looking for his cut."

Gene didn't know what to do. Put the money in his pocket.

Kearns took the revolver from Gene. Broke open the cylinder and clucked at the empty slots for bullets. "You're too honest for your own good."

He took a flat .25 automatic from his back pocket and disappeared it in Gene's hand. "An honest guy needs iron that works. This one's ready to go, though it won't damage anybody who's not kissing close."

Kearns walked toward the door. The crowd outside roared when Gibbons connected with a combo that stung the champion, than danced around the ring to escape a furious Dempsey.

"Mr. Kearns!" said Gene. "Who got all the money from the fight?"

"Gee kid, beats me."

Then he was gone. Outside, the crowd roared. Gene fled the counting room. Saw the door to his dressing room shake. Out of the door crack fell a knife blade.

Gene ran. Made it out of the roaring arena. A naked yellow eye baked the oiled air. He muscled his way through a dirt street jammed with crazed strangers. Two Martin boys set off a string of Chinese firecrackers. A man and two women sat on an overturned sausage peddler's cart, stuffing themselves with meat tubes they plucked from the ground. A tuxedoed redhead bounced off Gene and staggered away, his eyes whirling in his head. A cowboy shot his Peacemaker into the air and no one flinched.

Where are you, Billie? Got to be here! She's got to be here!

Firecrackers. A horse screamed and a fat woman laughed. The cowboy fired his pistol.

Car horn, was that a—

"Gene! Over here!"

Billie waved from the Ford's running board. Gene shoved his way to their getaway car that was pinned against the curb by a deserted truck. Parked vehicles jammed every road.

She grabbed Gene to be sure he was alive and real. "Where's Doyle? Where's...?"

"All gone wrong. No heist. Doyle killed Harry. He—"

165

Glass exploded in the car window.

Doyle: near the arena. He stood on a wobbly overturned pushcart, his gun hand shaking as he lined up for another shot over the sea of heads who didn't give a damn.

Gene grabbed her hand, held on to his life and plunged into the mad, milling crowd.

"One chance!" he yelled as he dragged her behind him. Every bone in his body wept. His legs shook. Lemonade he grabbed from a kid didn't cool the fire in his throat. "We got one chance! Get to Texas John! Not crooks! We're targets 'n' only he can save us!"

"His house is two miles across town!" But she ran with him.

By the time they'd fought their way to Main Street, Billie was more carrying Gene than running with him. They looked back and saw only the sea of people in their wake.

"Still there," gasped Gene. "He's still there somewhere. Won't stop. We can't stop."

The crowd became a solid wall of flesh at the east end of Main Street, an audience to the volunteers battling a ball of fire that had once been a tailor shop.

"Railroad tracks!" gasped Billie. "Nobody's there! We can go quicker along them!"

"But not straight to John's! That's maybe three football fields north of his house—"

"Only hope," she told him as they staggered to the steel rails. Hundreds of parked freight cars squatted on the tracks, diverted there for the passenger charters that hadn't come. A metal *clang!* shuddered the wall of boxcars beside them as the locomotive a thousand yards away got a *clear track* signal. Steel wheels creaked a slow revolution.

Gene pressed Kearns' close-in gun into Billie's hands. Shoved Kearns' money into her dress pocket. "Get on train! Can't make it farther. Can't run no more."

"Yes you can!" Billie grabbed his shirt. "Look! You can see

Texas John's house from here! Just up that hill!"

"Can't get up that hill 'fore Doyle catches us. You know he's out there, Hell-hound smelling us. He won't stop until he gets his blood. Till he gets me. But you: hop on this freight, open boxcar comin' up. Hide. Taking care of me will slow him down. He'll see me, stop for me. Enough so you can go. Get free."

"You can get away!" cried Billie.

"No. I can only do what makes me special. You said it. I save you. Only special you can do is make me love you. Let me be special and love you and get you on the train. You be special and do it. Don't let us both die as nothing."

"Too late," she said, looking past him, wrapping her grip around the pistol.

Doyle stood a hundred yards down the tracks.

Billie raised her gun—

Gene covered her hand with his: "That won't work until he's close enough to kiss."

The barrel of her automatic swung down along Gene's ribs. Billie hid the gun behind her.

"You have to let him get real close," said Gene. "He'll like that. Do that. For you. Not for me. He'll never let me get close to him again. But I won't just stand here and take it."

He stepped away from her grabbing hand. Took two steps forward as Doyle strolled toward him. Doyle stopped when he was about the same distance away as a sucker shot to a bank door. But instead of night, he had a broad daylight aim, though the sky had suddenly gone grey with rain clouds as Dempsey threw everything he had at Gibbons, yet had to settle for a clinch finish at the final bell, a decision victory instead of a knockout.

The freight train groaned and inched forward.

Gene Mallette brought both hands up in fists and dropped into the stance of a boxer.

Heard Doyle laugh and saw that man's solo hand clear his suit coat and snap straight out.

A crimson rose blew out Doyle's left ear and sprayed red on a passing boxcar. Doyle fell to the chipped rock track bed as the *crack!* of a German sniper's Mauser from a front porch on a hill a thousand yards away whispered to Gene above the rumble of the train.

No second shot came from the man who used to have a badge and who knew what his eyes saw. Gene stared at the house on the hill: whatever had happened up there was over. He and Billie went to the dead man. A million angels dropped tears on them as she helped Gene throw Doyle and the guns through open doors of crawling boxcars. Gene almost fell under the steel wheels, but she grabbed him and held on. The train rumbled toward the mountains and the ocean beyond. Gene ripped the medal off his neck and threw it onto the last boxcar out of nowhere.

THE MAN WHO BOXED FOREVER

by Edward D. Hoch

Simon Ark and I were in London on another matter when we first heard about Desmond "Dragon" Moore. A publishing friend of mine had given me two tickets to Moore's sold-out fight against Clayt Sprague for the heavyweight championship. It was a title that would go unrecognized in American boxing circles, but the winner was certain to become a top contender to challenge the Americans.

"We could delay our return by an extra couple of days if it interests you," I told Simon.

"Boxing as such holds little appeal, but this man Dragon Moore seems to be getting a great deal of press over here. Do you think Shelly could spare you for two more days?"

We'd been in England a week already while I met with a juvenile author and Simon took care of a matter up in Suffolk. I phoned Shelly with some trepidation that her perpetual annoyance with Simon Ark might surface. "Two more days? Is this some idea of Simon's, chasing after his goblins?"

"No, no." I explained about the prizefight and the free tickets.

"All right, I suppose two days more doesn't matter. Just remember we have the dinner party Saturday night for my sister's birthday."

"I'll be home long before that."

"Have fun. I'll look for you on Thursday."

As it turned out, it wasn't much fun.

The championship fight the following night was at London's new Barbican Arena. I realized at once that it was an upscale event, with the ringside seats occupied by men and women in proper evening clothes. Our seats were farther back in the front section, on the aisle, and we arrived halfway through the card. One of the preliminary bouts was in progress as we settled into our seats. "We are not dressed for this, my friend," Simon remarked. He was wearing a black suit, as usual, and could have passed for a priest with his intense expression and eyes that missed nothing.

"The people farther back aren't so fancy," I observed, turning to study the sell-out crowd. It was then that a man seated about four rows behind us in the adjoining section caught my eye. He looked vaguely familiar, but I couldn't place him until he got up at the end of the preliminary bout and came down to say hello.

"I'm Roger Russell," he said. "You probably don't remember me, but I did a sports book for Neptune about ten years ago and you were my editor."

"Sure, Roger! I thought you looked familiar. This is Simon Ark, Roger Russell." I was retired from publishing now, but still acted as a consultant for Neptune Books. Russell's opus, a coffee-table volume about the early days of sports in America, had been a mildly popular seller for the Christmas trade. He was a rugged, athletic-looking fellow, probably in his mid-forties now, and he wore his brown hair cut short to heighten the illusion of youth.

"Seeing Mr. Ark here, I suppose that means you're investigating the rumors too."

"What rumors would those be?" Simon asked him.

"Oh, about Dragon Moore being a lot older than he claims."

"We hadn't heard that," I admitted. "A London editor gave me the tickets."

"It's probably not true anyway," Russell said, putting a quick end to the conversation. "Good seeing you again."

"Same here."

When he'd returned to his seat, Simon Ark asked, "What are

those rumors about Moore's age?"

"Beats me. I don't follow boxing that closely. All I know is that he's a Creole from New Orleans who's done most of his fighting in England."

The ring bell sounded several times to signal the arrival of the fighters for the main event. Down our aisle came Dragon Moore, a bald, hulking giant of mixed race, grinning widely as he trotted into action. Seeing the flare of his nostrils, I remembered something else about him. He'd earned the nickname of Dragon because of a small dragon-shaped birthmark on his left cheek, and because he often seemed about to exhale fire. A limping gray-haired man followed along, apparently his trainer or manager.

On the opposite side of the arena a second boxer had appeared. Clayt Sprague was a limber Jamaican who seemed to move about more easily than Moore. He bounded into the ring with gloved hands raised, eliciting cheers from the packed house. Clearly he was the crowd's favorite. The fighters were called to the center of the ring to hear the referee's instructions, then retreated to their corners until the bell sounded for the start of the first round.

Both came out warily, like two jungle cats approaching one another, each seeking an advantage. At first only a few feints, and then light, testing blows were struck. Some in the crowd booed, wanting them to mix it up, but the round ended with barely a single serious punch having been thrown. In the second round Sprague went after the Creole, landing a stiff right followed by a rain of left jabs. Dragon Moore retreated, but only momentarily. Just before the bell ended the round he landed a savage blow to the jaw that sent Sprague's mouthpiece flying.

"The crowd likes it now," I commented. "It's a brutal business."

"It always has been, since ancient Greece. It was a sport in the first Olympic Games, and in Rome it was often part of gladiatorial contests. The boxers there wore metal-studded hand coverings designed to maim or kill."

After that blow the energy seemed to go out of Clayt Sprague. The Jamaican went through the motions for another two rounds, but in the fifth he went down hard and didn't move. Dragon Moore won by a knockout. Though most of the crowd had favored Sprague, they gave wild approval to the giant Creole.

"What did you think of it?" Roger Russell asked me on the way out. Simon had dropped behind us in the crowd.

I shrugged. "That Dragon is quite a fighter. How do you think he'd do back in America?"

"With the right publicity he could be a pop icon like Ali and Foreman and some of the others. He's got a lot of backstory going for him."

"What do you mean?"

The crowd was pushing from all sides as the place emptied out. A final bout followed, but hardly anyone remained for it. "The age thing, you know."

"I don't know," I assured him.

"I've got some clippings and things. Your friend Simon Ark is the one who should really see them. He's into this undead business, isn't he?"

"Undead? What in hell are you talking about?" He must have heard about Simon from someone, about how he sometimes claimed to have been a Coptic priest in first-century Egypt, prowling the earth ever since in search of evil, hoping for a confrontation someday with Satan himself. I'd met Simon more than forty years earlier when I was a young reporter, before my publishing days. My wife Shelly took a dim view of him, and chided me about believing in his myth of eternal life. I may not have believed it all, but when I studied his face and saw the tiny lines of age almost hidden there, I had to admit that he hadn't changed much in those forty years.

We'd reached the front entrance at last and Roger Russell shoved a card into my hand. "Meet me at this place tomorrow afternoon around two. Leather's Gym in Soho. Bring Ark with you.

There might be a book idea in this."

In the taxi on the way back to our hotel I recounted the strange conversation to Simon. "What did he mean by undead?" I asked. "Vampires?"

He smiled slightly. "I know of no vampire pugilists, my friend. Let us go to Leather's Gym tomorrow and find out."

The following day was cool and cloudy with occasional drizzle, typical of London in October. We took a taxi to Soho Square and walked two short blocks down Greek Street to the address on the card, arriving just at two o'clock. There a metal sign above the entrance advised us: LEATHER'S GYM — ONE FLIGHT UP — HOURS 10 TO 5. We followed the direction and found three gray metal fire doors with no names on them. I picked the right one on my second try and it slid open readily when I pushed.

We found ourselves in a large room dominated by a regulation prizefighting ring. Around the ring were rows of folding chairs and off to one side were punching bags and other training equipment. Through an open office door I could see a desk and computer. At first the place seemed empty, but suddenly I realized there was a man on the canvas in the center of the ring.

"Simon! It's Roger Russell!"

The man we'd come to meet was lying on his back, arms outstretched. His shirt was off and he was bare to the waist. Boxing gloves were laced onto each of his hands. The left side of his head had sustained a mighty blow that left it ripped and bloody. He was dead.

The police arrived within five minutes of our call. A brisk young man named Sergeant Willis came in a few minutes later and seemed to be in charge of the investigation. "Do you two work here," he asked, "or are you just hangers-on?"

"Neither one," I informed him. "We came to meet the dead man, a writer named Roger Russell."

"American, like you?"

"Yes."

An officer called out from the other side of the ring. "I think we have the murder weapon, Sergeant."

Simon and I followed him around to look at it. We saw a bloody leather hand covering, studded with bits of sharp metal. "A cestus," Simon said, giving a name to it. "They were used by Roman gladiators. The straps wrapped around the hand. Remember, my friend, I mentioned them just last night at the fight."

"What fight was that?" the detective wanted to know.

"Moore and Sprague," I told him. "We had free tickets. That's where I ran into the victim."

Someone else had entered the gym, a tall man with crew-cut black hair, wearing a single gold earring and a long leather coat. "What's going on here?" he asked in a deep Scottish brogue. "I go out to lunch and come back to find coppers all over my place!"

"I'm Sergeant Willis," the detective said. "There's been a murder here."

"Who?" the man asked. "Not Roger?"

"The dead man has been identified by these people who found him as Roger Russell."

"My God!" He ran past them and tried to climb into the ring but was restrained by the officers. "I left the place open because he said he'd be coming by."

"It appears that someone goaded him into a boxing match," Willis said. "He stripped to the waist and allowed himself to be laced into boxing gloves. Then, when he was relatively helpless, the killer struck him a deadly blow, wearing a studded leather hand covering."

"A cestus from ancient Rome," Simon added.

"Who are you two?" the bald man asked, appearing to notice us for the first time.

I introduced us and he did likewise. "Miles Leather. This is my gym."

"Does Dragon Moore train here?" Simon asked.

"I'll ask the questions, if you don't mind," Willis told him.

"Why do you want to know that?"

"Because we encountered the dead man at the Moore–Sprague fight last evening, and that's when he invited us to meet him here."

He turned back to Leather. "What about it? Do either of those fighters train here?"

"Moore does, when he's in the city. Usually he goes to his camp outside Brighton."

"Have you seen him today?"

Leather shook his head. "He never comes in right after a fight."

"Do you usually leave the door unlocked when you go out to lunch?"

"Roger phoned to say he was meeting someone here. I left it open for him when I went out at one."

"It was probably Simon and me," I volunteered. "He'd asked us to meet him here around two."

Willis made some notes and then led Miles Leather over to look at the murder weapon. "Did you ever see it before?"

"Not like that. I've seen kids from street gangs wearing studded gloves sometimes. I took one away from a guy at a soccer game once. Those people get crazy."

"What did you do with it after?"

"Threw it away," Leather told him. "It was nothing I wanted around."

The detective made another note. "How well did you know the dead man?"

"Pretty well. He was a journalist. You always like to be friendly with them."

"Was he living in London or just visiting?"

"He came over a couple of weeks ago to do research for last night's fight. He was writing something about Dragon Moore. It started out to be a magazine profile but he told me this week it might develop into a book."

"What hotel was he at?"

Leather hedged a bit. "I don't know. He might have been staying at a friend's flat."

"Do you have the address?"

"Roger was married, you know. Wife back in the States."

It was Simon who put it into words. "He was staying here with another woman."

"I guess so, yes. Her name is Tracy Kimball, but I don't know where she lives."

"We'll find her," Sergeant Willis assured him.

When he'd finished his questioning of Simon and me, he suggested we remain in London until the investigation was complete. When we returned to the street the drizzle had stopped and a ray of sunshine was fighting a winning battle with the clouds. We walked north toward Soho Square and almost at once we encountered an agitated young woman who stopped us with a question. "What's going on in there? I saw the police cars."

"An accident," Simon told her as we tried to keep on walking.

"A friend of mine was at Leather's Gym. Is that where it happened?"

I studied her more closely then. She was a tall, athletic-looking woman with chestnut hair and large brown eyes, probably around thirty but who could tell with women these days? I took a gamble and asked, "Would you be Tracy Kimball?"

The muscles of her face tensed. "What's happened to him?"

"Roger Russell is dead."

She would have fallen to the pavement if I hadn't caught her.

Simon hailed a taxi and within fifteen minutes we had her back to her flat in Bloomsbury. Simon had recounted the bare facts of Russell's murder without going into detail. "Are you feeling better now?" I asked.

"I think so. It was just a shock. I'd come over on the Underground with him and was waiting down the street." She passed a hand uncertainly over her face as if trying to clear away a mist. "You're the men Roger went to meet, aren't you?"

"Yes," I agreed. "We saw him at the fight last night."

"I waited in the Square for him. Leather doesn't allow women in the gym because the fighters walk around naked after they shower. Roger had some printouts of old newspaper and magazine articles he was going to show you. I think he had some with him, but most of them are still in my flat. Could you come up for a few minutes?"

"These are about Dragon Moore?"

"They're about old fighters."

She had Simon's interest now, and we followed her up to a third-floor flat. It was a big room cluttered with a single girl's furnishings. A double bed was visible in an alcove, and a small kitchen and bathroom completed the necessities. A bookcase held a surprising number of nonfiction titles, mainly memoirs written by journalists. One row was bookended by a statuette of a bare-knuckled fighter.

"Had you known Roger long?" I asked while she retrieved a laptop carrying case from some pieces of luggage in the alcove.

"We worked together at the *Times* for about six months, but then he decided to go back to his wife in America. He still stayed here when he was in town." She unzipped the case and took out a folder of clippings and photocopies. "This Dragon business had become a crazy obsession with him. Maybe it led to his death."

"In what way?" Simon asked.

She held up the folder. "Did you ever hear of someone living over a hundred and twenty years?"

It was an odd question to ask Simon Ark, with his own claim of something akin to immortality. "There have been cases," he answered vaguely. "Do I assume that Dragon Moore claims to be that old?"

"Not at all. He only insists he has no record of when or where he was born. He grew up in New Orleans and that's where

177

Roger did much of his research. There were no birth or baptismal records for any Desmond Moore at about the time he should have been born. But he did find these things on some of those odd Internet sites." She handed Simon the folder.

I looked over his shoulder as he read through the computer printouts. The top one was an account of a wrestling match between someone called the Masked Dragon and a Mexican with the unlikely name of Pancho Willa in Galveston in 1939. "This man's a wrestler!" Simon protested.

"But the story says he also boxed without his mask as Desmond Moore. That was Moore's name before he started calling himself Dragon."

"A mere coincidence," Simon suggested, turning to the next newspaper article. This one was much older, from 1892, and the tiny print described a bout in New Orleans between Dragon Moore and Reefer Foxx, one of the first to be fought since bare-knuckle fights were outlawed under the newly adopted Queensberry rules.

"Look at the picture on the next page," she instructed.

The picture was an old photograph of the sort often found in newspapers of the late nineteenth century. It showed a bald fighter with his boxing gloves raised in the traditional protective stance. The caption read, "The Creole Dragon Moore, one of the first to fight with gloves under the new rules."

I had to admit the illustration bore a remarkable resemblance to Dragon Moore. "I suppose it could be his great-grandfather or something, but there've been a great many boxers named Moore."

Tracy Kimball bent over the page and I caught a whiff of her perfume. "Look here. See this little birthmark on his left cheek? It's just like Dragon's."

"That could be a shadow," Simon told her. "It's difficult to be sure."

"Roger was sure." She flipped the page, propelling us further back into sports history. "This is a page from an old history of

the Battle of New Orleans in 1815. It describes bare-knuckle fighters entertaining troops before the battle. One of the most popular
was named Desmond Moore. See? Right here!"

"These pages only show that there were several men who
boxed briefly under that name."

Tracy lifted her eyes to meet Simon's. "Or one man who
boxed forever."

Later, when we'd returned to our hotel, I asked Simon Ark
what he intended to do. "I think I owe it to Roger Russell to look
into this affair further," he said. "He was killed while fighting someone, and the most likely suspect would seem to be Dragon Moore.
We must make a call on Mr. Moore."

The Creole boxer had left London for his training camp near
Brighton, and it was there that we tracked him down on that
Wednesday evening. Up close he was even larger and more threatening than in the ring, a massive mountain of muscle that threatened
to burst through the T-shirt he wore. "You the ones called from
London?" he asked, meeting us on the porch of his cottage after
dark. "What do you want?"

"My name is Simon Ark. We're looking into the death of a
journalist named Roger Russell."

"I know," the big man told us. "The police called from
London. They want me back there in the morning for a statement."
His voice carried the Creole tones one associated with the French
Quarter of New Orleans.

"Had Russell interviewed you?"

A shake of the head. "I wouldn't talk to him." He turned and
the light from inside fell across the birthmark on his cheek. It did
resemble a dragon, and it appeared identical to the photograph in
the old newspaper.

"Why not?" Simon asked. "Do you have something to hide?"

"He had crazy ideas about me."

"How old are you, Mr. Moore?"

The big man smiled, showing a gold tooth in front. "Twenty-five, thirty. Age does not matter."

"Did you ever box Roger Russell, even in fun?"

"'Course not! That would be a crime. My fists are classed as deadly weapons, at least in America. Probably over here too."

"Somebody boxed Russell in the ring at Leather's Gym today. What time did you and your entourage arrive here today?"

"They came this morning," he mumbled. "I drove down a couple of hours ago."

"Alone?"

"Sure, alone. I wasn't anywhere near Leather's Gym, if that's what you're thinking."

"Did you ever use a cestus?"

A sly smile played along Moore's lips and I knew he was familiar with the word. "Sure did! Back when I was a gladiator."

He was joking, playing along with us.

"Russell believed you fought in New Orleans a long time ago," Simon told him.

"I fought there, yes. I was fighting on the club circuit when I was sixteen."

"Bare-knuckles?"

"When I was a boy."

"Russell couldn't find any record of your birth or schooling."

The big man shrugged, wrinkling his brow in a frown. "Not unusual among my people. I was born when the time was right, and I was schooled in the streets."

"Do you remember the Vietnam War?"

"I remember them all. Vietnam, Korea, World War Two. I remember the Battle of New Orleans. I remember the Roman gladiators." But the smile was back on his face.

"Prove it to me," Simon challenged.

"You are not the police. I have answered too many questions already." He walked past us into the cottage, closing the door behind him. Our interview was over.

On the way back to London in our rented car, I asked Simon, "What's his game? Obviously he knows about the rumors and is playing along with them. Is he just trying to kid us or what?"

"I'm not quite sure," Simon admitted.

"That bald head makes it difficult to guess at his age."

He agreed. "If he has gray hair he might shave his head to hide that fact."

"Why would he kill Russell? To keep his age a secret?"

"These days being older could be good publicity for him."

"But two hundred years old?"

"I'm not ready to admit that," he said.

By the time we returned to our London hotel and had a late dinner I was ready for bed. In the morning I phoned Shelly again to tell her the police had delayed our return. "What about the party?" she asked.

"I'll be home before Saturday," I promised, none too sure of it at that moment. Sergeant Willis had just phoned to invite us to assist with their inquiry at Scotland Yard.

Simon and I arrived there before ten and were immediately ushered into an interview room where Willis joined us. "We now have the autopsy report on Mr. Russell," he said, flipping through the sheets of paper as he spoke. "It appears that he was hit at least twice in the right temple by this."

"Cestus," Simon Ark supplied.

"Cestus, yes, this studded hand covering. The initial blow would have knocked him out, and the second one killed him. You saw the shape his head was in. There was blood on his pants and even a spot on his right hand. It seems likely the killer must have been splattered too."

Simon thought about that. "Did you find his shirt? The one he removed for the fight?"

"No," the detective admitted. "I have a theory that the killer might have worn it to cover up blood on his own shirt."

"Possible, but not likely," Simon told him.

"Why not?"

"Russell wouldn't have been bare-chested unless his oppo-nent was too. And if the killer was bare-chested, he wouldn't have had blood on his shirt."

"Makes sense," the detective admitted. "I've got Dragon Moore and Clayt Sprague both coming in here this morning. I hope to learn something from them."

That puzzled me. "You don't seriously believe he would have been boxing with either of those two heavyweights, do you?"

"They might have been sparring. I've heard of writers doing crazier things than that for a story."

So had I, but I wasn't about to admit it to Sergeant Willis. Simon had a question. "Tell me something, Sergeant. Who is Dragon Moore's manager?"

"We're looking into that. His manager of record is Sheldon Ames, a former middleweight boxer. There's talk in fight circles that Ames is just fronting for Miles Leather." He asked a few more routine questions and then said, "That's all for now. Will you still be in London tomorrow?"

I nodded. "But we have to catch an evening flight back home."

As we left the office I saw the Jamaican fighter Clayt Sprague waiting his turn. Simon recognized him too, and went over to his chair. "We saw you fight Tuesday night. Good job."

"Not so good," Sprague answered through lips still badly swollen from the fight. "I lost." His speech carried the familiar Jamaican accents of an upper-class English education.

"Anyone would have lost against Dragon. He hardly seems human."

The boxer snorted. "He's human, all right. Next time we fight I'll mop the floor with him!"

"There are strange stories about Dragon Moore," Simon suggested.

"Sure! He's a hundred years old! Two hundred! I heard the stories. He's still human. And I've got a good right hand that can prove it."

"Did you know the writer who was killed at Leather's Gym?"

"Russell? He interviewed me a week or two ago. Asked me about these stories he'd been collecting. It was mostly garbage he downloaded from the Internet. I told him that."

"You didn't arrange to meet him at Leather's Gym yesterday?"

"Hell no!"

Sergeant Willis came out of his office then, surprised to see us talking with the boxer. "In here, Mr. Sprague," he ordered. "I'm conducting this investigation."

Simon and I beat a hasty retreat to the elevator.

Back on the street I grumbled to Simon, "It's a wonder you didn't get us arrested with that trick."

"I was only exchanging pleasantries with the man."

"Do you think he's involved?"

"Probably not. He's right-handed. We saw it at the fight and he just told us again."

"How does that exonerate him?"

"The killing blows were to Russell's right temple. If the two were facing each other those blows would have been delivered by a left-handed man."

"Meaning Dragon Moore," I said. "But a right-handed fighter could still deliver a powerful jab with his left hand, and wearing that glove it might have been enough to knock Russell unconscious. The second blow finished the job."

Simon Ark smiled slightly. "You're getting to be quite the detective in your later years, my friend. I've trained you well. What would you suggest as our next step?"

"A return to Leather's Gym."

"And why?"

"Sprague said Russell was getting some of those documents

about Dragon Moore off the Internet. I noticed a computer in Miles Leather's office."

"Very good. I won't remind you that every office in London probably has a computer these days."

"Still, Simon, I think Leather knows more than he's saying."

It was after noon when we reached the Soho gym, and a few boxers were working out on the punching bags. I'd half expected to see police crime-scene tape circling the ring, but there were no reminders of the previous day's killing. Miles Leather was in his office, wearing a brown turtleneck sweater. He rose from his desk and came out when he saw us enter.

"Mr. Ark, isn't it?" he addressed Simon, with a nod in my direction. I'd learned long ago that people often forget my name. "Have there been any new developments in the investigation?"

"We're following up some interesting avenues of investigation," Simon told him. One of the young boxers, his body glistening with sweat, had started jumping rope almost on top of us. "Is there someplace we can talk?"

"In my office."

Leather sat behind his desk while Simon and I took the other two chairs. Simon immediately produced the folded printouts from his pocket. "Do you know about these?"

"I've seen them."

"It would make a compelling myth, wouldn't it? A mysterious Creole heavyweight who might be two hundred years old, fighting for the championship of the world?"

"It might be good for publicity," Leather agreed.

"You're Dragon's manager, aren't you?"

His lips compressed into a hard line. "Sheldon Ames is his trainer and manager. He's called Shell."

"The police believe it's you."

"What difference does it make? I have a piece of him, sure. With the gym and all it's best not to advertise the fact. Sprague trained here for a bit too, along with Dragon, so Ames manages

Dragon and I stay on the sidelines."

"You may have planted those stories on the Internet your-self."

Leather shrugged. "Check them out if you want. They're all real stories."

I shook my head. "You're telling us Dragon Moore is two hundred years old?"

"I'm telling you that in this age of the Internet the public will believe most anything, at least for a short time. Dragon Moore is going to be a nine days' wonder."

"Fifteen minutes of fame is all you get anymore, not nine days."

"It may not last, but I'm going to make some money for him. And for me too, of course."

I could only shake my head. "We can sink your whole scheme with just a few words to the press."

He smiled. I almost expected a gold tooth like Dragon had, but there was none visible. "Tell them what you want. It's just more publicity."

"Did you kill Russell to keep him quiet?"

"Hardly! I was counting on him to break the story."

We left Leather in his office and were on our way out when we encountered a gray-haired man who walked with a slight limp. I remembered seeing him the night of the fight. "Hey, you blokes!" he called to us. "You looking for me?" His accent was decidedly Cockney, and he didn't look too friendly.

"I don't know," Simon Ark replied. "Who are you?"

"Shell Ames. I manage Dragon Moore. You fixing to hurt my boy?"

"Not unless he deserves it," Simon told him. "We're looking into the killing of Roger Russell."

"Dragon had nothing to do with that. He was at our training camp."

"He was here in London earlier that afternoon. He could

have met Russell before he left."

"But he didn't. I wouldn't let him. We were eating at the Café Royal last week when Russell and his girl came over to the table. He wanted to talk to Dragon then but I told him to get lost."

"What girl was that?" I asked innocently.

"Name o' Tracy something."

"Tracy Kimball?"

"I guess so."

"You see them around much?"

"Used to, when he was living over here. He was a collector then, had lots of old boxing stuff, a picture signed by Ali, boxing gloves used by Dempsey, a program from the Johnson–Jeffries fight in Reno. That's how he found all that old stuff about my fighter. You stay away from him, hear?"

"We are only seeking the truth," Simon told him.

Shell Ames reached down to touch his left knee. "That's what I used to say in my younger days. I was a pretty good middleweight then. One night I refused to throw a fight. They broke my kneecap with a lead pipe and I been a gimp ever since. So what did it get me?"

"You think something like that happened to Russell?"

He shrugged. "It can be a dirty business. Watch your step."

I glanced back to see Leather watching us from his office door. Then Simon and I hurried out.

Once on the street I hailed a cab. "I think it's time we gave up, Simon. I have to be getting home."

"One more stop, my friend. I believe Tracy Kimball might hold the key to this mystery." He gave the driver her address.

Tracy was just returning from the local grocer's when we arrived. We followed her inside as she unpacked and stored the butter and eggs. "What is it?" she asked. "What's happened?"

"We met Shell Ames," Simon told her.

"Shell—? Oh, Dragon's manager."

"He said you saw him with Dragon a couple of weeks ago."

"Roger did. I was with him."

"Do you know Ames well?"

"Not at all. Roger had mentioned him, but that was the only time we'd met."

"But you'd know him if you saw him."

"I'm sure I would."

Simon nodded, as if finally certain of his next course of action. "Come with us now to Leather's Gym. I want you to identify him."

"Roger told me women aren't allowed. He would never take me."

"The gym closes at five. We'll wait for him outside."

"I don't know..."

"It will help to find Roger's killer."

"Then I'll do it," she decided.

We were back at Leather's Gym a half hour later, waiting in the park down the street. I remembered our meeting Tracy there just after Russell's murder. Now we watched young fighters carrying gym bags leave the building after their workouts, perhaps imagining that one day they might be the next Dragon Moore.

After a long wait, five o'clock passed without any sign of Shell Ames. "Come on," Simon decided. "We're going up."

"But women aren't—" Tracy began.

"The place closes at five. If anybody's still up there, that's who we want to see."

I held the street door open for Tracy and she preceded us in silence up the steps to the second floor, giving me a nice opportunity to admire her legs. Then she entered the gym without hesitation. I heard Miles Leather's voice bellow out, "No women allowed!"

"It's after business hours," Simon pointed out as we entered behind her. "Is Shell Ames here too?"

The gimpy manager came out of the office. "What is all

this?"

Simon turned to Tracy. "Take a good look at these two men, Miss Kimball, and tell us which one is Shell Ames."

My expectation of a sudden blinding revelation was doused when she pointed out the man we knew to be Ames. "This one, of course. The other man is Miles Leather."

Before either of us could say anything a third man emerged from the office. It was Dragon Moore himself. "What is going on here? These are the people who came out to the training camp yesterday."

"Yes, just what is going on?" Leather asked.

Simon Ark took a step forward. "I have come to explain a most perplexing problem. This man we see before us, Dragon Moore, is rumored to be much older than he looks. Items on the Internet would have us believe he boxed and wrestled more than sixty years ago. A photograph of a boxer with the same name more than a hundred years ago shows the identical facial birthmark shaped something like a dragon. How could this be? Could your fighter possibly be that old?"

Dragon Moore merely smirked while Leather took a menacing step forward. "Have your say and get out of here. Take the woman with you."

"I'll make it brief," Simon promised. "Putting aside the possibility of a man past one hundred being able to box like a heavyweight in his twenties, we are left with only two explanations. Could the man in the picture, the nineteenth century Dragon Moore, be a great-grandfather of the present one, having passed the birthmark down through several generations? Upon reflection I discarded this explanation. That fact alone, if true, would have been enough of a hook to ensure wide press coverage. No, you wanted to make Dragon a real legend, with the press puzzling over the story and that birthmark for months to come."

"It's real," Leather insisted. "It doesn't wash off."

"It's a tattoo!" Simon thundered, pointing his outstretched

finger like Solomon rendering a biblical verdict. "A tattoo that deliberately copied the birthmark on the earlier Dragon Moore's face! Of course your man wasn't named Dragon or Desmond Moore when you first came up with this scheme, which is why there's no record of his birth in New Orleans. He had a different name then. You found that old photograph of a fighter who looked something like Dragon and persuaded him to change his name and get the tattoo, matched exactly to the photo, and began dropping hints on the Internet that he was over a hundred years old."

"Are you saying we killed Russell because he discovered our plan?" Leather asked.

"Hardly. Any story he wrote would only have stoked the publicity and prolonged the debate. The American matchmakers would have offered big purses to lure Dragon back across the ocean for a fight."

"Then who killed him?"

Simon walked over to the ring and climbed the steps, fitting himself awkwardly between the ropes. "The murder of Roger Russell had nothing to do with Dragon's story, and I think I can prove it. Would one of you join me in the ring, please?" When nobody moved, he said, "Tracy? How about you? I promise I won't throw a punch."

She climbed reluctantly into the ring and Simon positioned her exactly in the center. "You see, the mistake everyone made was in assuming that Russell was killed during a sparring match, but he couldn't have been."

"Why not?" Dragon asked.

"Because the autopsy found a spot of blood on his right hand, even though both his hands were covered with boxing gloves. You see, Russell's shirt was removed and the gloves put on him after he was dead."

Ames and Leather exchanged bewildered glances, and I was as confused as everyone else. "But his shirt would have had blood on it too," I argued.

189

"Exactly! And that's why it had to be removed by the killer. It couldn't have been left on the gym floor or draped over a chair to spoil the illusion of a fight. The autopsy mentions blood on his pants but none on his torso, another proof that he was wearing the shirt when he was killed."

"If he wasn't boxing, why did the killer use a cestus on him?" Ames asked.

"Again to heighten the illusion there was a fight in progress."

"How did the killer get him into the ring if they weren't going to fight?"

"Simply by asking him, as I just asked Tracy Kimball to join me here. Isn't that how you did it, Miss Kimball?"

Suddenly she threw a punch at Simon that might have hurt had it connected. He grabbed her arms and held them tight until I came to the rescue.

It was some time later, after Sergeant Willis arrived to take her into custody, before we heard the rest of Simon's story. "Love and money are usually the primary motives for murder," he told us. "She still loved Russell, but he'd stopped loving her. He was back with his wife in America and their affair was over. The murder weapon, the cestus, came from his own collection. At least part of it was still at Tracy's apartment, of course. We saw a statuette of a bare-knuckled fighter in her bookcase. She slipped the cestus into her purse and insisted on accompanying him to meet us at the gym. Then she lured him into the ring and hit him from behind. She had to hit him a second time to finish him off. She removed his bloody shirt and disposed of it later in a trash can. There were plenty of boxing gloves around the gym and she laced a pair onto his hands. Her idea was that we'd never suspect a woman of killing him in a sparring match."

"That's all you had to go on?" Sergeant Willis asked.

"That and one more thing. She claimed she'd never been

here before because they bar women, but when I lured her here this afternoon with a made-up story of identifying Shell Ames, she walked up those stairs and through the proper door without hesitation, even though there are three unmarked steel doors out there."

We caught the Friday night plane back home, and I arrived in time for Shelly's party.

THE TRIAL HORSE

by Clark Howard

When the knock on the door came, Joe Bell was lying on top of a moist sheet in his Jockey shorts, snoring quietly like the engine of a late-model car that was starting to miss. His bed was a pull-out couch in a grubby little apartment in Boyle Heights, just east of Los Angeles. There was no air-conditioning in the building, just window units called "swamp coolers" that produced barely cool air almost moist enough to drink. But Joe was a good sleeper, so the humidity didn't bother him. Gladys, his wife, bitched about it constantly, especially when she put hot curlers in her bleached hair getting ready to go to work at the Arabian Cafe at seven A.M. She sweated so heavily that she had to wait until she got to work to put her mascara on.

When the knock on the door persisted, Joe's quiet snoring stopped, and when it persisted even more, he opened his eyes, thinking: The landlady! Gladys didn't pay the fucking rent. He had almost made up his mind not to answer the knock when a voice outside called his name.

"Joe! Joe Bell! It's Race, man! Open the door!"

Joe hauled himself out of bed and opened the door. Race, a tall, rail-thin, gray-haired black man with scar tissue around both eyes, came in and closed the door. "Wha's up wit' you, man?" he asked. "You hung over?"

"No, man. I thought you was the landlady. Wait a minute—"

Joe went into his tiny bathroom, took a leak and rinsed his face with cold water. "What's going on, man?" he asked Race, drying his face as he came back into the living room.

"Danny Pitts broke his wrist yesterday in training."

"No shit! Sparring?"

"Yeah. Some blockhead just down from Stockton. Came in low with his head and Pitts caught him with a right hook that bent his hand all the way back. Could hear the dorsal snap clear 'cross the gym."

"Jeez. He had a fight with Avila coming up, too. Tough luck."

"Tough for him. Maybe good for you."

"What d'you mean?"

"Ortega wants to see you." He meant Gil Ortega, manager of fighters, matchmaker and owner of Ortega's Championship Gym.

"Me? What's he wanna see me for?"

"What you think, stupid? He gots to find a sub for Pitts."

"Yeah, but why me? Mus' be plenty of guys around he can get. Active guys. Hell, Race, I ain't had a fight in ten months."

"Yeah, but you gots a leg up on this slot, baby."

"Why's that?"

Race smiled. "'Cause you lily-white, son, and Ortega agreed to put a white fighter in against Avila. His last six wins have been over niggers, spics and slopeheads. Public wants to see him do damage to a white boy for a change." He studied Joe for a moment. There was some bulk around his middle. "What you weigh?"

Joe shrugged. "I don't know. One-seventy, seventy-two."

"Yeah, well, Ortega gonna want you to get rid of that baby fat. You gon' have to make one-sixty."

"When's the fight?"

"Three weeks from Friday. And it's on ESPN, baby."

"No shit!" Joe patted his excess weight. "I can make one-sixty by then. When's Ortega wanna see me?"

"Soon's you can get over there. Shave, get cleaned up. Wear a loose sport shirt outside your pants. Tell Ortega you weigh one-sixty-seven. Suck your gut in and keep your shoulders back." Race returned to the door. "I'll see you over there," he said, and left.

Joe went into the bathroom and stood in front of the mirror. He sucked his stomach in, braced his shoulders back and flexed his biceps. ESPN, he thought with a smile. Son of a *bitch!*

Ortega's Championship Gym was housed in a one-story terra-cotta–and–brick building on Soto Street near Cesar Chavez Avenue. In the sixty-odd years since it was built, it had been a wholesale grocery store, a free medical clinic, a Chicano zoot-suiter jitterbug dance hall, a youth center and a weekend flea market. For the past ten years it had been Gil Ortega's training gym for professional fighters. A weathered sign above the entrance read: ORTEGA'S CHAMPIONSHIP GYM—HOME OF FUTURE CHAMPIONS.

Gil Ortega was a big man, not fat but brawny big, with thick arms, eyes like bullet holes and a sweeping Zapata mustache. He was dressed in fresh gray sweats, watching a young Mexican kid work the speed bag, when Joe Bell walked up and stood silently beside him. Noticing Joe, Ortega bobbed his chin at the kid. "He's from Culiacan. Every kid comes up from there, I always hope might be another Julio Cesar Chavez. That there is called wishful thinking." He looked knowingly at a flowing Hawaiian shirt Joe wore outside his trousers. With one big hand, he patted Joe's stomach. "Who's the father?"

"Come on, Gil, I ain't in that bad a shape," Joe protested.

"No? What do you weigh?"

"One-sixty-seven."

"Bullshit. You weigh one-seventy-two, seventy-three. You think I fell with the last rain? Don't try to bullshit me." He walked away, saying, "Come on in the office."

They walked the length of the gym. It was a big, rectangular room, two training rings occupying the very center, one end outfitted with speed bags, heavy bags, full-length sparring mirrors, exercise pads, a rope training corner and various other accoutrements

195

of the trade. Beyond that area was a locker room and showers. Along one side of the main room, Ortega had installed metal bleachers for spectators who could pay a buck to watch the work-outs, two bucks if a titleholder was working.

At the other far end of the room was Ortega's office. Through a frosted-glass door, Ortega and Joe entered a small reception area where Ortega's wife sat at an ancient wooden desk sorting out file cards on which were neatly typed the records of practically every professional fighter in North and Central America and the Caribbean.

"Hi, Joey," Ortega's wife said, looking up.

"Hi, Stefi," Joe answered.

"How's Gladys?"

"She's okay."

"She still a blonde?"

"Yeah."

"Hmmm. She still working for that Arab?"

"Uh, yeah."

"She better watch out for that guy," Stefi warned. "He's got a heavy reputation with the ladies."

"Gladys can take care of herself," Joe said.

Joe followed Ortega into his inner office. Ortega sat down behind an incredibly cluttered desk, and Joe, taking a chair facing him, watched as he fished around in the clutter and came up with several sheets of paper stapled together. "Race told you about Pitts, right?"

"Yeah. Tough luck."

"I had him on ESPN on the undercard of the Hector Camacho Jr.–Vic Malloy card three weeks from Friday. He was going against Antonio Avila. You know him?"

Joe shrugged. "Seen him around is all."

"They call him 'The Anvil.' Fourteen and zip, fourteen KOs, nobody's gone past three with him. He and Pitts were set for eight. The ESPN people have agreed to cut it to six if I can find a suitable sub for Pitts. You interested?"

"Where's the fight at?" Joe asked. He didn't want to take any long trips. Stefi wasn't the first one he'd heard say that the guy Gladys worked for was a real cocksman, a player who put the moves on every woman he was around. Not that Joe didn't trust Gladys. He just didn't want to be away overnight, was all.

"It's at the Rialto in Indio," Ortega told him.

Joe nodded. That was okay. He could get back home after the fight. Indio was just a few miles past Palm Springs. The Rialto Resort and Casino was one of the new Agua Caliente tribe casinos. "How much?" he asked Ortega.

"Twenty-five hundred."

Joe grimaced. "Come on, Gil. How much was you paying Danny Pitts?"

"Six grand. But Pitts is twenty-two and three. He's still a contender. You're nineteen and nine. A trial horse. Plus which, Pitts has never been stopped. You been stopped twice."

"Only on cuts!" Joe protested. "And one of them was from a butt."

"Cuts, butts, don't make no difference. You been stopped twice, Joey. That's the record." Ortega sighed quietly and looked at one of Stefi's neatly typed cards on his desk. "Your last fight was ten months ago. You lost in six to Fredo Castro down in Albuquerque on that Johnny Tapia card. What you been doing since then?"

Joe looked away. "This and that."

"Race said you was doing day work on the piers down in San Pedro. And he said you was delivering telephone books for Pac Bell. And doing clean-up work for Alvarez Brothers Landscaping."

Joe kept looking away and did not answer. Presently, Ortega sighed again, a little more heavily this time. He wished to God he didn't love fighters as much as he did.

"Okay, I'll give you three grand. And I'll see if I can throw some sparring work your way in the gym after it's over."

"What if I win? You get me another match? For more dough?"

"You ain't gonna win."

"Yeah, but what if I do, Gil? What do I get?"

"If you win, I'll give you my wife, my Cadillac and the key to my safe deposit box." He leaned forward and his tone softened. "Forget about winning, Joey. Just give Avila a good fight for as long as you can. Try to take him past three rounds. Do that and I'll give you an extra five hundred." Ortega rose. "I'm gonna have Race train you. Come on, let's get you a locker and some gear."

After he left the gym, Joe went over to the Arabian Cafe to see Gladys. She was in the kitchen, getting salads ready for the lunch trade. When he told her about the Avila fight, she said, "Thank God! Now maybe we can move into an apartment with real air-conditioning. Hass told me he saw some vacancy signs down on Whittier Boulevard." Hass was her boss, Hassim Hamed, an Iranian who was constantly talking about raising venture capital to open an Arabian boutique restaurant in Beverly Hills. Joe did not like him much. He did not like the way Hamed was always covertly glancing at Gladys' breasts. And buttocks. And legs. When Joe complained about it, Gladys told him he was crazy. Hass, she said, was always a perfect gentleman toward her.

"When do you get paid?" Gladys asked. There was a time when her first concern had been how good a fighter the other guy was.

"The day after the fight."

"Oh." She sounded disappointed. Joe picked up on it.

"Why? We short again?"

"Yeah, but it's okay. Hass will give me an advance. He's good about that."

"I'll get an advance from Ortega. I don't want you asking Hamed."

"Why not, for God's sake?" she asked, annoyed. "I've asked him plenty of times before."

"You have?"

"Well, sure I have, Joe. Jesus! How do you think we make ends meet when you can't pick up any day work?"

"I don't know. I guess I didn't think."

"Well, maybe you better start," she told him. Her voice was an edge beyond annoyance now.

Hassim Hamed walked in from the front of the cafe. "Hello there, Joe," he said. He was tall, slim, thick black hair over a *cafe au lait* complexion and perfect teeth.

"Yeah, hiya," Joe said sullenly. He began to sulk. Hello there. What the fuck was wrong with just plain hello?

Hamed filled a tray with bowls of salads to put in the glass-doored refrigerator behind the lunch counter. Joe watched him, studying the man's flawless face. It looked like it was made of cocoa butter. Not a mark on it. Unlike Joe's own, which had a ridge of scar tissue above the right eye, a crescent-shaped scar on the left chin bone, and the beginning of some cauliflowering in the cartilage of his right ear.

"So, how have you been, Joe?" the Iranian asked.

"I'm okay," Joe said.

"Good. Very good," Hamed said. He smiled a dazzling smile and left with the tray. Gladys gave Joe a scathing look.

"I swear to God, you are so *rude*. Least you could do is be polite, for God's sake."

"You be polite to him," Joe said. "You're the one who works here." He went to the back door, which led to an alley. "I gotta go start training," he said, and left.

He took a bus to a multiplex down in Whittier and spent the afternoon watching two movies.

Joe started training with Race the next day at Ortega's Gym. He was glad it was Race that Ortega was letting get him in shape. Race was easy to work with, as long as a fighter did exactly what Race told him to do. Race didn't take any shit from fighters; he had been around the fight game a long, long time, since back in the days of Basilio and Fullmer and the real Sugar Ray—not Seales or Leonard, but the man himself, Ray Robinson. Race knew what it was all about.

"Firs' thing we gots to do is get that baby from off yo' middle," he told Joe. He wrapped Joe's body from armpits to hip bones with Saran Wrap, then bundled him in double sweats and started him on some rope work. Joe was usually good at rope work; he had a smooth, steady rhythm and even toe balance that he had learned from watching videos of Sonny Liston working the rope to the Harlem Globetrotters theme song, "Sweet Georgia Brown." But after ten months of gym inactivity, and bundled up the way Race had him, he felt and looked like a fat man climbing steep stairs. Race shook his head dismally at the sight of him.

"You some sorry-lookin' mess," he said when Joe began to pant. "Put the rope down and get over here on this exercycle."

As he pumped away on the cycle, with Race tightening and loosening the tension in increments, Joe asked, "Race, do you think I'm a trial horse?"

"Why you ax?"

"Ortega told me I was a trial horse. It's why he ain't paying me as much as he was paying Danny Pitts."

Race chewed on the inside of his mouth a bit before answering. "I reckon he might be pretty much right. You ain't no contender no more, fo' sure. But I'd say this: if you a trial horse, you a good trial horse."

That made Joe feel a lot better. He had never minded being anything, as long as he was good at it. Every once in a while he found some day work on a garbage truck, hanging on the back end as it went from house to house, pausing so that Joe and another guy could swing off and heft big trash barrels to empty them. Once, the driver had said that Joe was the best extra helper he'd ever had. It had made Joe feel good, even if it was about working on a garbage truck.

After the exercycle work, Race had Joe spar in front of a training mirror for ten two-minute rounds, with one-minute rests in between. Joe felt good being back in training again. The heavy, sweat-filled air of the gym was like a fragrance to him; the grunts of the men working out, mixed with the thud of leather training gloves against the canvas of the heavy bags, and the *thump-thump-thump* of speed bags, *tap-tap-tap* of rope work—it was like music. He had not realized how much he missed boxing. It was good to be part of it, even if Gil Ortega did call him a trial horse.

While Joe was working in front of the training mirror, three young Hispanic men, wearing white shirts buttoned up to the neck and baggy trousers, sauntered over from the bleachers to watch. They stood observing for a while, talking among themselves, and then one of them, who was fleshy but not quite fat, and who stood between the other two, said to Race, "Hey, how's your boy looking there, man? He going to be in shape for Avila?"

"What's it to you?" Race asked, annoyed. He did not like to be bothered when he was working. Fixing the younger man in a baleful stare, he asked, "You writin' a sports column or something, boy?"

"Hey, I ain't no boy, *hombre*," the young Hispanic said. "You trying to be funny?"

"If I was tryin' to be funny, I'd dress like you," Race said dismissively. "Get the hell out of here. Go on home and suck on your momma's titty."

"You *maiate*—!" the youth spat. In a blink, he had a four-inch handle knife out and open. Race did not flinch or get angry, even though he knew that a *maiate* was a large black roach that lived in manure. Race was cool.

Gil Ortega came out of somewhere and stepped between the two men. "That's enough," he said evenly. He bobbed his chin at the youth. "Paying spectators are required to stay in the bleachers. You're not allowed on the training floor."

"Do you know who I *am*, man?" the youth challenged.

"Of course. You are Mickey Morales."

"*Si!* And I am *La Familia!*"

A silence fell between them as Mickey Morales and his two friends waited for some reaction from Ortega. They got none. He remained as calm as Race did.

"Well?" Morales finally asked.

"Well what?" Ortega replied.

"Well, do you respect *La Familia* or don't you?"

"Of course. If I did not respect *La Familia*, I would not pay Chico Puente a monthly tribute to protect my business and all my employees. Do you know who is Chico Puente?"

Mickey Morales pursed his lips, then said, "*Everybody* knows who is Chico Puente, man." Chico Puente was the top boss of all *La Familia* members in Los Angeles County.

Ortega took some currency from his pocket and handed Mickey Morales three dollars. "Here's back the money you paid to get in. Don't come around anymore, and I won't mention to Chico Puente that you were being disruptive here. That way, there's no trouble for either of us. Okay?"

Morales took the money and smiled. "Sure, *ese*. Whatever you say." With a nod of his head, he led his two friends out of the gym.

"Try to be a little friendlier with the customers, will you, Race," said Ortega.

"Yassuh, boss man," Race replied. "Y'all wants me to dance a little jig for 'em, too?"

Ortega walked away, shaking his head resignedly.

"Get yo' ass back to work!" Race snapped at Joe. "I didn't call no time-out!"

"Yassuh, boss man," Joe said. He resumed training.

The next morning, Race wrapped and bundled Joe again and said, "You know where Evergreen Cemetery is?"

"Yeah, it's up on Lorena Street."

"Right. I wants you to go up to First and Lorena and jog all the way 'round the cemetery three times. Jog up there and back, too. Get!"

It was one mile to Evergreen Cemetery, one mile completely around it, and one mile back. In any other neighborhood except around the gym, Joe imagined he would have been the object of numerous curious looks, swathed as he was in heavy sweats garb and trotting along like a dray horse, but the people on the streets of East L.A. hardly noticed him. In a world of gang-bangers, drunks, day hustlers and old men wandering around with vacant stares, a scar-tissued pug doing road work didn't even raise an eyebrow. When he got to the area around the cemetery, it was still poor but less Skid Rowish; there were more Latina mothers out pushing strollers and dragging preschoolers along by the hand, and old women out with their own straw baskets to shop early for the best fruit and vegetables at market stalls.

Evergreen Cemetery was very old, some of its grave markers dating back one hundred and twenty-three years. As Joe diligently did his running, he took note of some of the more ornate and elaborately hewed tombstones, but would not interrupt his pace to pause and study any of them. Maybe some weekend, after the fight, he and Gladys could walk over and just leisurely stroll around, looking at the names and dates. There were undoubtedly generations of families buried there. It might be interesting.

It was just as he turned the corner on Lorena to begin his third lap that Joe saw Mickey Morales and his two friends strutting toward him. Experiencing a brief flash of anxiety, he then remembered, and was glad, that he had not said a word during the previous day's altercation in the gym. All he had to do now, he decided quickly, was be cool and not show any disrespect.

The three blocked his way. Morales, smiling, said, "Hey, man, how you doing?"

Joe paused and ran in place. "Good, man. You?"

"Me? I always do good, man. So do my homeboys here—

203

MURDER ON THE ROPES

Luis, Manny," he pointed to each of the others. "Hey, man, listen, no offense to you about yesterday, you know? We were jus' trying to see how you looked, since you going to be fighting Antonio Avila. He's our *carnal*, you know?" *Carnal* meant a street brother.

"I didn't know that," Joe said, panting a little.

"Sure, man. He's married to one of Manny's cousins," he bobbed his chin at one of his friends. "Hey, listen, man, how you like to make some extra money on this fight?"

Joe shook his head. "No offense, but I'm not interested."

"Hey, look, I don't mean take no dive, don't misunderstand me. I wouldn't disrespect you by asking you to go in the tank. But look, man, Avila going to take you anyway—you know it, I know it, everybody knows it. Fourteen fights, fourteen wins, fourteen knockouts, come on. See, we don't make no money on the *fight*. We make money on the *round*. And the *minute* of the round."

"No, sorry," said Joe. He tried to move around them, but they casually blocked his way.

"Look, man, it's money in the bank," Morales said. "And it ain't even like gambling; it's a *pool*, man. We get bets from all over; money goes down on first minute, Round One; second minute, Round One; third minute, Round One—you know, like that. But if we know ahead of time which minute of which round you going to fall, we close the book on it, see. Don't take any bets. We tell anybody who asks that bets were too heavy on that round and minute, so we can't take no more action. But see, really, we never take any. There's no payout at all. It's beautiful, man!"

"Yeah, but it ain't for me," Joe said. "I'm in the fight to *win*, man."

Luis and Manny laughed. Mickey Morales just shook his head in disbelief. "Come on, man, get real," he said. "Antonio's going to flatten you. Probably sometime in the first three rounds. You might as well make a little extra money for it." He leaned closer, confidentially. "Danny Pitts was in for a piece."

Joe's lips parted in surprise.

"I ain't shittin' you, man," Morales assured. "He was going to drop in the second minute of the second round. That's the round and minute we ain't been taking bets on."

Joe shrugged, as if the information was of no import. "Well, that's him, man, not me. I'm in it all the way. Sorry, man." This time he shouldered his way past them.

"Listen," Morales shouted after him, "jus' think about it, okay? We'll talk again!"

Joe started his last lap around the cemetery.

At supper a few nights later, Gladys said, "You'll have to eat out tomorrow night. I'm going to Beverly Hills with Hass."

Joe stopped eating. "Beverly Hills? What for?"

"He's going to look at some vacant properties that might be suitable for a boutique restaurant."

Joe grunted derisively. "Come on, Gladys. He ain't going to open no restaurant in Beverly Hills. That's just bullshit talk to impress you."

"That's what you think, Mr. Smart Guy," she retorted with a smirk. "His two older brothers are coming over from Tehran in a couple of days. They're going to finance him."

"When did all this come about?" Joe asked, almost indignantly.

"Just in the last couple days. See, Hass had a serious falling out with his father in Iran because his father didn't want him to come to the U.S. So Hass was kind of disowned for a while. But his two older brothers have been working on the father ever since to forgive Hass and help him succeed over here. Well, finally the father gave in. So Hass' two brothers are coming over with a line of credit for him to open a new place, real classy, in Beverly Hills."

"Oh." Joe fell silent and resumed eating his salad, which was dry except for one tablespoon of olive oil. He was down to one-sixty-six, with eleven days to go before the fight. He knew he would make one-sixty easy. And the dietary supplements that Race had him taking were keeping his red blood count up, so he wasn't losing any muscle strength, and his endurance was not affected.

After thinking about it for several minutes, Joe said, "I don't see why you have to go to Beverly Hills with the guy. Can't he look at places by himself?"

Gladys stiffened slightly. "He *wants* me to go along, Joe. I've been helping him with ideas and stuff."

"What does that mean, 'ideas and stuff'?"

"For the kind of place he wants. How it should be decorated, what color tablecloths and napkins, how the food servers should dress— "

"Food servers?"

"Waiters, Joe."

"Well, it seems to me you're just wasting your time, Gladys. You won't be working for him anyway. You can't go all the way to Beverly Hills to work. You'd have to take two or three buses to get there, leave at four o'clock in the morning if you worked the breakfast shift."

Gladys looked at him incredulously. "Joe, the kind of restaurant Hass is going to be opening won't be serving breakfast. It will be open for dinner only."

"So what are you going to all the trouble for? Even if it was closer, I don't want you working nights."

At that, Gladys fell silent. She began clearing the supper dishes, neither agreeing nor disagreeing with his last comment. Usually, Joe knew, when she assumed that attitude, it was because she took exception to a position of his, whatever it was, but was not prepared to argue about it just then. It always came up again later, after she'd had time to properly prepare her argument—and at that time she generally won the dispute. Now and then, when the issue was something that Joe was determined not to yield on, such as the idea she once had for Joe to become a fry cook for Hamed, he would press the matter and insist it be resolved immediately so it would not be on his mind. At those times, Joe won.

But he decided not to do that in their present disagreement, because he was pretty sure it would resolve itself without further argument when Hamed closed his cafe and moved to Beverly Hills. Gladys would be left behind, and that would be that. Tomorrow, Joe thought, he would ask Stefi, Ortega's wife, if she knew of any waitress jobs Gladys could get in East L.A. Maybe she could get on at one of the Mexican places. Then she wouldn't have to work for foreigners anymore.

The next day, as Joe was finishing his afternoon workout on the speed bag, Danny Pitts came into the gym with a cast on his right wrist. He walked over as Joe was using his teeth to pull off his training gloves.

"Hey, Joey," he said.

"Hey, Danny. How's the wrist?"

"Doc says it'll be as good as new in six weeks. I heard you got my slot against Avila. I'm glad you got a slot, but I ain't glad it's against Avila."

"I can prob'ly hold my own with him," Joe said.

"In your dreams," Danny replied. "I don't think I could hang in with Avila, and I'm better than you."

"In *your* dreams you're better than me," Joe scoffed. "I can kick your ass anytime, Danny."

"Shit, you can't kick my ass and you know it, Joey. Lonnie Green beat you in eight, unanimous, and I mashed Green in five."

"You didn't mash dick, Danny. You beat Green on a cut eye. I took him the distance—*and* I fought with the flu that night."

"Well, I ain't gonna argue the point with you, man. Fact is, I don't think both of us together could take Antonio Avila. They don't call him 'The Anvil' for nothing, man. Sucker hits like he's got concrete in both gloves. How much is Ortega paying you?"

"Enough, I guess. Not as much as he was paying you."

"You want to lay your purse on Avila? I know a guy over in El Monte that'll handle it for you."

Joe shook his head. "I don't bet against myself. It ain't right." He stepped over to a bench and opened a bottle of distilled water that was half full. In a long, continuous swallow, he drank it all, then wiped his mouth on the sleeve of his T-shirt. "Listen, Danny, I need to ask you something," he said, looking around to make sure no one was close enough to hear. "A kid named Mickey Morales had a talk with me. He mentioned you."

"You tell anybody about it?" Pitts asked at once, concerned.

"No, man. You think I'm fucking stupid, I'd talk about something like that?"

"I didn't think so, but I hadda ask," Pitts said. He stepped closer to Joe. "Us white fighters gotta stick together, man. Ain't that many of us left."

"Mickey Morales said he had a deal with you."

Pitts looked down at the floor. "Yeah, I was gonna go down in the middle of the second. Not a knockout; down three times for a TKO. Then, after the fight, I could complain that one of the knockdowns was really a slip, you know, and that Avila didn't really knock me out." Pitts shrugged. "It seemed like a good way to pick up some extra scratch, you know? Without getting hurt." He looked back up. "This guy hits like a fucking train wreck, man. I seen him against Derrell Carr and Julio Trejo. He broke both their jaws. He's a killer, Joey." Pitts quickly glanced around again. "Why don't you make a deal with Morales?"

"No," Joe shook his head. "I gotta go in to win, man."

"Look," Pitts said, "I'm gonna level with you. Morales asked me to come have a talk with you. Just to explain how it would work, with the three knockdowns and all. He wants you to come see him and have a talk, just the two of you. He lives in that new apartment building over on Floral and Carmelita, you know the one?"

"That big orange one?"

"Yeah. He asked me to ask you just to stop by. If he ain't in, his girlfriend will page him for you."

Joe was shaking his head the whole time Pitts was talking.

"No, that ain't for me, Danny. Forget it."

"Look, man," Pitts lowered his voice, "this kid is *La Familia*. He's low level, but still connected. He ain't just some fat punk. Joey, it is *serious* to mess with this guy."

"What serious?" Joe said, unimpressed. "The guy made me an offer. I turned it down. That's all. It ain't like I spit in his face, Danny."

"Okay, man," Pitts said with resignation, "it's your call. Antonio Avila is gonna mash you, man. Shit, he's being groomed to go for a title somewhere down the line: Vargas, Trinidad, Mosley, I don't know who. The guy's a killer. If you want to take that kind of punishment for what Ortega's paying you and not pick up nothin' on the side, it's your business, man." He looked at his watch. "Listen, I gotta split. Good luck, man."

"Yeah. Take care of that wrist. When all this is over, maybe we can get Ortega to put you and me in together. I'll kick your ass."

"You couldn't kick my sister's ass, you pussy," Pitts said over his shoulder, walking away.

The next afternoon, as Joe was walking up Soto Street on his way home after training, he saw Mickey Morales coming toward him. At first he did not think it *was* Morales, because the pudgy Latino was alone, absent the two homeboys Joe was accustomed to seeing him with. Joe tried to go past him, merely bobbing his chin in recognition but not pausing to speak. But Morales had other ideas. Casually he took Joe's arm.

"Hey, man, how you doing?" he said, smiling. "I was jus' thinking about you. Got a minute?"

"I have to make it quick," Joe said. "I'm on my way home to eat."

"Tha's cool," said Morales. He let go of Joe's arm and gestured toward the doorway of a vacant storefront. Joe stepped off the sidewalk with him. "I guess you didn't make out too good with Pitts, huh? He tol' me you didn't want to talk to me no more."

"I don't mind talking to you," Joe said. "I just ain't gonna buy into your proposition, is all. It's got nothing to do with you, man. It's the proposition I don't like."

"What if I was to cut you in for a little bigger piece than Pitts was getting? I had him in for fifteen hundred; I'll sweeten that to two grand for you."

"The amount of dough's got nothing to do with it," Joe said, shaking his head for emphasis. "I just don't go in the tank, period."

"Look, man," Morales said patiently, "it *ain't* going in the tank. Going in the tank is throwing a fight that you could win. You got no chance of winning this fight. Fourteen guys have gone up against Avila and none of them have gone past three rounds. That's why there's so much betting action not only on which round you'll go in, but which *minute*. But you wouldn't be going in the tank, man. You know and I know, *everybody* knows you gonna lose; all's you're doing is controlling *when* you lose."

"I'm sorry, man, I just can't do it." Joe started to walk away.

"Come on, man, wait a minute," Morales urged, taking Joe's arm again. "You really putting me on the spot, you know. We been taking bets on this fight for three weeks. We got bets covered on every minute of the first three rounds except for the second minute of the second round. If you don't go out in the second minute of the second round, *ese*, I'm gon' to lose a whole lot of money."

"That's your problem," Joe told him evenly. "I can't help you." He took another step, but Morales stopped him again, not with his hand this time, but with words.

"Say, man, how's your wife doing at that little cafe where she works? What's it called, the Arabian Cafe?"

Joe turned back, his expression hard and mean. "She's doing fine. You trying to say something?"

"Not me, man. I jus' asked how she's doing. I'm glad to hear she's doing fine. I hope she keeps doing fine, man. I'm the kind of guy likes to see everybody happy."

"Yeah, well, don't talk about my wife, see? She's got nothing to do with this."

Morales shrugged. "Sure, man. Whatever you say." He smiled at Joe. "Listen, we still got a few days to make a deal. You keep thinking about it, okay. We'll talk again."

Morales walked away, leaving Joe in the doorway. As he watched Morales walk off down the street, Joe's hard, mean expression morphed into a concerned frown. The words of Danny Pitts surfaced in his mind. *He ain't just some fat punk, Joey. It is serious to mess with this guy.*

At supper the next evening, Gladys asked, "You know a spic kid named Mickey?"

Joe tensed inside. "What about him?"

"He was in the cafe today. Him and a couple other young spic guys. They asked if I was your wife."

"What'd you tell them?"

"Well now, what do you think I told them, Joe?" Gladys asked sarcastically.

"Well, what'd they want? What'd they say?"

Gladys shrugged. "Nothing much. Just how you were doing in training, how you were feeling, stuff like that. They each had a Pepsi, sat around a while and left. The one named Mickey said to tell you hello for him."

"He didn't make no threats or nothing, did he?"

Gladys froze, a fork halfway to her mouth. Her eyes got wide. "Threats? Why would they make threats? What's going on, Joe? Are you mixed up in something?"

"No, I ain't mixed up in nothing. This guy is trying to get me to go in the tank in the second—"

"Oh, my God! Did you report it? Did you tell Ortega so he could tell the boxing commission?"

"No, because then they'd cancel the fight and I don't want the fight canceled. We need the dough. Especially if you're gonna be out of work."

Gladys looked down. "What if I could keep working for Hass?"

"I thought he was moving to Beverly Hills?"

"He is. We found a really nice vacant property on Olympic near Beverly Drive. It's not in the mainstream around Rodeo or anything, but it's perfect for a start-up place; you know, build up a clientele, build up a reputation. Hass wants me to work with him getting the place ready; you know, decorating, buying tables and linens and everything. Then he wants me to be his hostess when it opens. Greet customers, seat them, make sure service is satisfactory, that kind of thing—"

Joe fixed her in a flat stare. "You wanna work in Beverly Hills? Nights? You're crazy, Gladys."

She leaned forward eagerly. "Listen, Joe, it's a chance to get ahead. Hass will pay me good money. Why couldn't we find an apartment that was closer? Not in Beverly Hills, we couldn't afford that, but someplace close by, like West Hollywood or the La Brea area—"

"Where would I train, Gladys?" he asked. "They got any gyms out there?"

Gladys sat back and looked at him in disbelief. "How often do you think you're going to *have* to train, Joe? This is your first fight in ten months. You probably won't get another one for a year after you lose this one—"

"Who says I'm gonna lose?"

"Everybody says you're going to lose. You're not a contender anymore; you're not even a main-eventer. Stefi says you're a trial horse now."

"Stefi? When'd you talk to Stefi?"

"She called me from the gym today. She said you told her I'd be looking for a job soon and asked if she knew of anything. She called to tell me about an opening in a chili joint over on Eastern. Strictly a blue-collar joint, six to four, no weekends."

"Sounds good," Joe offered.

"To you maybe, not to me; I told her I wasn't interested. Anyway, getting back to you, Stefi said that Gil said that you should maybe start looking around for some other line of work. Stefi says Gil thinks you've got maybe two or three fights in you after this one, and then you'd be washed up. All you'll be able to get is four-rounders with kids starting out, and someday you'll end up punch-drunk, shining shoes on the street."

"That ain't gonna happen to me, Gladys," Joe said coldly. Pushing his unfinished salad away, he rose and pulled on an old sweater.

"What are you doing?"

"Going out for a walk," he said. "I got some thinking to do."

On Friday, the day before the fight, when Joe was halfway through his last training session, Race weighed him and he was down to one-fifty-eight.

"Okay," said Race, "we got a two-pound buffer. Watch what you eat for the rest of the day."

"Race, you think I can take this guy?" Joe asked, wiping the sweat off his arms with a ragged towel.

"Sure you can, boy," Race replied offhandedly.

"No, Race, I mean *really*. No bullshit. Can I take this guy?"

Race stopped what he was doing and stared thoughtfully at Joe Bell for a moment. In Joe's face and eyes he saw all the dreams and nightmares of every fighter he had ever known. Dreams of greatness, nightmares of failure. Taking more punches than they made dollars. A spirit strong and alive, an ego still thriving, in a body being slowly beaten to waste. And the pain, oh sweet Jesus, the pain—

"Look, Joey," Race said in the quietest tone Joe had ever heard him use, "I been around this here boxing game a long, long time. Two things I know. One, any fighter can beat any other fight-er of equal weight on just about any given night. All it takes is one perfectly timed, perfectly placed punch, and the other guy is out of it. I've seen world champions beat the shit out of challengers round after round after round, then get knocked cold in the last half minute of the fight. Second thing I know is this: usually the fighter who's younger, quicker, stronger, hungrier and meaner will win the fight. You ask me, can you take this guy? Yeah, sure. Will you? Probably not one chance in a thousand. I don't see no perfectly timed, perfectly placed punches in your future, Joe. Wish I did—but I don't."

"Do you think I can go six with him? Stay the distance?"

Now Race frowned. Six rounds. Eighteen minutes of fighting. Antonio Avila was young, strong, hungry and mean. But he wasn't particularly fast. Then again, neither was Joe Bell. But Joe might be just a lick faster. And Joe had a huge edge in ring experience: he had fought a hundred and ninety-four rounds in his career. Avila, because no one had ever gone past three with him, had fought thirty-nine.

"Yeah," Race decided, "you could take him the whole six. You'd have to run most of the time, and the spic crowd out in Indio would boo the hell out of you. You'd have to back off and take a lot of grazing shots. Do a lot of clinching and take a beating to the body. Catch a hell of a lot of power shots on your forearms and upper arms. But, yeah, I think you got a chance of taking him six. You gonna feel like a sixteen-wheel highway rig run over you when you done, but yeah, I think you can do it."

Joe smiled. "Thanks, Race." Impulsively he hugged the old black trainer. Race immediately pushed him away.

"Quit that, boy!" he chastised. "I don't like no boys be hugging me!" He looked up at a big Coors Beer clock on the gym wall. It was ten past noon. "Go on next door and eat. Mixed salad, no dressing, one hard-boiled egg, nothing to drink but water. Be back in half an hour. I want us to take one more pound off, jus' to be safe. Go on."

Before he left, Joe got a telephone number for Danny Pitts

214

from Stefi, and used the gym's pay phone to call him.

"Danny? Joe. I want you to put a bet down for me with that guy you know in El Monte. What kind of odds can you get on me taking Avila the distance?"

"You joking?" Pitts asked derisively.

"No, I ain't joking. What kind of odds?"

"A gazillion to one, man. No way you're gonna go six with Avila. *I* couldn't go six with him, and I can kick your ass."

"Look, I ain't got time to fuck with you, Pitts. You want me to take the bet someplace else?"

"Hell no, man, not if you're serious," Pitts said quickly. He got a small percentage of all losing bets he brought in. "I can probably get you thirty to one. How much you laying?"

"Three grand."

"Jesus, Joey! Are you sure you know what you're doing, man? Three long ones is a lot of scratch." Then a thought occurred to him. "Wait a minute. Is Avila in on this? Did you work something out with Morales? 'Cause if you did, man, I want in on it—"

"Avila and Morales got nothing to do with it, Danny. This is my call. I think I can do it. Put the bet down. If I lose, come over to the gym Sunday morning when I get my purse and I'll pay you off."

"Word of honor?"

"Word of honor."

"Okay, you got it, man."

"Thanks, Danny."

Joe hung up, feeling good, feeling loose, strong, *right*, like a winner. But when he walked out of the gym to go next door, all that good feeling vanished, because waiting outside, leaning up against the building, were Mickey Morales and his two homeboys, Luis and Manny.

"Hey, *hombre*," Morales said, "I'm going to give you one more chance to make some money with us."

Joe stopped and faced them, keeping far enough away to give himself punching room if he needed it. "I don't want no last chance," he said flatly to Morales. "What I do want is for you and your girlfriends here to stay the fuck away from my wife."

Morales shrugged. "I was thinking of going to see her today, man. You know, jus' to ask her to have a talk with you about this thing. Does she know you got a chance to pick up some easy money here? I mean, maybe she could reason with you—"

"You stay the fuck away from her!" Joe closed a fist and shook it in front of him. "I mean it, Morales."

Morales' eyes narrowed into a squint that made him look Asian. "You threatening me, *hombre?* You threatening somebody in *La Familia?*"

"I'm making a threat to you, punk! If my wife tells me you're in the cafe bothering her again, I'll come looking for you. I'll kick your ass good. Your two girlfriends here, too." He shook his fist at Luis and Manny. "I'll kick *all* your asses! Don't say you ain't been warned."

As Joe walked away from them, Morales yelled after him, "You jus' made a bad mistake, tough guy!"

Without looking back, Joe gave him the finger.

It was nearly six when Joe finished his last training session and showered and got dressed. He and Race went into Ortega's office.

"He weighs one-fifty-seven, boss," Race told the gym owner. "He's strong and sharp. Should give Avila a decent go."

"Okay," Ortega said to Joe. "Be here at nine in the morning and we'll drive out to Indio. Weigh-in's at two. Then we'll feed you good and get three, four pounds back on. Okay."

"Yeah, sure," said Joe. He swallowed briefly. "Say, Gil, can you let me have a couple hundred in advance. I need to pay the rent."

Ortega peeled two hundred off a roll of twenties and fifties. "Here. Don't be late tomorrow."

"An' eat light tonight," Race added. "Drink lots of water, flush yourself out."

"Yeah, sure. See you tomorrow."

Joe walked home, feeling good, feeling, as Race had said, strong and sharp. It felt good to have the excess weight off his midsection, to feel his rib cage and stomach taut and hard. He was aware of the strength in his biceps and forearms, his thighs and calves. He knew that today, if he had to, he could have flattened Morales *and* his two homeboys with no problem. They wouldn't have had time to pull out their handle knives before he had decked them all. That was the difference between a professional fighter and an ordinary guy: the timing, power and ability to land telling punches. That was why a professional fighter's fists were considered legally to be deadly weapons outside the ring. A fighter outside the ring was like an ordinary guy with a hammer or a tire iron in his hand. How you used what you had, and what you used it for, made a difference.

When he got to his apartment building, the landlady was sweeping the front hall. "Your wife said you'd have fifty dollars for me today," she told Joe.

"Yeah, sure." He gave the woman a fifty.

"She didn't say when she'd be back," the woman said.

"Huh?"

"Your wife. She didn't say when she'd be back. She left with three guys."

Joe turned cold inside. *Three guys.* "Uh, what—what'd they look like?"

"I don't know. Like Mexicans, I guess. They all look the same to me."

Joe hurried into their grubby little apartment. Everything looked all right. Nothing was missing, nothing out of place, nothing had changed.

Except Gladys wasn't there.

An image of Mickey Morales surfaced in Joe's mind. The words of Morales resounded in his memory. *You jus' made a bad mistake, tough guy!*

Beginning to seethe with anger, Joe dragged a canvas bag from the closet in the living room and rummaged around in it until he found a pair of old, worn training gloves, the knuckle padding flat and hard from hundreds of hours of concussion from the outside, dried sweat on the inside. Shoving them into his back pocket, he left the apartment and walked briskly down the street.

It took him fifteen minutes to walk to the new orange apartment building at Floral and Carmelita. In the foyer, he found the name M. MORALES next to the bell for apartment 206. Pushing the bell, he waited. Presently a voice through the intercom said, "Yeah?"

"It's Joe Bell. I wanna talk."

"Well, you finally got smart, huh?" the voice said contemptuously. "Come on up."

The inner door buzzed and Joe pushed through it. As he got to 206, the door was opened by a pretty Mexican girl with eyes like ripe plums and a belly that was five or six months pregnant. Morales, in his undershirt, holding a bottle of Corona, was standing in an overdecorated living room with black velvet bullfighting paintings on the wall. He was just putting down a portable phone.

"Can we talk in private?" Joe asked.

"Teresa," Morales said, "go visit your sister for a while. I'll call you when to come back." Teresa picked up a yellow plastic purse and left. When the door closed behind her, Morales asked, "You want a beer, man?"

Joe walked up close to him, pulling on the worn training gloves. "Where's my wife, you motherfucker?"

"What? I thought you came to talk about the fight, man—"

Joe slapped the bottle of Corona out of his hand and across the room. Some of it splashed across one of the velvet paintings.

"You *gringo puta*—" Morales snarled. *White pussy.*

Joe hit him a hard right to the mouth, splitting his lip. Blood spurted. A left to the eye opened a cut in the eyebrow. It began to seep.

"I warned you to stay away from her!"

A hard right dug low into his groin and Morales' eyes rolled back. He clutched himself with both hands and bent over. Joe drilled him hard, first to one ear, then the other. With a vicious uppercut, he straightened him up again, then rained four hard punches to the face. The flat, aged leather of the old training gloves contused flesh each time they struck. Morales tried to fall, but Joe held him up against a wall.

"Where is she, you spic cocksucker? If you don't tell me, I'll fucking kill you!"

Morales, choking on blood from a broken nose and his split lip, tried to speak but could not, and instead shook his head, which Joe took to mean refusal.

"I'll kill you! I'll kill you!"

Shots to the head, shots to the kidneys, shots to the liver, the solar plexus, the rib cage; then back to the head and face: under his punches, Joe felt Morales' sphenoid bone break, the mandible snap, then the zygomatic arch collapse on the left side. His face was pulp.

Suddenly Joe realized that Morales was limp; he was unconscious, only Joe's punches holding him up. That's when Joe knew he'd fucked up; Morales couldn't tell Joe where Gladys was now even if he wanted to.

Joe let the slack, flabby body in front of him slide down the wall to a sitting position, then tumble sideways with the arms twisted, as if Morales had been tied in some grotesque knot.

Gotta get out of here, Joe thought. He cracked the apartment door an inch; the hall was empty. At least I taught the son of a bitch a lesson.

Downstairs, as he was leaving the building, he ran into Luis and Manny. Sure, Morales had been using the phone when I got there, Joe remembered. He blocked the door to the building and shoved both of them back. "Where's my wife, motherfuckers?"

Both of them saw the bloodied training gloves on his hands.

"Your wife?" said Luis. "What you talking about, man?"

Joe shoved them again. "You know what I'm talking about! You took my wife! Where is she?" At that moment, he had visions of Gladys being gang-raped by every spic punk in East L.A. "Tell me where the fuck she is!"

"You crazy!" Manny said indignantly. "We ain't got your wife, man! You think we commit a *kidnaping* to fix a fight pool?"

"Kidnaping's a life sentence, man!" Luis exclaimed. "You think we crazy?"

While they were talking, both pulled out their handle knives and slid the blades forward.

"You better get the fuck out of the way, man, or you gon' get cut," Manny said. They moved cautiously around Joe toward the door. Joe was frowning now, uncertain.

"Where you get that blood on your gloves, man?" Luis asked. "If you did what I think you did, you in bad trouble, *hombre*."

They got around him and moved into the foyer. Luis used a key card to open the inside door.

Joe walked away, confusion shrouding him, questions beginning to form. He started trotting. The cool night air felt good against his sweaty face and neck. Somewhere along the way, he peeled off the bloody gloves and threw them in a trash can.

Back at his own apartment, Joe went into the bathroom and washed his face with cold water. It was when he was drying his hands that he saw the note. It was propped up against the aspirin bottle where she knew he'd find it; he always took an aspirin tablet at bedtime because he thought it thinned his blood and relaxed him while he slept.

Dropping the towel on the floor, he read the note:

> *Joe—I've left with Hass and his brothers. Sorry to do it like this, but I want to make something of myself. Just throw all my stuff out. Hass wants me to have everything new.*
>
> *Gladys*

220

P.S. Good luck with the fight.
P.P.S. I'll see a lawyer in the near future.

Joe sat down on the edge of the bathtub and stared at the note. Inside, he felt like his intestines were shriveling. His heart began to hurt. He wanted to cry, but he hadn't cried in so long he didn't know how anymore. Punches and pain do that. Fighters and abused kids learn not to cry.

After a while, he went into the other room, packed an old cardboard suitcase and left.

When he got to Indio at midnight, he walked from the shabby little bus station to the Aztec Motel, which was half a mile down the highway from the Rialto Resort and Casino, where the fight was to take place. After checking into a room, he sat on the bed, took a slip of paper out of his wallet with Race's phone number on it, and called him.

"I'm already in Indio, Race," he said. "I took a bus down. I was afraid I'd get car sick riding down in the morning. This way, I get a good night's rest and I'll be fresher for the fight."

"You on the level with me, boy?" Race asked suspiciously. "Ain't nothin' wrong, is they?"

"No, nothing's wrong. I'm a little nervous, is all."

"That's all? You sure?"

"I'm okay, Race."

"All right then. I'll bring all the gear down with Ortega tomorrow. You be at the Rialto for the weigh-in at two, understand? Don't you be late."

"I'll be there, Race. Don't worry." He paused a beat. "Listen, Race, thanks for all the help getting me ready."

"Ain't no call to thank me, boy. I jus' does what I gets paid to do, tha's all."

Yeah, sure, but the *way* you do it makes a difference, Joe wanted to tell him. The *way* you do it is special. But Joe knew that Race wouldn't want to hear any such talk as that, so all he said was, "See you tomorrow, Race," and hung up.

For a few minutes, Joe sat on the side of the bed, thinking about his situation. By now, Luis and Manny would have reported what happened, and someone in *La Familia*, probably that guy Ortega paid protection to, Chico something, would have decided what to do to him and when. He was in for a bad beating, he knew; maybe even a maiming of some kind: a smashed ankle that would leave him with a limp; broken fingers that he could no longer make a fist with; or a cutting, some kind of facial slashing that would leave a bad scar that people could see. *La Familia* liked to mark victims of retaliation to remind everyone that the price for disrespect was very high.

Because Mickey Morales had said that Joe's opponent tomorrow, Antonio Avila, was a member of *La Familia*, Joe was sure that nothing would be done to him until after the fight. No one was going to jeopardize Avila's rapidly improving record. "The Anvil" was probably being groomed for a multimillion-dollar pay-per-view fight with Oscar de la Hoya, the "Golden Boy," who had moved up to middleweight after losing three out of his last four at welter. It would be a battle for bragging rights between two products of the East Los Angeles streets. The winner would then face the winner of Felix Trinidad–Fernando Vargas for the undisputed one-fifty-four and one-sixty unified title. *La Familia* wasn't going to mess with plans like that just for immediate reprisal for a beating taken by one of its neighborhood underlings. Reprisal would come, to be sure, but in good time. Business first, then revenge.

What he had to do now, Joe knew, was psych himself up to go the full six with Avila. His three-thousand-purse bet at thirty to one would bring him ninety grand. With that kind of money, he could rent a nice apartment, with air-conditioning, and find Gladys and get her back. She would take him back if he had some serious money like that, he knew she would; she loved him. Maybe he could even get Ortega to talk Chico-whatever-his-name-was into working a deal to withdraw retaliation for the beating of Morales; maybe for a piece of Joe's winnings; *maybe* even for a quick, big money rematch with Avila, eight, even ten rounds, with Chico as co-promoter.

There were all kinds of possibilities. Joe intended to level with Ortega about everything as soon as the fight was over. Ortega would find a way to help him. Everything was going to be all right.

Unpacking the few things he had brought with him, Joe took a shower and pulled on a pair of clean sweatpants and a T-shirt. Outside, next to the motel office, he got a bucket of ice and from a vending machine bought two bags of pretzels and a Sprite. Back in the room, he changed from the sweatpants to his Jockey shorts, turned on the TV and stretched out to eat what was going to be his supper. He found a movie on TV, an old John Wayne picture where he was trying to rescue his niece who had been captured by Indians. Joe had already seen it a couple times before, but he decided it was good enough to watch again, so he left it on.

As he watched the movie and ate, he alternated soaking each hand in the bucket of ice to reduce any swelling from the punches he had hit Morales with. They would be all right by morning; lucky he had thought to wear the old training gloves. Despite all the problems, despite the fact that he had been mistaken, he was not sorry about the beating he had given Mickey Morales. He hated punks like that. All they did was make life harder for people who already had it hard enough. Joe was glad he had taught the son of a bitch a lesson.

When he got Gladys back, he knew he was going to have to forgive her for sleeping with Hassim, which he guessed she had already done. But he was sure he could do that. Pretty sure, anyway. Gladys was one of those women who was easily flattered by the attention of men; she had just been led astray, was all. He could forgive her. He loved her enough; he could do it.

Everything was going to be all right.

At one forty-five the next afternoon, Joe walked into the Rialto Resort and Casino ballroom, where the ring had been set up in the middle of neat rows of three thousand folding chairs. A medical scale was standing near the press row, and members of the Agua Caliente Tribe Athletic Commission, the referee and the ringside physician were standing around talking. Avila and his entourage were seated nearby. Ortega and Race were standing on the sidelines, looking nervous.

"Where the hell you been, boy?" Race asked indignantly when Joe walked up.

"What's the matter, I ain't late," Joe said.

Ortega looked relieved. "You okay?"

"Yeah, sure. Got a good night's sleep down the road."

"You eat today?" Race asked.

"Nope. I'm starving, man."

Ortega went over to the commissioners and they called everyone up to the scale. Antonio Avila was young, relaxed, toned, buff. He bobbed his chin at Joe. "How you doing, Bell?"

"Good. How you doing, Avila?"

"Good."

The fighters stripped down to their Jockey shorts. And took turns on the scale.

"Avila, one-fifty-eight," the referee announced. Then: "Bell, one-fifty-seven-and-a-half."

As Joe dressed, Ortega said to Race, "Take him into the restaurant and feed him. I'm going to hang around for Camacho Junior and Malloy to weigh in. There's some hostility between them; might be interesting."

"Showboating is all it'll be," Race replied cynically.

When Joe was dressed, he and Race went into the resort restaurant, which was glass-walled, palm-tree-lined, and built around a small lagoon on which ducks paddled about. They were shown to a table and Joe ordered a New York cut steak, home fries and a Caesar salad. "Can I have iced tea?" he asked Race.

"Sure. Drink all the caffeine you want for the rest of the day."

Race had a chicken salad plate. While they were eating, he

said, " 'Member that smartass spic Mickey Morales that Gil run off couple weeks ago?"

Joe's stomach tightened. "Yeah, what about him?"

"Somebody beat the piss out of him yesterday. They got him over in the county medical center. Sounds like he got busted up good and proper. Little prick prob'ly deserved it."

"Who, uh—who done it?"

Race shrugged. "Beats me. I just heard it from one of the guys that trains Avila. They all part of that *La Familia* bullshit. Mexican gangsters, that's all they are."

Nothing more was said on the subject. Race avoided discussing the impending fight; he wanted Joe's mind to relax and be fresh when he went into the ring. Instead, Race reminisced about the "old days," meandering casually, dropping names of "fine" trainers like Whitey Bimstein, Ray Arcel, Jack Blackburn; and tough middleweights, "Ones you'd have to kill to make quit," like Carmen Basilio, Gene Fullmer, Jake LaMotta, Tony Zale; and when title fights were fifteen rounds, and twelve-round fights were "elimination bouts" to decide who would get a chance to try fifteen with a titleholder; when there were no "pussy" titles: "junior" this and "super" that.

"A middleweight was a middleweight, by God," Race recalled. "He weighed between one-forty-eight and one-sixty, period. None of this one-fifty-four shit. There were *eight* divisions and *eight* champions, period. Now there's *seventeen* divisions and *five* titleholders in each one. That's *ten* times as many. It's ruining the game!" He chewed on the inside of his mouth for a moment, then asked, "You want another steak?"

Joe shook his head. "Can I have dessert?"

"Okay. Tapioca pudding or Jell-O."

"Come on, Race. Apple pie with a scoop of vanilla ice cream."

"Tha's too much sugar."

"Without the ice cream then."

225

"Okay."

Joe ordered his apple pie. When they finished eating, Race asked what kind of room Joe had at the motel. "Just a cheap little room," Joe said.

"Twin beds?"

"Yeah."

"Okay, we gon' down there and take us a nap. You wait here, I'll tell Gil."

A few minutes later, the two of them walked down the highway toward the Aztec Motel, and a little while after that, with the drapes drawn and the cooler on, they were stretched out on separate beds, the old black trainer and the getting-old white fighter, both scar-tissued, both ring-worn, both too weary, without realizing it, for what lay ahead that evening.

Race got Joe back to the resort's makeshift fight dressing room at four-thirty, got him into his protective cup, trunks, socks and shoes, and had him do some shadowboxing to begin warming up. Since it was an ESPN Friday Night Fights card, Joe and Avila would be the first fight to be televised. There were shorter, stand-by fights, four-rounders, to be put on in case of an early knockout in the opener. The main event would go on at seven local time, ten in the east.

After Joe had warmed up sufficiently, Race patted him dry with a towel, then one of Avila's cornermen came in and Race taped Joe's hands. The Avila man used a Magic Marker to sign both wrappings. Ortega would be doing the same thing in Avila's dressing room. Presently the referee arrived and spent five minutes going over the commission rules for the fight.

After all that was over, Race sat Joe on a stool and massaged his trapezius and deltoid muscles to loosen up Joe's punching ability and perhaps add a split-second to his speed. Afterward, he knelt in front of him, Joe's legs stretched out straight, and massaged inside each thigh the adductor magnus muscle, which was the first one to transmit from the brain to the legs the result of a damaging punch. When he finished, he got Joe into his twelve-ounce ring gloves and taped the laces down.

Before long, a young Indian ring assistant stuck his head in the door and said, "Joe Bell, ten minutes!" They could hear him step across the hall to another door, open it and say, "Antonio Avila, ten minutes!"

Race got Joe back on his feet, put punching pads on his own hands and said, "Okay, loosen up." Joe rose, went into his fighting stance and began hitting the pads wherever Race moved them: up, down, out, forward, back. Within five minutes, Joe had broken a good sweat again.

The young Indian came back to the door. "Ready for Joe Bell."

"Let's go," Race said, holding a terry-cloth robe with extra-big sleeves for Joe to put on. Race picked up his water bucket, water bottle and a rolled corner pack containing swabs, Vaseline, adrenaline chloride cut paste, an ice pack, sponge and other items he needed to work the corner. Ortega met them at the door and they made their way down a deserted hotel hallway into the crowded, converted ballroom, its folding chairs now about 80 percent filled with people.

Joe liked stepping into the rush of noise that met him. There was some scattered applause as he and Race followed Ortega down the aisle to the ring. Here and there, hands reached out to pat his back or shoulders, and some people said, "Good luck." A few called him by name, but most of the spectators didn't know who he was. Indio was Avila country; Joe was just the latest sacrifice.

When he got to the ring, he bobbed his chin at Teddy Atlas, who was one of the best two or three trainers in the business, and sidelined as an ESPN boxing commentator. Atlas grinned and winked at him. Once in the ring, Race said, "Move around, keep warm," and Joe began dancing and shadowboxing.

A couple of minutes later, a loud cheer went up from the crowd as Antonio Avila, in a tiger-striped silk robe, came trotting down the aisle with an entourage of seven, including a stunning Mexican girl in a low-cut, red-sequined sheath dress. When Avila got into the ring, he danced around, smiling and waving to the crowd on all four sides.

After that, as usual, everything seemed to go very fast. With both fighters in their respective corners, the bell sounded three times and ring announcer Jimmy Lennon Jr. took a microphone to the center of the ring and introduced the three judges, physician at ringside, timekeeper, knockdown counter, referee and lastly the two fighters. There was some polite applause for Joe, and another resounding cheer for Avila. Robes off, the fighters were called to the center of the ring for final brief instructions from the referee, then returned to their corners to await the opening bell. Race, from outside the ropes, massaged strong fingers on the back of Joe's head and said, "Move to your right—*only* to your right."

The bell sounded. Both men came out circling, jabbing lightly, testing the canvas under their soles, feeling out the opponent in front of him. Joe held his position, taking Avila's punches on his gloves, countering to the body when he could. Two of Avila's punches caught Joe on his forearms and hurt. Joe began moving backward and to his right. Avila patiently stalked, an almost bored expression on his face, an expression that said: *Do whatever you want to, man, but sooner or later I'm going to tag you.* Joe did not let it bother him. He noticed that Avila was moving flat-footed, so Joe began using his toes more, became more springy, and increased his head movement. Midway through the round, he saw Avila drop his left glove a couple of inches when he threw his right. Joe wasn't sure if it was a lapse in concentration on Avila's part, or a habit. He watched for it again. Presently it happened a second time, then a third. It was habit, Joe decided—and it was a flaw in the younger man's defense. In the final minute of the round, Joe watched for the left to drop, and twice when it did he threw a solid overhand right that caught Avila on the left temple. Neither blow had much effect on Avila, but Joe knew that if he could continue to land it, a cut might open. Meantime, Joe was continuing to take most of Avila's punches on his forearms and upper arms, both of which began to throb for a few seconds after each blow. The bell finally sounded, ending a slow, unexciting first round.

In the corner, Race worked in front of him with an ice bag and Vaseline, while Ortega, from the ring apron, talked in Joe's ear. "He's dropping his left," Ortega said.

"Yeah, I caught him a couple times." Joe took a swallow of water from Ortega. Race put the ice bag on each upper arm for fifteen seconds.

"Bof' times when you tagged him," Race said, "you stopped moving to the right and stood still. Don't do that. You *got* to keep movin' to the right!"

"Okay, Race."

The bell sounded and the fighters moved forward, circling again. Avila threw a hard right hand, Joe caught it on his glove, and countered with his own hard right over a lowered Avila left again. Joe's punch landed solidly and there were some cheers from the neutral spectators. I'm gonna bust this guy's left eye open, Joe thought. The next time it happens—

That was immediately. Another hard right from Avila that Joe deflected, and landed his own hardest right yet, again on the same spot next to Avila's left eye. Except that this time Avila followed with a second smashing right that caught Joe, flat-footed, not moving to the right, flush on the jaw.

Joe saw an odd flash of red in front of him, exploding like a splash of paint thrown at him. Then he was on the canvas, reaching with one glove for a ring rope to pull himself up. But his depth perception was gone now and all he did was paw at space. He could hear no sound at all—no crowd, no count, nothing; his temporal bone was in shock and both his inner ear and equilibrium were temporarily neutralized. Somehow he got to his knees, then pushed a foot in front of himself and tried to stand up. Instead, he tumbled sideways and fell back to the canvas.

Next thing he knew, Ortega and Race were lifting him to his feet and half-dragging him to the stool in the corner. Ortega held the ice pack on the back of his neck, while Race sponged him off and massaged his temples. The ringside doctor was next to Race, shining a penlight in Joe's eyes. His hearing returned and he heard the din of the crowd.

"What's your name, son?" the doctor asked.

Race gave him a quick drink of water, and he said, "Uh—Joe Bell—"

"Where are you, Joe?"

"Uh—Indigo or something—"

"Okay," the doctor said.

Race stood him up and helped him on with his robe. Joe heard the ring announcer saying into the microphone, "—forty-six seconds of Round Number Two, the winner, with his fifteenth consecutive knockout—"

Then Ortega and Race were supporting him as he walked back up the aisle and into the dressing room again.

Jesus, he thought along the way, that kid sure can hit.

Twenty minutes later Race took him out of a cold shower and helped him dry off. Joe was feeling all right again as he started dressing; he did not even have a headache. One of Avila's trainers came in. "Your boy okay?" he asked Race.

"He's okay," Race said.

Avila's trainer smiled. "We weren't sure that dropped left trick was going to work. Took us a month to teach Antonio to do it so he could drop a second right in. But it worked."

"Yeah," Race said. "Good strategy. Long as you fight somebody who don't keep moving to the right."

As he started to leave, Avila's trainer said, "Hey, you know that Morales kid I tol' you about, was in the hospital?"

"What about him?"

"A call came in during the fight. He died."

"Too bad," Race said, without a lot of sincerity.

Joe sat and looked down, tying his shoes, almost feeling as if Antonio Avila had hit him again. *He died.* Two little words, but my God—

Could it be? he wondered. Had he really beaten a man to death? Then he remembered what he had shouted at Morales: *I'll kill you, I'll kill you!* He finished tying his shoes and sat staring at his hands.

"Wha's a matter?" asked Race.

"Huh? Oh, nothing." Joe quickly took hold of himself. "I was just thinking about the fight. It happened so quick."

"You lucky it did," Race said. "A boy't can hit that hard, it's better to go down from one punch than take half a dozen shots to the head. That boy's a killer. How you feel?"

"I'm okay."

"They got a four-round back-up fight on now before the main. You wanna hang around and watch the main?"

Joe shook his head. *He died.* "I think I'll go back to my room and lie down."

"You want me to walk down wit' you?"

"No, I'm okay. You stick around and watch the main."

"Okay. You go lie down. Take a nap. Gil an' me'll pick you up in a couple hours. We'll stop somewhere on the way back to L.A. Get us a good dinner. Maybe Chinese, how's that sound?'

"Sounds good."

"Okay. See you later, Joe."

"Okay, Race."

Race walked out toward the ballroom-arena, and Joe left by the nearest exit, crossed the parking lot and walked down the highway. A single thought kept resounding in his head. *He died.* The two words beat like a bass drum in his mind. *He died, he died, he died—*

At the Aztec Motel, he counted his money. Out of the two

hundred Ortega had given him, he had ninety-four dollars left. He packed his suitcase and slipped out of the room, because he owed another thirty-eight dollars for the second day. Walking to the opposite end of the motel, away from the office, he crossed the highway and started back on the other side, toward the bus depot.

He died, he died—

There was a bus leaving for Los Angeles in thirty minutes. And one coming through heading for Phoenix in twenty. Joe went up to the ticket window.

"Can I get a seat on that Phoenix bus?"

"You bet," the agent said. "One way or round trip?"

"One way." There was a small black-and-white TV set on a desk behind the window, and Joe saw that the agent had the Friday Night Fights on. The main event had started. Hector Camacho Jr. was kicking Vic Malloy's ass.

"Thirty-two dollars," the agent said. Joe paid him and took the ticket he pushed forward.

An hour later, in a window seat on the dimly lit Greyhound bus, staring at his reflection in the window as the black California desert along Interstate 10 raced backward outside, Joe shook his head sadly. What a tough break, he thought. Just when he was on his way to becoming a first-rate trial horse.

LONG ODDS

A Toby Peters Story

by Stuart M. Kaminsky

A hard right to the midsection. It was more than a jab. It was hurled concrete behind a lightly bandaged hand in a thin padded glove. It was the first punch of the fight.

The big kid doubled over in pain. He looked surprised. I wasn't. I had seen Archie Moore fight before. They called Moore "The Mongoose." He was a patient stalker who moved forward in his baggy pants, arms crossed in a style he called "armadillo."

Moore was just thirty, but he had already had more fights than five pros put together had in an entire lifetime. Less than a decade later he'd become the light heavyweight champion of the world and hold the title for a record eleven years. He'd also go on to become the only fighter who faced both Rocky Marciano and Muhammad Ali in the ring. Tonight, however, he was an up-and-coming crowd favorite with a great record.

Before the kid could come back to reality, Moore got in fast, hit hard, bobbed away from a wide right and landed a short right to the chin that had the kid limp and ready to give up or go down.

I was ringside in Moore's corner, a white towel draped around my neck over a white T-shirt, watching the fight, though I was supposed to be watching the crowd.

I looked like a typical cornerman, flat nose, somewhere

over forty, a touch of gray at the temples, around a hundred and eighty pounds. I looked more like a washed-up middleweight than a private detective, which was fine for the job. My job as a second, if the fight went for more than one round, was to step into the ring between rounds with a stool, a bottle of water and a bucket for Moore to spit in. My job as a private detective was to find the person who had told Moore to take a dive or die.

The other man in Moore's corner was an old-timer named Charlie Otis. Charlie was a big old-timer, a black man with short white hair who had sparred with Jack Johnson. Charlie had a belly now and the air of a Buddha. Nothing seemed to bother him. His job was to fill in the corner for fighters whose regulars were busy somewhere else or who couldn't afford to come along because the purse wasn't enough to make it worthwhile.

It didn't look as if the fight would go more than one round. It didn't look as if it would go more than one minute. The kid hadn't landed a single punch.

Moore followed the right to the chin with a looping left to the side of the head. The big kid staggered back, looking for something or someone he might recognize. Moore backed up, hoping the kid would fall, but he was either game, embarrassed or too confused to know that his best chance to survive with teeth was to go down, collect some sympathy and whatever he was being paid.

The referee, a little guy with almost no hair wearing a sweat-dampened long-sleeved shirt, stepped up to the kid, looked into his bleary eyes and heard the crowd calling for the fight to go on. The referee knew where his cash was coming from. He motioned for the fight to continue.

The day before the fight Moore, a squat, determined and compact brown man who was a good forty pounds lighter than the kid he was closing in on, had come to the closet I call my office. He had to go through the dental torture chamber of Sheldon Minck, D.D.S., to get there.

There were two names on the door to our offices. One, in

big black letters, read "Sheldon Minck, D.D.S." From time to time Shelly added a bunch of initials to impress the trade that happened to be looking for a dentist on the sixth floor of the Farraday Building in downtown Los Angeles. "S.S.C., F.C.V." were the current letters. Below Shelly's name, in small letters, was "Toby Peters, Private Investigator."

I had a California license and everything that came with it. In my case, everything was a telephone booth–sized office with a window overlooking an alley, a small desk, two chairs, a painting on one wall, a photograph of my father, me, my brother and our dog, a German shepherd named Kaiser Wilhelm. The photograph was more than thirty-five years old.

The war news was good. The Russians were pushing the Nazis back across the Dnieper. The RAF and the U.S. Air Force had shot down a hundred and four Nazi fighters in three days. Douglas MacArthur was on New Guinea waiting for the Aussies and Americans to take New Britain so he could make that landing in the Philippines he had promised.

Moore had called, said he got my name from Joe Louis (who had been one of my clients) and said he had to talk to me. Twenty minutes later he sat across from me in my office while a patient in Shelly's dental chair moaned and Shelly sang something that might have been "Anything Goes."

"I got a call," Moore said. He was wearing dark slacks, a white shirt and a dark zippered jacket. "I've got a fight tomorrow night at the Garden. Some kid called Sailor Jack Sweets."

"A call?" I asked.

"Guy said I should carry the kid till the third and then go down and stay down."

"Throw the fight," I said when he paused and looked out the window.

"Throw the fight," he agreed. "I go down, guy says I find a wad of bills in my locker. I win and I'm dead inside half an hour after the fight."

"Tell the cops?"

He shook his head no.

"I got in trouble when I was a kid," he said. "Did twenty-two months in a reformatory back East. I've got a record. I've got no proof about this call and I don't want trouble with the California boxing commission."

"So...?"

"I'm not gonna lose," he said. "Even if I did I know there wouldn't be a wad in my locker. It's probably just someone hoping I'll fold. No real threat, I guess. But..."

"You want..."

"You in my corner," he said. "Watching my back. One night's work."

"Fifty dollars," I said.

Moore nodded, stood, held out his hand. I took it.

I had questions. The odds in the fight must have been at least ten to one on Moore, maybe more. Maybe a lot more. Any bookie would smell a dead rodent if someone plunked down big money on the kid. So if money were being placed against Moore it had to be private or in pieces, laid off, covered. Still, an upset would have meant trouble for whoever was threatening Moore. Someone would have to be more than a little nuts or a lot desperate or both. I agreed with Moore, it was probably a bluff, but for fifty bucks why take chances.

It was a little over thirty seconds into the first round.

The big white kid with the hairy chest and confused blue eyes took another right to the chin without raising his arms to protect himself. The kid staggered back across the ring and into the ropes. Moore brushed his left thumb against the side of his nose and strode after the big kid who looked at the referee. The referee motioned for him to defend himself. He still hadn't thrown a punch.

The crowd was big, the usual for a Friday night. Lots of sweat. Kids in uniform. Fight fans of all ages. A few celebrities, including Lucille Ball, Warner Baxter and Lou Costello, were at ringside. There were more women than before the war but just as much smoke blocking sight and lungs. I checked the first two rows around me for the tenth time. I'd made the rounds checking out the rows on the side of the ring. Our gambler, if he was there, could have been anyone sitting there or anyone not sitting anywhere, but it seemed likely whoever had told Archie Moore to take a dive would be watching or have someone watching. The fight wasn't being broadcast.

As the kid looked for angels or for some sign that told him he was still among the living, I was looking for a very angry face somewhere in the crowd. I didn't find one. Moore strode in with a looping left and a right to the midsection. The fight hadn't gone long enough for sweat to spray the first rows and the timekeeper. The kid was going down. I hoped he didn't have the heart to get up. He was more than outclassed.

"Toby," a voice came at my side. Shelly Minck stood next to me. He was sweating more than the fighters. Shelly was short, nearly bald, pudgy and wearing thick glasses on his nose and a cigar in his mouth. He looked like a confused baby.

"I think I spotted him," Shelly said, starting to lift his hand to point. I reached up and put the hand back at his side. Shelly's arms are remarkably strong. Years of pulling out teeth, occasionally the right ones.

"Just tell me," I said, glancing at Moore, who had stepped back to let the big kid sink to his knees. The audience groaned. There were boos. This was Sailor Jackie Sweets about to fall flat on his face in Round One. Never mind that Jackie Sweets wasn't really a sailor and his name wasn't Jackie Sweets. He was a symbol. We were winning the war in Europe and the Pacific. He was supposed to win it in the ring, pull off a big upset. Never mind that only a few bigots, misguided patriots and drunks had bet on him, plus of course the guy who had called Archie Moore. The crowd wanted a victory. They wanted the American flag waving. They wanted to sing "Anchors Aweigh."

237

Jackie, whose real name was Bengt Forsberg, was about to sink into the California canvas. Bengt was eighteen years old, had been in the States for three weeks. He had come to California with his mother by way of Australia. Sailor Jackie Sweets couldn't speak anything but Swedish. But he did plan to enlist in the U.S. Army if his mother would let him. I got all this from an *L.A. Times* sports reporter named Scruggs Martin who owed me more than a beer or two.

"Third row, over there," Shelly said, no longer pointing but making such broad movements of his head that a few people took their eyes off the ring where the referee was counting and looked at this man at my side who was having a seizure. I followed the aim of the binoculars Shelly wore to a group of standing, chanting fans urging Sweets to get up off his knees. Sweets shook his head to clear it. The crowd thought he was shaking his head no. A half a hot dog sandwich came flying into the ring, missing the fallen warrior's head by inches but catching the referee in the chest. He looked as if he were bleeding mustard.

Sweets got to his feet doing a confused shuffle dance as the referee wiped his gloves on his chest. The referee said something to the kid. Even if he had been able to understand English, I didn't think he was close enough in time and space to answer.

Archie Moore was in the far corner, looking as if he were thinking of a high peak in Tibet. I glanced at Otis. He was thinking of the same peak. I looked at Shelly.

"Look, look," he whispered.

I looked.

"That's Sonny Tufts," I shouted.

Shelly shook his head and shouted, "Behind him."

At least that's what I thought he shouted. There was too much noise to hear him. Sweets was about to fall on his face again without a punch. Moore ran over and caught the kid before he crashed and smashed his nose even more than Moore had done in the brief fight.

Sonny Tufts and the crowd sat back down in disgust. Then I saw. He hadn't stood with the crowd. The man had remained seated, a rolled-up program in his hand. I wasn't sure what the look on his face meant but anger came pretty close. He was lean, wearing a brown sports jacket, no tie. His hair was dark, combed to one side to make it look like there was more of it than reality told him in his mirror each morning. From here, he looked about my age, pushing fifty maybe, but that was the end of the resemblance. I'm reasonably solid, with a face that looks as if it had taken more punches than the battered pug who was standing just outside the ring, waiting for the official announcement of Moore's victory before he stepped through the ropes to take a beating for a few bucks.

I look like a boxer or someone who ran into an industrial-size refrigerator one time too many. The angry guy with the rolled-up program looked like a crooked lawyer in the second half of a Monogram double feature. He had a little mustache and a little chin and something that was clearly bothering him.

"That's him," Shelly said.

"Sit down," someone behind us called. He was talking to us. I didn't sit down. I watched the pug climb into the ring as soon as the referee raised Moore's hand in victory. The crowd applauded politely. The confused Swedish kid was helped out of the ring and the angry guy who looked like a movie lawyer made his way down the row he was sitting in. He was moving fast.

"I said, sit down," the someone behind me said again. I turned. The guy speaking was one of the sailors. He wasn't a kid. He looked like a retread from the Big War and probably was. He was also big. Big voice, big gut.

"You a cook?" I asked, watching the lawyer escape from the row he was in and start up the aisle, barely missing a fat woman juggling three beers.

The sailor was sitting with three younger guys in uniform. They all started to laugh. I had nailed him.

"Yeah, I'm a cook. Now sit the hell down. Your guy won. Now get out of the way."

One of the young sailors tugged at the older guy's sleeve. The older guy was obviously a line of beers into the night.

"That's Tony Zale," the kid said, looking at me. The lawyer was getting away.

"No," said the navy cook. "He ain't."

"He is," said Shelly. The crowd around Moore's corner was watching us. Moore bounced back to the corner, waiting for the official announcement. Otis climbed slowly into the ring, handing him a towel.

The crowd around us was looking at the sailor and me. We promised to be more interesting than the fight that had just ended or the one that was about to begin. A rumble went through the crowd. Tony Zale was in the audience. I hurried after the fleeing lawyer, Shelly behind me.

We almost slammed into four men. Three of them were white and too old for war. They waited to start one of their own with a little Negro man arguing with them in the aisle. Shelly and I parted them in pursuit of the man I could no longer see ahead of us. One of the white guys grabbed my arm.

"Watch where you're going," he said. He wasn't big, but he had friends. Everyone wanted a fight. It was contagious, an arena of frustration.

"Watch who you're talking to," Shelly said. "This is Tony Zale." The three white guys looked at me unsure. I didn't look much like Zale, but where had they seen Zale? In a ring? In a little newspaper photograph? The guy let go of my arm. The Negro man was holding his ground. I grabbed his arm and hurried him along with us.

"Don't need your help, Mr. Zale," the little man said. He looked older with his face a few inches from mine.

"I apologize," I said. The little Negro looked back at the three guys in the aisle. Two of them stood with their arms folded, glaring at us. We had the audience. Even the pug with the smashed face who had climbed into the ring for the next fight was looking in our direction.

"You know what he said?" the little man shouted.

"No," I answered, hustling him into the corridor behind the seats and looking around in both directions.

"He said the big sailor took a dive, that Archie didn't hit him that hard. You believe that?"

"I believe he said it," I said. "I saw the punch. The kid didn't dive."

"You should know," the man said with satisfaction. "You should know."

"There," shouted Shelly, pointing to my left. The angry guy with the bad hair was bucking the light traffic moving back toward their seats as the bell sounded for the introductions. The crowd booed. Shelly waddled. I ran. I had a bad back. Sometimes I coddle it. Sometimes I challenge it with handball games and workouts with the punching bag at the Y on Main. For someone who's hit the bag and looked the way I looked and loved the sport of boxing as much as I did, I should have a better record in my occasional battles for my clients. I looked like a better fighter than I am but I had one advantage. I didn't give up. I didn't give up when I was being beaten for a client who had paid me fifty bucks to cover his back and I didn't give up when I went to my knees. Archie Moore had never punched me but I knew I was dumb enough to get off my knees if I had been that kid.

I didn't give up. That's what people paid me for. That's what Archie Moore was paying me for. I ran. There was a row of taxis waiting with cabbies standing around talking. The crowd wouldn't be getting out for another couple of battles. The angry guy got in the first taxi in line. I caught up with him as he closed the door. I opened it. I could hear Shelly in the distance behind me gasping.

"Who the hell are you?" asked the guy, looking at me at an angle like a bird. I slid in next to him as the cabbie got in and looked back at us with "Where to?" The cabbie needed a shave. He didn't need trouble.

"Why'd you leave before the last fight?" I asked.

The angry guy touched his head to be sure the few strands of hair were still Wildrooted down.

"What?"

"Where to?" the cabbie repeated.

"Why did you leave?" I repeated.

"This man is crazy," the guy in the backseat said to the cabbie. The cabbie looked at me and shrugged.

"Could be," he said. "I'm turning on the meter. You want to sit here and talk? Jake by me. You decide you want to go somewhere? Let me know."

"I'm getting a cop," the man next to me said, reaching for the door. "Fine," I said. "Then you can explain why you looked angry when Moore won the fight."

"None of your damned business," he said, looking at the cabbie, who was humming and looking out the front window.

"Let's find that cop," I said, opening the door.

"Okay. I lost a lot of money," the guy blurted out. "If you plan to rob me, I've got twelve dollars which I'll get back from this cab company if I have to sue them right up to the Supreme Court." I closed the door.

"You bet on the kid," I said.

"Yes."

"Why? He didn't have a chance."

"I was told otherwise," he said.

"By who?"

"By whom," the man corrected. "Look, my name is Jerry Litwiller. I'm a writer at Paramount. A guy at the Wilshire Bar and Grille said Sweets was going to win. He was sure. I'm down to my last twelve dollars after losing fifty on that fight. I'm having a bad night."

"Turn it into a screenplay," I said. "Who was this guy who told you to bet on the Sailor?"

Shelly was at the window now, leaning over and looking in,

his breath steaming the glass. He was breathing hard and heavy.

"You're crazy, you know that?" the writer said.

"I've been told that before," I said. "The guy in the bar. His name." The writer laughed twice and shook his head.

"Colley Tillman," he said. "Works at the Madison Square Athletic Club. Knows all the fighters. Trains some."

"Sweets?"

"Sweets, yeah," Litwiller said.

"He thought his boy was going to beat Moore?"

"Let's put it this way, he thought Moore was going to lose. He didn't just think it. He said he knew it."

"Fix?"

Litwiller shrugged. "Who knows? What difference does it make? He was wrong. You going to tell me what's going on?"

"You going to turn it into a movie?" I asked, opening the door again.

"Who knows?" he said. "I'm desperate and I'm nearly broke."

And you're losing your hair fast, I thought and got out, nudging Shelly out of the way. The door closed and the cab pulled away.

"He the guy?" Shelly asked.

"No, but he gave me a lead." I headed back toward the arena.

"A clue?" asked Shelly, following me.

"A lead."

"I'm hungry," said Shelly.

"Get a hot dog and a beer," I said, hurrying back through the open gate and into the corridor. The crowd inside groaned. They were getting a lot to groan about and not much to cheer. I headed for the dressing room, leaving Shelly to consider his options, a hot dog and beer or his loyalty to our job. Moore was in Dressing Room Three. It was small, a dozen full-length metal lockers, a low wooden bench at an odd angle, a table with a tattered and padded leather top. Moore sat on the table, Charlie Otis taking off his gloves.

"You okay?" I asked.

"Kid can't fight," Moore said. "I couldn't have carried him three rounds even if I had wanted to. I think I broke his jaw. I'll check when I get changed. You find...?"

"I'm close," I said. Otis turned to look at me.

"Crazy damned business," he said. "How many kids you think died in the Pacific today? Guess. Seventy? Hundreds? And this happens?" I guessed the 'this' was the threat to his fighter. I didn't stop to find out. There were a few guys smoking in the hallway. No reporters, no fans. It wasn't like the movies. There were no beautiful girls in tight dresses. There were no girls.

I tried Dressing Room Two. Before I opened the door, I heard a woman's voice behind it scream, "Henry!"

I went in. The old pug with the face flatter than mine who was supposed to be in the fight after Moore's sat dazed on a table like the one I had just seen. He was alone, wearing a shiny purple robe and a towel over his head. His eye was swollen shut.

"Henry Aldrich!" called the woman from the little plastic Philco radio on the table next to the pug. He was listening to *The Aldrich Family*.

"Coming, mother," came the cracking teenage voice on the radio.

"I love this show," the pug said and then added, "You ain't Zale," pointing a gloved hand at me.

"No," I said.

"Damn," the pug said, shaking his head. "You see what I did."

"No," I said, starting to close the door.

"I won the damned fight is what I did," he said. "Won the damn fight. One round. I go in there raw meat for a kid with seven wins and no losses and flatten him. And who saw it?"

"Missed the chance of your career," I said.

"I'll get more," he said. I closed the door and went for Door Number One. There were five people in the kid's locker room, which was smaller than the other two I had just been in. The Swedish kid was lying on his back, eyes open, blinking from time to time and admiring a squashed bug on the ceiling.

"Tillman?" I asked, looking at the faces.

"He's not here," said a big, older version of the kid looking at the ceiling. The accent was clear. One of the people in the room was a woman. She held the dreamy kid's gloved hand. She was obviously Mom, and Mom had clearly had enough of boxing and people who lived in and near it. She glared at me and said something in Swedish to the three men near her.

"Tillman," I repeated.

"I think you go now," said the father. I nodded and left the room.

Bluff, I told myself. The threat against Moore was just a bluff. Tillman, or someone he knew, put down a few bucks on the kid and made the call to Moore. There would be no follow-up, no knife or bullet in the back and there would have been no wad of bills in Archie Moore's pocket if he had dived. That's what I told myself. It made sense, but that wasn't what I was being paid for.

There was one man who had been in the Swede's corner who was not among the people in his dressing room. I figured him for Tillman. He had been wiry, probably around forty and tough looking. He wasn't in the hall. I started opening doors, closets and a small office with no windows. I could hear a roar of voices, moans and phlegmy laughter ahead of me. Another early finish. There were nights like that. The fights were over.

I went back to Archie Moore's dressing room. Moore was up now, coming out of a small shower stall with a thin curtain, a white towel around his waist. Otis wasn't there but Shelly was, sitting on the wooden bench finishing off a hot dog, a beer perched on the bench next to him.

"He's protecting me," said Moore with a small smile Shelly couldn't see.

"I can protect your teeth too when this is over," Shelly said. "I've got an idea for a rubber thing you can put in your mouth, protect your teeth when you're fighting. Doesn't interfere with your breathing."

"I can't afford to have people laughing at me when I'm in the ring," said Moore, toweling himself off.

"You can't afford to lose more teeth," said Shelly. "Let 'em laugh. Win the fight. Show great protected teeth. We can make thousands. We'll call them the Archie Moore Mouth Protectors. You get five percent on each protector sold."

"No thanks," said Moore.

"Shell," I said. "We're looking for someone, remember." To Moore I said, "You know a guy named Tillman?"

"I know him to nod to," said Moore, reaching for a locker door. Moore opened the door. Tillman fell out, missing the boxer by inches. Moore stood in his towel, looking down at the fallen corner-man. Shelly jumped into action. The corpse's eyes and mouth were open, looking in awe at a spot on the wall.

"Let me take a look," he said, pushing his glasses up his nose. "I'm a dentist." I looked at the door and then at Moore. "He's dead," said Shelly.

I stepped past the corpse, looked in the empty locker and kicked the locker shut.

"We can see that, Shel," I said. Shelly stood up.

"Why'd you open that locker?" I asked Moore.

"I thought...my things. I thought my clothes were in there."

I opened the next locker. There were Moore's clothes. I pushed it shut.

The dressing room door opened, letting in the sound of the departing, disgruntled crowd. They were going home at least an hour earlier than they had expected.

Otis stepped in and looked at the corpse, nothing showing on his face, and closed the door. He had a couple of Pabst Blue Ribbon beer bottles in his hand.

"You see someone come in here?" I asked Otis and Moore. Both shook their heads no.

"He's very dead," said Shelly, looking down at the corpse.

"This is bad," Moore said, looking at the dead man.

"Worse than you think," I said. "Tillman was the guy who called you and told you to throw the fight."

"Nothing for it," said Moore with a sigh. "We call the cops."

"I'll get 'em," said Shelly, moving toward the door past Otis, who just stood looking down at the dead man.

"Hold it, Shel," I said.

"How'd they stuff a man in a locker?" said Otis, shaking his head. "And when? I ain't been gone two minutes and Archie..."

"I was in the shower. Someone must have killed him while I was in the shower. Curtain closed. I didn't hear anything but water."

Shelly had his hand on the doorknob. He looked at me and pushed his glasses back up his nose.

"Okay, come back with a cop, Shel," I said.

"Right. Why don't I just tell them they want a cop in Archie Moore's dressing room and then I'll go home," said Shelly, opening the door.

"Come back with them, Shel," I repeated firmly.

"I'll come back. I'll come back," he said and left the room, closing the door behind him.

"I better get dressed," Moore said, moving toward the locker with his clothes. "What are we gonna tell 'em?"

"The truth," I said.

"You put things together and figured Tillman for trying to get me to dive. The cops will figure it too. Then they're going to come up simple. Two and two makes me a killer."

"No," I said. "Two and two makes Otis a killer."

"Me?" asked Otis, calmly still clutching the bottles of beer.

"No time for anyone else," I said. "I was gone no more than three or four minutes. Tillman left the ring with the Swede."

"Could have been somebody come in while I was out," said Otis.

"Otis didn't kill the guy," Moore said, readjusting his towel, beads of water still clinging to his chest and forehead.

"You asked how the killer could have stuffed Tillman in the

247

locker," I said to Otis. "When you came in, the lockers were closed and Tillman was on the floor. No one said he had been in a locker."

"I just..." Otis began looking at Moore and me.

"What happened?" I asked. "Make it quick. Shelly'll be back with a cop or ten in a few seconds."

Otis slumped down on the low bench and placed the beers gently next to him. He was shaking his head.

"He come in when Archie was in the shower," Otis said softly. "Mad as hell. He had a gun. Told me to get out of the way. Said some fool thing like Archie had messed up his life. He pushed me out of the way. Figured an old man wouldn't be much trouble. Figured wrong. I'm old but some things you don't forget. They just come back. I hit him hard, pit of the stomach with a left. Then a cross to his face. Missed. Hit him in the neck. Went down hard. Think I busted his windpipe. I stuffed him in the locker. Figured we'd just leave him there. Might take days before they found him."

"Where'd you go?" I asked.

"Got rid of his gun," said Otis, shaking his head. "Picked up two beers to cover."

The door flew open. Shelly led in a pair of uniformed cops, both retreads from earlier times helping out for the duration of the war, doing crowd control at the fights.

"What happened?" said one of the cops, a thin guy with a pink Irish face.

"He tripped," I said.

"He..." Shelly began.

"Tripped," I repeated. "Came in to congratulate Mr. Moore. Tripped, the bench was in the middle of the floor. He went flying over. Nothing we could do."

"You saw it?" asked the cop, looking at each of us.

"Mr. Otis and I saw it," I said. "Mr. Moore was taking a shower. Dr. Minck wasn't here."

"I wasn't here," Shelly repeated emphatically.

The Irish cop moved over to the corpse and went down on

one knee.

"Must have hit something," he said.

"Fell against the side of the table," I said. "Weird. Hit his neck."

"Yeah," said the cop, getting up. "I know him. Name's Tillman. He was in that kid's corner tonight. Tillman's not the kind to come and congratulate someone who beats his boy."

"Not unless he had a few bucks on the winner," the second cop said. He was even older than the Irish veteran and looked as if he belonged in the gang of bandits in a Bob Steele Western.

"Who knows?" said the Irish cop.

He looked at Otis for a long beat and then at Moore. Their eyes met and held.

"Heard nothing?"

"Not a thing," said Moore.

"Then I hope you don't mind if I ask you one more question?"

Moore shook his head to show that he didn't mind, but the Irish cop had a knowing look on his face.

"You sign a poster for me?" he asked. "I'll tear one down in the hall. I save 'em. For my son when he gets back from the war. I told him you were gonna be a champ."

"Happy to," said Moore.

The cop smiled and looked at Tillman's corpse.

"Shame," he said. "No place in the world's safe anymore."

"No place," I agreed. "A beer?"

"Why not?" said the cop.

Otis handed a beer to each of the cops. The Irish cop held up his bottle and said, "To the end of the war."

"And the memory of the fallen," added the other cop.

I felt like saying "Amen" but I just stood watching Shelly shake his head in confusion.

DREAM STREET

by Mike Lupica

Vinny noticed that some of the cable channels, especially the ESPN one that put on the old-time shit, helped him remember things. Sometimes, when they'd show wall-to-wall boxing the week of some big fight, he'd find himself sitting there and watching the rematch between him and Dream Street in Boston. And there'd be some small moment, some little sequence of punches, and he'd surprise himself, the way he surprised Dream Street that night, when he went southpaw on him in the middle rounds.

Vinny Tavernese wished sometimes there was a cable channel he could turn on that would tell him which room he'd left his fucking reading glasses in, or where he'd put his wallet.

He forgot things more and more. It scared him, and nothing had ever scared him, not the other guy in the ring, not the Mob, not even Madeline, his second wife. But now he'd be on Second Avenue, walking south, and he'd stop for the light at Forty-ninth and suddenly he couldn't remember where he was going, or why he was even out. And he'd just buy the papers and go home until he remembered. Only sometimes he didn't remember. One of his doctors, a couple of doctors ago, told Vinny he should try writing himself notes.

And Vinny said, "Yeah, that's a good one, doc. Except what kind of dumb asshole am I gonna feel like when I can't remember who sent them to me?"

Maybe that's what he ought to do with Dream Street, just write him a letter, ask him straight out once and for all, why he didn't come out for the fifteenth that night at the Garden.

Vinny'd watched the whole fight the other night, forgetting the last time he'd watched it start to finish, thinking to himself that the black-and-white film seemed to be fading or something, he felt like he was looking through a screen door. Or maybe his eyes were going too, along with everything else, no matter what the doctors said.

He moved his chair up until it was right on top of the TV when it was time for the fifteenth round, Don Dunphy saying that the fight had been everything people wanted, that it was too close, that it might come down to these last three minutes.

The close-ups weren't too good in those days, but they were up on Vinny's face pretty good now, both eyes nearly closed as he waited for Dream Street in the middle of the ring.

The ref, Ralphie Iannelli, has his back to Vinny, you can see him pointing.

What the fuck? Vinny says, plain as day, you didn't have to be some kind of professional lip reader.

Now Iannelli is talking again, trying to raise Vinny's arm, except this is where he went a little nuts, waving his arms like a madman, even as Iannelli was telling him he won the fight.

Vinny didn't need the pictures on the ESPN oldies channel telling him what came next, because this was one part he'd never forget, no matter how many brain cells he'd lost taking ten shots to the head waiting to throw one big one himself.

Ralphie Iannelli grabbed him and leaned over and said, "Dream Street says he's sorry."

Sorry? Vinny turned off the set now, went and stood at the window and stared downtown, at the building where the *News* used to have its offices, where he'd go sometimes and have coffee with Bill Gallo, the *Daily News* cartoonist, and a fight guy from even before Vinny's time. Dream Street says he's sorry? Vinny was the one who'd always been sorry, more than forty years sorry, that he didn't get to finish the fucking job.

Oh, he remembered everything about that night in '59 like it was yesterday. Of course, remembering yesterday, that was another story. He'd be making an appearance for the beer company upstate someplace, and he'd be talking about some fight he'd seen the week before between a couple of Mexicans with tattoos all over them, up and down their arms and even on their necks and backs, and he'd completely lose his place and have to fall back on *schtick.*

"Hey," he'd say, "I get more confused sometimes than that Holyfield when he hears somebody yell, 'Daddy!'"

That would get him a laugh, and then he'd go with material he knew by heart, stories about him and Dream Street in Boston, because even the young guys in the crowd wanted to hear about it; because it turned out to be one of those sports events people talked about forever. When they started making lists at the end of the century, greatest this, greatest that, it was still Vinny vs. Dream Street in Boston at the top of the boxing list, then the Thrilla in Manila, when Frazier didn't come out for the fifteenth, and then the rest of them, Hearns vs. Leonard and Louis vs. Conn and Graziano vs. Zale.

But somehow, all this time later, it was as if they both won. Well, he didn't win shit, Vinny thought now, staring at the lights all the way down Second, wondering what he was going to do with the rest of the night.

"I won," Vinny said in the empty apartment, pounding a fist into his chest.

So how come he was the one who ended up feeling like a bum?

How come Dream Street Stone, who quit on his stool, how come he was the one who ended up having the dream life?

"Your PSA count has gone up a little bit again," the young doctor said, the chart from Vinny's annual physical in his hands.

MURDER ON THE ROPES

"We'll take another one in a few months, but at your age I don't think there's anything to worry about."

The doctor was a nice colored kid. Dr. Hudson. Vinny couldn't remember if he'd asked him his first name and forgotten, or had just never asked. Vinny thought he looked a little bit like Jeter, the Yankee shortstop, light-complected, but Hudson had his head shaved. You could never tell with the coloreds, at least the modern ones, whether they were going bald or just liked the look.

Vinny could remember the first colored guy he ever fought with a shaved head, way before guys like Zora Folley did it. Parker Gillespie. Vinny got ahead of him on points early and then tried to see after that if he could hit him enough shots on top of his head to make it bleed, see if the blood came spurting out like it would from a water fountain.

God, he was a crazy bastard in those days.

What year was that?

"PSA," Vinny said. "How great is this, having to worry all the time about something that sounds like an airline out West?"

"If you were thirty years younger, the number might worry me," Hudson said, "but frankly at your age, it's pretty normal."

"You say."

"Mr. Tavernese." No matter how many times Vinny corrected him, he'd still sound out the "e" at the end sometimes. "You worry too much."

"I still get these goddamn headaches."

Hudson sighed now. It always felt like a body shot to Vinny. "We've done an MRI. We've done a CAT scan. There is nothing. The only thing wrong with your head that I can see is all the scar tissue around the eyes."

"You're tellin' me I'm just supposed to forget what I can't remember?"

"Memory loss is a part of aging. For you. For me. For the world, Mr. Tavernese." Again with the loud "e."

"Call me Vinny," he said.

The kid looked over his shoulder at the clock behind Vinny, trying to look casual, like he was looking out the window, so he didn't have to look at his watch.

Vinny said, "I'm more worried about my memory than my prostate, okay? Hell, you want my prostate, I'll bend over right here, take it, I don't need it anymore."

"Mr. Tav...Vinny," he said. "I told you. We've run all the tests we can run, there's none of the markers we usually get for Alzheimer's. It's just a product of age and, well, what you used to do for a living." He cleared his throat, like it was something he'd learned in medical school. "Having seen what's happened to others from your line of work, I think you should stop worrying and consider yourself quite lucky, at least in that area."

"Lucky," Vinny said. "Yeah, that's me, Mr. Lucky. You ever see that one? Cary Grant and Laraine Day. You ever hear of her? She was married to my friend Leo Durocher."

He knew the kid wasn't listening anymore. There was always a point where Vinny got talking about something and he knew he'd lost him.

"Don't worry so much about the forgetting," Dr. Hudson said now, standing up behind his desk, officially letting Vinny know they were through. "It happens to all of us. The other night, I was on my way out to a date and spent twenty minutes looking for my apartment key." He smiled, though the smile didn't seem to have a hell of a lot to it. "You're a great storyteller, Mr. ...Vinny. When I've got more time, and I certainly wish I did today, you have a wonderful memory about scenes and events and even conversations that happened in what is almost another life for you."

"The one I liked," Vinny said.

"You are not losing your mind. Trust me."

"That was what my last accountant told me," Vinny said.

Hudson came around the desk now, put a hand on Vinny's shoulder. "Besides," he said, "as long as you've been around, there must be a few things you're happy you can't remember."

"That part you got right, doc," Vinny said. "Life's a son-ofabitch, ain't it? Sometimes the stuff that drives you goddam crazy is the stuff you can't forget."

The sportswriters called him and Dream Street "Beauty and the Beast."

Vinny was about five-foot-seven in those days, before he started to shrink, built like one of those old Checker cabs, with a nose that had gotten mashed young, and the scar tissue that always fascinated the docs already lumping up around his eyes, making him look older than he was. But he didn't think he was a bad-looking guy. It's why he hated that Beast shit. "How come," he'd say to the writers when they'd be sitting around with him up in the Catskills, after watching him train, "how come if I'm such a beast I got so many good-looking broads throwing theirselves at me?"

"It's your charm and way with words," Jimmy Cannon told him once. "Not to mention your bank account."

Vinny said, "You're tellin' me I get as much as I do on account of I'm rich?"

Cannon said, "No, I'm just telling you you get more than you should."

"You ain't no leading man yourself," Vinny said, "even if you did go out with Betty Hutton."

"Joan Blondell," Cannon said.

"You still ain't much better lookin' than me," Vinny said.

"Yeah, I am," Cannon said. "Know why, kid? When I punch my typewriter, it doesn't punch back."

Cannon liked him. So did Red Smith and Bill Heinz. They just seemed to love Augusta (Dream Street) Stone more, just about all of them saying he was the most beautiful boxer they'd ever seen, writing him up in the papers as if they were queer for him. Nothing against Vinny. He was tough. He could hit and take a punch and kept coming. They didn't call him dumb, think of him as just another dumb Wop fighter, but they didn't have to, Vinny could read between the lines, sometimes better than he could read the lines themselves.

Dream Street, though, he was the artist, he was the thinking man's fighter, he was poetry in motion. Vinny Tavernese, that dumb Wop bastard, he'd keep coming, no matter how much punishment he took, how much the other guy rearranged his face, as long as he won the fight. It was different with Dream Street. Even when he was young, he talked about being in the movies when he was through boxing, that's why he had to protect that pretty mug of his.

"I did get hit in the head once or twice," Dream Street would say in that snooty way he had. "Didn't like it *at* all."

He was a handsome bastard, even Vinny had to admit that, with smooth skin the color of a light coffee, almost light enough to pass, maybe that's why he dated so many white women, even in the old days. Dream Street, even after the second fight, was the one who did the cigarette commercials. He was the one to open the restaurant in Harlem, a couple of blocks from the Apollo. Dream Street was the one who drove around New York City in a cream-colored Caddy with the top down, just waiting for somebody to snap his picture, and sat with Jack Paar on the old *Tonight Show*.

They spent a little time together, promoting both fights, but Vinny never felt like he got to know him. It was like Dream Street couldn't bring himself to drop his guard even when the two of them were alone.

"Vincenzo," he'd say, pronouncing it perfectly, Vin-*chen*-zo, "I do believe if we weren't trying to beat each other's brains out, we could have some laughs together."

Only they never did.

Afterward, after both of them were retired, people'd say to Vinny, "What was Dream Street really like?"

Vinny'd say, "He hit hard and wouldn't go down."

And they'd say, "No, away from the ring."

"There wasn't no away from the ring for us," Vinny told them.

He'd gone forty years telling himself the thing had to be on the square, that nobody could have bought Dream Street Stone, that if they had, you couldn't keep something like that a secret, somebody would've gave it up. That's what he'd tell himself. Only now he couldn't get it out of his head how Dream Street came on at the end of the fourteenth.

Now Vinny, who lived inside his own head more and more, as cluttered as it was, had convinced himself Dream Street had one more round in him in Boston.

Problem was, no one seemed to know where the hell Dream Street was, or what had happened to him the last few years.

"Maybe it was at Graziano's funeral I saw him the last time," Bill Gallo was saying in the back room of P.J. Clarke's. "How long ago was that? Five years? I'd have to look it up."

"You talk to him?" Vinny said.

"I don't think so," Gallo said. "I just remember that he still had that smile. Now that I think of it, him and May came in late. The only time I saw them was when they were coming up the aisle, then I never saw them again, I figured they must've slipped out the side during Communion."

May Stone, the former May York, had been a singer at the Apollo in the fifties, another light-skinned colored the way Dream Street was, as pretty to look at as anybody Vinny'd ever seen. Almost as pretty as Dream Street thinks *he* is, that's what the boys at the gym used to say. They'd gotten married after he retired, not too long after the second fight with Vinny, and had been together ever since. There was a famous line May got credit for, when she and Dream Street were packing up their Los Angeles house to go live in Italy, when Dream Street was about to hit it big making Westerns over there. They were in what he called his Trophy Room, boxing up trophies and photographs and the rest of the shit you accumulate, and May was looking at the famous white robe Dream Street always wore into the ring.

"Augusta," she said, because that's what she always called him, Augusta, "why do you keep this old thing, it's all covered with blood?"

"Not my blood," he was supposed to have said back to her.

He had been a winner at everything he touched his whole life, from the time he came down from Harlem to win his first amateur tournament at the old Garden on Fiftieth Street. He won all his professional fights after he came back with his gold medal from the Melbourne Olympics in '56. He won May York and the hearts of just about the whole world.

Vinny never said it to anybody, not even his friends, because he knew how stuff got around, but he used to think: Jesus, people treat me like I'm the nigger here.

Dream Street Stone won everything except his second fight with Vinny Tavernese and then never fought again.

"You ever wonder why he didn't come out for the fifteenth?" Vinny asked Gallo, sitting there in his bow tie and his checked sports jacket, just about the sweetest guy he ever met around the fight game.

"Didn't he say something about how that was the closest to death he ever came?" Gallo asked.

"That was Frazier, after the Thrilla in Manila."

"Well," Gallo said, "you must've asked him why he didn't."

"This thought that maybe the thing wasn't legit didn't get into my head until lately," he said. "And you know how it is with this hard head of mine, when a thought does get in there, it's pretty fucking hard to ignore."

"You're saying you never wanted to ask him before."

"I never did," Vinny said. "But I'd like to now, if I could ever find the guy."

"Forty years after the fact," Bill Gallo said, "you're worried that maybe the greatest fight that ever was—a fight you won—

wasn't on the level?"

"I still got a hard head," Vinny said.

They'd decided to meet up at Clarke's because they used to go there a lot in the old days. Only now it was like a lot of places, Vinny didn't know anybody. Frankie, the funny little guy who used to work the door of the back room, was gone, and Danny Lavezzo, the owner, had passed on a few months ago. Vinny didn't even know any of the waiters. He'd looked around when he came in the front door, off Third Avenue, trying to spot some of the pasty-faced Irish guys who used to take such good care of him, even after he retired. Only they were gone, too.

He told Gallo it was really his old trainer, Mike Altamero, who started putting these ideas in his head, right before he died of lung cancer. He got Gallo laughing, telling him what it was like even at the end, Mike doing everything he could to shoo the young nurse he had taking care of him round-the-clock at his little apartment down on Horatio. He'd send her out to buy more paperbacks for him, then as soon as he'd see her on the street, he'd have Vinny open the window for him so he could have a smoke out of the pack he kept hidden under his mattress. And out of nowhere one day, talking about the old days—what the hell else were they going to talk about?—Mike blew some smoke out the window and said, "You ever think he dumped that last one?" knowing Vinny knew which last one he meant and who he was talking about. Vinny could still picture him now, a Mets cap on his bald head, wrapped in a blanket, coughing so hard Vinny started to worry that maybe you could *catch* cancer from a guy sucking on a Lucky Strike. The cigs had killed him, and even at the end he was still holding on to them like they were some kind of lifeline. Vinny'd asked him, "Why would he dump it? I was as ready to go as he was. I was afraid he'd *breathe* on me hard and I'd go down." Vinny told Gallo he shook his head that day, no, no, no, saying, "Why dump a fight three minutes from the end?" And Mike Altamero had looked at him and said, "Maybe that's the best time you can dump it, because then nobody says a word."

"What if I'd gone down before that?"

Mikey pointed at him with the Lucky and said, "No, that's the thing, you dumb guinea bastard. He knew, on account of the bastard was smart. He *knew* you and he knew himself, especially after fighting you once already. He knew he couldn't put you down."

In Clarke's Vinny said to Bill Gallo, "I asked him why he was bringing this shit up now, and he looked at me and said, when you start moving toward the dancing lights, looking for that soft landing on the other side, you gotta ask all the questions, whether you get answers or not."

Gallo said there was a guy at the paper could maybe help Vinny track down Dream Street, one of their columnists, a kid named Frank Sann. He went over to the phone booth they still had in the back room, came back a couple of minutes later, smiling. It occurred to Vinny that Gallo looked a lot younger than he did, even if they had to be about the same age. It must be the work keeps him going, drawing every day, still writing his boxing column on Sunday.

"Frank reminded me, he did that long piece on you last year, on the anniversary of the second fight," Gallo said. "He said he'd love to help, if he could put you and Dream Street together after all these years it might read like some kind of *Sunshine Boys* of boxing. You remember that one?"

"George Burns and Walter Matthau played those old Jew comics," Vinny said. "Didn't Matthau just die?"

Gallo nodded.

"Sometimes when a guy like that dies, I'm surprised, 'cause I had him for dead already," Vinny said. He looked at Gallo. "You didn't tell him the real reason I want to see him, did you?"

"You want to tell him, tell him. I just told him you needed help finding him."

Vinny tried to signal for the check, but Gallo reached over, gently grabbed his hand, said the paper was paying for lunch.

"Maybe it was Mikey talking about those dancing lights," Vinny said. "Maybe I can see them myself sometimes. Who the hell knows? All I know is that there's a big difference between Mikey and me. I want to do more than ask the questions."

Vinny finished the last of his espresso and said, "I need an answer here."

Frank Sann sat at the kitchen table in Vinny's apartment with one of the other ESPNs, the all-news one, on in the background, and said that it was the goddamnedest thing, but that Dream Street Stone seemed to have disappeared.

"You're telling me no one knows where he is," Vinny said.

"Somebody knows where he is," Sann said. "I just haven't found that somebody yet. But I will, just give me more than a day."

Sann was another kid too young to have seen him fight, in his thirties, a good-looking kid with short hair already going to gray a little bit, and one of those neat little beards all the young guys were starting to wear. And Gallo said this was the best young guy in the business now, not just a good writer but somebody who wouldn't quit. I figured, Gallo told Vinny, I couldn't screw around, I better find a guy for you willing to go the distance.

"I did finally hook up with Dream Street's accountant this morning," Sann said. "Only he acts like this is a spy movie, or he's in the Secret Service. He said that Mr. and Mrs. Stone were doing just fine, they had just been traveling extensively since Mr. Stone's retirement from what the little dork called the entertainment industry. Beyond that, he couldn't help me and good day."

"Jesus," Vinny said, "he hasn't been in anything in about twenty years. Where they been traveling nobody can find them, the moon?"

"I'm going to do another Internet sweep this afternoon," Sann said.

He'd brought them coffees from the Starbucks around the corner. Vinny wouldn't have been caught dead in there himself, but he had to admit he was starting to acquire a taste for some of that chocolate mochaccino.

"Sweep," he said. "When I was a kid, sweep was what you did at the bar to earn a nickel."

Sann took out his notebook, tossed it on the table between them.

"Same shit's in there today as yesterday," he said. "They sold the flat in Rome, what was their home base when he was in the movies over there, a long time ago. Sold the house in Los Angeles about five years ago. They still own what used to be their summer house, out in the Hamptons. His Hollywood agent is dead. So's his lawyer. The only person I've talked to who's had any contact with him lately, or at least says he has, is this snippy accountant."

Sann lit a cigarette now, Vinny thinking, Okay, *now* he looks like a sportswriter. In the old days, they all smoked, even Vinny between fights. Sann offered him the pack now and Vinny shook his head. The way he felt lately, all the things he was sure were wrong with him, he was sure he'd have lung cancer by dinnertime if he even smoked one.

"Do me a favor before I go," Sann said, "play this out for me."

Vinny waited. Sann had that tone he took with him already, in person or on the phone, a little like the colored doctor's tone, talking to him slowly and patiently, the way he would some slow kid.

"You find Dream Street. *We* find him. You walk up, ring his doorbell. Then what? You tell him you were in the neighborhood, you thought you'd drop by after thirty years, or whatever the hell it is? You think he's just going to come out with it, that the most famous fight of all time was fixed, and by him?"

"Yeah," Vinny said, "I do."

"You do."

"I'm gonna tell the guy I won't tell, that I just have to know. I'm gonna tell the guy I can't die not knowin'. I'm gonna tell him all that and then I'm gonna ask him one other question."

Vinny'd worked hard to talk better his whole life, all the way back, knowing everybody used to make fun of him, but sometimes it still came out "ax" him a question.

"What question is that?" Sann asked.

"I'm gonna ask him who the better man was that night."

Vinny tried to explain all of it to Frank Sann then, surprised at how fast the words came out of him, and how well, as if somebody else was doing the talking for him. Everybody knew Dream Street was on the way out, this was going to be his last big score in the ring, he'd already gotten a couple of parts, one in a pretty good John Wayne Western, and he didn't want to take any more chances on ruining that pretty face of his. It was one of those times, the Friday night fights starting to die off on television, when people figured boxing was about to die anyway. Dream Street figured the real money was in the movies. So this was it, a chance for him to go out on top, make his hero's exit, go out to Hollywood with his wife, May, like he'd always said he was going to.

But Vinny knew he could take him. Vinny was no genius outside the ring, but he didn't get to be champ in the first place not knowing how to fight. He'd figured out early there was a difference between getting punished and getting hurt. Dream Street could punish him, but he couldn't hurt him. And Mikey Altamero was right: he couldn't put him down. Vinny knew Dream Street was prettier and faster, and people rooted for him the way they'd root for Ali late in his career, when they really came around on him, forgetting how they hated his ass when he was this wise-ass colored kid out of Louisville.

He told Sann all that, and more.

"You know why I'm the people's champ?" Dream Street said at the last press conference in Boston before the fight. "Because the people, they love the Dreamer."

Vinny leaned into the mike they'd put in front of him at the table—he forgot which Boston hotel it was—and said, "Don't worry, you're gonna get all the dreaming you want come Saturday night."

Dream Street came back with, "No wonder the Mob could never get their hooks into you, Vincenzo. Even if they asked you to do some business, they were afraid you wouldn't understand the question."

They never did get their hooks into him. They sure tried, though. There was the day at the apartment Vinny and Madeline had on Central Park West, in the same building John Garfield lived in, maybe a month before the Dream Street fight. Joey Spada, who'd gotten into boxing as one of Frankie Carbo's lieutenants, just showed up at the door, having greased the doorman, with a suitcase full of money.

Vinny explained to him one more time that he hadn't taken all those shots to the head so he could be another Joey Spada whore.

"*Whore*," Joey said, grinning that shit-eating grin of his, "not *hoo-er*."

"Well, you'd know," Vinny said.

"How about this, smart guy? How about I put the word out after Dream Street beats your ass you threw the fight anyway? Then watch you go around denying it the rest of your life."

"Nobody'll believe it."

"Why's that?"

"Because I'm not smart enough to know how to lose."

"So maybe then I got to come up with other ways to fuck with you," Spada said and walked out the door with the suitcase, Vinny never even asking how much was in it.

The last time he heard from them was in Boston, three nights before the fight. Spada didn't quit either, at least until somebody finally shot him up so much he looked like one of those dummy targets they use in shooting galleries. A kid in a topcoat that was too long for him, a snap-brimmed hat like all the wiseguys wore in those days, knocked on Vinny's door at the Parker House. Didn't even introduce himself.

"My boss wants I should ask you a question."

Knowing Vinny knew who his boss was.

Vinny, standing there in his boxer shorts with the stupid

hearts on them some old girlfriend had given him, just eyeballed him.

"He wants to know if you had a change of heart."

Vinny shook his head slowly, side to side. If the kid made any kind of move he was going to drop him.

"That being the case, he asked I should remind you about something he told you not so long ago."

"Such as?"

"Such as there's more than one way to teach a dumb bastard —his words, not mine—a lesson."

Vinny thought at the time it was just another way of Spada and the boys threatening him and had pretty much always thought of it that way—whenever he *did* think of it, anyway—until Mikey Altamero had to get him all worked up about Dream Street a couple of weeks before Mikey passed.

"Now you know everything I know, which frankly ain't one whole hell of a lot," Vinny said to Frank Sann. "That night in Boston, that's really all I got left. Most of the money's gone, the wives are long gone, even my kid, Vincent, he died of a stinkin' drug overdose when he was a year out of college. I don't want anybody runnin' a benefit for me, I don't want you helping me out on account of you feel sorry for me. I just want to know if it was on the square."

"You say it's all you've got," Sann said. "Then why put it at risk?"

"'Cause I don't want somethin's not mine," Vinny said.

Sann called the next morning first thing, said he'd found Dream Street. Just like that. He'd pick Vinny up out front of his building in half an hour, he had to rent a car first.

"Where?" Vinny said.

"That summer place I told you about, in the Hamptons."

"How'd you find out?"

"A cop out there knows somebody who knows somebody who did some landscaping for May Stone. They saw him."

"How's he doing?"

"What, you want everything? I didn't ask how he was doing.

These guys don't know how he's doing, just that his privet needed trimming. They saw him for a minute on the back deck. He waved and smiled. That was it."

"They're sure it was him?"

"It was him."

"Sonofabitch," Vinny said and Sann said, "If you say so," and hung up.

Now they were at Exit 55 on the Long Island Expressway. Sann said it was about another hour from there. He'd been listening to one of the sports stations when Vinny got in the car and before they were even through the Midtown Tunnel, Vinny was ready to throw himself out the window if he didn't change the station, the whole thing sounded to him like all three of his marriages combined.

"Can I trust you?" Vinny said.

"What did Bill Gallo say?"

"He said yes."

"He ever lie to you?"

"Never."

"He's not lying now."

"If he tells me he dumped it, I don't want it in the paper."

Sann didn't turn, just grinned as he watched the road. "No shit."

"Then what's in this for you?"

Sann said, "A reunion piece that'll make 'em cry. Maybe there's even a short story in it, or a novel."

Vinny leaned back and thought about what he was going to say while Sann talked about Dream Street Stone, as if he had to share everything he'd found out the last couple of days. How he'd gone to Italy in the late sixties when the good movie parts started to dry up for him over here, and became a huge star, sort of like a black Clint Eastwood, not as big as Eastwood in his spaghetti Westerns, but still a cult figure on his own, the mysterious black man in black. Vinny knew some of that, but not that Dream Street had made nine movies in nine years.

"Like that Marvelous Hagler would do later on," Vinny said. "The colored bald guy who fought that great fight against Hearns?"

"Marvin Hagler wasn't as big as Dream Street was in the sixties," Sann said.

In the early eighties, Dream Street came back to the States, even got himself a good recurring role in a cop show, *Midtown North,* playing a detective just trying to hang on, live through the last year on the street before his pension.

"Then the show became a hit, and then that cop had to put off his retirement for another six years," Sann said. "You ever watch it?"

Vinny said, "Coupla times. I kept waiting for Dream Street to do that little foot shuffle thing he did, *bing bing bing,* and get the jab in the bad guy's face. But he'd just shoot them and look bored doing it."

"When the show finally went off," Frank Sann said, "Dream Street pretty much faded from public life, as they say."

"Me too," Vinny said. "I just didn't go anywheres."

They got off at Exit 70, took the connector road at Manorville, got on Route 27 East, which finally became a two-lane road in Southampton. They went past Southampton, and then through this little town with a huge windmill on the right, and then past a shopping center and were on their way into the town of Bridgehampton when Sann took a left. "Shortcut," he said, "guy at the paper who comes out here summers told me when I gave him the address."

Now they were on a road called Butter Lane, taking that to the end, taking a right when Sann said, "Okay, this is Scuttlehole," talking to himself more than Vinny, who could've been in fucking Iowa. All Vinny wanted to know is which way the ocean was. Sann said they would've had to go right off 27, they were heading north now, toward a town Vinny'd never heard of called Noyack.

"You see any of those beautiful people, you tell me," Vinny said.

Sann said he was on the lookout.

It took about forty more minutes and two wrong turns that took him into Sag Harbor both times, but now they were on a long road that went back into some woods, and coming up on a nice two-story house, what Sann said was built "saltbox" style, whatever that meant. He stopped about a hundred yards from the house, where the dirt-road driveway began.

"You're just going to go up, ring the doorbell?" Sann said.

Vinny shrugged. "You know what they always said about me. I got no couth."

May Stone, looking young still to Vinny, looking young and pretty, made it easy for him, smiling when she opened the door, as if she'd been expecting him. No shock, no surprise, just a smile as she came out on the porch and gave him a hug.

"Vincenzo," she said, the way Dream Street used to, "please come in."

It was an elegant-looking room, Vinny thought, not that he knew what any of the furniture was, or the paintings on the wall. There was one big table with a fancy lamp on it, surrounded by photographs of Dream Street and May, none from boxing, just them looking young and happy and made for each other.

She asked if she could get him something and Vinny said no, no thanks, he knew he was intruding, but that's what old people did, right?

"You never did stand on ceremony," she said. "In or out of the ring."

"I didn't know any better."

May Stone said, "I've got a million questions, but I guess the only one that matters is, to what do we owe this surprise?"

Vinny said, "I came to ask him a question." He looked around, aware now of how quiet the house was. "Is he here?"

Vinny saw something in her eyes now, something he couldn't read, he'd never been any good at reading women especially. Jesus, look at the record.

"He's not...he's not himself," she said finally.

She started to say something else and Vinny put up his hand, trying to keep things light, saying, "None of us are, except you, May, from the looks of you."

Vinny saw May Stone looking toward the back and before she could say anything he said, "Is he out there? Let me surprise him, I promise I won't be long."

May said "Surprise" now, trying to make it sound happy, the way you would at a party. Vinny thought it came out sad-sounding instead. Then she walked him through the kitchen to the back door and pointed to where Dream Street Stone was, out there at the other end of the backyard, which finally ended at a small duck pond. He was sitting by himself, in a big wooden chair, wearing a leather jacket with the collar pulled up.

"Vinny..." May said.

"Don't worry," Vinny said, "it's my turn to talk."

He walked across the lawn, rehearsing what he wanted to say, knowing he was only going to get one shot to get it right. When he was about twenty feet away from where Dream Street sat, he said quietly, "Hey, you want to go a few?"

Dream Street Stone turned around, the smile that the whole world loved once still on his face, a lot heavier than Vinny remembered, his hair snow white, but still a handsome bastard, no signs on that face that he'd ever been in any kind of fight in his life.

"Hey," Dream Street said, still smiling. "Hey you," and came over and shocked Vinny by hugging him.

"Hey," Dream Street Stone said again, and sat back down in the chair, turning it so it would face Vinny, still smiling.

"You okay?" Vinny said, and then shook his head, thinking. There was a great fucking icebreaker. "Of course you're okay," Vinny said, "you've still got May, look at you, sitting out here like the lord of the manor."

"You," Dream Street said again, looking happy as a kid.

And then it just came right out of Vinny, the way it had with Frank Sann that day at the apartment, not like he rehearsed exactly but right from his gut.

"Listen," he said. "I'm an old man. We're both old men." He looked at the water, not wanting to stare into Dream Street's smile just then, watching the ducks float lazy-like on the water instead, barely making a ripple on it. "Somebody once told me that late at night was the hour when guys told each other the truth. You know? Well, maybe it's the same way when you get late into your goddamn life, no matter how much you bullshitted yourself when you were younger, you want the truth now, you don't have the energy to lie. Now I know you're gonna think I'm crazy"—Vinny laughed, feeling like he was talking to himself, maybe just for himself—"hell, you probably always thought I was a little crazy, the way I kept coming, but there's something been bothering me all these years about the second fight in Boston. I forget things sometimes, it scares the shit out of me the way I forget things, maybe someday I won't even be able to remember this conversation, but I got to know something, once and for all. If I'm insulting you by asking the question, well, I apologize."

Vinny took a deep breath, the April morning too cold for his old bones, making him feel like it was still winter out. "I got to know why you didn't come out for the fifteenth round basically," Vinny said.

He turned now, looking right at Dream Street, who wasn't smiling the way he had been, a frown on his face now, as if Vinny had confused him somehow.

"You want to get up and pop me a good one for asking, go ahead, I probably deserve it for even asking the question. Maybe it's not even a question at all, now that I think about it. Maybe I'm begging you to please tell me that nobody got to you, that you just didn't have nothing left."

Dream Street Stone didn't say a word. All you could hear was the sound of one of the ducks behind them. But then the frown melted away, and he was smiling again.

"Hey," he said, getting up out of the chair again, giving Vinny another hug. "Hey you."

Vinny Tavernese had always thought of himself as a dim bulb, at least without boxing gloves on. His last year of school had been the seventh grade, their choice. But now he knew.

"You know who I am, Dream?" he said.

"Hey!" Dream Street said, brighter and louder than before. "Hey you!"

This time it was Vinny's turn. He hugged Dream Street Stone as hard as he could. When he finally pulled back, he saw May standing there.

"How long——?" Vinny began.

"Too long."

Vinny said, "He doesn't know——?"

"Not even me."

There were two chairs like the one Dream Street Stone was sitting in. May pulled them closer to him, and gestured for Vinny to sit down. He thought briefly about Frank Sann sitting there in the car, wondering what was happening. He'd go get him soon enough. He stared at Dream Street Stone, the smile frozen on his face as he watched one of the ducks go airborne, his eyes as empty as the house behind them, as still as the trees all around them.

"Talk to him," May said. "He doesn't know what you're talking about, but it seems to make him happy. Talk to us both, Vincenzo, about the old days," she said, taking his hand.

Now Vinny smiled.

"Don't worry," he said. "I remember everything."

THE MAN WHO FOUGHT ROLAND LASTARZA

by Joyce Carol Oates

And in that instant the Armory is silent. Every uplifted face still, frozen. Overhead lights are reeling like drunken birds. Where my eye is bleeding there's a halo of red light. No pain! Never pain again! Only this strange, wonderful silence. A giant black bubble swelling to burst. It was the moment I died, and I was happy.

This is not a very pretty story, and not just because it's about boxing. In a way, it's only incidentally about boxing. Its true subject is betrayal.

A story about the only person I've known, close to me, lodged deep in my memory like a beating heart, who took his own life.

Took his own life. These clumsy words. But words are what we say. We try our best, and words fail us.

Took his own life. This was said about Colum Donaghy, my father's friend after he died at the age of thirty-one in September 1958. Colum would be spoken of in two ways depending upon who the speaker was, how close to Colum and how respectful of his memory. To some, he would always be *the man who fought Roland LaStarza.* To others, he would be *the man who took his own life.*

My heart beat in fury when I heard them speak of my father's friend in that smug, pitying way. As if they had the right. As

273

if they knew. "Where'd he take his life to, if he took it!" I wanted to shout at them. "You have no right. You don't know."

In fact, no one knew. Not with certainty.

My own father, who'd been Colum's closest friend, hadn't known. The shock to him was so great, he never truly recovered. He would remember Colum Donaghy's suicide his whole life. But it was rare for him to speak of it. My mother warned us children: *Don't ask your father about it, you hear? Not a word about Colum Donaghy.* As if we required warning. You could see the hurt of it in my father's face, and the rage. *Don't ask. Don't ask. Don't!*

Colum's parents and relatives, especially the older Donaghys, could never accept it that he'd shot himself deliberately, at the base of his skull. They were Roman Catholics, to them *taking your own life* was a mortal sin. No matter the evidence of the county coroner's report, the police investigation, no matter how circumstances pointed to suicide, they had to believe it was an accident, but they refused to talk about that, too. My father said it's necessary for the Donaghys, let them think what they need to think. Like all of us.

Forty years ago. But vivid in my memory as a dream unfolding before my eyes.

And now my father has died, just five days ago. Which is to say New Year's Day of this new era 2000. "Outlived Colum by forty years so far," my father said last time I visited him. Shaking his head at the strangeness of it. "Christ, if Colum could see me now! Older than his father was then. Old people made him nervous. But maybe we'd have a laugh together, once he saw it was me."

"Know what? I'm betting on myself."

Colum Donaghy was a man who liked to laugh, and he laughed, telling my father this. Seeing the look in my father's face.

It was his Irish temperament, was it? Colum's first instinct was to laugh, as another man might steel himself against surprise. His eyes were pale blue like washed glass, and didn't always reflect laughter. There was a part of him held in reserve, calculated, wary. But when Colum entered a room it was like a flame rising, you couldn't turn your eyes away. He had a deceptively childlike face to which something had happened. Something with a story to it. A misshapen nose and scar tissue above his left eye like an icicle, that seemed to wink at you. There was a pattern of tiny scars like lacework in his forehead. A scattering of freckles like splashes of rain on his pale, coarse skin, and reddish blond hair, ribbed and rippled and worn a little long in the style of the day. And sideburns that offended the elder Donaghy men and older boxing fans (except if you kept Billy Conn in mind, flashy Billy as a model for Colum Donaghy). Colum had a rougher, wilder ring style than Conn, for sure. There were some observers who praised Colum for his natural gifts and for his "heart" but worried the boy had never learned to seriously box, he was all offense and not enough defense; whatever strategy his trainer had drilled into him before a fight he'd lose as soon as he got hit, and started throwing punches by instinct. Colum was a natural counter-puncher, that look of elation in his face like flame. *Now you hit me, now I can hit you. And hit, and hit you!*

At the time of his fight with Roland LaStarza in May 1958 in the Buffalo Armory, Colum was thirty years old, weighed one hundred eighty-seven compact, muscled pounds, and stood five feet ten and a half inches tall. Colum was such a forceful presence in and out of the ring, you were inclined to forget that he was a "small" heavyweight, like Floyd Patterson, like Marciano and LaStarza, and had shortish legs and a short reach, built powerfully, in the torso with the muscular stubby arms and smallish hands, that in a later era of Sonny Liston, Muhammad Ali, George Foreman, giant black heavyweights who have dominated the heavyweight division since, would have handicapped him from the start. And like most Caucasian boxers, he bled, and scarred easily, like his boxer friend in Syracuse he so admired, Carmen Basilio with his wreck of a face, Colum wore his scars proudly as badges of honor. *I wanted to stay pretty, I'd have been a ballet dancer.* Colum Donaghy was a natural light heavy, but there was no money in that division. And in the fifties, fighting in arenas and armories and clubs in Buffalo, Niagara Falls, Rochester, Syracuse and Albany, a few times in Cleveland, once as far west as Minneapolis, and St. Catharines, Ontario, Colum Donaghy looked good. Even when he lost on points, he looked good. And in Yewville, where he'd lived all his life, where he was known and liked by everyone, or almost everyone, he looked good. That quick, easy, boyish smile, the slightly crooked front teeth. His nose had been broken in an early Golden Gloves fight, rebroken in the Navy, where he'd made a name for himself as a light heavyweight, but it was a break that softened his hard-boned face and made you think, if you were a girl or woman and inclined to romance, that here was a "tough" man who wished for tenderness.

Like my father Patrick Hassler, whom nobody called "Pat," Colum was a man of moods. Gaiety, and sobriety, and melancholy, and anger smoldering like an underground fire. Maybe the moods were precipitated by drinking, or maybe the drinking was a way of tempering the moods. These were men you couldn't hope to know intimately, unless you already knew them; their friendships were forged in boyhood. If you hadn't grown up with Colum, you'd never truly be a friend of his, he'd never trust you and, as Colum had many times demonstrated, you couldn't trust him.

He confided in my father, though. Close as brothers they were and protective of each other. My father was the only person Colum told about betting on himself in the LaStarza fight, so far as my father knew, though after Colum's death rumors would circulate that he'd owed money to a number of people, including his manager, who'd been advancing him loans for years. Colum surprised my father with the revelation that he wasn't just going to win the fight with LaStarza, he was going to knock LaStarza out. His trainer was preparing him to box, box, box the opponent but Colum sure as hell wasn't going to box a guy who'd managed to keep Marciano at arm's length for ten rounds in their title fight, made Marciano look like an asshole, for sure Colum wasn't going to pussyfoot with the guy but go after him at the bell, first round, surprise the hell out of him, get him into a corner. "Believe me, I know how," Colum told my father seriously. "You can bet on me. This time. No fucking up this time. Maybe a TKO, a KO. See, I can't risk going the distance and lose on points. So I'm going to win the smartest way." Colum paused, breathing quickly. He had a way of watching you sidelong, narrow-eyed, cagey and alert as a wild creature. "Shortest distance between two points, see? I'm going to bet on myself."

My father was troubled by these revelations. He tried to dissuade his friend, not from winning the fight but from trying for a KO that might be disastrous; and from betting on himself if he was betting serious money. "You could lose double, man."

Said Colum with his easy smile, "No. I'm gonna win double."

They were our fathers, we did not judge them.

The bond between them was they'd been born in the same neighborhood in Yewville, New York, in the same year, 1928. Their families were neighbors. Their fathers worked in the same machine shop. They belonged to the same parish, St. Timothy's. Colum Donaghy and Patrick Hassler, high school friends who'd enlisted together in the U.S. Navy in 1949 and were sent to active duty in Korea the following year, there was that bond between them of which they had no need to speak.

These were not men who were sentimental about the past: they survived it.

Of Colum's Yewville children (the mysterious rumor was he had others, outside his marriage) it was Agnes I knew. Or wished to know. She was a year behind me in school. With her father's fair, whitish skin that never darkened in summer, only burnt. With her father's cold blue eyes that could laugh, or drill through you as if you didn't exist. For a long time Agnes was *the girl whose dad is*

Colum Donaghy the boxer, and she basked in that renown, then so suddenly she became *the girl whose dad took his own life,* and her eyes shrank from us, all of the Donaghys were like kicked dogs. I was drawn always to Agnes, Agnes who was so pretty, but Agnes shunned me, hatred for me shone in her eyes and I never knew why.

Nothing so disturbs us as another's hatred of us. Our own secret hatreds, how natural they seem. How inevitable.

Colum Donaghy would say zestfully, "Before a fight, I hate a guy's guts. I just want to wipe him out. After a fight, I could love 'im to death."

Our fathers were young in those years, in their early thirties. They were of a generation that grew up in the Depression, they'd been made to grow up fast. Most of them had dropped out of school by the age of sixteen, were married a few years later, began having kids. Yet they would remain boys in their souls, restless, hungry for more life. "Boxing is a kid's game, essentially," my father said. "That's why it's deadly, kids are out for blood."

They were our fathers, we had no way of knowing them. We adored them and were fearful of them. Their lives were mysterious to us, as our mothers' lives and our own lives could never be. *I'm just a woman, what the hell does it matter what I think,* I'd overheard my mother once saying, laughing wanly over the phone to a woman friend, and this did not seem a misstatement to me, or even a complaint exactly. No man would ever make such a remark. I knew that my father was co-owner of a small auto and truck repair and gas station, and I knew that Colum Donaghy supplemented his irregular boxing income by driving a truck, working in a local quarry, a lumberyard. I knew such facts without understanding what they might mean. None of us children had any idea what our fathers earned yearly. How much a boxer made, for instance.

A locally popular, much-loved boxer? Whose picture was often in the *Yewville Post* and the *Buffalo Evening News* sports pages?

Our fathers were to us their bodies. Their male bodies. So tall, so massive-seeming, like horses magnificent and dangerous, unpredictable. They were men who drank, weekends. At such times we knew to recognize the slurred voice, the flare of white in the eye sudden as a lighted match, nostrils quivering like those of a horse about to bite or kick—these were signs that alerted us, prepared us to flee, as the casual lifting of a hand at a window will send birds flying to safety in the trees. Young, we learned that the male body is beautiful and dangerous and not to be trifled with.

The safest time with these adult men was when they were drinking and laughing, maybe celebrating one of Colum's fight victories, and he'd be treating his friends to cases of beer in someone's backyard. It was a time of good luck and celebration and they'd smile to see a child appear; to be hoisted with a grunt onto a knee or onto a shoulder for a piggyback ride. Grinning Colum Donaghy would extend his muscled right arm out straight from the shoulder, make a fist and invite a child to swing from his wrist, he was so *strong*. No other man so strong. If you were a little older, and if you were a girl, and even just a little pretty, he'd make you blush with flattery, your own dad would smile and it was a time of perfect joy rushing into your face like heated blood to be recalled forty years later. And your dad, Patrick, having to agree yes, you weren't half bad-looking, and Colum Donaghy fixing his sly blue eyes on you, saying with a wink, *This little girl takes after her ma, not her pa, eh?* And all the men laughed, your dad the loudest.

When Colum Donaghy died the obituaries in the papers would end with *Colum Donaghy is survived by.* How strange those words seemed to me! *Survived by.* Only just close family members were named, of course.

The friends who loved him were not named. My father Patrick Hassler was not named.

After Colum's body was found twelve miles from Yewville, off a country road near farmland owned by Donaghy relatives, Yewville police questioned Colum's male friends, and it was my father who'd had to admit to police that the handgun Colum used to shoot himself was one he'd owned since Korea. No one in the

Donaghy family admitted knowing that Colum had this gun hidden away somewhere, certainly his wife hadn't known. My father was sickened by having to give such testimony. He believed it was like kicking Colum when Colum was down, defenseless. It outraged him to speak of Colum Donaghy to strangers.

My father believed that a man has a right to privacy, dignity. After death, as before.

Patrick Hassler was two inches taller than Colum Donaghy, bigger-boned, with heavy sloping shoulders and a fatty-muscled torso and long sinewy arms, big hands, weighing well over two hundred pounds, you'd think of the two that he was the heavyweight boxer, not Colum Donaghy the smaller man, but you'd be mistaken. Size has nothing to do with boxing skills. You're born with the instinct or you are not. You're born with a knockout punch or you are not. When they were in their twenties Colum and my father sparred together a few times at the Yewville gym where Colum trained, both men in boxing trunks, T-shirts, protective headgear and wearing twelve-ounce gloves, and someone (my mother?) took snapshots of these occasions. My father marveled at how fast Colum was, it was impossible to hit him! Colum invited my father to hit him hard as he could, and my father tried, he tried, throwing wide awkward punches that, even if they landed, were merely glancing blows to be deflected by Colum's raised gloves or elbows, of no more force than a child's slaps, and within five minutes my father, who believed himself in decent physical condition was flush-faced and panting, and his eyes brimmed with hurt and indignation and frustration. Colum was no Willie "The Wisp" Pep, not a graceful boxer, yet still he scarcely needed to move his feet to avoid my father's blows, without seeming effort he slipped blows thrown at his head, moving back then and laterally, and everyone in the gym crowded around the ring cheering him in mock encouragement—"Get him, Hassler! Nail that Mick bastard!" And Colum laughed and ducked and swerved back inside with a flurry of left jabs to Patrick's body gentle as love taps (he would afterward claim) that nonetheless left the larger man's fleshy sides flaming and his ribs aching for days. Patrick was panting, "God damn you, Donaghy, stand still and fight!" and Colum laughed, saying, "That's what you want, Hassler? I don't think so."

Snapshots of these sparring matches were kept under the glass top of a cocktail table in our living room. For years. They'd been taken in the early fifties. So anyone visiting us who had not known of Colum Donaghy would ask who that was with Patrick, and the short reply was *An old friend of Patrick's, who'd once fought Roland LaStarza in Buffalo.* If my dad was present, there was no longer reply.

After Colum died my mother wondered if she should remove the snapshots, how heartbreaking they were, my dad and his friend posed in the ring with their arms around each other's shoulders, grinning like kids. But she was afraid to ask my dad point-blank. Just to bring up the subject of Colum was risky. And who knows, it might set off my dad to discover one day that the snapshots were gone from the cocktail table, he had a quick temper and after he'd stopped drinking he was anxious and edgy as a spooked horse, so the snapshots remained there in our living room for years.

There were many more snapshots with Colum Donaghy in them, in our family photo album.

Say there's this special place somewhere on Earth. Where the inhabitants know ahead of time when they will die. The exact hour, minute. Not only this, they know when Earth itself will end. The Universe will end. How's their way of living going to differ from ours?

I'll tell you: they would measure time differently.

Like they wouldn't be counting forward from the past. No first century, second century, twentieth century, et cetera. Instead, they would be counting backward from the end. People saying, What's the date, the date is X. (X years before the end.) Somebody saying, How old am I, I'm X. (X years before he dies.)

And how'd these people get along, what kind of civilization would they have? I believe they would be good to one another. They would be kind, decent. Not like us! But they would like to laugh, too. Have good times, celebrate. Because, see, they wouldn't need to wonder about the future. They would know the future from the day of their births, they would be at total peace with it.

Colum Donaghy was one to say strange things. He'd get this glimmering look in his face. After an out-of-town fight where he'd managed to win, but just barely; and took some hard punches to the head and body. A cruel welt on the underside of his jaw, fresh scar tissue in his eyebrow. Such a Goddamned bleeder, Colum joked he started to bleed at the weigh-in. Maybe it was funny? But a white man's face can get used up, hit too many times. What's being done to the capillaries in the brain, you don't want to think. Colum liked to say with a shrug, *There's fights where even if you win, you lose.*

This was a fact nobody much wanted to know. Not in Yewville or Buffalo among Colum "The Kid" Donaghy's admirers. His trainer and his manager surely didn't want to know. It was nothing to be discussed. Like enlisting in the Navy, being sent overseas to Korea, for sure you might get killed, you accept that possibility.

A kid just going into boxing, fighting in the Golden Gloves at age fifteen, fourteen, as Colum had done, he won't know it. A young guy just turning pro, he won't want to know it. And by the time he knows it, could be he's a legendary champion like Joe Louis, Henry Armstrong, it's too late for him to know it.

Even if you win, you lose.

You win, you lose.

And what of fixed fights, another fact of boxing in the fifties nobody liked to acknowledge. That of bribed referees and judges. A boxer wants to win, it's his life on the line, Colum used to flare his nostrils saying every time he stepped into the ring he was fighting for his life, but there are boxers who have given up wanting to win, their spirits have been broken, there's a deadness in their eyes and they know they're being hired to fight and lose, they're being hired as "opponents" to showcase another guy's skills, some hot young kid on the way up. Their paydays are about over, and they know it. So they will sign on, and go through the motions of fighting for four, five, six rounds, then suddenly they're on the ropes and the crowd is wild for blood, they're down, they're struggling to get up, on their feet seeming dazed but with their gloves uplifted so the referee won't stop the fight, and the young kid rushes them with a flurry of hard, showy punches, and another time they're down, and this time counted out. And it isn't the case that the older boxer has been bribed, or the fight's been fixed, not exactly. But the outcome is known beforehand. Like a script somebody has written and the boxers act out.

In the fifties, in any case. A long time ago.

If you rebelled, past a certain age, if you were a midlevel boxer who'd never made the top ten ranking in your division and your name no longer generated ticket sales, you were in trouble. It would be said of you you're *washed up*. You're *on the skids*. If you persisted in being a maverick, your career was over, you were out *on your ass*. If you talked carelessly and word got back to the wrong people, you might be *dead meat*.

So Colum said unexpected things. Interviewed in the *Buffalo Evening News* after he'd won a locally big, money-making match when he was in his mid-twenties, he'd said in reply to a reporter's question about alleged criminal connections with boxing that he'd fire his manager if he heard even that the man was taking calls from "those s.o.b.'s." (This was a time when boxers of the stature of Graziano, Zale, Robinson were being subpoenaed by the New York State Athletic Commission investigating bribe offers to fix fights.) A few years later, interviewed prominently in the *Yewville Post* before the LaStarza fight, which would be the biggest fight held in the Buffalo Armory since an aging Joe Louis came

283

through in 1951, Colum promised the boxing crowd "exactly what they deserved." Which meant—what?

And with his friends Colum said even stranger, more enigmatic things that no one knew how to interpret. Saying he was a Mick, he knew not to trust anybody at his back. Saying when his big payday finally came, he'd be giving money to the IRA back in Belfast, Ireland—"So those poor bastards can get some justice there." Saying he wasn't scared of anybody in the ring, white, black, spic, but anybody out of the ring, he was. My dad and the others never knew if they were expected to laugh, or whether all this was dead serious.

Like when after a few beers Colum got onto one of his subjects, which was time. *This special place on earth where the inhabitants know ahead of time when they will die.* Talking so intense, excited. And his friends tried their best to follow. My dad said it was like some puzzle in the newspaper, Einstein and atomic physics and sending men to the moon. You could sort of follow it, but you only thought you were following it. Actually, you were lost. You couldn't repeat a word of it. And Colum was like that, talking faster and faster, and you'd be like trying to keep up with him in the ring. Quick as you might be, Colum was quicker. "See? A man would say, you asked him how old he is, 'I'm X years.' Like me, Colum Donaghy, might be five. By which it's meant, 'Five years till I die.' Instead of saying my age measured from when I was born, I'd say my age measured from when I would die, see? 'Five' means five years left to live."

Colum's buddies shook their heads over this logic. If it was logic.

Mike Kowicki pulled a face. "So? What the hell's that supposed to mean? I don't get it."

Otto Lanza, who was generally conceded the most educated of the guys, he'd graduated from high school and owned a cigar store that also sold newspapers and paperback books, shook his head reprovingly. "Kind of morbid, ain't it? Thinking that way."

"It's the opposite of 'morbid'!" Colum said. "It's what you call 'hy-po-the-sis.'" Colum pronounced this word, which surely had never before been uttered at the Checkerboard Tavern bar in its history, with care.

My dad said, "What's the point, Colum? We're listening."

Colum said, like a child who's just discovered something, "The point is, see, if we could know how things turn out, how they end, we would experience time differently. We would count backward from the end, see? Like a boxer knowing how a fight was going to end, which round, he'd know how to pace himself, what kind of mind-set to go into it with. See?"

"Wait," my dad said, "he knows how it's going to end, what's the point of trying? If he's going to win, he wins; if not, he can't. Why'd he do anything at all? Why even show up?"

The others laughed. "Just collect his purse," Otto Lanza said sagely.

But Colum was shaking his head, annoyed. A slow flush came into his face. Maybe this was a factor he hadn't considered, or maybe it was far from the point of what he was trying to say; the reason he was so involved. "See, if we knew these things, we'd behave better. Like my last fight, I KO'd the guy in eight rounds, but I was pretty sloppy in the first rounds, I kept getting thrown off stride, I could've tried harder, looked better. See? I could've won with style."

"You won by a KO, so what? You don't get more money, winning with *style*."

Colum considered this. My dad said afterward that for sure, Colum was thinking hell yes, you do get more money if you've got style, eventually you get a lot more money. Because you get matched with top contenders and your purses improve. But that was a subject of a certain fineness or subtlety Colum wouldn't have wanted to acknowledge. The difference between "The Kid" Donaghy and, for instance, LaStarza, Marciano, Walcott. He said:

"See, if we *knew*, we wouldn't be *guessing*. Making mistakes.

If you were going to marry your wife, from the start when you first met her, you'd treat her a helluva lot better. Right? If you knew how you'd be crazy for your kids once they got born, you wouldn't be, you know, scared as hell ahead of time. That's what I mean." Colum looked at his friends in his strange squinting way, as if daring them to disagree. And they were sort of conceding the point or anyway had gotten beyond a serious wish to contest it. What the hell? Let Donaghy talk. They loved "The Kid" when he was in his weird moods and insisting upon buying rounds of beers, dropping ten-dollar bills on the bar like he had pockets of them, an endless supply.

"The crappy thing about dying is you only get to do it once," Colum added. "The second time, see?—you'd go with style."

The man who fought Roland LaStarza, in Buffalo back in the fifties. Whatever happened to him?

A boxer who's going to be a champion is on the rise from the first fight onward. He's going to win, win, win. He's going to win his amateur fights, he's going to win his first pro fights. He's protected from harm or accident by a luminous light enveloping his body, like Athena protected her soldiers in the Trojan War. He will not be seriously hit, he will not feel his mortality. He will not be matched with fighters who might beat him, too soon. His career is a matter of rising, ascending. To him, it feels like destiny. It does not feel as if it's being arranged by human beings. Money changes hands, but it isn't a matter of money. Is it?

These boxers rise through their ranks undefeated. They win by spectacular KO's, or failing that, they win on points. They win, consistently. The future champion is *one who wins*. If two future champions are fighting in the same division at the same time, their canny managers will not make a deal for them to fight, too soon. Because the big payday is somewhere ahead.

Then there are the others who are not going to be champions.

They win, and they lose. They have a streak of wins, and then suddenly they lose. They lose again, and then they win. Their careers are what you'd call *erratic, up-and-down.* They do predictable things in the ring because their boxing skills are limited, like a small deck of cards. But they do unpredictable things, too, because their boxing skills are limited, like a small deck of cards. And sometimes there's a wild card in the deck.

This was Colum "The Kid" Donaghy.

He began boxing as a kid of fifteen, in 1943. He fought his last fight in September 1958.

Never would Colum Donaghy be ranked among the top ten in his division. In the Navy, he'd been a light heavyweight winner and he'd looked good against that tough competition. In the places like the old Buffalo Armory, matched with men like himself, boxers with showy aggressive skills and little or no defensive strategies, he'd looked very good, crowds loved Colum "The Kid" Donaghy. And grinning happily out at them, covered in sweat like cheap glittering jewels and an eye swollen shut, blood dribbling from a nostril as the referee held his gloved hand high amid a deafening roar of cheers, yells, applause, "The Kid" loved them.

There's these weird times, Christ! It's like I could bless everybody I see. Like I'm a priest or something, and God gave me the power to bless. My heart is so full, feels like it's going to burst.

Know what I mean? Or am I some kind of dope or something?

It's like I got to go through what I do, hitting, and being hit, hurting a guy, and being hurt, before I can bless those people? Before I can feel that kind of, whatever it is, happiness.

Next day, anyway, it's gone. Next day I'm feeling like shit, can't hardly get out of bed and my eye swollen shut and I'm pissing blood and the fucking phone better be off the hook, fuck it I don't want any interference in the household.

"That poor woman. I don't envy her."

So the Yewville women spoke of Colum Donaghy's wife Carlotta. She was a brunette Susan Hayward look-alike from Niagara Falls. She hadn't any family in Yewville, and few women friends. A glamorous woman when you saw her ringside, and photographed in the papers beside her husband, but at other times she looked what you'd have to call almost ordinary, shopping at Loblaw's, pushing a baby in a stroller and trying to hang on to a toddler's hand to prevent him from rushing into the street.

"When he brought her here to live, she looked so *young*."

When Colum wasn't in training, it's true Colum did drink. Coming off a fight, whether he'd won the fight or lost, he'd start to drink pretty seriously. Because now it was normal life, it was the life of normal, average men, men who worked at daily jobs, in garages, in lumberyards, driving trucks, taking orders from others, trying to make money like you'd try to suck moisture out of some enormous unnameable thing pressing sucker-lips against it filled with revulsion for what you did, what you must do, if you wanted to survive. *These times, it's like I saw into the heart of things. The mystery. And there's no mystery. Just trying to survive.* It was known that Colum and Carlotta had married within a few weeks of meeting, crazy for each other but prone to quarrels, misunderstandings. Each was an individual accustomed to attention from the opposite sex. It was known that Colum loved his wife very much, and their children. If he lost his temper sometimes, if he frightened them, still he loved Carlotta very much, and their children.

Yet sometimes, specific reasons unknown, Colum would disappear from Yewville to live in Buffalo. He had many friends there, men and women both. Sometimes he'd only just move out of his house and live across town. Friends took him in, eager to make room for Colum Donaghy. Rarely did he pay rent. He'd stay in a furnished apartment in downtown Yewville near the railroad yard, which was also in a neighborhood of Irish bars where Colum "The Kid" was very popular, his boxing photos and posters taped to the walls. For a few weeks, or maybe just a few days, he'd live apart from his family; then Carlotta would ask him to return, and Colum would promise that things would be different, he loved her and the kids, he'd die for them he vowed, and he meant it. Colum Donaghy was a man who always meant the words he uttered, when he uttered them.

Sometimes it was Carlotta who left Yewville, took the children to stay with their grandparents in Niagara Falls. And it was Colum who went to bring them back.

"She's taking a chance. Him with that temper. And his drinking—"

"What kind of woman would stay with him? You can't trust that kind of Irish."

Always there seemed to be women in Colum's life, so naturally there were misunderstandings. There were complications, crises. There were threats of violence against Colum and occasional acts of violence. Scuffles in the parking lots of taverns, aggrieved husbands and boyfriends accosting Colum so he had no choice but to "defend himself," once breaking his fist on a stranger's jaw, so an upcoming fight had to be postponed. Another time, in a woman's house in Albany, police were called to break up a fight involving Colum and several others. "What can I do? These things happen." A man who's a boxer is attractive to both men and women, they want to be loved by him or hit and hurt by him, possibly there's little difference, they only know they yearn for something.

When he wasn't actively in training, and in the rocky aftermath of a fight, never mind if he won or lost, Colum was restless and edgy as a wild creature in captivity; drank and ate too much, to the point of making himself sick; couldn't sleep for more than an hour or two at a time, walking the nighttime streets of Yewville, or driving in his car aimlessly; waking at dawn not knowing where he was, on a country road miles from home, having fallen asleep at last. He was happiest drinking with his friends, watching the Friday night fights on TV, at a local bar. At such times carried out of himself in a bliss of excitement, subjugation. For he understood he was in thrall to boxing: to that deep rush of happiness, that blaze of life, that only boxing could give him. And he wanted even the yearning that swelled up in him as he watched the televised fights, broadcast from fabled Madison Square Garden, the very center of the professional boxing world, where he'd been waiting, waiting, waiting to be called to fight, waiting so badly he could taste it. Colum Donaghy waiting for his turn, his chance, his payday. Though money had little to do with it, except as a public sign of grace. *A specially ordered canary-yellow Buick convertible, he'd buy. A new house in a better part of town. Something for his parents, who deserved better than they'd got from life so far? A week in Miami Beach?* Colum "The Kid" Donaghy, who wasn't getting any younger. Some of the kids in the gym, eyeing him. Maybe he's slowing down. Waiting for five years, waiting for eight years, ten years. But his manager Gus Smith was just a local Buffalo guy, in his sixties, near obese, cigar smoker with a goiter for a nose, good-hearted and decent but second-rate, unconnected, whom nobody in the boxing business owed favors, and the truth was Colum's record was not that impressive, he'd thrown away fights he should have won, thrown away opportunities because he had other things on his mind, like women, or Carlotta giving him grief, or he owed money, or somebody owed him, too many distractions, he'd become one of those wild Mick brawlers the crowds cheer even when they lose, so losing was too often confused with winning. Like gold coins falling through his fingers, those years. There was the hot exhilarating rush seeing the coins fall, and no way of guessing one day they'd all be gone.

So he was waiting, he was a hungry Irish kid waiting all his life. *If there's some other world, fuck it I expect I'll be waiting there too.*

His record going into the fight with LaStarza in May 1958 was forty-nine wins, eleven losses and one draw. LaStarza's record was fifty-eight wins, five losses. But two of LaStarza's losses, in 1950 and 1953, were to Rocky Marciano, who would be the single heavyweight boxer in history to retire undefeated, and the second match with Marciano was for the heavyweight title. And LaStarza had mixed it up for Marciano for ten rounds before he was TKO'd in the eleventh.

Colum said excitedly, "That fight?—LaStarza came close. If it'd been a decision, he'd won. Shows it can be done, the Rock ain't invincible."

True, LaStarza may have been ahead on points through ten rounds of the fight, but only because, and this is a big only, he'd boxed a cautious fight, determined to keep the stronger Marciano at bay as you'd keep a coiled-up cobra at bay, if you were lucky, wlth a pole. But Marciano was relentless, always pushing forward, always aggressive, maintaining a steady pace, not fast, deliberate, dogged, knowing what he was going to do when he was in a position to do it. With Marciano as with Louis, the cagiest opponent could run but he couldn't hide. It was only a matter of time. "Like that story we read in school," my dad said, "a guy is caught between a pit and a pendulum, and it's only a matter of time."

Now Colum knew this, or should have known, but didn't want to admit it. He was eccentric like many boxers, he took contrary views that in oblique ways were satisfying to him if mystifying to others. Watching the Marciano–LaStarza fight on TV, in a bar with my dad and their friends, he was too restless to remain still, moving about excited, panting, calling out instructions to LaStarza as if he were ringside. "C'mon! Nail 'im! Use that right!" Each time the bell rang signaling the end of a round Colum would snap his fingers: "LaStarza." Meaning LaStarza won the round. When, in Round Nine, Marciano slipped to the canvas, Colum protested the referee should have ruled it a knockdown; and when, in Round Eleven, Marciano knocked LaStarza through the ropes and out onto the ring apron, Colum protested it was a push, a foul. Sure, Marciano threw a few low blows. His ring style lacked finesse. But the knockdown was a clean one and everybody knew it, just as everybody including LaStarza understood that LaStarza had lost that fight. If he'd kept on his feet for fifteen rounds with Marciano hammering away at him to the body, to the head, to the arms, practically breaking the man's arms and leaving them weltered in bruises like battered meat, LaStarza might have been permanently injured.

But Colum, stubborn and contentious, seemed to have been watching a different fight. This was years before the deal with LaStarza was even being dreamt of by Colum's manager, yet Colum seemed to foresee that one day he might fight Roland LaStarza, forget Marciano for now, it was his unconscious wish to build up LaStarza, the man who'd been a serious heavyweight title contender for years, and would be taking home a pretty decent purse from the night's fight, and Colum Donaghy three hundred fifty miles away in upstate western New York is hungry for some of this, it's his turn, his time, how badly he wants to be fighting in Madison Square Garden in these televised Friday night fights, broadcast throughout the entire United States, and people in Yewville and Buffalo crowded around their sets and cheering him on. "See? LaStarza came pretty close. It can be done."

My dad said when he heard this, he just looked at Colum, didn't say a word. Because already in his imagination Colum was beyond LaStarza, he'd fought and beaten LaStarza and was ready to fight the legendary Marciano himself. That was the meaning of *It can be done.*

"Oh, Colum! Come *on.*"

I'm remembering the time I came home from school, I was in sixth grade at the time, and my mom and Colum Donaghy were talking earnestly together in the kitchen. They were drinking beer (Molson's, out of bottles) and talking in rapid lowered voices, Colum in a freshly laundered white T-shirt, khaki pants, gym shoes seated at the Formica-topped kitchen table, my mom leaning back against the rim of the sink, and in my memory she's wearing a cotton dress with a vivid strawberry print, short sleeves and a flared skirt, and her slender legs are pale and bare, and her feet in open sandals because it's a warm day in late May. And her hair that's chestnut brown is soft and curly around her face as if she recently washed it. And she's laughing, in her tentative nervous way. "Oh, Colum! Come on."

I wondered what they'd been talking about, my mother breathless and girlish. Where usually she's preoccupied, and two sharp vertical lines run between her eyebrows, even when her face is in repose.

It was vaguely known to me that my dad and mom had been engaged to be married twice; that something had gone wrong, some misunderstanding, in that murky region of time before my birth that both fascinated and repelled, and my mom had been "in love with" Colum Donaghy; and this "love" had lasted for six months, and had then ended; and again my dad and mom were together, and engaged, and married quickly. They were both so young, in their early twenties. They'd gone away from Yewville with no warning to be married by a justice of the peace in Niagara Falls, surprising and outraging their families. *Like it was something to be ashamed of, and not proud. Marrying that girl after she'd left him for Donaghy. Taking her back, after Donaghy.*

How I knew these facts, which could not have been told to me directly, I have no idea. I would no more have asked any relative about such things than I would have asked my proud, touchy father how much he made a year, repairing cars and trucks and selling gas out on the highway. I would no more have asked my mother a personal question than I would have confided in her the early-adolescent anxieties of my own life.

Had she left Donaghy, or had Donaghy left her.

This was not a question. This was a proposition.

My mother's name was Lucille, "Lucy." When I was a little girl and saw this name spelled out, I thought it was a way of spelling "lucky." And when I told my mom this she laughed sadly and ran her fingers through my hair. "Me? 'Lucky'? No. I'm Lucy."

But later she hugged me, she said, "Hey, I am lucky. I'm the luckiest girl in the world to have *you*."

I was the oldest of Lucy and Patrick Hassler's three children, and the only girl. A daughter born within a year of their run-away wedding. If there were whispers and rumors in Yewville about who my father truly was, I did not know of them. And if I knew of them by way of my malicious girl cousins, I did not acknowledge them. I never did, and I never will.

Now my mother Lucy has been dead for nine years, and my father Patrick for five days.

That May afternoon was a delirium of wind! The air was filled with tiny flying maple seeds, some of them caught in my hair. I'd been running, I pushed through the screen door into the kitchen and there were Colum Donaghy and my mom talking earnestly together, and my mom was laughing, her nervous, sad laugh, unless it was a hopeful laugh, which my brothers and I rarely heard, and my mom was wearing lipstick which rarely she wore, and seeing me she quickly straightened her back, her startled eyes appeared dilated as if looking at me, her daughter, she saw no one, nothing. As if in that instant she'd forgotten who I was.

Colum Donaghy turned to me, smiling. If he was surprised at me bursting into the kitchen breathless, he didn't give a sign. He smiled:

"H'lo there, honey."

I muttered a greeting. I was very embarrassed.

They talked to me about nothing, my mother's voice was eager and bright and false as a TV voice trying to sell you something you don't want. I walked through the kitchen and into the hall and upstairs, my heart thudding. Out of a small oval mirror on my bedroom wall, a mirror my father had made for me framed in wood painted pink, there glared my ferocious eleven-year-old's face.

"I hate you. All of you."

A sensation of pure loathing rose in me, bitter as bile. At the same time I was hoping they'd call me back downstairs. I understood that I could not be a girl as beautiful as Colum Donaghy's wife Carlotta or pretty as Lucy my mother; I understood, as surely as if my sixth-grade teacher had spelled it out in chalk on the blackboard of our classroom, that no man like Colum Donaghy would ever look at me as he'd been looking at my mother when I pushed through the screen door.

Still, the words echo in memory. So lightly tossed off, fleeting as breath. *H'lo there, honey.*

After thirty a boxer's legs begin to go, and fast. If he's a brawler who hasn't taken care of himself, a crowd pleaser who trades blows confident the crowd will always adore him for holding nothing back, his legs will go faster. His punch he'll keep till the end. Maybe. But the legs, the legs wear out. Breath wears out. By the age of thirty-five you're an old man, by the age of forty you're unspeakably old. Colum Donaghy was thirty years old by the time he fought Roland LaStarza in the Buffalo Armory. But LaStarza was thirty-one. Both boxers had been young for a long time. Still, Marciano had retired undefeated two years before at the age of thirty-three, in his prime. Or nearly. So it didn't always mean that boxers beyond thirty were *old*. That their lives were speeding by like landscape glimpsed from a car window.

"It isn't a matter of old, young," Colum argued, "it's got nothing to do with calendar age. Look at Willie Pep, Archie Moore. Look at Walcott, thirty-eight when he won the fucking title."

My father said, "So you got plenty of time, you're thinking, eh, Donaghy?" The men laughed, listening.

Colum said, "That's right. If it happens soon."

Then in the late winter of 1958, the deal was made.

How much negotiating had gone into it, how many calls between Gus Smith and Roland LaStarza's manager, what the exact payment would be for each boxer and what sort of promises were made not in the contract, no one except a very few individuals would know. Certainly the boxers would not know. But a deal was made at last, and the media were notified: a match between LaStarza and Donaghy was set as the main card for a Saturday evening of boxing, May 20, 1958, in the Buffalo Armory.

The most exciting local sports news of the year! Colum Donaghy, the popular heavyweight who'd never moved away from his hometown, Yewville, was scheduled to fight a major heavy- weight, an Italian glamor figure who'd "almost beaten" Marciano for the title and who was still a highly regarded contender and a TV favorite. (Or at least he'd been before his year of inactivity and losses to obscure fighters in places like Cleveland, Akron, Miami Beach.) How'd it happen, such a coup?

Gus Smith, interviewed locally, had a terse answer to this question: "It happened."

Colum called my father to tell him the good news before it broke. My father said, "This is great news, Colum. Congratulations." Trying to keep the dread out of his voice.

"Fucking fantastic, ain't it?"

"Colum, it is."

"Me and Carlotta, we're going out to celebrate tonight. At the Top Hat." The Top Hat was a well-known glitzy nightclub in Buffalo where individuals known in the media as *sports figures,* and their noisy entourages, often gathered on weekends. "You and Lucy want to join us? My treat."

"That sounds good, Colum. Let me check with Lucy and get back to you."

"Hey." Colum caught the signal. "Aren't you happy for me, Hassler?"

"Sure I'm happy for you."

"You're thinking—what? I can't beat LaStarza?"

"No."

"You're thinking I *can?*"

My father paused just a little too long. Colum said angrily: *"I'm going to win, fuck it! I can beat LaStarza."*

"Right. If anybody can, you can, Colum."

"What's that supposed to mean? Fucking condescending!"

"You can beat LaStarza, sure."

"You don't exactly sound overjoyed."

My father would recount how he'd been tongue-tied. Almost shy. Sweat breaking out on his forehead, in his armpits. Damned glad Colum couldn't see him, he'd have been madder than hell. "Colum, sure I am. It's just a surprise. It's—terrific news, what we've been waiting for, but a surprise. Isn't it?"

Colum muttered, "Maybe to you, man. Not to me."

"Colum, it's just that I wonder—"

"Save yourself the effort, okay? *I'm* not."

Colum slammed down the receiver, that was that.

Patrick would wonder, *What was happening, and what was going to happen?*

Because there was something fishy about the deal. Something in the evasive way Gus Smith talked about it, which wasn't characteristic of the garrulous old man. And there was something in the vehement way Colum kept insisting, as the weeks passed, that he was going to win the fight, not on points but by a knockout; he'd give LaStarza the fight of his life, Colum boasted, and make the New York boxing crowd, those bastards, take notice of him. "It's my turn. I always deserved better." Colum confided in my father he wasn't going to follow his trainer's instructions, boxing LaStarza in the opening rounds, he was going to go straight at him, like Dempsey rushing out against Willard, or tearing into Firpo. Like LaMotta, Graziano.

"LaStarza's manager looks at my record, thinks Donaghy is a pushover. Sure. It's a miscalculation in my favor. They see a fucking lousy draw in St. Catharines, Ontario! To a Canuck! So why should LaStarza train hard? This Donaghy is a small-town punk. I saw in the paper, LaStarza isn't in the best condition, after a year off. You hear things. Marciano almost broke his arms, shredded the muscles, he could hardly lift them afterward. And money he owes. It's just a payday for him up here. But me, I'm fighting for my life." Colum grinned, showing his crooked teeth. "See? *I can't lose.*"

You never knew how Colum meant these words. He couldn't

lose because he was too good a fighter, or he couldn't lose because losing this fight was unthinkable.

The fight that ended in a draw in St. Catharines, Ontario?

Until the LaStarza fight, this had been the worst luck of Colum Donaghy's career. When he'd been twenty-seven, working in the Yewville stone quarry to support his young family, forty back-breaking hours a week, therefore Goddamned grateful for any fight Gus Smith could arrange, anywhere. Colum would fight guys who outweighed him by twenty, even thirty pounds, for five hundred dollars. For four hundred. Three-fifty! Sure he'd take a chance, fighting in some place he didn't know, across the border in Ontario with a boxer he'd never heard of except he liked the name: O'Hagan. Between the Canuck O'Hagan and the Yank Donaghy they'd sell out the house, right?

A dozen or more of Colum's Yewville friends, including my father, drove to see the fight, and ever afterward it would be one of their tales of outrage and sorrow, Goddamn how Colum had been cheated of a win. It was an eight-round fight and Colum had won at least six of those rounds, beating up on his fattish thirty-six-year-old opponent who'd lost his mouthpiece in the last round, but managed to stay on his feet so the fucking local judges wouldn't allow the local favorite "Irish" O'Hagan to lose, declaring a draw. A draw! The judges had slipped out of the arena when the referee announced the decision, there were cheers, and a scattering of indignant boos, but the cheers drowned out the boos, and O'Hagan looking shame-faced (both eyes swollen shut, nose broken) waved to his fans even as a sullen-faced Colum Donaghy climbed out of the ring indignant, like a rejected prince and stalked away. Sports reporters for every U.S. paper agreed it had been a shameful episode. The New York State Athletic Commission was going to investigate, though it had no Canadian jurisdiction. Local headlines made Colum a hero, briefly: HEAVYWEIGHT DONAGHY CHEATED IN CONTROVERSIAL ONTARIO DECISION. In interviews Colum made it a point to be good-natured, philosophical. "At least they didn't stiff me, loading O'Hagan's gloves with buckshot." He laughed on WBW-TV, showing his crooked, slightly discolored teeth, the shiny scar tissue winking above his eye. "What can you expect from Canucks. They don't have a democracy like we do."

All I thought of was him. Him standing between me and what I wanted to make my life perfect.

The eight weeks Colum was in training, he avoided his old friends. He saw my father only a few times, when my father dropped by the gym, and he barely saw his wife and children. Long hours each day he spent at the gym, which was in downtown Yewville near the railroad yard. Often he slept and ate at his trainer's house, which was close by, his trainer was a soft-spoken monkish Irishman in his seventies, though looking much younger, never married. Each morning Colum got up at 4:30 A.M. like clockwork, to run deserted country roads outside Yewville, six miles before breakfast, and each night by 9 P.M. he went to bed exhausted. On Fridays he made an exception, stayed up to watch the TV fights. He ate six meals a day, his life had become almost purely his body. It was a peaceful life in its obsessive, narrow way. A monk's life, a fanatic's life. As a fighter he was focused exclusively upon the coming fight and upon the figure of his opponent, who was no longer merely another man, human and limited, vulnerable and aging, but a figure of demonic power, authority. Like a monk brooding upon God, so Colum brooded upon Roland LaStarza. Pummeling the heavy bag, throwing punches *whack! whack! whack!* in a dreamy trance. *Him! Standing between me and what I want.*

In the past Colum had not liked training. Hell no! Sure, he'd cheated. The random drink, even a smoke. Slipped away for a night with his friends. A night with a woman. This time there was none of that. He'd vowed. *What I want to make my life perfect, I can taste in my mouth like blood.*

Each day the drama was sparring. Yewville men and boys

dropped by to watch. Women and girls drifted in. They were crazy for Donaghy, there was an atmosphere of arousal, anticipation. The smell of male sweat, the glisten of bodies. In the background as in a film slightly blurred, the walls of the old gym were covered in posters of bygone fights in the Buffalo Armory, some of them faded to a sepia hue, dating back to the forties when the gym had been built. Most of the boxers' names were unknown, forgotten. Colum took no notice. He was fierce and alive in the present, in his vision he was climbing into the ring to confront LaStarza, he took little notice of his immediate surroundings for they were fleeting, insubstantial. In the ring, his body came alive. Where he'd been practicing his robot-drill, now he came alive in a quite different way. Each of his sparring partners was a vision of LaStarza. Each of them must be confronted, dealt with. Colum performed, and the onlookers called out encouragement and applauded. The bolder girls asked to have their pictures taken with Colum, and sometimes he obliged, and sometimes no. He was quirky, unpredictable. A good-natured guy except sometimes he was not. You dared not expect anything of him. A promise made one day, sure he'd be happy to oblige, next day no. That was the way with boxers of his temperament. Sometimes his trainer shut the doors against visitors, no one was welcome, not even Colum's friends. No one!

In the ring, in Colum's familiar, safe place. In the ring protected by ropes. In the ring in which there are rules, manners. No absolute surprises. He was shrewdly letting his sparring partners hit on him, his chin, his head, his body, to prepare him for LaStarza's hammer blows that had knocked out twenty-four opponents so far and had visibly shaken Marciano. A wicked left hook to the body and a right cross to the chin that were almost of Marciano's caliber.

But I can take it. Anything he's got.

It was as if Colum knew, his trainer would afterward say, that this would be the last time he'd train so hard, he meant to give it all he had. Colum Donaghy never held back, his trainer would claim of him, even in the gym. By the week of May 20 the odds were nine to one in favor of LaStarza.

"What the hell, it's my advantage. I'm betting on me."

He confided in Patrick Hassler, but no one else was to know: not Colum's manager, not his trainer, not his wife. My father dreaded to ask Colum how much he was betting, and Colum told him: "Three thousand." My father laughed out of sheer nerves. "Why three thousand, man?" Colum said frankly, "That's the most I could borrow." He laughed at the sick look in my father's face.

"Colum, my God. Are you sure?"

"Sure what? I'm going to win? Yes. I'm sure."

"Are you sure it's a good idea, to bet? So much?"

"Why the fuck *not?* It's like seeing into the future, you can figure backward what's the smart thing to do. Say I didn't, I'd be kicking myself in the ass afterward."

That was true, my father had to concede. If Colum was certain he was going to win. Why then, why not bet?

Colum said, "Nine to one odds, fantastic. You should bet, if you're smart. Three times nine is twenty-seven thousand, not bad for a night's work, is it? Plus the purse."

He spoke dismissively of the purse, for it wasn't the big payday he'd long envisioned. LaStarza was getting twenty-five thousand for the fight, and Donaghy was getting eleven thousand. So the newspapers said. Exactly what Colum's purse was, my dad didn't know. Public announcements of purses were always inflated. And Colum wouldn't see more than sixty percent of whatever it was, in any case. His manager took a big cut, his trainer, his cutman, his sparring partners and others. And then there was the IRS.

Colum, are you sure, man? This bet? You don't want to be making a mistake here.

Look: best you mind your own business, man. You think you do, but you don't know shit about me.

And that turned out to be true.

We drove to Buffalo for the fight, a crowded carload of us. Dad and some of the Hassler relatives. I was the only girl. My mom stayed home.

These weeks, my mother had refused to read about Colum in the papers. Even his smiling photo on the front page of the *Yewville Post* she thrust from her with a pained look. To my disgust I overheard her tell my father, "I don't think she should go with you. It isn't a healthy environment for a twelve-year-old girl. All those men! Such ugliness. You know what boxing is. Even if Colum isn't hurt, she will remember it all her life. And if—he gets hurt—" my mother's voice trailed off. My father said only, "She wants to go, and she's going."

She wants to go, and she's going!

Sharp as pain, the happiness I felt hearing this. For I had not expected my father to say such a thing. Like Colum, my father was an unpredictable man. You could not plead with him, you could not reason with him, he made decisions as he wished, and they were inviolable.

At that time in my young life I'd begun to hate my mother as always I had loved her so.

I hated her for wanting to keep me a girl, weak like her. I loved my father for taking me into his world that was a man's world. There, weakness was not tolerated, only strength was valued. I could enter this world only as Patrick Hassler's daughter but I wanted nothing more, this was everything to me.

Driving to Buffalo, my dad and the others talked only of the fight. Everybody wanted Colum Donaghy to win and was anxious of what would happen. What my dad must have known of Colum he would not reveal to these men, he spoke as if he knew Colum only at a distance. "It would be Donaghy's break of a lifetime, if he wins. But he's got to win. His manager says he's being 'looked at' for Madison Square Garden, to see how he'd perform on TV, but Colum is thirty years old, let's face it. He's fighting LaStarza, and LaStarza is still a big draw. He's on the skids, but still tough. You have to figure nobody in the boxing business wants LaStarza to lose just yet. Which means nobody in the boxing business wants Donaghy to win. Which means they don't think Donaghy can win, or will win."

One of my uncles said, incensed, "This wouldn't be a fixed fight, would it? Jesus."

My father just laughed.

"What's that mean? It's fixed, or—what?"

My father said, annoyed, "I don't know what it will be. I hope to Christ Colum survives it."

From the backseat I asked him if Colum Donaghy could win. I wanted almost to cry, hearing him say such things he'd been saying.

He said, "Sure Colum could win. Maybe he will. Maybe what I'm saying is bullshit. We'll hope so, yes?"

"Ladies and gentlemen, our main event of the evening: ten rounds of heavyweight boxing."

The vast Armory was sold out, thousands of spectators, mainly men. In tiers of seats rising to nearly the ceiling. The smoke haze made my eyes sting. The sharp sound of the bell. Sharp, and loud. Because it had to be heard over the screams of the crowd. It had to be heard by men pounding at each other's heads with their leather-gloved fists.

The ring announcer's voice reverberated through the Armory. My teeth were chattering with excitement. My hands were strangely cold, the palms damp. I felt a tinge of panic, that I had made a mistake to come here after all. I was twelve years old, young for my age. My heart beat light and rapid as a bird's fluttering wings.

God, please don't let Colum Donaghy lose. Don't let him be hurt.

Beside me my father was quiet. He sat with his sinewy arms folded, waiting for the fight to begin. I understood that no matter how calmly and dispassionately he'd been speaking in the car, he felt very differently. He was fearful for Colum's sake, he could not bear it that a man he loved like a brother might be publicly humiliated.

Injury, defeat, even death: these would be preferable to the abject humiliation of a boxer knocked down repeatedly, knocked down and knocked *out*.

At ringside in the row ahead of us there was the brunette in a showy electric-blue velvet costume, the bodice spangled with rhinestones, her face heavily made up: Carlotta, Colum Donaghy's wife. Tonight she was glamorous indeed. Her curled hair was stiff with spray, she wore rhinestone starburst earrings. She was seated with Colum's Buffalo friends, whom my father did not like and did not know well. Always she was glancing over her shoulder, seeing who might be watching her, admiring and envying her, she was Colum Donaghy's wife, his fans were eager to see her and there were photographers eager to take her picture. She smiled nervously, laughing and calling out greetings, her mascara-rimmed eyes bright and glazed. She saw my father, her eyes snagged on him, where we were seated in the third row a short distance away. Carlotta Donaghy staring at my father with an expression of— what? Worry, pleading? Seeming to signal to her husband's friend, *Well! Here it is, here we are, nothing will stop it now.* Quickly my father raised a hand to her. *Nothing to worry about, Colum will give him hell.*

I would see Colum's wife and another woman suddenly rise from their seats and leave the Armory by the nearest exit, midway in the fight. The tension was too much for her, her nerves could not bear it.

In his white satin robe Colum Donaghy was the first to enter the ring amid deafening applause. And how pale Colum's skin, milky pale, set beside the other boxer's olive-tinted skin. Roland LaStarza! Abruptly there he was. In black satin robe, black trunks. A pelt of dark hairs on his torso, arms, legs. He weighed only a few pounds more than Colum Donaghy but he looked heavier, older and his body more solid. His face was impassive as something carved from wood. His eyes were veiled, perhaps contemptuous. Wherever this was he was, this ring he'd climbed into, this drafty, crude hall filled with bellowing and screaming strangers, he was LaStarza, the TV LaStarza, a popular heavyweight from the Bronx, he was in western upstate New York on business. He had no sentiment for the occasion. He knew no one in Buffalo, he had not gone to school in Buffalo, there was no neighborhood here to claim him. The Italians adored him, but he was LaStarza from the Bronx, he could tolerate their noisy adoration, but nothing more. His trainer had no need to talk to him earnestly as Colum Donaghy's trainer was talking to him, trying to calm him. LaStarza would do what he had to do to defeat his opponent. He would not do more, and he would not do less. In his career of more than ten years he had rapidly ascended the heavyweight division in the way of a champion-to-be. He had basked in victory and in praise, he fought for years before losing his first fight and that had been no disgrace, for he'd lost to Marciano, and still a young boxer he'd fought Marciano the champion for the title and again he'd lost, he'd ascended the glass mountain as far as his powerful legs would carry him. He knew: his moment was behind him. Now he was in upstate New York; this was not a televised bout. His manager had younger, more promising boxers to promote, another rising champion-to-be. LaStarza would have to accept this deal, he'd turned down similar deals in anger and contempt but now he had no choice, he was thirty-one years old. He'd never fully recovered from the beating Marciano had given him. That public humiliation, the terrible hurt to his body and to his pride. He would win this fight, he would dispatch his opponent whom the morning before, at the weigh-in, he'd scarcely acknowledged. One of those thin-skinned Mick bleeders. Their noses crumple like cheap aluminum cans, their eyes bruise and swell. Their blood splashes like a tomato being burst. At the weigh-in the men had been photographed together for local papers and for TV sports news, shaking hands. Bullshit! The pose pained LaStarza, classy LaStarza, as a bad smell would pain him. He did not despise this Colum Donaghy, he had no thought for the man at all.

While Colum Donaghy bounced about the ring in his white

satin robe with golden trim, shadowboxing, displaying himself to cheering fans. Almost shyly he smiled. A boy's smile, tentative and hopeful. He was one who knew himself adored yet could not entirely trust it, the adoration. He was one who required constant reassurance, nourishment from the crowd. For how milky pale he was: his torso and sides shone clammy white beneath fair reddish hairs. The scar tissue in his face was obscured by bright glaring lights, his skin appeared almost smooth as a boy's. *Is it wrong that a boxer smiles before a fight?* I was very frightened for Colum Donaghy, and for my father seated grim and tense beside me.

I recalled Colum in our kitchen a year ago. The lowered voices of adults. What had they been talking of so earnestly, why had my mother been laughing, what did it mean? I would never know.

The myriad small mysteries of childhood. Never solved. Never even named.

For all of the adult world is mystery, you will never comprehend it. Yet you must surrender to its authority. One day, you must enter it yourself.

The bell rang! That loud, sharp sound.

The first round began.

Colum Donaghy, fair-skinned, in white trunks, moved swiftly to his darker-skinned opponent, and amid shouts and screams the long-awaited fight at last began. From the first, it was a surprise: for Colum rushed at LaStarza, throwing a flurry of punches, as LaStarza moved away and to the side, raising his arms to ward off the fast pummeling blows, trying to use his jab. The boxers circled each other, Colum was pressing forward, always forward. He rode the wave of the crowd's excitement, he threw a right cross that swung wide of its target, he grappled with LaStarza and the men fell into a clinch. This was the pattern of the first rounds: Colum would push forward, La Starza would elude him while catching him with quick, sharp jabs, blows Colum seemed capable of absorbing, though a swelling began above his right eye. In the third round Colum came out fast and anxious and by apparent luck struck LaStarza a short, hard blow to the midriff, his powerful left hook he'd honed to perfection in the gym, and LaStarza reacted in surprise, in a flurry of blows pushing Colum back into the ropes. There was a scuffle and before the referee could break it up the crowd screamed, for LaStarza had slipped, one knee to the canvas, pushing himself up at once, and the referee didn't call a knockdown, which precipitated boos, and more aggressive tactics on Colum's part. The rounds were furious yet how slow time had become: the harder I stared at the boxers above me in their brightly lighted pen, the more exhausted and unreal I felt. Everything was so much more vivid than on TV. The live fight was nothing like the TV fight, which was so small and flattened, in black-and-white images. And with broadcasters continually talking. In the Armory, there were no broadcasters to explain what was happening. Much of the time I could not seem to see. My senses were overloaded. The thud of blows, the squeaking-scuffing sounds of the boxers' shoes on the canvas, the blood splattered on both men's chests and like raindrops onto the referee's white shirt, the deafening crowd noises and the referee's shouted commands—*Break! Break! Box!*—all were numbing, exhausting. Between rounds my eyelids drooped. My father and others shouted to one another, and shouted encouragement to Colum in his corner. I watched Colum Donaghy sitting in his corner as his seconds worked swiftly to prepare him for the next round. I saw his flushed, battered-looking face glisten with beads of water, a sponge squeezed out onto his heated head. Like an animal he seemed, a racehorse, purely physical, and strangely passive, so long as he was seated and these others labored over him. It had not seemed to me, maybe I had not wished to see, how Colum's eye was swelling shut, how his face was cut, but there was his cutman deftly treating his wounds, sticking something like a pencil up into his nostrils in a way to make me feel faint. I asked my father if Colum was winning, for it seemed to me as to the crowd that he was, yet I dreaded some more expert knowledge, and indeed my father said only, frowning, "Maybe. He's ahead." This was a mysterious answer, for if Colum was ahead, wasn't he winning?

In the next rounds the boxers were more guarded, cautious. They were conserving their strength, covered in sweat and often breathing through their mouths. Colum's face was pinkened, as if flushed with health and excitement, LaStarza's was darker, heavy with blood yet still impassive with that carved-wood look. The older boxer was beginning to know that his opponent was going to give him serious trouble, the knowledge had sunk gradually in. A boxer wants to think that while his well-aimed blows are intentional, his opponent's are accidental and won't be repeated. But LaStarza saw that Donaghy was strong, clumsy and determined, a dangerous combination. The action erupted into flurries and then slowed into clinches. At the start of the seventh round Colum seemed to have regained his strength, and fought furiously, striking LaStarza on the right temple, following with his left, and there was LaStarza rocked back onto his heels. Screams on all sides, my father and his friends leaping to their feet, a wave of delirium, was LaStarza about to go down? But no. The moment passed. Yet the pace of the fight had accelerated. My eyes stung from the bright lights, the hectic action, a haze of cigarette and cigar smoke. Midway in the round Colum slowed, breathing through his mouth, and in that instant LaStarza swarmed upon him, a right to the head that made Colum's eyes roll, a body blow like a sledgehammer. Yet Colum returned these with fierce blows of his own, and again delirium swept the crowd, for there was Colum in a frenzy pressing his opponent backward, relentless backward; yet unknowingly he lowered his left glove as he threw a right cross, and LaStarza like a man trying to wake from a dream swung blindly at him over the dropped left, and struck him above the heart, a blow that might have killed Colum if LaStarza had had his full strength and weight behind it. The round ended in a flurry of blows and a repeated ringing of the bell as the fighters fought on unhearing.

The crowd erupted in applause for the fury of the fight.

Our way of thanking the fighters for—what? This mysterious gift of themselves they were giving us.

Daddy! Take me home, take me out of here. These words I could no more have uttered than I could have uttered obscenities.

It was seen that LaStarza, sitting slumped in his corner, was bleeding thinly from a cut above his left eye. It was seen that Colum leaned forward to spit into a bucket and in the dazzling light that seemed magnified what he spat with an expression of disdain was tinged with red.

Another time I leaned over to ask in my father's ear if Colum was winning, I was desperate to know, but this time my father shrugged me away like a bothersome fly, frowning and indifferent. He was smoking a cigar, gripping the ugly dark glowering stub between his teeth.

At the start of the eighth round Colum came rushing to LaStarza as if bringing him something precious—a clumsy downward-chopplng blow to the head, which LaStarza only partly blocked. Next Colum pushed forward with head lowered, bull-like, taking punches even as he threw punches, of varying degrees of strength and accuracy. Already at the start of the round, blood glistened in his nose. The deft, assiduous labor of Colum's cutman had been outdone. There was LaStarza backed into a corner, now into the ropes, warding off Colum's wildly flung blows, which fell onto his arms and shoulders. LaStarza's ribs were reddened in welts. Colum swung and missed, another time swung and missed, but LaStarza's reflexes were slowed, he wasn't able to take advantage. My father said, as if thinking aloud, yet so that I might overhear, "This is the turn," and his face was somber, unsmiling. I wondered: What did *the turn* mean? One of the boxers wasn't able to fight back, to defend himself? Was the fight nearly over? *God, please, end it now, please let Colum win.* I shut my eyes, hearing the ugly *whack! whack!* of body blows. I had no idea who was being hit. I was dazed, sickened, the roaring of the crowd was so loud, I'd been pressing my hands against my ears without knowing. The referee struggled to pull the men apart. Their skins seemed sticky, adhesive. Again, again, again. Each man grappled, seeking advantage, hitting the other short, chopping rabbit punches on the back of the neck. The referee's white shirt was now gray, soaked through with sweat as well as blood splattered. His ridiculous bow tie was crooked. *Break! Box!* I would hear those shouted angry-sounding commands in my sleep. LaStarza seemed to be dropping by degrees out of the active fight, like a man observing himself at a distance; protecting himself, yet offering little offense now. It would seem that Colum had won most of the rounds—hadn't he? Colum "The Kid" Donaghy? His fans were cheering, inflamed with excitement. Both fighters had bloodied, bruised faces. LaStarza was clearly winded, yet like any experienced boxer he was dangerous, always danger-ous, crouching in a corner, eyes glaring like a rat's. He would not go down, his will was unyielding. It was his opponent's will to send him down to the canvas but he would not, yet his knees buckled suddenly, the crowd again erupted. There was a palpable pressure, you could feel like billowing waves of heat, that the fight come to an end immediately, a climax, no one could bear enduring it any longer. Was this the knockdown? Colum struck LaStarza and LaStarza lurched forward into a clinch and amid deafening screams the bell rang signaling the end of the round. Colum continued pum-meling blindly and the referee shouted *Bell! Bell!* He would deduct a point from Colum for hitting after the bell.

My throat was raw, I had not known I was screaming.

The last two rounds were very different. As if a flame had been burning higher and higher, but now a dampening wind blew upon it, the flame lost its power, its luster. Colum tried to press his advantage as before but he'd lost momentum now. His legs were slower, sluggish. He threw combinations of punches intermittently, like a robot LaStarza lashed out, yet both seemed to be losing their concentration. Now Colum, wrenching out of a clinch like a death grip, was the one to slip on the blood-dampened canvas and fall to one knee, and immediately pushed himself up with a grimace of pain, had he injured his knee, the referee stopped the fight to examine Colum, staring into his eyes, the crowd erupted in boos, was the referee going to call the fight? Award a TKO to LaStarza? *Was the fight fixed?* The crowd yelled its displeasure, the referee squinted into Colum's eyes in a pretense of concern but had no choice finally except to nod, to wave the men on, yes the fight would continue.

Both men came out exhausted in the tenth and final round. Both men had difficulty raising their arms. It seemed now that LaStarza had been pacing himself more shrewdly than his opponent, yet still he had little strength left. He hit Colum with a combination of blows, none of them very hard, and Colum stood his ground, shaking his head to clear it. The men staggered like drunks trapped in some bizarre hellish ritual together. They had been together a very long time, neither would ever forget the other. It was possible to see both struggling men, near naked and gleaming with sweat, as noble; and at the same time as defeated. Midway in the round LaStarza managed to hit Colum with what remained of his fearful right cross, and Colum countered with what remained of his fearful left hook, a short, curving blow that looked more powerful than it could have been, since LaStarza staggered but didn't collapse, grabbing on to his opponent like a drowning man. In the final ten or twelve seconds of the fight LaStarza seemed completely dazed and the crowd was chanting *Col-um! Hit him! Col-um! Hit him!* but Colum, who was the crowd's favorite, was too exhausted, his muscled arms hung by his sides like lead. He'd punched himself out, my father would say afterward. He had nothing left.

The bell rang.

The moment I died, and I was happy.

Following that fight of May 20, 1958, which would live long in ignominy in local memory, pervasive as the smoke- and chemical-tainted air of industrial Buffalo, Colum Donaghy would fight once more in September of 1958, in Syracuse. That fight, against an opponent of a very different stature than Roland LaStarza, he would win on points, narrowly. Five days later he was dead.

In the night Colum drove into the countryside. On a lane near his relatives' farm he parked, walked a short distance from his car and shot himself at the base of the skull. The county medical examiner stated he'd died instantaneously. He'd used a .32-caliber Smith & Wesson revolver, unregistered, for which he had no permit. No one in the Donaghy family admitted of knowing of the gun's existence. But my father Patrick Hassler, interrogated by police, had to tell them Colum had brought the gun back with him from Korea. He'd won it playing poker.

Had he been in the game with Donaghy, he was asked.

Not me, my father said. I don't play poker, I'm a man without that kind of luck.

Patrick was deeply ashamed to be questioned by police, for he understood that he was betraying Colum Donaghy simply by speaking of him as he did. Yet he believed he had no choice. Despite the ruling of suicide, there were questions about Colum's death; there was a distrust of individuals associated with professional boxing, and the LaStarza episode was occluded by rumor, scandal. My father didn't volunteer to tell police, however, that Colum had told him he'd borrowed three thousand dollars to bet on himself.

Had Colum Donaghy ever spoken of taking his own life, my father was asked.

Not to me, he told them. We never talked about that kind of thing.

My father was stricken with grief at Colum's death. He was stunned, he was baffled, he was ashamed. You could see the vision in his eyes shrunken to pinpoints. You could see he'd aged within days, his ruddy skin now ashen, tight. This was not a man to speak of his feelings, this was not a man who wanted sympathy. Like a dangerous sleepwalker he moved among us, his family. My mother took care that we did not disturb him. Sometimes he was absent for days. He'd go on drinking binges. My mother wept in secret. Late at night we heard her on the telephone downstairs, pleading. *Have you seen Patrick? If you see Patrick...*

When Colum shot himself he'd knelt in the country lane. In the darkness. He'd aimed his gun carefully. The bullet to enter at the base of the skull, tearing upward through the brain. Yet his hand must have shaken. It can't be so easy to *take your own life* and throw it away like trash. He was missing for two days before he was found lying on his side in the lane, the fingers of his right hand curled stiffly around the revolver handle. He was found by two teenaged boys out hunting. They'd seen the car first, then found the body. They'd recognized Colum Donaghy, they said, at once.

The man who fought Roland LaStarza.

That first terrible day at school it was being said that Colum Donaghy had died. Agnes was called out of class, her mother had come to bring her home. Later it would be said that Colum had shot himself with a gun. He'd taken his own life, and that was a sin. A terrible sin. When we saw Agnes Donaghy again, two weeks later, it seemed that another girl had taken her place. Not so pretty, with eyes ringed in sorrow. Even her freckles had faded.

The cruelest among us whispered, Good! Now she knows.

Knows what?

How it is to be like everybody else. Not the daughter of Colum Donaghy.

In my father's face that was shut like a fist we saw the sick, choked rage. He would never speak of it. But sometimes he would say, "I hope they're satisfied now. The bastards." Meaning the boxing crowd. Gus Smith, too.

The judges had ruled the LaStarza–Donaghy fight a draw. A draw! Sports reporters had given it to Donaghy, clearly he'd won six or seven rounds. He'd punched himself out by Round Ten, but by then LaStarza was finished, too. The referee, interviewed, said evasively it had been a close fight, and a fair decision. One of the judges was from Rochester, the others were from New York City. No one could discuss the fight with my father. Colum refused to be interviewed afterward. He refused to see a doctor. A few weeks later he moved out of his home to live downtown near the railroad yard and the gym and the bars. He had a very young girlfriend from Olean, he spoke of quitting boxing. He complained of headaches, blurred vision. Still he would not see a doctor. He worked part-time at the quarry. He reconciled with Carlotta, and moved back home. Evidently he wasn't quitting boxing: Gus Smith signed him on for a fight in Syracuse, in September.

After that night in the Buffalo Armory, I never saw Colum Donaghy again. Though I would see his picture in the papers and on TV often. Sometimes when my father came home I was wakened, and listened for what I could hear. There was always wind, wind from the north, from Canada and across Lake Ontario and the sound interfered with the sounds from my parents' bedroom. My mother's voice was anxious, lowered. "How could he, oh God. I can't sleep thinking of it, I can't believe it." And my father's voice was inaudible, his words were brief. My mother often cried. I wanted to think that my father comforted her then. As she'd comforted me when I'd been a little girl and had hurt myself in some childhood mishap. I wanted to think that my father held my mother in his strong, sinewy arms like adults in movies, that they lay together in each other's arms, and wept together.

Mostly I heard silence. And beyond, the wind in the trees close about our house.

"I never wanted you to know how close to the edge we were in those days, honey. See?"

The edge. What was the edge?

He made a cautious gesture with the back of his hand. Approaching the edge of the table. It was not the Formica-topped kitchen table at which Colum Donaghy had sat, decades ago. A newer table, sleek and still shiny, though my mother Lucy was not the one to sponge it down any longer.

The edge of things, Daddy meant. The edge of civilization.

At Christmas 1999, I went to visit my father in Yewville. He was living alone in the old house, stubborn and remote from his grown children. He lived in just two rooms, the upstairs was closed off, unheated.

He was seventy-two. His life, he said, had rushed past him without his exactly knowing.

He hadn't voluntarily seen a doctor since my mother's death nine years before, of cancer. He blamed the Yewville General Hospital for her death, or spoke as if he did. A malevolent *they* presided over such institutions. *Goddamned bloodsuckers.* A year before, he'd had a heart attack on the street and had been rushed to the emergency room of the very hospital that had killed his wife, he vowed he would never again return. He was subject to angina pains, he had bad knees, arthritic joints, yet he still smoked, and he drank ale by the case. He boasted to his children he kept "emergency medicine" in the house for his private use when things got bad. He would not be hooked up to machines as others had been. He would not be "experimented on" like a monkey. He laughed telling us these things, he gloated. Sometimes when we spoke of helping him sell the house and prepare for the future, he was furious with us, slammed down the phone receiver. But sometimes he listened attentively. It was "about time for an overhaul," he conceded.

His grown children took turns visiting with Patrick Hassler, when he would have us. Usually he was feuding with two of us, and friendly with the third. In December 1999, I was the one allowed to visit.

My father greeted me warmly, his mood was upbeat, his breath smelled strongly of ale. Seventy-two is not old but my father looked old. His skin was tinged with melancholy. His shoulders were stooped. He'd lost weight, his flesh seemed shrunken on him, loose and wrinkled like an elephant's skin. He wasn't a tall man any longer, he'd become a man of average height. A man who has punished himself? We sat in the kitchen talking. The subject was selling the house, and what to do next. We were sidetracked by reminiscing of course. When I returned to Yewville always I was returning to the past. The city had not changed much in decades, it was economically depressed, frozen in the late fifties. The prosperity of subsequent decades in America had bypassed this region. Here, I was in Colum Donaghy's era. A thrill of something like panic, horror swept over me. For never had I understood. Why. Why that man so admired by so many had killed himself. He'd won his last fight. He had not lost the fight with Roland LaStarza, everyone knew. And he'd been only thirty-one years old.

I did not want to think that, at the age of thirty-one, a man's life might be over.

In Yewville, I stayed in a motel and visited my father for only a few hours each day. He seemed to want it this way, his privacy and his isolation had become precious to him. On the second day of my visit, he brought out the old photo album and we sat at the kitchen table looking through it together. I knew not to bring up the subject of Colum Donaghy and yet—there we were calmly looking at snapshots of him, and of my father with him, and of others, everyone so young and attractive, smiling into the camera. I was deeply moved by the snapshots taken in the gym, cocky-looking Colum and his friend Patrick in boxing trunks, headgear, arms around each other's shoulders, clowning for the camera. So young! Here were two men confident they had much life yet to live, and surely they had every right to think so. Except, seeing Colum Donaghy, and seeing that the date of the snapshot was February 1954, in that instant I was compelled to think of September 1958.

Four years, seven months to live.

My father said slowly, "It's like Colum is still with me, sometimes. I can hear him. Talk to him. Donaghy was the only person to make me laugh." Suddenly my father was confiding in me? He spoke calmly but I knew he was trembling.

So we talked of Colum Donaghy, and of those days. Forty years Patrick had outlived Colum, good Christ! That was a joke on them both. That was something to shake your head over. I said, "It was one of the mysteries of that time, Daddy. Why Colum killed himself. Just because he hadn't won that fight with LaStarza? But he hadn't lost it, either. He was still a hero. He must have known."

My father said, "Hell, I'm an old man now, I want to tell some things that couldn't be told before. Colum didn't kill himself, honey."

"What?"

"Colum Donaghy did not kill himself. No."

My father spoke slowly, wetting his parched lips. I stared at him in disbelief.

"Colum was killed, honey. He was murdered."

"Murdered? But—wasn't the gun his?"

My father hesitated, rubbing his eyes with both hands. His face was discolored by liver spots, deeply creased and fallen. "No, honey. The gun was not Colum's. Colum owned no gun."

A chill came over me. A terrible subterranean knowledge like a quickened pulse. And my father glancing at me, to see how I was taking this.

He would tell me now, would he! An elderly man on the brink of the grave, with nothing to lose. Even his fear of God he'd long ago lost.

The thought came to me swift and unbidden. *He is the one who killed Colum Donaghy.*

I could not accuse him. Before this man, I would always be a stammering child.

He saw me staring at him. With a frowning, finicky gesture he smoothed the wrinkles in one of his shirt sleeves. The shirt had been laundered and not ironed, and fitted him loosely. "I had to tell the police what I did, honey. It would've been my life, too. I'd been

317

warned. Gus Smith warned me. And Colum was gone, nothing would bring him back. Jesus, when he opened up like he did in the eighth round! It was a beautiful thing but—he was a dead man from that point onward. See, they'd told him what to do. What not to do. They were paying him, and he'd agreed. He was to fight like hell but LaStarza was going to knock him out. All this I knew, but not directly. Colum hinted to me he was going against his manager and his trainer, and LaStarza's backers, he'd even bet on himself to win. He'd intended all along to win. He was a—" My father's voice quavered. It was rare for him to speak at such length, and so vehemently. But now, words eluded him. "—so Goddamned stubborn *Irish*."

But I was left behind in this. I'd heard, but hadn't absorbed what I heard. "Daddy, I don't know what you're saying. Who killed Colum?"

"Who, exactly? Their names? Hell, I don't know their names."

"But—who hired them?"

My father shrugged. Shook his head, disgusted. "Some sons of bitches in New York, I suppose."

"But you told police—"

"Hell, you couldn't trust the police either. Boxing was part of the rackets, there were payoffs, high-ranking cops and judges and politicians. I said what I said, I didn't have a choice. I had you kids to think of, and your mother. Yeah, and I was afraid, too. For myself."

"Daddy, I'm just so—stunned. All these years...Colum was your closest friend."

"Colum knew what boxing was! Goddamn, he wasn't born yesterday. He wasn't any saint. Nobody forced him to sign on for the LaStarza fight, he knew what it was. LaStarza might not have been told, he only had to fight for real. But Colum! He thought he could win, and impress everybody, and everybody would love 'The Kid,' and the New York promoters would sign him on. He could take

LaStarza's place, he was thinking. Marciano's! But he'd underesti-
mated LaStarza. That was his second mistake. He didn't pace himself the way a boxer is trained to, he punched himself out by the
tenth round and couldn't KO his man so it went to the judges. They
called it a draw. It stank, everybody knew it was rotten, but there it
was. A draw, and nobody won. But Colum lost." My father spoke
disgustedly, shoving the photo album away from him.

"So the judges were bribed."

"Hell, those bastards wouldn't even need to be bribed.
They'd have naturally done what was expected of them."

"Daddy, I can't believe this! You loved boxing."

"I loved some boxers. I loved watching them sometimes.
But boxing—no, I didn't love boxing. Boxing is business, a man selling himself to men who sell him to the public. Christ!"

I was impatient suddenly. "And you never sold yourself,
Daddy, I suppose?"

"For your mother and you kids, sure I did," he said. "I sold
myself however I could. Just owning that garage, that barely made
a living, I had to pay 'protection' to s.o.b.'s in Niagara Falls. If I hadn't
paid them they'd have firebombed me. Or worse."

"You? Extorted?"

"Hell, it wasn't only me. Maybe it's different now, the police
will protect you. But in those days, no. If I'd told anybody that
Colum had been murdered, and the gun wasn't his—" His voice
ceased suddenly, as if the strength had drained from him. He was
rubbing his eyes in a way uncomfortable to see, as if wanting to
blind himself.

"Daddy, I feel sick about this. I—don't know what to say."

"We sold ourselves however we could," my father said
angrily, "and so have you kids in your different ways. What the hell
do you know?"

"It was all a lie then? Colum never took his own life—his life
was taken from him, and you knew, Daddy. And you didn't try to get
justice for him."

"'Justice'! For who? What's that? 'Justice'—bullshit. I'd have been shot too, or dumped in the Niagara River. You'd have liked that better?"

I was upset, revulsed. I stood and walked away. Suddenly needed to escape this airless kitchen, this house, Yewville. My father reached for me but I eluded him. I fled outside, he followed me. The ground was crusted with snow that looked permanent as concrete. Our breaths steamed. My father said, close to pleading now, "I didn't want you, your mother or anybody, to know how close we were to the edge in those days. It was Colum, it could've been me. I wanted to shield you, honey."

One day I would understand, maybe. But not then. I told him I'd talk to him later, I'd call him, but I had to leave Yewville now. Driving away I was shaken, stunned as if my father had hit me. I was filled with a sick, sinking sensation as if I'd bitten into something rotten, the poison was activated in me, unstoppable.

The last time I saw my father alive.

Not Colum Donaghy but Patrick Hassler, the sole person close to me who has taken his own life.

Taken his own life. But where?

My father died early in the morning of New Year's Day. He'd swallowed two dozen painkillers, washed down by ale. His heart, the medical examiner ruled, had simply given out; he'd never regained consciousness; his death was *self-inflicted.*

If I knew better, I told no one.

I would live with what I knew, and I would bear it.

He'd left behind items designated for us, his children. His survivors. There was a shabby envelope with my name printed carefully on it, and inside were the old, priceless photos of Colum Donaghy. One I hadn't seen before was of Colum and my father and me, posed in front of a car with a gleaming chrome grille. The date was 1950, I was four years old. Colum and Patrick were each leaning against a front fender of the car, and I was propped on the hood, smiling, legs blurred as if I'd been kicking at the instant the picture was taken. (By my mother?) I was a blond, curly-haired little girl in a pink ruffled dress. Both men were holding me so I wouldn't fall. I saw that a stranger, studying this snapshot, the three of us in that long-ago time of June 1950, could not have guessed with certainty how we were related, which man might be the little girl's father.

THE PROBLEM OF LEON

by John Shannon

Jack Liffey had been there at Stinkey's the evening Leon Krane set his fists on his hips, all five-six of him, and screeched out to the near end of the college bar, "Come on! I'm like a rubber, I take all sizes!"

The man-mountain middle linebacker from the school team, Kaz Kristowski, had swiveled around with one eye slitted. "You talking to me, pussy?"

This was well after the wave of mysterious thefts that struck the dorm their freshman year, in fact it was into the junior year, after most of them had completely lost track of Leon. But one of the endemic pastimes their first semester had been trying to figure out just what made this odd Leon Krane tick. Or, rather, why it was so very hard to *like* Leon Krane. They had whole sitting-on-the-bed late-night bull sessions on the subject: What is it about a human being that makes him the absolute standard of cringe? Why was the Smithsonian Likability Lab flying guys out to study Krane and zero their instruments? I think Wittgenstein himself would have trouble with this one. Who the hell's Wittgenstein, for crap's sake?

That's the way it went.

Leon wasn't stupid, but he was ineffably unpleasant and tiresome and permanently aggrieved, and he'd clearly been off somewhere, maybe stuck in the bathroom trying to comb his long black recalcitrant hair, when sense of humor had been handed out.

Leon never smiled, hardly ever got the point of jokes, and if he did get them, he just shrugged and passed on to some other subject he wanted to talk about. It was Jack Liffey's opinion that maybe Krane got the jokes well enough, but he just didn't feel he *belonged* enough to have a right to laugh. Jack Liffey tried to talk the guys in Walker Hall into making an effort to include Leon in the Vultures, see if he'd maybe get more bearable, but he almost got ostracized himself for the suggestion.

"You want to go room with the Krane, spaz?"

On the Krane question, the majority tended to the view that it was indeed lack of a sense of humor pure and simple that made someone unlikable. But Jack Liffey wasn't so sure. He thought it might have something to do with the way Krane insisted on bringing up subjects that were really of no intrinsic interest, like the different breeds of grass seed used for racetracks or how ants follow trails of formic acid, and the way he talked about them in a nagging aggrieved way, as if he knew in advance you weren't going to be interested. But, really, other people could talk about those same subjects and you didn't mind, you actually listened. Leon could open his mouth, get out a few words—"You know, eastern white oak is much better for furniture than red oak"—and moss would start to grow on the walls.

Who could say, really? On the late-night philosophical level in the dorm, it was far more entertaining to gab about sex or their lost childhood religions or foreign films like *Last Year at Marienbad*, which were just beginning to come to college towns then.

The upshot was that for the whole first semester Krane became the target of their RFs. The expression meant ratfucks, or malicious pranks. People burned his philodendron with lighter fluid. They gummed up his doorlock. They put fiery Mentholatum in his pound-off Vaseline. They sent love letters to undesirable girls in his name, and vice versa. They put a cherry bomb in a roll of wet toilet paper and blew it off in the middle of his room one Friday night so when he came back on Sunday evening several thousand little hardened wads of papier mâché were stuck to every surface, even his pajamas hanging over the chair. It actually got quite mean, and one night during finals they took his door off and hid it in the basement and the poor guy slept the night with a red-hot steam iron by his bed, threatening to scald anyone who set foot in his room.

By the time they came back from break for the second semester, the Vultures—that is, the south wing of Walker—seemed to have grown weary of tormenting anyone quite that humorless about it, and they just started taking Krane for granted as a permanent annoyance, but *their* annoyance, like a buzzing fluorescent in the hall or a balky car that was hard to start in the cold.

"Jesus, let's hold this discussion down at the coop where the Krane can't horn in."

Just as Leon was fading from their ken as a butt of pranks, things started to disappear. A bright red Raleigh bicycle locked to the pipe rack out front. A 45-rpm record player, complete with a rare collection of British Shadows records. One night Jack Liffey's Hermes Baby portable typewriter—a prized memento from his dad—vanished right out of his locked room. That tore it for him and before an enraged mob of vigilantes gathered in the snackroom he volunteered to track down the thief. Of course, a lot of them suspected Leon right off, but Jack Liffey felt that was just too obvious a scapegoating. He set elaborate baited traps, a gift box left outside a door or a dorm room left provocatively open, and he even skipped the homecoming game to wait in a darkened bathroom, door ajar, his eye to a toy periscope trained on the quiet hall. The thief was far too clever for any of that. Right under his nose, a nice Bulova vanished from a dresser to mystify them all.

Through all this, they watched Leon carefully and noticed a few new things about him. He cut corners a bit. Nothing really big, but he wouldn't pull his share of tidying the snackroom. If you left your door open Thursdays he'd swipe the fresh towels off your bed rather than walking over to the laundry ladies to swap his own. They suspected him of copying term papers, too, but nobody felt like snitching him out on that, and for all the amateur detective efforts, there was nothing at all to tie him to the bigger thefts.

Barney Monroe plopped down on Jack Liffey's bed one night. "I grew out of being an Episcopalian a long time ago, man, but this guy is gonna reanimate my faith, I swear. He's walking evidence of evil at work in the world."

"Isn't that a bit operatic?"

"You know that retarded townie who hangs out at the Sugar Bowl?"

"Uh-huh."

"I saw the Krane make her do an errand for him, and then he refused to give her the nickel he offered and laughed at her when she started sputtering."

"That's what you call pure evil?"

"It's getting worse every day, I swear."

"Look, even if you're right," Jack Liffey said, "I mean, say he's getting worse, say he's even the sneak thief. What do you gain by calling it evil? He was probably abused as a kid, or his mom died young, or she ignored him. He's selfish, he's needy inside, he's lacking in social graces, sure, he's really unpleasant to get cornered into a discussion with, but there's reasons for everything. Calling it evil just mystifies it."

"What do you say about guys who rape and kill little girls then?"

"They're psychopaths. They're sick. How does calling it evil explain anything? It's just a label so you can forget about it."

"I don't know, man. Sometimes there just isn't sufficient reason."

"That's medieval. There's always a reason."

"If you feel that way, why don't you befriend the guy? Maybe you can save him," Barney Monroe challenged.

That shut him up for a moment. "Somebody probably

should try it," he heard himself say. "You'd get a lifetime supply of positive karma out of it."

He didn't make any public commitment, but the next day, there he was, going down the hall toward Krane's room. The door was open, and Krane was listening softly to what was apparently a rebroadcast of the BBC's *Goon Show* on the radio and actually laughing aloud to himself, but it wasn't like any laugh he'd ever heard before. There was no enjoyment at all in it. It was as if he were just doing it to prove to himself he knew how to laugh, like anybody else.

Jack Liffey cleared his throat. "Spike Milligan's great, isn't he?"

Leon Krane looked up with his characteristic truculence. "What do you know about Spike Milligan?"

"There was an FM station in L.A. that played the *Goon Show* all the time. "

"You probably had a fancy FM radio." FM was still fairly rare then.

"I made it from a kit, an Eichler."

"Yeah, I'll bet your dad bought it for you and helped you build it, too. Guys like you had all the advantages."

This was not turning out the way Jack Liffey had expected, but he pushed on. "Actually, my dad's a longshoreman. I don't think I merit this silver spoon stuff. I'm here on scholarship." It was an expensive private college, and Jack Liffey was still feeling a bit overwhelmed competing with all the prep school boys who'd read so many things—Camus, Nietzsche, Thomas Mann—he'd barely even heard about.

"Me too. Of course. I never had a dad. Ma had to sell cosmetics door-to-door."

"That's an honorable trade."

Leon snorted. "Sure it is," he said sarcastically. "Everybody thinks she was a door-to-door whore just because she didn't marry my dad."

Actually, as far as Jack Liffey knew, *everybody* didn't know a thing about Krane's mom and wouldn't have cared. There didn't seem to be any way to offer a conversational gambit that would calm him down. Then he remembered the calculus book in his hand. This had been the ploy. Krane was a math major.

"I wondered if you could look at this calculus problem with me." He knew the answer perfectly well, of course.

"I see, Jackie old son, that's what this is about. Well, let's see if we can't put our heads together and figure it out."

He'd been very close to walking out of the room then, but he decided to give it just a *little* more of the old college try, even with the Jackie-old-son business. But Krane insisted on explaining the entire basis of differentiation, why calculus had been invented in the first place, stopping now and then to comment on the *Goon Show* that he'd left running on his cheap little transistor in a maddening distraction, and finally he labored the simple problem to death in a hectoring voice that suggested you were an idiot if you had to go through all the steps.

"Thanks a lot, Leon. I get it now."

Experiment over. He would have to live with his own meager supply of karma, as it were.

"Anytime, Jackie old son. My door's always open."

Barney Monroe saw him come out of the room fast and fuming and accosted him later. "Had a nice little chat, did we?"

"Fuck you, Bar."

"Whoa. So you're not a saint after all, Jack."

He never tried again, of course. Monroe was right. Eighteen-year-olds, even those with the best of intentions, rarely try that hard for sainthood.

The next fall, when they came back for their sophomore year, they were dispersed to various dorms and town apartments and Jack Liffey lost track of Leon Krane. The next he heard of him, the school weekly was reporting that Krane had become a pretty good flyweight boxer, at the very lowest weight class, under 112 pounds. Apparently he had begun his boxing career like Irish Jim O'Brien, head down and flailing, but had become a lot better under tutelage. Boxing was not a big sport at the college, but they sent their better candidates twice a week to a famous gym in the nearest town with a barrio. Leon learned to keep his head up and put some control into his flailing, and he was so fast and so relentless that he turned out to be good enough to beat all the town Chicanos and eventually go into Golden Gloves one weight up.

By their junior year Jack Liffey was living with Barney Monroe off campus, and whenever the topic of Leon's career came up in the paper, Barney referred to him as "your pal."

"I see your pal beat somebody called Oscar 'The Dog' Avila in Whittier. He must've been good if he had a nickname."

"Jesus, your pal, that all-purpose affable boxer guy, he made it to the state championships."

"This is rich, they've got an interview with your pal after he took some Golden Gloves title. Mr. Krane, to what do you owe your storied success? And this pal of yours, no slouch with the wit, old Leon replies, I banish weakness."

I banish weakness became Barney Monroe's catchphrase for a while, his all-purpose formula for acing exams and snagging Friday night dates.

"Oh, man, getting up for eight o'clock French class is murder. But *I banish weakness*."

But soon the Krane question pretty much fell out of sight in all its forms until that fateful night at the end of their junior year when the feisty little boxer barged into Stinkey's and called out the linebacker. They never even knew why.

After the challenge, Kaz Kristowski sloped down off his barstool and advanced on Leon Krane like a big mountain cat forced to attend to some pesky rodent.

"Here's your chance to split, man," the big linebacker offered softly, in a dead flat voice. He might have been a little drunk. "You don't even cast a shadow in my world."

Leon Krane's head topped out about chest level on the bigger man, and he was literally less than half his weight. Kristowski must have run to 270 easy, and a lot of it was weight-training muscle then, no matter what he would look like in another ten years.

"Eat my shit-caked shoes, Polack."

Kristowski took one big swing that seemed to go half-hearted before it got all the way to Krane, as if his large fist was having second thoughts of its own. They say the secret to a bar fight is not size or strength, not even a knowledge of dirty punches, knees to the groin and gouges that break skin, but simple speed, getting in as many blows as quickly as you can, and speed is what Krane had in spades. I don't think anyone there could have counted the number of times he hit the big linebacker's startled face in his first flurry. Even talking of a first flurry gives a false impression, because Krane just didn't stop. He was relentless, hammering away in a *rat-tat-tat* of lefts and rights that stunned the bar into silence with its bottomless ferocity. With all Krane's training the punches had force, too, snapping the big man's head back and forth.

Kristowski windmilled a couple of times in a bewildered response and then went down hard on one knee. Still, Krane didn't let up. He pounded away, evading the big flat hands Kristowski threw up to protect his face. Krane went in through those defenses as if they weren't there and just kept hammering over and over, always at the man's head, until the big man sagged down into a crouch, then crumpled onto his side, bellowing and emitting strange animal noises. Krane dropped to his knees and continued to punch the man's face. Blood was spattering around now and the tormented voice changed pitch and became a wail of distress.

Jack Liffey couldn't stand to see any more of the beating, and he wasn't alone jumping to his feet. A half dozen people converged to grab at Krane's pummeling fists and pull him off.

"That's enough, Leon. *Enough.*"

"You'll kill him."

Leon halted his attack as if a switch had been thrown, and

his face instantly went cool and neutral as he stared down at his bleeding handiwork, the linebacker's face already going puffy. In retrospect Jack Liffey felt that might have been the spookiest moment of all. Anyone could understand loss of control, a person lashing out in rage or humiliation or some kind of emotional frenzy, but to think that Krane's whole homicidal attack had been a kind of willed and calculated battering was too alarming for words, took one back to the whole discarded notion of evil at work in the world.

After that night, though, Leon Krane became something of a taboo subject throughout college. The hideous beating, the strange cold personality, his social isolation and his descent into a netherworld of off-campus working-class gyms were all unsettling facts without anyone finding in them a lesson that was simple enough and comprehensible enough to make the human condition seem any less troubling. Krane-ness, the Krane Problem became a true quandary, an unpleasant bump in the mattress that made no sense, and the young man's mind generally shies from anything that cannot be contained in a simple topic sentence.

This Krane silence, the moral hush that surrounded the idea of him, was sealed for good when neither of the bar brawlers returned to college for the senior year. It was rumored that Krane had gone off to become a professional boxer, while poor Kristowski never really recovered from all those head blows and went into a seminary in the Midwest, probably the only one of them all who was destined daily to contemplate the mystery of Leon Krane.

"Jack? Jack Liffey?" came the voice on the phone.

"That's my name."

"You probably remember me as Leon Krane. You were the only guy in college ever nice to me. I need your help. I hear you find kids."

It took a while to make the connection. It had been over thirty years since he'd even thought about the name. Wherever

331

Krane had gone after that fateful bar fight, Jack Liffey had finished college, done two years of graduate school before the draft, spent his Vietnam year in a radar trailer, then bummed around the world before settling in as a technical writer in L.A. and working his way up to the corner office in a big aerospace building in El Segundo and a salary in the high sixties. He married a bit late, refurbished a lovely suburban bungalow in Redondo Beach, had a wonderful daughter and then lost it all to the aerospace exodus at the end of the Cold War. Drink and anger cost him the marriage and house, and the only thing that had pulled him out of his self-destructive funk was discovering he had an unexpected talent for locating missing children. He didn't make much money at it, but it was a calling that let him climb out of bed in the morning feeling he was on the plus side of existence. That was worth a lot at the time.

Krane gave him an address in East L.A. "One other thing, Jack. My name is Léon Carne now, it has been for a long time. You may know me as Carnito."

It did ring a bell, something to do with the sports pages that he never more than glanced at, and Jack Liffey called up his friend Art Castro, a walking encyclopedia of sports trivia, for a little fill-in.

"Someday maybe you could give me a call when you don't need something from me, Jack."

"What is this, *The Godfather*? I'll take you to see the Pasadena Penguins play."

This was a standing joke between them. "There is no Pasadena Penguins."

"The Whatevers, then."

"Carnito was a pretty good featherweight for a long time, even went up and fought as a lightweight at the end. He could take a punch, and he was blazingly fast. Lovely to watch in his prime. Almost took the title from Antonio Esparragoza, but he was starting to slow down by then. Speedy Carnito was a big local favorite on the Eastside, like Oscar de la Hoya. You've heard of him?"

"Vaguely."

"I didn't even know he wasn't a Latino until I read a piece on him in the *Times*. Doesn't matter though. We're not racists. Hell, the founder of the Mexican Mafia was a white guy. You Irish guys used to be big in boxing."

Jack Liffey didn't really think of himself as Irish, but he allowed Castro his conceit. "We got busy being cops and presidents."

"What a moral collapse. See you at the fights, Jack."

The house was on the shoulder of a hill in a bit of county area just east of the city limits called City Terrace. In a radius of ten miles there would be very little English spoken, and all the mini-markets sported that strange angular gang-banger writing he could never read. Every other house on this particular block was a pleasant enough 1930s bungalow, maybe a little threadbare but with tidy gardens. Krane's address was a prime example of the process called mansionizing. You build on a second story, slap fanlights over all the windows, stucco everything in some obscure earth tone between peach and beige and make sure there are two really pompous columns rising up both stories a-flank the front door. It gave him the creeps, and on that street looked like a zebra in church, but he wasn't there as an architectural critic.

There was a picket fence, and his first hint that something might be wrong within was the dogs, three pit bulls trying insanely to get at him through the pickets. Some pit bulls are just dogs, but these were crazed little werewolves out for his blood.

A short man came down the stoop quickly and made for the dogs. *"Perros! Pendejos! Quieto!"*

He tried for a real kick, but the dogs dodged and fell into growls as they slunk away, with resentful backward glances. The man might have been Krane, he had the long black hair, though he had a broken nose now, a deeply lined face, a bushy mustache and the little underlip beard that musicians call a jazz-dab. The smile gave him away, that same humorless grimace Jack Liffey remembered from ancient history.

"Jack, it's good to see you." His hand was leathery and strong.

"Leon. Or what should I call you?"

"That's fine. I became Carne legally a long time ago. And you know Mexicans, they like their *diminutivos*. I fought as Carnito, Little Meat. Speedy Little Meat."

"Almost a world champion, I hear."

Apparently that wasn't a happy subject, because he ignored it and beckoned up to the house. A short round woman waited deferentially inside the door, like a servant. The second bad sign was her black eye. It was fading, but Jack Liffey didn't like the implication.

"Prepare café," he said without introducing her, and she hurried away, down a spotless hallway.

There was a glass trophy case in the living room, with a lot of silver pugilists on pedestals with their dukes up, some spangled belt buckles the size of UFOs and a couple sets of dangling bronzed boxing gloves. There was also a silvery plaque on the top shelf that almost sent Jack Liffey into a double take: *I banish weakness.* He hadn't stayed in touch with Barney Monroe, who'd become a hot-shot surgeon at Cedars-Sinai, but the plaque immediately called up an image of Barney's sardonic grin, and he felt like ringing him up to let him in on the joke. Or to ask him for help with the moral dilemma he sensed gathering about him. Apparently you still couldn't get near Leon Krane-Carne without something dark and metaphysical tapping you on the shoulder.

Leon's face set into a grim stare. "My oldest boys became boxers, too. They're doing okay, and they're strong boys. My daughter even tried her hand at it before she got married. But my youngest went a different direction. I've tried everything, but Ramon actually *wants* to leave himself vulnerable to every wind."

"What sort of winds would those be?" Jack Liffey asked.

They locked eyes for a little while, and something flitted past behind Leon's, something he wasn't going to talk about. "Just find him for me. He's a minor and I don't want him out there getting hurt."

THE PROBLEM OF LEON

The woman brought a tray of coffee and set it on a low table.

"Are you Leon's wife?" Jack Liffey asked.

"*Si, señor.* Rosaura Sanchez Carne."

Jack Liffey stuck out his hand with a smile and she seemed startled but took it briefly and limply, and then poured the coffee and hurried away.

"You got to get used to things being different in different communities, Jack."

He was about to mention the big difference of the black eye, and then decided he could use the money for this job and let it go. "Do you have any idea where Ramon has gone?"

"Yeah, it's a Korean cult with a headquarters in Hollywood. They think the world is going to come to an end at summer solstice next year. God knows what they'll have their members doing to get ready for it."

"You know, I don't kidnap kids, or deprogram."

"He's a minor. He's got to come home."

Leon agreed to a fee and gave him an address for the cult, and Jack Liffey finished off his coffee in one long pull so he could get out of there and think about this job and all the ambivalences trotting up around him like pit bulls.

"One thing, Leon. Remember that football player you demolished at Stinkey's?"

"Sure." He grinned, and there was almost enjoyment in it. "His parents threatened to sue me until they saw how ludicrous it would look in court, Goliath standing beside me."

"What was it about?"

"He called me a faggot."

"Were you the thief?" Jack Liffey added lightly, as if it hardly mattered.

Leon stared back at him for a long time. "If I was, you rich pricks deserved it."

It took Jack Liffey several days to satisfy himself that Ramon Carne had never joined the Hankook Gideon's 300 Church of the Last Glorious Days. No one on earth but a hard-core Korean millenarian would get within hailing distance of those wild-eyed chanting loonies, he thought. It was probably a misdirection the boy had let slip to his father on purpose. Jack Liffey tried the Gay and Lesbian Alliance, on the obvious hunch, but the boy hadn't gone there either. In a week he'd finally tracked the boy down to Zapata Graphics in Boyle Heights, an art center run by Liberation Theology nuns.

"I can't let you see him, Mr. Liffey," Sister Erasmus insisted in a cluttered studio where a number of young people labored away at silk-screen presses and other tasks. The sister was heavy-set and a bit frowzy, but seemed quite kindly.

She didn't wear a habit or the airplane hat, none of them did anymore, but there was something about her that screamed *nun* at you, maybe the sense of peace and confidence.

"I promise you, I have never taken a child home against his or her will. Especially if there's a danger of abuse. Ever. But Ramon is a minor and I've got to at least talk to him. I'm functioning here as an officer of the court." That was gibberish but it often worked.

"All right. You may talk to him, but only in my presence."

She led him up a worn stairwell, past a lot of posters of brightly colored Mexican village scenes and cartoony low-rider sedans, the East L.A. trademark. She knocked politely and waited for an invitation before ushering him into a small studio with a cot and a tiny fridge in the corner. The resemblance was so obvious there was no doubt. He was like a slightly more Latino version of Leon, short and frail with soulful brown eyes and a very solemn demeanor.

Ramon was dabbing at a watercolor of a giant hibiscus on an easel. Around the walls and leaning against furniture were similar big flowers, each with four or five lines of poetry inscribed on it in a cursive hand. As Sister Erasmus whispered to the boy, Jack

Liffey glanced at the nearest poem, beside the stalk of a big water-spotted iris.

Cooling rain at dusk.
The croak of frogs beyond
A wall that divides the calm
Within from the noisy threat of time
Advancing.

Almost a haiku, he thought, and not at all the mawkish teenage twaddle he would have expected.

"Mr. Liffey," the boy advanced and held out his hand.

"Lovely poem. Truly. And the flower."

"Thank you," the boy said gravely.

Jack Liffey explained his ground rules: that he found errant children, he never did anything against anyone's will, and right now he only wanted to talk. While Sister Erasmus kept a discreet distance, the boy walked him around the studio and explained how he had found exactly what he wanted to do in life, exactly where he fit comfortably in the world. In another year he could go to art school and in the meantime he could stay at the center. His silk screens were already selling and he could support himself.

"If the subjects were a little odder, they would call me a concept artist, but some people compare me to Sister Corita. I don't reject that."

"What went wrong at home?"

The boy puffed his cheeks and shook his head a little. "You mean, in addition to everything? Maybe if I painted jet planes or tanks or just boxers, dad would have accepted it, though, honestly, he didn't want me to be an artist of any kind. Opening yourself up that way is weakness."

"He has a thing about weakness, doesn't he?"

"Oh, yes." The boy shook his head sadly again. "It's his devil. You must be strong, and strong has a very special meaning to him. Closed up. Hard. Mean. Self-sufficient."

The boy looked at Jack Liffey for validation or at least understanding. "Afraid," Jack Liffey suggested.

The boy smiled at last. It was a bit spooky, Ramon's sense of inner peace. "Yes. My brothers and my sister Lula accepted everything he forced on them and built their lives around his obsessions. They may be all right eventually, if other people love them enough, but they are very wounded people. Mom and I had a special bond and it protected me. But he took it out on her."

"Do you hate him?"

"Oh, no. I don't hate."

Jack Liffey told him about Leon Krane's hard time in college. He wondered if he could somehow establish an understanding between father and son that would be sure to get him back on the karma gravy train. They went on talking for a long time and the boy gave him a vivid sense of what it must have been like to ride out his strange family life. Not only was his father forcing a particular vision of masculinity on him, but much of that stiffness was reinforced by the macho culture that had surrounded him—the very culture that had probably drawn his father to East L.A. in the first place. To resist all that, he seemed to have drawn a lot of strength from his mother and from the example of a pacifist priest he met who had been through the civil rights movement.

"Father Gregg told me you can only resist power with love. I think I can love Dad, it's tough, but I know I can't be around him. It would wreck me and destroy Mom. Are you going to make me go back?"

Jack Liffey stared at a beautiful golden columbine over a tattered sofa, and the first line of its poem:

I know there is no protection...

He wasn't much for garden flowers, but this one grew wild along mountain streams and he'd always loved it.

"I won't make you do anything. But I have to talk to your dad. Maybe he'll see what a wonderful son he has."

The boy shrugged. "I think you're overestimating his flexibility."

It plagued him for two days. Leon Krane-Carne called and called, and he put him off because he simply did not know what to do. He wanted to try to get Leon to allow his son to develop in his own way, but deep in his heart he knew it was far too late in life for that. His son was a total repudiation of whatever adjustments he had made with his private gods to save his own life. In the face of unremitting harassment, he'd closed his shutters against everything the boy now represented. Leon Krane-Carne was set in concrete by now. Yet, the boy was technically still a minor, and if he refused to tell Leon where his son was, the man would just hire somebody else to find him. The boy hadn't been that hard to find.

There was no ducking it. He had to talk to Leon and try to solve this exasperating problem.

The mother hovered across the living room, eavesdropping in trepidation. She clearly hoped the boy had permanently absented himself from his father's control and was afraid that Jack Liffey was going to drag him back.

"So where is he now?"

"It's not that easy, Leon." He explained that the boy had found a studio space to work and was supporting himself by selling his art.

"He's a minor."

"Would you let him go to art school?"

"That's none of your business. This is my son we're talking about."

As he'd feared, Leon was starting to bridle and turn belligerent.

"Did you ever think that there might be other kinds of

strength than yours? Gentle and determined strength. Like Cesar Chavez, maybe."

"What's this crap? I hired you to find my boy."

"I found one of the brightest, most resilient boys I've ever met. He is radiant with a kind of inner love. He might be a goddamn saint, for all I know. But he thinks all you want to do is knock it out of him."

Léon Carne pointed harshly toward his wife, and the woman made a wounded little *eep* sound and scuttled out of the room, and then he walked to the front door and locked the deadbolt ominously with a key and pocketed the key.

"Where is my son?"

"I sure wish I could reconcile you two." Jack Liffey felt a certain responsibility for what this man had become. One little change could turn around a life. Maybe if he'd tried harder back in college... "I tried to be your friend once, Leon, and you wouldn't even take a half-step toward me."

The small man glared at him. "Don't you judge me! I was a contender for the world featherweight title! I built this house. I raised a family. I made something of myself, which is more than you ever did. You fucking lowlife failure."

"Yeah, I'm a failure, Leon. But I know decency when I see it. I won't give you a child to ruin."

"You remember Kaz Kristowski and what I did to him?"

"Of course I do."

"I'm going to pound you into a pulp until you tell me where my son is."

Jack Liffey raised his palms. "I'm not a fighter. That's not fair."

"I don't give a shit about you. I want my boy. I want to save him from becoming a weakling. I've got to make it so people like you can't pick on him."

"I don't know why people picked on you, Leon. Honest to God, I don't. I wish I could have stopped it. But right now Ramon is stronger against it than you ever were."

"Where is he?"

The small man advanced on him and Jack Liffey had no illusions about standing up under his relentless punches. He was beginning to wonder again about the immanence of evil in the world, and wonder if he was about to learn something about it the hard way. "Please don't do this."

"Where is Ramon?"

Jack Liffey pointed behind the man. "That frying pan is going to hurt."

Leon Krane-Carne whirled, but his wife was not there with a frying pan and as he turned back, Jack Liffey swung with all his might. It turns out that there is one dirty trick from the world of bar fights that almost always works. If you clutch a roll of pennies in your fist and sucker-punch someone square on the jaw with it, the guy will go down.

Jack Liffey yelped at the punch, since it broke two of his knuckles. But Leon Krane-Carne deflated all at once and slumped like a medium-size sack full of doorknobs, out cold, his jaw broken in three places.

You did me one favor in life, Jack Liffey thought, looking down at this broken form. You probably gave me my first training as a detective.

"Call an ambulance," Jack Liffey said to Rosaura Sanchez Carne, who had come back into the room. There was time now to warn the kid to hide somewhere better. And as long as the pennies stayed a secret, he didn't think this particular almost-world-champion was ever likely to haul him to law over a one-punch amateur KO.

As it turns out, there are some problems that just plain have no reasoned solution, he thought, wincing as he pocketed the penny roll, and the problem of Leon was one of them.

MIDNIGHT EMISSIONS

by F.X. Toole

"Butcherin' was done while the deceased was still alive," Junior said.

See, we was at the gym and I'd been answering a few things. Old Junior's a cop, and his South Texas twang was wide and flat like mine. 'Course he was dipping, and he let a stream go into the Coke bottle he was carrying in the hand that wasn't his gun hand. His blue eyes was paler than a washed-out work shirt.

"Hail," he said, "one side of the mouth'd been slit all the way to the earring."

See, when the police find a corpse in Texas, their first question ain't who done it, it's what did the dead do to deserve it?

Billy Clancy'd been off the police force a long time before Kenny Coyle come along, but he had worked for the San Antonia Police Department a spell there after boxing. He made some good money for himself on the side—down in dark town, if you know what I'm saying? That's after I trained him as a heavyweight in the old *El Gallo*, or Fighting Cock gym off Blanco Road downtown. We worked together maybe six years all told, starting off when he was a amateur. Billy Clancy had all the Irish heart in the world. At six-three and two-twenty-five, he had a fine frame on him, most of his weight upstairs. He had a nice clean style, too, and was quick as a sprinter. But after he was once knocked out for the first time? He

343

had no chin after that. He'd be kicking ass and taking names, but even in a rigged fight with a bum, if he got caught? Down he'd go like a longneck at a ice house.

He was a big winner in the amateurs, Billy was, but after twelve pro fights, he had a record of eight and four, with his nose broke once—that's eight wins by KO, but he lost four times by KO, so that's when he hung 'em up. For a long time, he went his way and I went mine. But then Billy Clancy opened Clancy's Pub with his cop money. That was his big break. There was Irish night with Mick music, corned beef and cabbage, and Caffery's Ale on tap and Harp Lager from Dundalk. And he had Messkin night with *mariachis* and folks was dancin' *corridos* and the band was whooping out *rancheras* and they'd get to playing some of that *norteña* polka music that'd have you laughing and crying at the same time. For shrimp night, all you can eat, Billy trucked in fresh Gulf shrimp sweeter than plum jelly straight up from Matamoros on the border. There was kicker, and hillbilly night, and on weekends there was just about the best jazz and blues you ever did hear. B.B. King did a whole week there one time. It got to be a hell of a deal for Billy, and then he opened up a couple of more joints till he had six in three towns, and soon Billy Clancy was somebody all the way from San Antonia up Dallas, and down to Houston. Paid all his taxes, obeyed all the laws, treated folks like they was ladies and gentlemen, no matter how dusty the boots, how faded the dress, or if a suit was orange and purple and green.

By then he had him a home in the historic old Monte Vista section of San Antonia. His wife had one of them home decorating businesses on her own, and she had that old place looking so shiny that it was like going back a hundred years. His kids was all in private school, all of them geared to go to U.T. up Austin, even though the dumb young one saw himself as a Aggie.

So one day Billy called me for some "Q" down near the river, knew I was a whore for baby back ribs. Halfway through, he just up and said, "Red, I want back in."

See, he got to missing the smell of leather and sweat, and the laughter of men—he missed the action, is what, and got himself back into the game the only way he could, managing fighters. He was good at it, too. By then he was better'n forty, and myself I was getting on—old's when you sit on the crapper and you have to hold your nuts up so they don't get wet. But what with my rocking chair money every month, and the money I made off Billy's fighters, it got to where I was doing pretty good. Even got me some ostrich boots and a *El Patron 30X* beaver Stetson, *yip!*

What Billy really wanted was a heavyweight. With most managers, it's only the money, 'cause heavies is what brings in them stacks of green fun-tickets. Billy wanted fun-tickets, too, but with Billy it was more like he wanted to get back something what he had lost. 'Course, finding the right heavyweight's like finding a cherry at the high school prom.

Figure it, with only twenty, twenty-five good wins, 'specially if he can crack, a heavy can fight for a title's worth millions. There's exceptions, but most little guys'll fight forever and never crack maybe two hundred grand. One of the reason's 'cause there's so many of them. Other reason's 'cause they's small. Fans like seeing heavyweights hit the canvas.

But most of today's big guys go into the other sports where you don't get hit the way you do in the fights. It ain't held against you in boxing if you're black nowadays, but if you're a white heavy it makes it easier to pump paydays, and I could tell that it wouldn't make Billy sad if I could get him a white boy—Irish or Italian would be desired. But working with the big guys takes training to a level that can break your back and your heart, and I wasn't all that sure a heavy was what I wanted, what with me being the one what's getting broke up.

See, training's a hard row to hoe. It ain't only the physical and mental parts for the fighter what's hard, but it's hard for the trainer, too. Fighters can drive you crazy, like maybe right in the middle of a fight they're *winning*, when they forget everything what you taught them? And all of a sudden they can't follow instructions from the corner? Pressure, pain and being out of gas will make fighters go flat brain-dead on you. Your fighter's maybe sweated off six or eight pounds in there, his body's breaking down, and the jungle in him is yelling quick to get him some gone. Trainers come to know how that works, so you got to hang with your boy when he's all alone out there in the canvas part of the world. He takes heart again, 'cause he knows with you there he's still got a fighting chance to go for the titties of the win. 'Course, that means cutting grommets, Red Ryder.

Everyone working corners knows you'll more'n likely lose more'n you'll ever win, that boxing for most is refried beans and burnt tortillas. But winning is what makes your birdie chirp, so you got to always put in your mind that losing ain't nothing but a hitch in the git-along.

Working with the big guys snarls your task. How do you tell a heavyweight full-up on his maleness to use his mind instead of his sixty-pound dick? How do you teach someone big as a garage that it ain't the fighter with the biggest brawn what wins, but it's the one what gets there first with deadly force? How do you make him see that hitting hard ain't the problem, but that hitting *right* is. How do you get through to him that you don't have to be mad at someone to knock him out, same as you don't have to be in a frenzy to kill with a gun? Heavyweights got that upper-body strength what's scary, it's what they'd always use to win fights at school and such, so it's their way to work from the waist up. That means they throw arm punches, but arm punches ain't good enough. George Foreman does it, but he's so strong, and don't hardly miss, so he most times gets away with punching wrong. 'Course he didn't get away with it in Zaire with Mr. Ali.

So the big deal with heavies is getting them to work from the waist down as well as from the waist up. And they got to learn that the last thing that happens is when the punch lands. A thousand things got to happen before that can happen. Those things begin on the floor with balance. But how do you get across that he's got to work hard, but not so hard that he harms himself? How do you do that in a way what don't threaten what he already knows and has come to depend on? How do you do it so's it don't jar how he has come to see himself and his fighting style? And most of all, how do you do it so when the pressure's on he don't go back to his old ways?

After they win a few fights by early knockout, some heavies get to where they try to control workouts, will balk at new stuff what they'll need as they step up in class. When they pick up a few purses and start driving that new car, lots get lazy and spend their time chasing poon, of which there is a large supply when there is evidence of a quantity of hundred-dollar bills. Some's hop heads, but maybe they fool you and you don't find that out till it's too late. Now you got to squeeze as many paydays out of your doper that you can. Most times, you love your fighter like he's kin, but with a goddamn doper you get to where you couldn't give a bent nail.

Why shouldn't I run things? the heavy's eyes will glare. His nose is flared, his socks is soggy with sweat, his heart's banging at his rib cage like it's trying to bust out of jail. It's 'cause he don't understand that he can't be the horse and the jockey. *How could anyone as big and handsome and powerful and smart as me be wrong about anything?* he will press. Under his breath he's saying, *And who's big enough to tell me I'm wrong?*

When that happens, your boy's attitude is moving him to the streets, and you may have to let him go.

Not many fight fans ever see the inside of fight gyms, so they get to wondering what's the deal with these big dummies who get all sweaty and grunty and beat on each other. Well, sir, they ain't big dummies when you think big money. Most big guys in team sports figure there's more gain and less pain than in fights, even if they have to play a hundred fifty games a year or more, and even if they have to get those leg and back operations that go with them. Some starting-out heavies get to thinking they ought to get the same big payday as major-league pitchers from the day they walk into the gym. Some see themselves as first-round draft picks in the NBA before they ever been hit. What they got to learn is that you got to be a hungry fighter before you can become a championship fighter, a fighter who has learned and survived all the layers of work and hurt the fight game will put on you. Good heavyweights're about as scarce as black cotton.

There're less white heavies than black, and the whites can be even goofier than blacks about quick money. Some whites spout off that 'cause they're white, as in White Hope, that they should be getting easy fights up to and including the one for the title. If you're that kind—and there's black ones same as white—you learn right quick that he don't have the tit or the brains to be a winner under them bright lights.

Though heavies may have the same look, they're as different from each other as zebras when it comes to mental desire, chin, heart, and *huevos*—*huevos* is eggs, but in Messkin it means balls. Getting heavies into shape is another problem, keeping them in shape is a even bigger one, 'cause they got these bottomless pits for stomachs. So you work to keep them in at least decent shape all the time—but not in punishing *top shape*, the kind that peaks just before a fight. Fighter'd go wild-pig crazy if he had to live at top shape longer than a few days, his nerves all crawly and hunger eating him alive. And then there's that blood-clotting wait to the first bell. See, the job of molding flesh and bone into a fighting machine that meets danger instead of high-tailing from it is as tricky as the needlework what goes into one of them black, lacy deals what Spanish ladies wear on their heads. Fighting's easy, cowboy, it's training what's hard.

But once a trainer takes a heavy on, there's all that thump. First of all, when the heavy moves, you got to move with him—up in the ring, on the hardwood, around the big bag. You're there to guide him like a mama bear, and to stay on his ass so's he don't dog

348

it. All fighters'll dog it after they been in the game a while, but the heavies can be the worst. They got all that weight to transport, and being human, they'll look for a place to hide. A good piece of change'll usually goad them. But always there is more training than fighting, and the faith and the fever it takes to be a champ will drop below ninety-eight-point-six real quick unless your boy eats and sleeps fight. 'Course, no fighter can do that one hundred percent. Besides, there's the pussy factor. Which is part of where the punch mitts come in. They'll make him sharp with his punches, but they're also there to help tire him into submission come bedtime.

The big bag they can fake if you don't stay on them, but a trainer with mitts, calling for combination after combination, see that's for the fighter like he's wearing a wire jock. But for the trainer, the mitts mean you're catching punches thrown by a six-foot-five longhorn, and the punches carry force enough to drop a horse. And the trainer takes this punishment round after round, day after day, the *thump* pounding through him like batting practice and he's the ball. I can't much work the mitts like I once did, only when I'm working on moves, or getting ready for a set date. But even bantamweights can make your eyes pop.

Part of the payoff for all this is sweeter'n whipped cream on top of strawberry pie. It's when your fighter comes to see himself from the outside instead of just from the in. It's when all of a sudden he can see how to use his feet to control that other guy in the short pants. It's how a fighter'll smile like a shy little boy when he understands that all his moves're now offense *and* defense, and that he suddenly has the know-how to beat the other guy with his mind, that he no longer has to be just some bull at the watering hole looking to gore. And that's when, Lordy, that you just maybe got yourself a piece of somebody what can change sweat and hurt into gold and glory.

Getting a boy ready for a fight is the toughest time of all for trainers. After a session with the mitts, your fingers'll curl into the palms of your hands for a hour or so, and driving home in your

Jimmy pickup means your hands'll be claws on the steering wheel. The muscles in the middle of your back squeeze your shoulders up around your ears. Where your chest hooks into your shoulders, you go home feeling there's something tore down in there. Elbows get sprung, and groin pulls hobble you. In my case, I've got piano wire holding my chest and ribs together, so when I leave the gym shock keeps on twanging through me. By the time I'm heading home, I'm thinking hard on a longneck bottle of Lone Star. The only other thing I'm thinking on is time in the prone position underneath Granny's quilt.

See, what we're talking about here is signing on to be a cripple, 'cause when you get down to it, trainers in their way get hit more than fighters, only we do it for nickels and dimes, compared. So what's the rest of the deal for the trainer? Well, sir, after getting through all the training and hurting, you live with the threat that you could work years with a heavy only to have him quit on you for somebody who's dangling money at him now that you've done the job that changed a lump of fear and doubt into a fighter. But like I say, a good heavy these days only has to win a few fights for a shot at the title. If he wins that, he's suddenly drinking from solid gold teacups. As the champ, he will defend his title as little as once. But the payoff can be *mucho* if he can defend a few times. So when the champ gets a ten-million-dollar payday, the trainer gets ten percent off the top—that's a one-million-dollar bill. That can make you forget crippled backs and hands.

'Course the downside can be there, too. That's when your heart goes out to your fighter as you watch helpless sometimes as he takes punches to the head that can hack into his memory forever. And your gut will turn against you when one day you see your boy's eyes wander all glassy when he tries to find a word that he don't have in his mouth no more. You feel rotten deep down, but you also love your fighter for having the heart to roll the dice of his life on a dream. And above all, you see clear that no matter how rotten you feel, that your boy never had nothing else but his life to roll, and that you was the lone one who ever cared enough to give him the only shot he would ever have.

Yet the real lure, when you love the fights with everything that's left of your patched-up old heart, is to be part of the great game—a game where the dues are so high that once paid they take you to the Mount Everest of the Squared Circle, to that highest of places, where fire and ice are one and where only the biggest and best can play, *yip!*

Trainers know going in that the odds against you are a ton to one. So why do I risk the years, why do I take shots that stun my heart? Why am I part of the spilt blood? Why do I take trips to Leipzig or Johannesburg that take me two weeks to recover from? B.B. King sings my answer for me, backs it up with that big old guitar. *"I got a bad case of love."*

Anyway, all I was able to get Billy was what was out there, mostly Messkins, little guys wringing wet at a hundred twenty-four and three-quarters, what with us being in San Antonia. But there was some black fighters, too, a welter or a middleweight, now and then. Billy treated all his fighters like they was champs, no matter that they was prelim boys hanging between hope and fear, and praying hard the tornado don't touch down. If they was to show promise, he'd outright sponsor them good, give them a deuce a week minimum, no paybacks, a free room someplace decent, and eats in one of his pubs, whatever they wanted as long as they kept their weight right. If a boy wasn't so good, Billy'd give 'em work, that way if the kid didn't catch in boxing, leastways he always had a job. People loved Billy Clancy.

See, he'd start boys as a dishwasher, but then he'd move 'em up, make waiters and bartenders of them. He had Messkin managers what started as busboys. He was godfather to close to two dozen Messkin babies, and he never forgot a birthday or Christmas. His help would invite him to their weddings, sometimes deep into Mexico, and damned if he wouldn't go. Eyes down there would bug out when this big *gringo*'d come driving through a dusty *pueblo* in one of his big old silver Lincoln Town Cars what he ordered made special. Billy'd join right in, *yip!*, got to where he could talk the lingo passable, good enough to where he could tell jokes and make folks laugh in their own tongue.

Billy Clancy'd be in the middle of it, but he never crossed the line, never messed with any of the gals, though he could have had any or all of 'em. The priests would always take a shine to him, too, want to talk baseball. He never turned one down who come to him about somebody's grandma what needed a decent burial, instead of being dropped down a hole in a bag.

One time I asked Billy why he didn't try on one of them Indian-eyed honeys down there. Respect, is what he said, for the older folks, and 'specially for the young men, you don't want to take a man's pride.

"When you're invited to a party," said Billy, "act like you care to be invited back."

That was Billy Clancy, you don't shit where you eat.

My deal with Billy was working in the gym with his fighters for ten percent of the purse off the top. No fights, no money. I didn't see him for days unless it was getting up around fight time. But he'd stop by, not to check up on me, but just to let his boys know he cared about them. Most times he was smoother than gravy on a biscuit, but I could always tell when something was pestering him. 'Course he wouldn't talk about it much. Billy didn't feel the need to talk, or he saw fit not to.

I know there was this one time when the head manager of all Billy's joints in San Antonia took off with Billy's cash. Billy come into his private office one Monday expecting to see deposit slips for the money what come in over a big weekend. Well, sir, there was no money, and no keys, and no manager, but that same manager had held a gun on Billy's little Messkin office gal so's she'd open the safe. The manager had whipped on the little gal, taped her to a chair with duct tape to where she'd peed herself, and she was near hysteric.

Billy had some of his help make a few phone calls, and damned if the boy what did Billy didn't head for his hometown on the island of Isla Mujeres way down at the tip of Mexico, where he thought he'd be safe. Billy waited a week, then took a plane to Mérida in the Yucatán. He rented him a big car with a good AC and drove on over to the dried-out, palmy little town of Puerto Juárez on the coast that's just lick across the water from what's called Women's Island.

He hung out a day or so in Puerto Juárez, until he got a feel for the place, and so the local police could get a good look at him. Then he just pulled up in front of their peach-colored shack, half its palm-leaf roof hanging loose. He took his time getting out of his rental car, and walked slow inside. Stood a foot taller than most. He talked Spanish and told the captain of the local *federales* his deal, made it simple. All he wanted was his keys back, and he wanted both the manager's balls. The captain was to keep what was left of the money.

That night late, the captain brought forty-six keys on three key rings to Billy's blistered motel. He showed Polaroids of the manager's corpse what was dumped to cook in the hot water off the island, and he also brought in the manager's two *huevos*—his two eggs, each wrapped in a corn tortilla. Billy Clancy fed them to the wild dogs on the other side of the adobe back fence.

Billy checked out some of the Mayan ruins down around those parts, giving local folks time to call the news back to San Antonia. Billy got back, nobody said nothing. Didn't have no more problems with the help stealing now he'd made clear what was his was his.

There was only one other deal about Billy I ever knew about, this time with one of his ex-fighters, a failed middleweight, a colored boy Billy'd made a cook in one of his places. Nice boy, worked hard, short hair, all the good stuff. First off, he worked as a bar-back. But then the bartenders found out the kid was sneaking their tips. They cornered him in a storeroom. They had him turned upside down, was ready to break his hands for him, but then he started squealing they was only doing it 'cause he's black. Billy heard it from upstairs and called off his bartenders, piecing them off with a couple of c-notes each. He listened to the boy's story, and 'cause he couldn't prove the boy was dirty, he moved him to a different joint, and that's where he made a fry cook out of him. The kid was good at cooking, worked overtime anytime the head cook wanted. But then word come down the kid was dealing drugs outta the kitchen. Billy knew dead bang this time and he had one of his cop friends make a buy on the sly.

See, Billy always tried to take care of his own business, unless when it was something like down in Mexico. Billy said when he took care of things himself, there was nobody could tell a story different from the one he told. So he waited for the boy outside the boy's mama's house one night late, slashed two of his tires. Boy comes out and goes shitting mad when he sees his tires cut, starts waving his arms like a crawdad.

Billy comes up with a baseball bat alongside his leg, said, "Boy, I come to buy some of that shit you sell."

Boy pissed the boy off something awful, but he knew better than to challenge Billy on it. So the boy tried to run. He showed up dead, is what happened, his legs broke, his balls in his mouth. No cop ever knocked on Billy Clancy's door, but drugs didn't happen in any of Billy's places after that neither.

It was a couple years after that when Dee-Cee Swans collared me about this heavyweight he'd been working with over at the Brown Bomber Gym in Houston. I said I wasn't going to no Houston—even if it was to look at the real Brown Bomber himself. Dee-Cee said there wasn't no need.

Henrilee "Dark Chocolate" Swans was from Louisiana, his

family going back to Spanish slave times, the original name was Cisneros. Family'd brought him as a boy to Houston during World War Two, where they'd come to better themself. Henrilee's fighting days started on the streets of the Fifth Ward. He said things was so tough in his part of town that when a wino died, his dog ate him. Dee-Cee was a pretty good lightweight in his time, now a'course he weighs more. Fight guys got to calling him Dee-Cee instead of Dark Chocolate, to make things short. Dee-Cee said call him anything you want, long as you called him to dinner.

He wore a cap 'cause he was bald-headed except for the white fringe around his ears and neck. He wore glasses, but one lens had a crack in it. He had a bad back and a slight limp, so he walked with a polished, homemade old mesquite walking stick. It was thick as your wrist and was more like a knobby club than a cane. But old Dee-Cee still had the moves. The time, between now and back when he was still Dark Chocolate, disappeared when Dee-Cee had need to move. Said he never had no trouble on no bus in no part of town, not with that stick between his legs. Dee-Cee had them greeny-blue eyes what some coloreds gets, and when he looked at you square, you was looked at.

Way me and him hooked up was chancy, like everything else in fights. 'Course we knew each other going way back. Both of us liked stand-up style of fighters, so we always had a lot to talk about, things like moves, slips and counters. Like me, he knew that a fighter's feet are his brains—that they're what tell you what punches to throw and when to do it. Since there was more colored fighters in Dallas and Houston, that's where Dee-Cee operated out of most. But he had folks in San Antonia, too. He showed up again, him and a white heavyweight, big kid, a Irish boy calling himself "KO" Kenny Coyle. What wasn't chancy was that Dee-Cee knew I was connected with Billy Clancy.

Dee-Cee got together with Coyle, trained him a while in Houston after working the boy's corner twice as a pickup cutman in a Alabama casino. The way the boy was matched, he was supposed to lose. See, he hadn't fought in a while. But he won both fights by early KOs, and his record got to be seventeen and one, with fifteen knockouts. Coyle could punch with both hands at six-foot-five, two hundred forty-five pounds, size sixteen shoe. His only loss came a few years back from a bad cut to his left eyelid up Vancouver, Canada.

The boy'd also worked as sparring partner for big-time heavyweights, going to camp sometimes for weeks at a time. That's a lot of high-level experience, but it's a lot of punishment, even when you're bone strong, and sometimes you could tell that Coyle'd lose a word. Except for the bad scar on his eyelid, and his nose being a little flat, he didn't look much busted up, so that made you think he maybe had some smarts. He was in shape, too. That made you like him right off.

Dee-Cee was slick. He always put one hand up to his mouth when he talked, said he didn't want spies to read his lips, said some had telescopes. He was known to be a bad man, Dee-Cee, but that didn't mean he didn't have a sense of right and wrong. Back before he had to use a cane, we got to drinking over Houston after a afternoon fight—it was at a fair where we both lost. Half drunk, we went to a fish shack in dark town for some catfish. Place was jam-packed. The lard-ass owner had one of them muslim-style gold teeth—the slip-on kind with a star cutout that shows white from the white enamel underneath? Wouldn't you know it, he took one look at my color and flat said they didn't serve no food. Dee-Cee was fit to be tied—talked nigga, talked common, said Allah was going to send his black ass to the pit along with his four handker-chief-head ho's. Old muslim slid off the tooth quick as a quail when Dee-Cee tapped his pocket and said he was going to cut that tooth out or break it off.

We headed for a liquor store, bought some jerky and ended up out at one of them baseball-pitching park deals drinking rock and rye and falling down in the dirt from swinging and missing pitches. People got to laughing like we was Richard Pryor. Special loud was the hustler running a three-card monte game next to the stands, a little round dude with fuzzy-wuzzy hair. He worked off a old lettuce crate and cheated people for nickels and dimes. Not one of them ever broke the code, but old Dee-Cee had broke it from the git. He watched sly from the fence as the monte-guy took even pennies from the raggedy kids what made a few cents chasing down the balls in the outfield.

Dee-Cee put on his Louisiana country-boy act, bet a dollar and pointed to one of the cards after the monte-guy moved the three cards all around. 'Course Dee-Cee didn't choose right, *couldn't* choose right, so he went head-on and lost another twenty, thirty dollars. Then he bet fifty, like he was trying to get his money back. The dealer did more slick business with his cards, and Dee-Cee chose the one in the middle—only this time, instead of just pointing to it and waiting for the dealer to turn it face-up like before, Dee-Cee held it down hard with two fingers and told monte-man to flip the other two cards over first. Dee-Cee said he'd turn his card over *last*, said he wanted to eyeball *all* the cards. See, there was no way for nobody to win. The dealer knew he'd been caught cheating, and tried to slide. Dee-Cee cracked him in the shins a few times with a piece of pipe he carried those days, and pretty soon, wouldn't you know it?, the monte-man got to begging Dee-Cee to take *all* his money. Dee-Cee took it all, too. 'Course he kept his own money, what was natural, but he gave the rest to the ragamuffins in the field—at which juncture the little guys all took the rest of the night off.

Dee-Cee got me off to the side one day, his hand over his mouth, said did I want to work with him and Coyle? He told me Coyle maybe had a ten-round fight coming up at one of the Mississippi casinos, and I figured Dee-Cee wanted me as cutman for the fight, him being the trainer and chief second. I say why not?, some extra cash to go along with my rocking chair, right?

But Dee-Cee said, "Naw, Red, not just cutman, I want you

wit' me full-time training Coyle."

I say to myself, *A heavyweight what can crack, a big old white Irish one!*

Dee-Cee says he needs "he'p" 'cause as chief second he can't hardly get up the ring steps and through the ropes quick enough no more. 'Course with me working inside the ring, that makes me chief second *and* cutman. I'd done that before, hell.

Dee-Cee says he chose me 'cause he don't trust none of what he called the niggas and the beaners in the gym. Said he don't think much of the rednecks neither. See, that's the way Dee-Cee *talked*, not the way he *acted* toward folks. Dee-Cee always had respect.

He said, "See, you'n me knows that a fighter's feet is his brains. My Irish boy's feet ain't right, and you good wit' feet. We split the trainer's ten percent even."

Five percent of a heavyweight can mount.

Dee-Cee said, "Yeah, and maybe you could bring in Billy Clancy."

Like I said, Dee-Cee's slick. So I ask myself if this is something I want bad enough to kiss a spider for? See, when a fan sees the pros and the amateurs, he sees them as a sport. But the pros is a business, too. It's maybe more a business than a sport. I liked the business part like everybody else, but heavyweights can hurt you like nobody else. So I'm thinking, do I want to chance sliding down that dark hole a heavyweight can dig? Besides, do I want to risk my good name on KO Kenny Coyle with Billy Clancy? I told Dee-Cee I'd wait a spell before I'd do that.

Dee-Cee said, "No, no, you right, hail yeah!"

See, I'm slick, too.

What it was is, Coyle was quirky. He'd gone into the Navy young and started fighting as a service fighter, started knocking everybody out. He won all of the fleet and other service titles, and most of the civilian amateur tournaments, and people was talking

Olympics. But the Olympics was maybe three years away and he wanted to make some money right now. Couldn't make no big money or train full-time in the Navy, so one day Coyle up and walks straight into the ship's Captain's face. Damned if Coyle don't claim he's queer as a three-dollar bill. See, the service folks these days ain't supposed to ask, and you ain't supposed to tell, but here was Coyle telling what he really wanted was to be a woman and dance the ballet. Captain hit the overhead, was ready to toss him in the brig, but Coyle threatened to suck off all the Marine guards, and to contact the President himself about sexual harassment. Didn't take more'n a lick, and the Captain made Coyle a ex-Navy queer. Coyle laughed his snorty laugh when he told the story, said wasn't he equal smart as he was big? Guys said he sure was, but all knew Coyle wasn't smart as Coyle thought he was—'specially when he got to bragging about how he stung some shyster lawyers what had contacted him while he was still a amateur. See, they started funneling him money, and got him to agree to sign with them when he turned pro. He knew up front that nobody was supposed to be buzzing amateurs, and he got them for better'n twenty big ones before he pulled his sissy stunt on the Navy. When they come to him with a pro contract, he told them to stick it, told them no contract with a amateur was valid, verbal or written, and that he had bigger plans. He had them shysters by the ying-yang, he said, and them shysters knew it. Coyle laughed about that one, too.

Too bad I didn't hear about the lawyer deal until we was already into the far turn with Coyle. By the time I did, I already knew Kenny was too big for his britches, and that he was a liar like no different from my cousin Royal. If it was four o'clock, old Royal'd say it was four-thirty. Couldn't help himself.

Coyle's problem as a fighter was he'd not been trained right, but he was smart enough to know it. His other trainers depended on his reach and power, and that he could take a shot. The problem with that is that you end up fighting with your face.

What I worked on with him was the angles of the game, distance, and how to get in and out of range with the least amount of work. The big fellows got to be careful not to waste gas. But where I started Coyle first was with the *bitch*. See, the bitch is what I call the jab, that's the one'll get a crowd up and cheering, you do it pretty. *Bing! Bing!* Man, there ain't nothing like the bitch. And Coyle took to it good, him being fed up with getting hit. With the bitch, you automatic got angles. You got the angle, you got the opening. *Bang!* Everything comes off the bitch. I got him to moving on the balls of his feet, and soon he was coming off that right toe behind the bitch like he was a great white going for a seal pup. *Whooom!*

See, when you got the bitch working for you is when you got the other guy blinking, and on his heels going backward, and you can knock a man down with the bitch, even knock him out if you can throw a one-two-one combination right. Coyle picking up the bitch like he did is what got me to think serious on him, 'specially when I saw how hard he worked day in, day out. On time every day, nary a balk. Dee-Cee and me both started counting fun-tickets in our sleep but both of us agreed to pass on the ten-round Mississippi fight until I could get Coyle's feet right.

Moving with Coyle, like with the other heavies, is easy for me even now. 'Cause of their weight, they get their feet tangled when they ain't trained right, and I know how to back them to the ropes or into a corner. I don't kid myself, they could knock me out with the bitch alone if we was fighting, but what we're up to ain't fighting. What we're up to is what makes fighting boxing.

Billy Clancy got wind of Coyle and called me in, wanted to know why I was keeping my white boy secret. I told him Coyle wasn't no secret, said it was too soon.

"Who's feedin' him?"

"Me and Dee-Cee."

Billy peeled off some hundreds. I'd later split the six hundred with Dee-Cee.

Billy said, "Tell him to start eatin' at one of my joints, as much as he wants. But no drinks and no partyin' in the place. When'll Coyle be ready?"

"Gimme six weeks. If he can stand up to what I put on him, then we'll see."

"Will he fight?"

"He better."

Once I got Coyle's feet slick, damn if he didn't come along as if he was champion already. When I told Billy, he put a eight-round fight together at one of the Indian reservations on the Mississippi. We went for eight so's not to put too much pressure on Coyle, what with me being a new trainer to him. We fought for only seventy-five hundred—took the fight just to get Coyle on the card. When I told Coyle about it, he said book it, didn't even ask who's the opponent. See, Coyle was broke and living in dark town with Dee-Cee, and hoping to impress Billy 'cause Dee-Cee'd told him about Billy Clancy having money.

Well, sir, halfway through the fifth round with Marcellus Ellis, Coyle got himself head-butted in the same eye where he'd been cut up Vancouver. Ellis was a six-foot-seven colored boy weighing two-seventy, but he couldn't do nothing with Coyle, 'cause of the bitch. So Ellis hoped to save his big ass with a head-butt. Referee didn't see the butt, and wouldn't take our word it was intentional, so the butt wasn't counted. Cut was so bad I skipped adrenaline and went direct to Thrombin, the ten-thousand-unit bovine coagulant deal. Thrombin stopped the blood quicker'n morphine'll stop the runs, but the cut was in the eyelid, and the fight shoulda been stopped in truth. But we was in Mississippi and the casino wanted happy gamblers, so the ref let it go on with a warning that he'd stop the fight in the next round if the cut got worse.

Dee-Cee got gray-looking, said he was ready to go over and whip on Ellis' nappy head with his cane.

I told Coyle the only thing I could tell him. "They'll stop this fight on us and we could lose, so you got to get into Ellis' ass with the bitch and then drop your right hand on him and get *respect!*"

All Coyle did was to nod. He went out there serious as a diamondback. Six hard jabs busted up Ellis so bad that he couldn't think nothing but the bitch. That's when Coyle got the angle and, *Bang!* he hit Ellis with a straight right that was like the right hand of God. Lordy, Ellis was out for five minutes. He went down stiff like a tree and bounced on his face, and then one leg went all jerk and twitchy. We went to whooping and hugging. That right hand was lightning in human form. But what it was that did it for me wasn't Coyle's big right hand, it was the way he stuck the *bitch*, and the way Coyle *listened* to me in the corner.

Billy wanted to sign him right then, but I said wait, even though I knew Coyle was antsy to get him a place of his own. Besides, we had to wait a month and more to see if the eye'd heal complete. It took longer than we thought, so Billy started paying the boy three hundred a week walking-around money. Folks at the casino was so wild about that right hand coming outta a white boy that Billy was able to get twenty-five thousand for Coyle's next fight soon's a doctor'd clear his eye. And sure enough, Coyle was right back in the gym when the doctor gave him the okay. But he had some kind of funny look to him, so I told him to go home and rest. But no, Coyle kept showing up saying he wanted to get back to that casino. How do you reach the brain of a pure-strain male hormone when he's eighteen and one with sixteen KOs? But one morning when me and Dee-Cee was out with him doing his road work, we got a surprise. Coyle started pressing his chest and had to stop running. Damn if he didn't look half-blue and ready to go down. Me and Dee-Cee walked him back to the car, both holding him by a arm. I thought maybe it was a heart attack. We hauled ass over to Emergency. They checked him all over, hooked him up to all the machines, checked his blood for enzymes. Said it wasn't no heart attack, said it was maybe some kind of quick virus going around that could knock folks down. Coyle wanted to know when he'd be able to fight again in Mississippi, and I told him to forget

Mississippi till he was well. On our way out, the doctor got me to the side to tell me he wasn't positive Coyle was sick.

I said, "What does that mean?"

Doc said, "I'm not sure. Just thought you might want to know."

After a couple of days rest Coyle was back in the gym, but then he had to stop his road work outta weakness again. He looked like a whipped pup, so I figured he had to have something wrong. He said, "But I can't fight if I don't run, you said it yourself."

I said, "You can't fight if you ain't got gas in your tank, that's what that means. Right now, you got a hole in your tank."

"I need dough, Red."

He was a hungry fighter, it's what you dream about. And there he'd be the next day, even if he coughed till he gagged. You never saw anybody push himself like him. But by then, the fool could hardly punch, much less run. But he still wanted to train, said he didn't want us to think he didn't have no heart.

I said, "Hail, boy, I'm worried about your brain, not heart. You got money from the last fight. Rest."

He said, "I sent all but a thousand to my brother for an operation, he's a cripple."

Well, later on I learned he'd pissed all the money away on pussy and pool, and there wasn't no cripple. But at that time I was so positive Coyle had the heart it takes that I just grabbed the bull by the horns and told Billy it was time. Billy could see the weak state Coyle was in, but on my good word it was a virus, Billy signed Coyle up to a four-year contract. On top of that, he gave Coyle a one-bedroom poolside apartment in one of his units for free. Said he'd give Coyle twenty-five hundred a month, that he'd put it in the contract, no payback, until Coyle started clearing thirty thousand a year. Said he'd give Coyle sixty thousand dollars under the table as a signing bonus soon's he was well enough to get back in the gym. Coyle wanted a hundred thousand, but settled for sixty.

Billy said, "That's cash, Kenny. So you don't have to pay no taxes on it."

"I'll get you the title, Mr. Clancy."

"Billy."

I looked at Dee-Cee, knew the head of his dick was glowing same as mine. Damned if Coyle wasn't back in the gym working hard and doing road work in only three days. Billy's word was good, and I was there when he paid Coyle off in stacks of hundreds. Money smells bad when you get a gang of it all together.

Wouldn't you know it? Old stinky-head went right out and spent the whole shiteree on one of them new BMW four-wheel-drive deals what goes for better than fifty thousand. Coyle got to bragging about the sports package, the killer sound system, how much horsepower it had. Who gives a rap when you can't afford tires and battery? Buying them boogers is easy, keeping them up what's hard.

Besides, it was about that time that Coyle's knees went to flap like butterfly wings. See, the ladies took one look at Coyle and thought they had the real deal, what with him having that big car and flashing hundreds in the clubs.

Dee-Cee said, "How many times you get you nut this week?"

Coyle said, "That's personal."

Dee-Cee said, "So you been gettin' you nut every night."

Coyle said, "No, I ain't."

Dee-Cee said, "You is, too. If it was one or none, or even two times, you'da said so."

Coyle looked at me like he'd never heard such talk.

I said, "He's sayin' when your legs get to wobblin', you been doin' it too much. He's saying that when your legs're weak that your brain gets to wonderin' why's it so hard to keep itself from fallin' down. That's when your brain is so busy keeping you on your feet that it don't pay attention to fightin'. Son, you got to have your legs right so your mind can work quicker than light, or you end up as a opponent talkin' through your nose, and the do-gooders wants to blame us trainers. No good, it's you and your dick what's doin' wrong."

Coyle said, "I'm a fighter livin' like a fighter."

Dee-Cee said, "Way you goin', you won't be for long."

I said, "Dee-Cee ain't wrong, Kenny."

Dee-Cee said, "Boy, you can fuck you white ass black, but that ain't never gonna make you champ of nothin'."

Coyle snorted, said, "I'll be champ of the bitches."

Dee-Cee said, "You go out, screw a thousand bitches, you think you somethin'? Sheeuh, you don't screw no thousand bitches, a thousand bitches screw you—and there go you title shot, fool."

Coyle said, "Fighters need release."

Dee-Cee said, "*Say what?* All you got to do is wait some. You midnight emissions'll natural take care of you goddamn release!"

I said, "Look, we're tryin' to get you around the track and across the finish line first, but you're headin' into the trail on us."

"Yeah," said Dee-Cee, "workin' wit' you be like holdin' water in one hand."

Coyle thought about that and seemed to nod, but next day when he come in his knees were flapping same as before.

Come to find out, Coyle wasn't worth the powder to blow him to hell. Billy found out Coyle had been with three gals in the stall of the men's toilet at one of his hot spots—that they'd been smoking weed hunched around the stool, *yip!* Billy didn't jump Coyle. But instead of seeing him as a long-lost White Hope in shining armor, he saw him same as me and Dee-Cee'd come to—like a peach what had gone part bad. So, do you cut out the bad part and keep the good? Or do you shit-can the whole deal? Billy decided to save what he could as long as he could.

Billy told Coyle to flat take his partying somewhere else, like he was first told. If I know Billy, there was more he wanted to say, but didn't. 'Course big old Coyle didn't take it too good, and wanted to dispute with Billy. So Billy said not to mistake kindness for weakness. Coyle got the message looked like, and was back in the gym working hard again—he wanted that twenty-five hundred a month. We figured the bullshit was over, leastways the in-public bullshit. But who could tell about weed? And who knew what else Coyle was messing with? By then, I got to feeling like I was a cat trapped in a sock drawer.

I told Coyle that what he'd pulled on Billy wasn't the right way to do business.

Coyle said, "He's makin' money off me."

I said, "Not yet he ain't."

That's when things got so squirrelly you'd think Coyle had a tail.

First thing what come up was that stink with the plain-Jane cop's daughter who said Coyle knocked her up—said Coyle'd gave her some of this GHB stuff that's floating around that'll make a gal pass out so deep she's a corpse. Cop's daughter said the last thing she remembered was that she was in Coyle's pool playing kissy-face. Next thing she knew she was bare-ass on the floor and Coyle was fixing to do her. She said she jumped up and fled.

Coyle claimed that he'd already done her twice, said she was crying for more.

See, it wasn't until it come out she was pregnant that she told her daddy, who was a detective sergeant of the San Antonia P.D. She was a only child, and Daddy had them squinty blue eyes set in a face wide in the cheekbones what the Polacks brought into Texas. That good old boy got to rampaging like a rodeo bull, and right about then his neighbors got to thinking about calling Tom Bodette and checking into a Motel 6.

Once Daddy'd killed a half bottle of Jim Beam, he loaded up a old .44 six-gun, put on his boots and hat, and went on over to shoot Coyle dead.

Coyle told Daddy he loved plain-Jane more than his life itself, said that he wanted to marry her.

Cop was one of them Fundamentals and figured marrying

was better'n killing, so he let Coyle off.

Arrangements was made quick so the girl could wear white to the altar and not show. But then Coyle ups and says he'd have to wait till after the kid was born, that he wanted a blood test to prove he was the real daddy. The cop went to rampaging again and was fixing to hunt Coyle down, but he was took off the scent when his daughter stuck something up herself. Killed the baby, and liked to killed herself. The family was in such grief that Daddy started to drink full-time. The girl was sent off to live with a aunt up Nacogdoches. The cop had to go into one of them anger management deals or get fired from the force. 'Course Coyle slapped his thigh.

Second deal was about sparring, and was way worse for me'n Dee-Cee than the cop-daughter deal. All of a sudden Coyle started sparring like he never done it before. Everybody was hitting him—middleweights we had in with him to work speed, high school linemen in the gym on a dare, grunts for God's sake. The eye puffed up again, and we had to take off more time. All of a sudden Coyle's moving on his heels instead of his toes, and now he can't jump rope without stumbling into a wall. A amateur light heavy knocked him down hard enough to make him go pie-eyed, and Dee-Cee called the session off. Most times like that, a fighter's pride will make him want to keep on working, but not Coyle. He was happy to get his ass outta there. Billy heard about it and quick got Coyle that second Mississippi fight for seventy-five thousand. Got Coyle ten rounds with a dead man just to see what was what.

The opponent was six foot tall, three hundred twenty-eight pounds, a big old black country boy from Lake Charles, Louisiana, who couldn't hardly scrawl his own name. But in the first round, with his damn eyes closed, he hit Coyle high on the head with an overhand right and knocked him on his ass. Me and Dee-Cee couldn't figure how he didn't see the punch coming, it was so high and wide. Coyle jumped up, and to his credit, he went right to work.

Bang! Three bitches to the eyes, right hand to the chin, left hook to the body, all the punches quick and pretty. The black boy settled like a dead whale to the bottom, and white folks was dancing in the aisles and waving the Stars and Bars. It was pitiful, but Coyle strutted like he just knocked out Jack Johnson. Me and Dee-Cee was pissed, and our peters had lost their glow. Dressing room afterward was quiet as a gray dawn.

Coyle took time off, not that he needed the rest. He came back for a few days, then it got so he wasn't coming in at all. If he did, he'd lie around and bullshit instead of work. You could smell weed on him, and his hair got greasy. Now all our fighters started going flaky. Sweat got scarcer and scarcer. There was other times Coyle'd come in so fluffy from screwing you wished he didn't come in at all. Gym got to be a goddamned social club what looked full of boy whores and Social Security socialites. What with Coyle lying around like a pet poodle, Billy's other fighters started doing the same. Some begged off fights that were sure wins for them. You never want a fighter to fight if he's not ready, but when they're being paid to be in shape, they're supposed to be in shape, not Butterball goddamn turkeys.

I tried to get Coyle to get serious, but he kept saying, "I'm cool, I'm cool."

I said, "Tits on a polar bear's what's cool."

That went on for three months, but I wasn't big enough to choke sense into him. Besides, no trainer worth a damn would want to. Fighters come in on their own, or they don't come in. Billy wanted a answer, but I didn't have one. How do you figure it when a ten-round fighter hungry for money pulls out of fights 'cause of a sore knuckle, or a sprung thumb, or a bad elbow? Course old Coyle didn't volunteer for no cut in pay.

One day he was lounging in his velour sweatsuit looking at tittie magazines. He said to turn up the lights. I said they was turned up. He said to turn them up again, and I said they was up again. Coyle yelled at me the first and last time.

"Turn 'em all the goddamn fuck up!"

"Boy," I said, and then I said it again real quiet. "Boy, lights is all the goddamn fuck up."

He looked up. "Oh, uh-huh, yeah, Red, thanks."

About then I figure Kenny don't know shit from Shinola.

Vegas called Billy for a two-hundred-thousand-dollar fight with some African fighting outta France. He had big German money behind him, and he was a tough sumbitch, but he didn't have no punch like Kenny Coyle. Coyle said he'd go for the two-hundred-thousand fight in a heartbeat.

I knew there had to be some fun in all this pain. We whip the Afro-Frenchie and win the next couple of fights, and we're talking three, maybe five hundred thousand a fight. Even if he loses, Billy's got all his money back and more, and me and Dee-Cee's doing right good, too. If we win big, we'll be talking title fight, 'cause word'll be out that there's some big white boy who could be the one to win boxing back from the coloreds. The only coloreds me and Dee-Cee gave a rap about was them colored twenties, and fifties, and hundreds that'd make us proud standing in the bank line instead of meek. Like I say, the amateurs and the pros ain't alike, and Billy's figuring to get his money out of Coyle while he can. Me and Dee-Cee's for that, 'specially me, since it gets me off the hook.

But neither one of us could figure what had happened with Coyle, so we got Billy to bring in some tough sparring partners for the Frenchie fight to test what Coyle had. Same-oh same-oh, with Coyle getting hit. But when he hit them, *damn!*, they'd go *down!* A gang of them took off when Coyle threw what that writer guy James Ellroy calls *body rockets* that tore up short ribs and squashed livers. But it was almost like Coyle was swinging blind. Usual-like, you don't care about the sparring partners, they're paid to get hit. But the problem was that Coyle was getting hit, and going *down*, too. He'd take a shot and his knees would do the old butterfly. We figured he'd been smoking weed, or worse—being up all night in toilets with hoochies.

Dee-Cee said, "Can't say I didn't tell him 'bout midnight emissions, but no, he won't listen a me."

But Coyle wasn't short on wind, and he looked strong. Me'n Dee-Cee'd never seen nothing like it, a top guy gets to be a shot fighter so quick like that, 'specially with him doing his road work every dawn? Hell, come to find out he wasn't even smoking weed, just having a beer after a workout so's he could relax and sleep.

Seeing all our work fall apart, I figured we was Cinderella at midnight. Me and Dee-Cee both knew it, but we still couldn't make out why. Then Dee-Cee come to me, his hand over his mouth.

Dee-Cee said, "Coyle's blind in that bad eye."

I said, "What? Bullshit, the commission doctors passed him."

"He's blind, Red, in that hurt eye, I'm tellin' you. I been wavin' a white towel next to it two days now, and he don't blink on the bad-eye side. Watch."

Between rounds sparring next day, with me greasing and watering Coyle, Dee-Cee kind of waved the tip of the towel next to Coyle's good eye and Coyle blinked automatic. Between the next round, Dee-Cee was on the other side. He did the same waving deal with the towel. But Coyle's bad eye didn't blink 'cause he never saw the towel. That's when I understood why he was taking all them shots, that's when I knew he was moving on his heels 'cause he couldn't see the floor clear. And that's why he was getting rocked like it was the first time he was ever hit, 'cause shots was surprising him that he couldn't tell was coming. And it's when I come to know why he was pulling out of fights—he knew he'd lose 'cause he couldn't see. He went for the two-hundred-thousand fight knowing he'd lose, but he took it for the big money. I wanted to shoot the bastard, what with him taking Billy's money and not saying the eye'd gone bad and making a chump outta me.

The rule is if you can't see, then you can't fight. I told Dee-Cee we got to tell Billy. See, Billy's close to being my own kin, and it's like I stuck a knife in his back if I don't come clean.

Dee-Cee said to wait, that it was the commission doctor's fault, not ours, let them take the heat. He said maybe Vegas won't find out, and maybe the fight will fuck Coyle up so bad he'll have to retire anyhow. Billy'll still get most of his money back, Dee-Cee said, so Billy won't have cause to be mad with us. That made sense.

But what happened to mess up our deal permanent was that the Vegas Boxing Commission faxed in its forms for the AIDS blood test, said they wanted a current neuro exam, and they sent forms for a eye exam that had to be done by a ophthalmologist, not some regular doctor with a eye chart. Damned if Coyle wasn't sudden all happy. He couldn't wait once he heard about the eye test. Me and Dee-Cee was wondering how can he want a eye test, what with what we know about that eye?

Sure enough, when the eye test comes in, it says that Coyle's close to stone blind in the bad eye, the one what got cut in Canada. The nuero showed Coyle's balance was off from being hit too much in training camps, which is why he couldn't jump rope, and why he'd shudder when he got popped. The eye exam proved what me and Dee-Cee already knew, which is why Coyle was taking shots what never shoulda landed. What it come down to was the two-hundred-thousand-dollar fight was off, and Coyle's fighting days for big money was over. It also come down to Billy taking it in the ass for sixty grand in signing money that was all my fault. And that ain't saying nothing about all the big purses Coyle coulda won if he had been fit.

Turns out that the fight in Vancouver where Coyle got cut caused his eye to first go bad. The reason why word didn't get loose on him is 'cause Coyle didn't tell the Canadian doctors he was a fighter, and 'cause it was done on that Canadian free health deal they got up there. The eye doc said the operation was seventy percent successful, but told Coyle to be careful, 'cause trauma to the eye could mess it up permanent. What with him dropping out of boxing for a couple of years the way fighters'll do when they lose, people wasn't thinking on him. And the way Coyle passed the eye test in Alabama and Mississippi was to piece off with a hundred-dollar bill the crooked casino croakers what's checking his eyes. When later on he told me how he did it, he laughed the same snorty way as when he told how he played his game on the Navy.

That's when I worked out what was Coyle's plan. See, he knew right after the Marcellus Ellis fight that the eye had gone bad on him again, but he kept that to himself instead of telling anyone about it, thinking his eye operation in Canada won't come out. That way, he could steal Billy's signing money, and pick up the twenty-five hundred a month chasing-pussy money, too. I wondered how long he'd be laughing.

Only now what am I supposed to say to Billy? After all, it was my name on Coyle what clinched the deal. It got to be where my shiny, big old white boy was tarnished as a copper washtub. I talked with Dee-Cee about it.

Dee-Cee said, "You right. That why the schemin' muhfuh come down South from the front!"

See, we surprised Coyle. He didn't know the tests had come back, so me and Dee-Cee just sat him down on the ring apron. Starting out, he was all fluffy.

Dee-Cee said, "Why didn't you tell us about the eye?"

Coyle lied, said, "What eye?"

Dee-Cee said, "Kenny, the first rule's don't shit a shitter. The eye what's fucked up."

Coyle said, "Ain't no eye fucked up."

"You got a fucked-up eye, don't bullshit," said Dee-Cee.

"It ain't bad, it's just blurry."

"Just *blurry* means you ain't fightin' Vegas, that's what's muthuhfuckin' blurry," Dee-Cee said, muscles jumping along his jaw. "I'm quittin' you right now, hyuh? Don't want no truck with no punk playin' me."

Coyle's eyes started to bulge and his neck got all swole up and red. "You're the punk, old man!"

Coyle shoved Dee-Cee hard in the chest. Dee-Cee went down, but he took the fall rolling on his shoulder, and was up like a bounced ball.

Dee-Cee said, "Boy, second rule's don't hit a hitter."
Coyle moved as if to kick Dee-Cee. I reached for my Buck, but before it cleared my back pocket, Dee-Cee quick as a dart used his cane *bap! bap! bap!* to crack Coyle across one knee and both shins. Coyle hit the floor like a sack full of cats.

"I'll kill you, old man. I'll beat your brains out with that stick."

Dee-Cee said, "Muhfuh, you best don't be talking no *kill* shit wit' Dark Chocolate."

Coyle yelled, "Watch your back, old man!"

Dee-Cee said, "Boy, you diggin' you a hole."

Dee-Cee hobbled off, leaning heavy on his cane. Coyle made to go after Dee-Cee again, but by then I'd long had my one-ten out and open.

I said, "Y'all ever see someone skin a live dog?"

I had to get Coyle outta there, thought to quick get him to the Texas Ice House over on Blanco, where we could have some longnecks like good buds and maybe calm down. Texas Ice House's open three hundred sixty-five days a year, sign out front says GO COWBOYS.

Coyle said, "Got my own Texas shit beer at home."

Texas and *shit* in the same breath ain't something us Texans cotton to, but I went on over to Coyle's place later on 'cause I had to. I knocked, and through the door I heard a shotgun shell being jacked into the chamber.

I said, "It's me, Red."

Coyle opened up, then limped out on the porch looking for Dee-Cee.

Coyle said, "I'm gonna kill him, you tell him."

Inside, there was beer cans all over the floor, and the smell of weed and screwing. Coyle and a half-sleepy tittie-club blond gal was lying around half bare-ass. She never said a word throughout. I got names backing me like Geraghty and O'Kelly, but when I got to know what a sidewinder Coyle was, it made me ashamed of belonging to the same race.

I said, "When did the eye go bad?"

Coyle was still babying his legs. "It was perfect before that Marcellus Ellis butted me at the casino. But with you training me, hey baby, I can still fight down around here."

"You go back to chump change you fight down around here."

"My eye is okay, it's just blurry, that's all, don't you start on me, fuck!"

"It's you's what's startin'."

"This happened time before last in Mississippi, okay? And it was gettin' better all by itself, okay?"

I stayed quiet, so did he. Then I said, "Don't you get it? You fail the eye test, no fights in Vegas, or no place where there's money. Only trainer you'll get now's a blood sucker."

Coyle shrugged, even laughed a little. That's when I asked him the one question he didn't never want to hear, the one that would mean he'd have to give back Billy's money if he told the truth.

I said, "Why didn't you tell us about the eye before you signed Billy's contract?"

Coyle got old. He looked off in a thousand-yard stare for close to a minute. He stuttered twice, and then said, "Everybody knew about my eye."

I said, "Not many in Vancouver, and for sure none in San Antonia."

Coyle said, "Vegas coulda checked."

I said, "We ain't Vegas."

Coyle stood up. He thought he wanted to hit me, but he really wanted to hide. Instead, he moved the shotgun so's it was pointing at my gut.

He said, "I don't want you to train me no more."

I said, "Next time you want to fuck somebody, fuck your mama in her casket, she can't fuck you back."

That stood him straight up, and I knew it was time to git. As the door closed behind me, I could hear Coyle and the tittie-club blonde start to laugh.

I said to myself, "Keep laughin', punk cocksucker—point a gun at me and don't shoot."

I drove my pickup over to Billy's office next day, told him the whole thing. It wasn't far from my place but it was the longest ride I ever took. I was expecting to be told to get my redneck ass out of Texas. He just listened, then lit up a Montecristo contraband Havana robusto with a gold Dunhill. He took his time, poured us both some Hennessy XO.

He could see I felt lowdown and thought I'd killed his friendship.

I said, "I'm sorry, Billy, you know I'd never wrong you on purpose."

Billy said, "You couldn't see the future, Red, only women can do that, and that's 'cause they know when they're gonna get fucked."

Billy put the joke in there to save me from myself, damned if he didn't. I was ready to track Coyle and gut him right then. But Billy said to calm down, said he'd go over to Coyle's place later on. I wanted to go, said I'd bring along Mr. Smith and Mr. Wesson.

"Naw," said Billy, "there won't be no shootin'."

When Billy got to Coyle's, Kenny was smoking weed again, had hold of a big-assed, stainless steel .357 MAG Ruger with a six-inch barrel. Billy didn't blink, said could he have some iced tea like Coyle was drinking. Coyle said it was Snapple Peach, not diet, but Billy said go on'n hook one up. Things got friendly, but Coyle kept ahold of the Ruger.

Billy said, "Way I see it, you didn't set out to do it."

Coyle said, "That's right, Ellis did it."

Billy said, "But you still got me for sixty large."

Coyle said, "Depends on how you look at it." He laughed at his joke. "Besides, nobody asked about my eye, so I told no lie. Hey, I can rhyme like Ali, that's me, hoo-ee."

Billy said, "Coyle, there's sins of commission and there's sins of omission. This one's a sixty-thousand-dollar omission."

Coyle said, "You got no proof. It was all cash like you wanted, no taxes."

Billy said, "I want my sixty back. You can forget the free rent and the twenty-five hundred you got off me every month, but I want the bonus money."

Coyle said, "Ain't got it to give back."

Billy said, "You got the BMW free and clear. Sign it over and we're square."

Coyle said, "You ain't gettin' my Beamer. Bought that with my signing money."

Billy said, "You takin' it knowin' your eye was shot, that was humbug."

Coyle said, "I'm stickin' with the contract and my lawyer says you still owe me twenty-five hundred for this month, and maybe for three years to come. He says you're the one that caused it all when you put me in with the wrong opponent."

Billy'd put weight on around the belly, and Coyle was saying he wasn't dick afraid of him.

Billy didn't press for the pink, and didn't argue about the twenty-five hundred a month, didn't say nothing about the lost projected income.

"Then tell me this," Billy said, "when do you plan on gettin' out of my building and givin' back my keys?"

Coyle laughed his laugh. "When you evict me, that's when, and you can't do that for a while 'cause my eye means I'm disabled,

I checked."

Billy laughed with Coyle, and Billy shook Coyle's left hand with his right before taking off, 'cause Coyle kept the Ruger in his right hand.

Billy said, "Well, let me know if you change your mind."

"Not hardly," said Coyle, "I'm thinkin' on marrying that cop's daughter. This here's our love nest."

Me and Dee-Cee was cussing Coyle twenty-four hours a day, but Billy never let on he cared. About a week later, he said his wife and kids was heading down to Orlando DisneyWorld for a few days. On Thursday he gave me and Dee-Cee the invite to come on down to Nuevo Laredo with him Friday night for the weekend.

Billy said, "We'll have a few thousand drinks at the Cadillac Bar to wash the taste of Coyle out of our mouths."

He sweetened the pot, said how about spending some quality time in the cat houses of Boys Town, all on him? I said my old root'll still do the job with the right inspiration, so did Dee-Cee. But he said his back was paining him bad since the deal with Coyle, and that he had to go on over Houston where he had this Cuban *Santería* woman. She had some kind of mystic rubjuice made with rooster blood he said was the only thing what'd cure him.

Dee-Cee said, "I hate to miss the trip with y'all, but I got to see my Cuban."

I told Billy he might as well ride with me in my Jimmy down to Nuevo Laredo. See, it's on the border some three hours south of San Antonia. I had a transmission I been wanting to deliver to my cousin Royal in Dilley, which is some seventy-eighty miles down from San Antonia on Highway 35 right on our way. Bllly said he had stuff to do in the morning, but that he'd meet me at the Cadillac Bar at six o'clock next day. That left just me heading south alone and feeling busted up inside for doing the right thing by a skunk.

I left early so's I could listen to Royal lie, and level out with some of his Jack Daniel's. When I pulled up in front of the Cadillac

Bar at ten of six, I saw Billy's bugged-up Town Car parked out front. He was inside, a big smile on him. With my new hat and boots, I felt fifty again, and screw Kenny Coyle and the BMW he rode in on. We was laughing like Coyle didn't matter to us, but underneath, we knew he did.

Billy got us nice rooms in a brand new motel once we had quail and Dos Equis for dinner, and finished off with fried ice cream in the Messkin style. Best I can recollect, we left our wheels at the motel and took a cab to Boys Town. We hit places like the Honeymoon Hotel, the Dallas Cowboys, and the New York Yankey. Hell, I buried myself in brown titties, even ended up with a little Chink gal I wanted to smuggle home in my hat. Spent two nights with her and didn't never want to go home.

I ain't sure, but seems to me I went back to the motel once on Saturday just to check on Billy. His car was gone, and there was a message for me blinking on the phone in my room, and five one-hundred-dollar bills on my pillow. Billy's message said he had to go on over to Matamoros 'cause the truck for his shrimps had busted down, and he had to rent another one for shrimp night. So I had me a mess of Messkin scrambled eggs and rice and beans and a few thousand bottles of Negra Modelo. I headed on back for my China doll still shaky, but I hadn't lost my boots or my *El Patrón* so I'm thinking I was a tall dog in short grass.

There seems like there were times when I must a blanked out there. But somewhere along the line, I remember wandering the streets over around Boys Town when I come up on a little park that made me stop and watch. It happens in parks all over Mexico. The street lights ain't nothing but hanging bare bulbs with swarms of bugs and darting bats. Boys and girls of fourteen to eighteen'n more'd make the nightly *paseo*—that's like a stroll on the main drag, 'cause there ain't no TV or nothing, and the *paseo's* what they do to get out from the house to flirt. In some parts, the young folks form circles in the park. The boys' circle'd form outside the girls' circle and each circle moves slow in opposite directions so's the boys and the girls can be facing each other as they pass. The girls try to squirt cheap perfume on a boy they fancy. The boys try to pitch a pinch of confetti into a special girl's mouth. Everybody gets to laughing and spitting and holding their noses but inside their knickers they're fixing to explode. It's how folks get married down there.

'Course, getting married wasn't on my mind. Something else was, and I did my best to satisfy my mind with some more of that authentic Chinee sweet and sour.

Billy was asleep the next day, Sunday, when I come stumbling back, so I crapped out, too. I remember right, we headed home separate on Sunday night late. Both of us crippled and green, but back in Laredo Billy's car was washed and spanky clean except for a cracked rear window. Billy said some Matamoros drunk had made a failed try to break in. He showed me his raw knuckles to prove it.

Billy said, "I can still punch like you taught me, Reddy."

Driving myself home alone, I was all bowlegged, and my heart was leaping sideways. But when it's my time to go to sleep for the last time, I want to die in Boys Town teasing the girls and learning Chinee.

I was still hung over on Monday, and had to lay around all pale and shaky until I could load up on biscuits and gravy, fresh salsa, fried grits, a near pound of bacon, three or four tomatoes, and a few thousand longnecks. I guess I slept most of the time, 'cause I don't remember no TV.

It wasn't until when I got to the gym on Tuesday that I found out about Kenny Coyle. Hunters found him dead in the dirt. He was beside his torched BMW in the mesquite on the outside of town. They found him Sunday noon, and word was he'd been dead some twelve hours, which meant he'd been killed near midnight Saturday night. Someone at the gym said the cops had been by to see me. Hell, me'n Billy was in Mexico, and Dee-Cee was in Houston.

The inside skinny was that Coyle'd been hog-tied with them plastic cable-tie deals that cops'll sometimes use instead of handcuffs. One leg'd been knee-capped with his own Ruger someplace else, and later his head was busted in by blunt force with a unknown object. His brains was said to hang free, and looked like a bunch of grapes. His balls was in his mouth, and his mouth had been slit to the ear so's both balls'd fit. The story I got was that the cops who found him got to laughing, said it was funny seeing a man eating his own mountain oysters. See, police right away knew it was business.

When the cops stopped by the gym Tuesday morning, I was still having coffee and looking out the storefront window. I didn't have nothing to hide, so I stayed sipping my joe right where I was. I told them the same story I been telling you, starting off with stopping by to see old Royal in Dilley. See, the head cop was old Junior, and old Junior was daddy to that plain-Jane gal.

I told him me and Billy had been down Nuevo Laredo when the tragedy occurred. Told him about the Cadillac Bar, and about drinking tequila and teasing the girls in Boys Town. 'Course, I left out a few thousand details I didn't think was any of his business. Old Junior's eyes got paler still, and his jaw was clenched up to where his lips didn't hardly move when he talked. He didn't ask but two or three questions, and looked satisfied with what I answered.

Fixing to leave, Junior said, "Seems like some's got to learn good sense the hard way."

Once Junior'd gone, talk started up in the gym again and ropes got jumped. Fight gyms from northern Mexico all up through Texas knew what happened to Coyle. Far as I know, the cops never knocked on Billy Clancy's door, but I can tell you that none of Billy's fighters never had trouble working up a sweat no more, or getting up for a fight neither.

I was into my third cup of coffee when I saw old Dee-Cee get off the bus. He was same as always, except this time he had him a knobby new walking stick. It was made of mesquite like the last one. But as he come closer, I could see that the wood on this new one was still green from the tree.

I said, "You hear about Coyle?"

"I jus' got back," said Dee-Cee, "what about him?"

One of the colored boys working out started to snicker. Dee-Cee gave that boy a look with those greeny-blue eyes. And that was the end of that.